HISTORICAL

Your romantic escape to the past.

Miss Georgina's Marriage Dilemma

Eva Shepherd

Wedded To His Enemy Debutante

Samantha Hastings

MILLS & BOON

MISS GEORGINA'S MARRIAGE DILEMMA
© 2024 by Eva Shepherd
Philippine Copyright 2024
Australian Copyright 2024
New Zealand Copyright 2024
First Published 2024
First Australian Paperback Edition 2024
ISBN 978 1 867 29971 4

WEDDED TO HIS ENEMY DEBUTANTE
© 2024 by Samantha Hastings
Philippine Copyright 2024
Australian Copyright 2024
New Zealand Copyright 2024
First Published 2024
First Australian Paperback Edition 2024
ISBN 978 1 867 29971 4

MIX
Paper | Supporting responsible forestry
FSC® C001695
FSC www.fsc.org

Published by
Harlequin Mills & Boon
An imprint of Harlequin Enterprises (Australia) Pty Limited
(ABN 47 001 180 918), a subsidiary of HarperCollins Publishers Australia Pty Limited
(ABN 36 009 913 517)
Level 19, 201 Elizabeth Street
SYDNEY NSW 2000 AUSTRALIA

Printed and bound in Australia by McPherson's Printing Group

Miss Georgina's Marriage Dilemma

Eva Shepherd

MILLS & BOON

After graduating with degrees in history and political science, **Eva Shepherd** worked in journalism and as an advertising copywriter. She began writing historical romances because it combined her love of a happy ending with her passion for history. She lives in Christchurch, New Zealand, but spends her days immersed in the world of late Victorian England. Eva loves hearing from readers and can be reached via her website, evashepherd.com, and her Facebook page, Facebook.com/evashepherdromancewriter.

Visit the Author Profile page
at millsandboon.com.au for more titles.

Author Note

Miss Georgina's Marriage Dilemma is the third book in the Rebellious Young Ladies miniseries, featuring four unconventional young women who became firm friends when they met at Halliwell's Finishing School for Refined Young Ladies.

As the daughter of a wealthy industrialist, Georgina Hayward takes pride in the fact that she has only one skill: enjoying herself. While her parents expect her to marry a titled man, she prefers to spend the Season making sport of the men who pursue her so they can get their hands on her generous marriage settlement.

Then she meets Adam Knightly, the Duke of Ravenswood, an impoverished widower with three children, who is in need of a wife. Georgina's commitment to only marry a man who loves her and is not interested in her dowry is severely challenged.

I hope you enjoy *Miss Georgina's Marriage Dilemma* as much as I enjoyed writing it. I love hearing from my readers and can be reached at evashepherd.com and Facebook.com/evashepherdromancewriter.

DEDICATION

To everyone who enjoys a happy ending

Chapter One

Somerset, England, 1895

After successfully negotiating five Seasons, her single status firmly intact, Georgina Hayward could not believe her parents were still trying to match her with supposedly suitable men.

What was wrong with them? Were they incapable of understanding the simple fact that she did not want them to find her a husband? She'd thought by now they would have realised she would not be married off to some fortune-hunter who fell in love with her immediately on hearing the size of her marriage settlement. Nor would she marry a man with a title just to advance the family's position in Society.

She paced her bedchamber, her fury growing with every step.

Her father was not an unintelligent man. After all, the grandson of a humble baker did not become one of the richest men in England without having a certain amount of intelligence.

Her teeth clenched more tightly together. And it might be better if they weren't so rich. While she loved all the nice things money provided, if her father hadn't bought all those properties, businesses and whatnot in an endless quest to get richer and more influential, and if her mother had been content to remain in that quaint Park Lane house where Georgina had been born, rather than aiming to have the best estate, the best balls, the best everything, maybe life would be easier. At least for Georgina. Then she wouldn't be paraded in front of an endless stream of men who were all but salivating at the thought of getting their hands on her dowry.

Georgina shuddered. Why, oh, why could her parents not understand the simple concept that if Georgina married—and that was an *if*, not a *when*—it would be to a man of her choosing? A man who loved her and she loved in return. A man who wanted her for herself and cared nothing for her dowry, unlike all those grasping men she met during the Season.

She stopped pacing and glared out of the window, as if showing her anger to the entire world, then recommenced pacing the well-worn path across the Oriental rug.

When she had informed her parents at the beginning of the first Season what her conditions regarding marriage were to be, they had looked at her as if *she* were the simple one.

Unbelievable.

Instead of doing as she emphatically commanded, they had tried to interest her in Baron this, the Earl of that or the Viscount of something else.

And they were still at it.

Even more unbelievable.

The Season hadn't even begun and they had invited some penniless, widowed duke to their estate in Somerset, and told her he was absolutely perfect for her, when they all knew the only thing perfect about him was his title.

Well, her parents and that toothless old codger were going to have to be taught a lesson. It was time to take action and show them she was not to be trifled with.

The Duke would arrive, expecting to find a docile young woman who was bedazzled by the prospect of becoming a duchess. Meanwhile, she would be hundreds of miles away, entertaining anyone who would listen with a daring tale of how she had thwarted her parents' plans yet again and put a grasping member of the nobility firmly in his place.

But first, like a princess imprisoned in a tower, she had to escape her evil captives.

Fortunately, unlike most princesses in towers, she was not helpless and knew exactly how to gain her freedom, and she didn't need a handsome prince to help her do it.

To that end, she bundled up her skirt, leant out of the window and looked down at the gardens below. She had climbed out of this window countless times as a young girl to flee from her mother, her nanny and her annoying older brother. And she could do it again now. After all, it was only two storeys.

Only two storeys.

A knock at the door caused her to drop her skirt and stand up straighter, as if proving she was not guilty of the crime she was yet to commit.

'Miss Georgina, please, you must let me in so I can

finish dressing you,' her lady's maid pleaded through the locked door. 'And your mother wants to talk to you in the drawing room as soon as you are ready.'

'I'm perfectly capable of dressing myself, Betsy.' She looked down at the frilly dress her mother had insisted she wear to meet the Duke, bedecked with ribbons, ruches, laces and a ridiculous number of pearl buttons.

That was the problem.

That was why climbing out of the window seemed so daunting. When she was a child, she would have worn a plain dress, one that caused less hindrance when climbing trees, or down the occasional drainpipe.

She had to change, but did not need a lady's maid in order to do so.

'Oh, miss, you're not going to do anything foolish, are you?' Betsy pleaded.

She stared indignantly at the closed door. 'No, I certainly am not.' Betsy's lack of faith in Georgina never failed to amaze her.

'Please, miss.' The lady's maid rattled the locked doorknob.

'And tell Mother I will be down presently.' She smiled to herself. She was not lying to Betsy. She *would* be down presently. She just wouldn't be using the stairs to do so and would not be appearing in the drawing room.

The doorknob turned again. That was followed by a *hmph* of disapproval, then Betsy's skirts swishing off down the hallway.

Georgina rushed to the wardrobe, pushing aside gown after overly ornate gown to find something more suitable to wear.

Then she saw it, stopped her frantic pursuit and smiled in triumph.

She pulled out the uniform she had purchased from the chambermaid for what she suspected was an exorbitant price so she could play a prank on her brother, Tommy, a few weeks ago. It was perfect.

With much wriggling, squirming and squeezing, she eased herself out of her gown and corset, pulled on the simple brown dress and placed the floppy white cap on her head. Then she flipped off her embroidered silk slippers and tied on the much more practical black boots.

There was nothing stopping her now.

She looked back out of the window. The side of the house appeared to have grown higher while she had been distracted. But she had been left with no other choice. She pushed up the sash window as high as it would go and climbed onto the windowsill.

She edged herself over the sill, turned onto her knees and angled her body in an attempt to reach the first bracket on the drainpipe. As a child she had been able to scurry down this drainpipe like a circus acrobat. Surely it would be easier now. After all, her legs were much longer. But it seemed her bravery had diminished at the same rate at which her body had grown.

Slowly, tentatively, she edged her foot along the outside wall until it made contact with the drainpipe, then just as slowly, just as tentatively her foot slid downwards to find the first bracket that attached the cast iron pipe to the outside wall.

She sighed with relief as her foot reached its destination. Not looking down, she edged herself slowly out of the window, her feet steadying her as her hands left the sanctuary of the windowsill and grasped hold of the drainpipe.

There was no going back now. She clung to the drainpipe as if her life depended on it, and tried not to think about how her life did literally depend on it. Now was also not the time to think about how she weighed so much more than she had when she was a slip of a girl. Nor was it time to wonder whether the drainpipe would cope with her added weight. And it was certainly not time to admonish herself for eating all those cream cakes and chocolates that were responsible for the added weight.

She looked down at the ground swirling beneath her, gripped the drainpipe tighter, stared at the stonework so close to her nose and told herself to never, ever look down again. Instead, she looked up, at the window above her.

Should she return to her bedchamber? Even as a child she had not mastered the art of climbing back into her room, and there was no wisdom in trying to learn a new skill now at the advanced age of three and twenty.

Down it would have to be. Her hands scrabbled down the pipe until she reached the next bracket. Once she had a secure grasp, she slid her feet further down until she made contact with the bracket beneath. In this awkward manner she slowly made it down the pipe.

When her feet reached the firm ground she took a brief moment to celebrate her victory, then dropped down behind the shrubbery.

She was still not free. She had to escape the estate. Maintaining her crouched position, she moved along the side of the house. It was inelegant, and she suspected she resembled a waddling duck, but it was the only way she could avoid being seen by anyone who might look out of one of the multitude of windows at the front of the house.

Her father had been so proud when he had moved the family into the Somerset estate he had purchased from an impoverished viscount. Georgina had also loved the house and had enjoyed playing in the enormous gardens, but with her thighs screaming as she continued her awkward progress, she wondered why a house needed to be so big, why it had to have so many rooms, and why the windows on the lower floor had to be quite so close to the ground.

Finally, she made it to the corner of the building. She stood up, shook her legs to release the tension, then sprinted to the large, red brick building that held her final means of escape. She entered the stables and said a silent thanks to her brother for providing her with a way to race across the countryside as free as a bird. Her parents had disapproved of the gift, claiming no good would come of it. They were wrong. Much good was to come of it. It would allow her to put as much distance as possible between herself and the greedy old Duke.

She quietly wheeled her bicycle out of the stable and down the path, holding her breath as if that would somehow quieten the sound of rubber on gravel. The moment she reached the elm trees that lined the path, she mounted her bicycle and pedalled faster than she had ever pedalled before.

Not stopping to see if there were any carts or carriages travelling along the country lane, she flew around the corner and continued pedalling. Her lungs cried out for a rest, but her legs kept pumping. She would not stop until she reached the village. Then she would take a train and travel as far away from Somerset, the Duke and her irritating parents as it was possible to travel.

Sailing around another corner, she smiled to herself. Freedom was near at hand.

Her smile disappeared. She stopped pedalling and whirled to a halt. Where was the village? When they travelled by coach it was always such a short distance. She couldn't remember there being so many corners, so many long stretches of road. But there was nothing for it. She pushed off again and forced her legs to continue, albeit at a less hectic pace.

She reached another corner and still no village, just another long stretch of hedge-lined country road.

Wheezing to a halt, she climbed off her bicycle, threw it into the hedge and glared at it. It was supposed to be her ticket to freedom and instead she was stuck on this country road, miles from anywhere, her legs aching, her lungs gasping, and by now her family had probably noticed her missing and were mounting a search party.

She looked back down the lane and her blame turned towards her father. He had probably bought an estate so far out in the country for just this reason, so she would be trapped. She sank down beside her abandoned bicycle and placed her head in her hands. It was all so unfair.

Adam Knightly, the Duke of Ravenswood, looked out of the carriage window as it drove along the country road and told himself, yet again, that he would not be dispirited. He was resigned to his fate. He had to be. He had been left with no other choice. If he'd been given some warning, he might have been able to find another, less desperate solution to his predicament. But with his father's sudden death he had not only inherited the Dukedom, but also the burden of seemingly insurmountable debts. He needed money, and he needed it immediately. Too many people's livelihoods depended on the Ravenswood estate. Too many tenant farmers and villagers risked losing the tied cottages their families had lived in for generations. Too many tradesmen were owed far too much money and risked going into bankruptcy. They could not be left to suffer because of his father's profligate ways.

Despite his resolve, he huffed out a despondent sigh. He had to marry an heiress. That was the only answer. He tried to take some small solace in the knowledge that he was not the first aristocrat to have to resort to this method to save the family fortune. Nor would he be the first man who had to marry for duty. He would finally be doing just what his father had expected of him when he had first taken a wife.

The old Duke had been furious when Adam had gone against his wishes and not only married a woman with no dowry but had fallen in love with and married the daughter of a tenant farmer. Now he knew why. It wasn't an objection to his beloved Rosalie that had angered his father. It wasn't because the old man was a snob, although there were definitely elements of that. It was because the Duke knew the family was desperate for money.

Well, now Adam would have to do what his father wanted. He watched the scenery pass him by, his mood sinking lower the closer he got to the Hayward estate.

Marriage. It was the last thing he wanted. When Rosalie had been taken from him so early and so cruelly, he had known he would never marry again, and had vowed he would love her until the day he died.

And now, a short five years since her death, he was already being forced to take another bride.

He had married Rosalie for love, and no one would ever replace her in his affections. He still loved her with all of his heart and she never left his thoughts. This marriage was not a complete betrayal of his vow, but it certainly felt like it.

He would do his duty, as would Miss Georgina Hayward. Just like countless couples before them, they would find a way to make this work. And from what Mr Hayward had said, she would make a suitable bride for a man such as himself.

Her father had described her as a dutiful young woman, one who only wanted the best for her family and was honoured to have the opportunity of becoming a duchess. He had said she was amiable, gentle and would make a perfect mother for his three children. If he had to marry again, he could want for nothing better than such a young woman.

His carriage turned a corner and out of the window he spied a maid in a state of some distress. He signalled to the coachman to stop.

As he climbed out of the carriage, Adam told himself he had stopped because it would be wrong to pass by a female in need of help, but deep down he knew there was another reason. He'd welcome any delay if it could put off the coming ordeal, even for a few moments.

'May I be of assistance?' he asked the dishevelled young woman.

'Yes, yes, you can,' she said, standing up and giving him a beaming smile. 'I have to get to the village and I'm afraid I've run out of puff.' She pointed towards the abandoned bicycle.

She did indeed give the impression of someone who had run out of puff. Her cheeks were a bright shade of pink and her strawberry blonde hair, most of which had fallen out of her bun, was stuck to the top of her forehead and neck. Adam also couldn't help noticing she was rather pretty, with dimples on each flushed cheek and a somewhat delightful smile.

But something about this scene was not right. He looked from the maid, who was now brushing down her uniform, to the bicycle, tossed carelessly into the hedgerow, and back to the maid. The shiny black bicycle was new. Could a maid afford such a contraption? Her accent was not what he would expect of a servant, and the way she boldly looked him in the eye was not the usual behaviour of a maid.

And young women did not usually ask strange men for a ride in their carriage, or even speak to men without a formal introduction.

Her uniform restored and her hair tucked back into her cap, she looked back at him. Her smile quivered slightly as he watched her with growing curiosity, and she bobbed a belated curtsey.

'I'd be ever so grateful for your assistance, sir,' she said, her accent suddenly taking on a curious Irish lilt.

Whatever was going on, Adam had neither the time nor the inclination to work it out. She was a young woman, alone in the countryside, and she wanted his help. That was all that really mattered.

He signalled to the open door of the carriage. Her smile returned and she climbed in.

'What of your bicycle?' he asked as she settled herself on the padded leather bench.

'Oh, don't worry about that. Someone will pick that up later.'

Again, it made no real sense, and again it was not Adam's business. He signalled to the coachman and climbed back inside and took his seat on the bench across from her. The carriage was now filled with the delicate scent of lily of the valley. This maid, it appeared, was not averse to helping herself to her mistress's expensive perfume.

The coachman manoeuvred the carriage on the narrow country lane so they could go back to the village. They travelled for a moment in silence, the young maid looking out of the window, still with that pretty smile on her lips.

'May I ask why you need to get to the village with such urgency?' he asked.

The smile faded and she frowned. 'I had to get away from the Hayward family.'

She now had his undivided attention. If something untoward had happened to this young maid at the Haywards' home he was eager to know. The father had seemed like an honourable man, but how a man acted when he was conducting the business of securing a title for his daughter and how he treated his servants could be two very different matters.

'Were you treated badly?'

She nodded rapidly. 'They're terrible people. Tyrants. The things they expect me to do, it's appalling. I'm not a piece of chattel. They don't own me and I won't do it.' She lifted her chin in defiance.

Adam's fists clenched so tightly his nails dug into his flesh. This was an abomination. Servants, particularly young female servants, could be so vulnerable.

'Then you did the right thing in running away.' Adam knew for a young woman in her position, that was all she could do. The law would always be on the side of the master, never the servant. If she had stolen a bicycle so she could flee for her own safety, then in his eyes there was no crime, even if the constabulary might not see it that way.

She leant towards him, as if including him in her conspiracy. 'I plan to run away, as far as I can. I'll take the first train that comes along and hopefully make it all the way to one of those islands at the top of Scotland, or maybe I'll leave the country. No one will ever find me if I run away to America.'

'I believe you need a better plan than that.' He doubted the Haywards would pursue an errant maid all the way to the Shetland Islands or abroad, and it would be unwise for a young woman to travel such a distance unaccompanied. Particularly this young woman, who hadn't even made it to the local village without throwing herself on the mercy of a complete stranger. 'Is there not someone closer at hand with whom you can stay? A family member or a friend?'

She nodded slowly. 'Yes, you're right. I'll take the train to London and hide out with Irene Huntington.'

Adam frowned. 'You know the Duchess of Redcliff?'

She stared at him, her eyes wide, those flushed cheeks turning a deeper shade of pink. 'Well, no, not as such. I mean, well, you know, I worked in her house and—' she shrugged one shoulder '—I know the housekeeper and I'm sure she'll give me employment.'

'That sounds like a sensible idea.'

'Hmm,' was all she said in response, and she looked out of the window, her blushing cheeks now becoming almost scarlet, and the colour moving down to encompass her neck.

Again, it was a peculiar reaction, and again it was none of his business. All he had to do was to make sure she was safely on her way.

The carriage arrived at the station, and he asked her to wait while he bought her a ticket to London. She opened her mouth to object, but he held up his hand to still her words.

He was soon back, with the ticket and some bad news. 'I'm afraid the next train does not leave for another hour.'

'Oh.' She frowned and looked over her shoulder as if expecting to see the Haywards in pursuit. 'Oh, well, never mind. I suppose it won't matter. And thank you so much for buying my ticket. You didn't have to, you know. I do have money.' She patted her pockets and frowned, obviously finding them empty.

He helped her down from the carriage. 'Perhaps we can have a cup of tea in the tearoom while we wait.'

'Oh, are you going to stay with me?' Her face lit up with a pretty smile, and those dimples deepened. She really was too sweet, too pretty and too innocent to be left alone in the world.

'Yes, and perhaps I should send a telegram to the

Duchess of Redcliff so someone can meet you at the station upon your arrival.'

'No, no need,' she said. 'I wouldn't want to put you to any more trouble. Let's just have that cup of tea, shall we?'

With that, she took his arm in a surprisingly familiar manner and led him towards the tearoom, as if taking a gentleman's arm was a perfectly acceptable thing for a maid to do. But her odd behaviour mattered not. He would buy her a cup of tea, put her on the train, perhaps provide her with some money so she could get transport to her new employer's residence, then forget all about her and get back to his real reason for being in Somerset.

'Good morning, sir,' the woman behind the counter said. 'What can I get for yourself and Miss Georgina?'

Adam looked back at the young maid, who was seated at a table and staring out of the window at the travellers and railway workers passing by along the station platform.

'Miss Georgina?' he asked, turning back to the tea lady. 'Are you familiar with my companion?'

'That I am. My sister works up at the Hayward estate. Is Miss Georgina on her way to a fancy dress party or on her way home from one?' She smiled at him, her eyes bright with anticipation as if about to hear an amusing story.

'Yes. She is in fancy dress.' It was all he was prepared to say to the disappointed woman as he placed his coins on the counter then returned to his seat.

Miss Georgina smiled at him. He had been duped, and not just by this so-called escaping maid. He remembered clearly how Mr Hayward had described his daughter.

She was amiable, gentle, would make a perfect mother to his children and was excited about the prospect of marriage to a duke. The man was lying on all counts. Nothing about her behaviour was that of a young lady eager to marry. Quite the reverse.

Thank goodness he had seen the real Miss Georgina Hayward and knew how desperate she was not to wed. Otherwise, they both could have made a terrible mistake. But he had been inadvertently drawn into her strange charade, and that was a situation that needed to be put right immediately.

Chapter Two

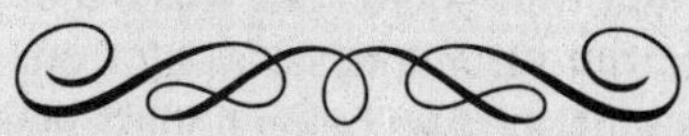

This was all going rather well. Georgina decided she should disguise herself as a maid more often. It provided one with so much freedom—she was all but invisible. This gentleman hadn't even asked for her name, which was fortunate because, in her haste to escape, she hadn't thought far enough ahead to come up with an alias. She looked out of the window at the country station, at the people clasping their suitcases and waiting patiently for the train to puff its way around the corner. If anyone on the train should ask, she would say she was Agnes Bull, or perhaps Molly Scunthorpe, or maybe Bertha Ramsbottom.

She looked back as the gentleman took his seat, and wondered whether she should introduce herself now and try out her new name. She smiled across the table at him. Her rescuer really was rather dashing, and so handsome, with those dark brown eyes and coal black hair. If she had to be saved by a man, she could think of none better than one with chiselled cheekbones and a strong jawline. It would be better if those sculptured lips smiled on occasion, but perhaps heroes who rescued damsels in distress weren't supposed to smile or laugh.

'As the train is going to be another hour, it might be best if I took you to the next station so you can get a connecting train to London,' he said, his expression still deadly serious.

Georgina was about to say it was no bother to wait, but he was right. The sooner she was out of this village and on the train to London, far away from her family, the better. And if she was being honest, she was rather enjoying her time with her dashing, earnest saviour and was more than happy to prolong her time in his company.

'That would be ever so good of you, kind sir. If it's not too much trouble that I'm putting you to,' she said, remembering to use her new maid's way of speaking.

With no further explanation, he stood up and walked towards the door. She looked over to the counter, where the woman was still preparing their tea. It was all a bit rude, to both her and the tea lady. But now was hardly the time to give him a lesson in manners, so she stood up and dutifully followed him out of the tearoom. And, bad manners aside, what choice did she really have but to follow along? After all, he still had her train ticket and she had foolishly left home without her reticule.

She scowled slightly. Father was, unfortunately, right about *one* thing. She really did need to start thinking things through a bit more carefully. Next time she staged a daring escape she would make sure she had plenty of money for the journey. Then she would not have to rely on the kindness of strange men. She could have sent her own telegram to Irene, and the message would contain no confusing mention of maids, unknown men or the request for employment. But then, if she'd planned ahead, she would not have met this kind and not the least bit strange man. She nodded in satisfaction. It had all worked out in the end and Father was wrong to criticise her yet again.

He strode across to his waiting carriage and opened the door. She waited for him to offer her his hand. No hand was proffered so she clambered inside. He joined her, shut the door and signalled to the coachman. Her knight in shining armour had suddenly become a bit of a grump, but not to worry. She would soon be miles away in London. Away from her rescuer, away from the greedy Duke, away from her family and away from attending yet another insufferable Season.

She gave a little shudder at the thought of the looming Season. If she went into hiding at her friend Irene's London townhouse, she would not endure being placed on display yet again. She would not be subjected to all those down-on-their-luck nobles assessing her flaws and attributes to see whether she was worthy enough to become their bride.

And to think the first Season had started off so promisingly. Her father had pulled strings and called in favours so his daughter could be presented at Court. She had been so excited when she had lined up in her white gown with all those daughters of the aristocracy and taken her curtsey in front of Queen Victoria. She had then expected to be the belle of the ball, that men would be lining up to dance with her. She had expected to have fun flirting with countless handsome men and to be inundated with proposals from love-struck suitors.

Instead, the only men who'd paid her any attention were those everyone knew were in desperate need of money. Yes, they flirted and charmed, but in such a manner she would have to be a halfwit not to see the real reason behind their interest. And even if she had been a half-wit, she would not have been able to ignore a conversation she'd overheard between the Duke of Cromley and his eldest son.

'I don't care if she is the most vacuous woman you've ever met. And if her looks don't appeal to you, then think of the vast fortune she will bring to the family and all we can do with it. Now, ask her to dance again, before one of those other blackguards bags her dowry.'

Georgina had been flabbergasted. She hadn't even wanted to dance with John Cromley, and certainly would not consider marrying him. He was such a bore. And yet he thought she would be flattered by his attentions, just because he would one day become a duke.

After overhearing that outrageous conversation, she had been unsure whether to give Cromley a stern telling off, or to thank him for opening her eyes to what the ball was really about. It was merely a place where men could scrutinise what was on offer that Season so they could make the most advantageous marriage.

Well, if all those men were interested in was her marriage settlement, then she wanted nothing to do with any of them.

She blinked away the annoying tears that had sprung to her eyes and looked out at the scenery. Then she saw a sight that drove out all thoughts of Cromley, Seasons and dowries.

'What?' she gasped as she pointed out of the window. 'We've just passed my bicycle.' She turned in her seat as her abandoned bicycle disappeared from view around a corner. 'We need to turn around. We're going the wrong way. This is not the way to the next village.'

'Perhaps now would be a good time to introduce ourselves,' he said, rather than informing the coachman of his mistake.

'What? Now? Yes, all right. I'm Agnes Ramsbottom. How do you do?'

'No, you're Miss Georgina Hayward and I am Adam Knightly, the Duke of Ravenswood.'

Georgina's lips formed an O shape, but no words came out. He continued to stare at her, those dark brown eyes boring into hers while Georgina racked her brain to come up with an explanation for her behaviour. None came. She lurched forward to pull open the door. She had never tried leaping from a moving carriage before, but desperate times called for desperate measures, and this most decidedly counted as a desperate time.

The handle didn't move. She wriggled it harder. It still didn't move. And neither did the Duke. He sat completely still, his face expressionless, those brown eyes still staring at her without pity.

'You've locked the door. Are you holding me prisoner? What sort of man has a lock on his carriage door?'

'I have a lock on the door to stop my son from trying to climb out of the carriage when it is moving.'

'You have no right to lock me in.'

'I made the decision to do so as it appears you are just as likely to do something foolhardy without thought of the consequences. Just like my son. He, of course, does have the excuse of being only five years old.'

She scowled at him. She had thought him kind and considerate, but he wasn't. He was arrogant, rude and as awful as she'd expected the Duke of Ravenswood to be. Although she hadn't expected him to be so young. What would he be? Late twenties, early thirties? Nor had she thought he'd be so handsome, but none of that mattered, not when he had the audacity to actually hold her captive.

'Stop this carriage now and let me out,' she demanded.

'I will take you home to your parents, where you belong.'

'So you can marry me and get your grubby hands on my dowry?' She looked down at his hands, which were definitely not grubby. In fact, they were rather attractive hands, strong, with long lean fingers.

Her gaze flicked back up to his face and she lifted her chin high. 'Well, that is not going to happen. I am not one of my parents' chattels and I will not marry anyone just because they say so.'

'I'm returning you home to where you will be safe. And you can rest assured I have no intention of marrying you or anyone else against their will.'

'Good,' she stated defiantly. It might have been nice if he'd put up a bit of an argument, but still, she had what she wanted and should be content. 'Now that we've agreed there will be no marriage, you can let me out, and go back to wherever you came from.'

'Dorset.'

'What?'

'That is where I come from.'

'Good, well, go back there. Now.'

'Your parents invited me for the weekend, to meet

you and to see whether a courtship between us would occur. I accepted the invitation. It would be remiss of me not to arrive.'

'But I have no interest in being courted by you or anyone.'

'I am well aware of that. And you will be pleased to know that I too have no interest in a courtship.'

'Why not?' Georgina blurted out, affronted by so immediate a rejection. He wanted a dowry. She had a dowry. Wasn't that all men like him ever saw when they looked at an unmarried heiress? Or did he think himself too handsome, too grand, too superior for the likes of her?

His long, tapered fingers indicated her attire.

She looked down at her dull brown, sack-shaped uniform, which was far from flattering.

'I'm not really a maid, you know. I don't usually dress like this, but I could hardly climb down a drainpipe dressed in a fancy gown, now, could I?'

One eyebrow rose slightly. 'I am now well aware that you are not a maid. But I am also aware that you are… how shall I put this…rather impetuous and indulge in behaviour that is perilous. I have a young son and two impressionable daughters. I need a wife who will be responsible and a good influence on them, not someone who climbs drainpipes.'

Georgina glared at him, although it was hard to deny she was impetuous or that she did, when the occasion demanded, behave perilously. Not when she was sitting across from him dressed as a maid, having just admitted to him the manner in which she'd escaped her home.

'But I come with an enormous dowry,' she said instead, her words dripping with sarcasm. 'That's usually enough for most men to overlook my long list of flaws.'

'I'm not most men.'

Georgina could not argue with that. He was definitely more attractive than any man she had met before. And more something else. Manly? Commanding? Something she couldn't quite put her finger on. But, whatever it was, it did not excuse his rude dismissal of her.

'But you don't deny you were after my dowry.' He had criticised her, now she was determined to show him up for the sort of man he really was. One who had no right to look down his nose at her, albeit a rather elegant, imperious nose.

'No, I don't deny it.'

Georgina frowned. How could one argue with a man when he agreed with one?

'Well, I think it's appalling to marry someone just for their money,' she said. That was what she would focus on—self-righteous indignation—and not the fact that he did not appear to be the slightest bit insulted by her accusation.

'I agree.'

'You do not. You already said you were after my dowry.'

'I agree that it is wrong to marry just for money.' He huffed out a deep sigh. 'Unfortunately, my financial position means I have to marry a woman who brings with her a substantial amount of money.' His jaw tightened, although his exasperation no longer seemed to be with her.

'Why? I suppose you gambled away all your wealth and now you want to do the same with mine.'

He flinched at the accusation. Good. She had hit the

nail on the head, as they said, and shown him up for the man he really was.

'You're right that the family fortune was gambled away, but not by me. I have never entered a gambling den, attended a racecourse or shuffled a pack of cards in my life.'

She didn't doubt it. He was far too humourless for that.

'It was my father who was the gambler, and as a result I inherited a dukedom collapsing under the weight of crushing debts, one carrying mortgages more than ten times the size of the estates' annual incomes.'

'Well, why don't you just sell them?' she fired back, determined not to feel sorry for him. 'Wouldn't that be the decent thing to do, rather than marrying for money?'

'That is exactly what I would do if legal restrictions did not mean no part of my inheritance can be sold and it all has to stay in the family. I inherited debt, but I do not want to pass on that burden to my son, nor do I wish to put at risk the futures of the tenant farmers, whose families have lived on the estates for generations, by selling off the land on which they live.'

'Then get a loan from someone, a bank or something.' Georgina lifted her chin higher, pleased that she knew about such things. 'That's what Father always does when he starts a new business venture.'

'Do you not think I have tried?'

She shrugged. Money, banks, finance… She knew such things existed, but that was the limit of her knowledge. Arguing with her father for an increase in her allowance was the closest she ever came to such matters. But the Duke's money troubles did not mean she would forgive him, although whether she was still annoyed with him for seeking an heiress or rejecting her, she was no longer entirely sure.

'Banks lend to your father because his businesses are viable propositions that will make them a good return on their investment. They do not loan to dukes who already have enormous debts throughout the land, whose estates are unprofitable because they are still using farming methods that have changed little since the Middle Ages, whose home is in desperate need of repair, whose…' He sighed loudly. 'No bank or financial institution will lend money under such conditions. So I am forced to marry an heiress who is desirous of a title.'

'Oh…' was all Georgina could say.

'But, as I am to marry again, I also require a wife with whom I am compatible, who is content with this arrangement, and one who will make a good mother for my three children.'

'Oh,' she repeated.

'Your father assured me you would be agreeable to this arrangement, but you are correct. You are not a chattel and I will not marry anyone against their will.'

'Hmm,' was all she could say to that. Then she turned back to him as another thought occurred to her. 'So how do you intend to find your perfect heiress now that I've failed to live up to your expectations?'

He hissed out a sigh through clenched teeth. 'I will do what every other unmarried man in search of a bride does. I will attend the Season and see who is available.'

His doleful expression suggested he found the thought of attending the Season as pleasurable as she did.

'They're awful, aren't they?' Georgina said, dread of what was to come driving out her irritation with him.

'I have never attended, so can't say.'

'Really? But how did you meet your first wife?'

'It wasn't during the Season,' he said, turning to look out of the window as if to inform her that the manner in which he'd met his wife was none of her concern.

'Well, you're about to discover just how truly horrible the Season can be. Everyone dresses in their finest clothes, all being so terribly polite, while at the same time manoeuvring and manipulating to catch the man with the highest title or the lady with the biggest dowry.' She gave a mock shudder to emphasise the horror.

He did not respond nor did he look happy.

'If it's any consolation, while you're in search of your heiress I'll be fending off men after my fortune.' She frowned at the thought. 'Men who don't care about my countless faults or whether I want to marry them or not.'

He still made no response but continued staring out of the window. Apparently, her problems were no consolation at all. Well, he was soon going to discover for himself how ruthless mothers and debutantes could be, particularly when there was a handsome unwed duke for the taking.

She smiled to herself as a wonderful source of amusement occurred to her. 'I could help you,' she said.

He didn't answer, merely turned to look at her, his eyebrows raised, as if he couldn't possibly see any way in which she would be helpful.

'If you tell me all the qualities you are looking for in your heiress, I can let you know which young lady possesses those qualities. Believe me, debutantes can be very deceptive when they're looking for a husband. They'll all pretend to be the perfect bride for you, until they get you up the aisle. Only then will you discover what a terrible mistake you've made. Oh, the stories I could tell you. There was one young lady who—'

'I believe I am perfectly capable of seeing through deception.'

'Really? You thought that I was a maid who needed your help.' She sent him a satisfied smile.

He merely hmphed in response, then drew in a deep breath and exhaled slowly. 'And if you do help me, what will you be expecting in return?'

An image of the Duke taking her in his arms, holding her close against him and kissing her long and slowly flashed into her mind, causing heat to explode onto her cheeks.

'Nothing. Nothing at all,' she burst out to cover her embarrassment.

'Nothing?'

'It will provide me with a diversion from the tedium of another Season,' she said, her words tumbling over each other. 'Do you know how boring the Season can get, especially when you've attended five, like I have?'

He made no response, but signalled for the coachman to stop at the large gold and black gates, still bearing the Viscount's crest, that led to her family home. 'After your own deception, it might be best if you don't arrive home in my carriage. I suspect that, along with your attire, would be difficult to explain to your parents.'

'Yes, right. It will be our little secret.'

Before he could respond, she climbed out of the carriage and rushed down the pathway, hoping he had not noticed her burning cheeks and had no inkling that a decidedly inappropriate and unwanted image had crashed into her mind completely uninvited.

Chapter Three

Adam watched Miss Georgina dart to the nearest tree in the row of elms lining the long path that led to the house, peek out, then dash to the next one. She continued this bizarre behaviour until she reached the edge of the house. Then she bent low, scuttled around the side of the building and disappeared from view.

She really was an unusual young lady. But she was also right. He was hopelessly ill-prepared for the Season. The ease with which she had fooled him showed just how easy it would be for any young woman with an eye on his title to deceive him. He'd had his suspicions when he'd found her on the side of the road but had never for one moment thought she would be a wealthy heiress in disguise, and that it would be *him* she was fleeing from.

And that wasn't the only worrying aspect of their encounter. Despite her being wholly unsuitable as a wife for him or a mother to his children, he could not deny that there was something about her he found damnably attractive.

But that was not enough. He needed a wife who had a level of maturity—someone quiet, who would unobtrusively fit in with his household and cause him no disruption. Hopefully, he would meet a young lady who genuinely possessed these qualities early in the Season and his search would be a short one.

But how was he going to ensure that he did find such a bride? If he could be attracted by a young lady who was so patently unsuitable, did that mean he was in danger of having his head turned by any pretty young thing with an endearing smile, and of forgetting what he really needed in a wife?

Perhaps it was merely that he had been five long years without a woman in his life. That too, unfortunately, made him vulnerable. Loath as he was to admit it, perhaps her assistance in his quest was not quite so ridiculous.

He waited a few moments longer to ensure she had made it inside safely, then signalled for the coachman to take them up to the house. This was going to be an absurd encounter. Everyone was going to be deceiving each other. The Season hadn't even begun and already he had encountered a disheartening level of what Miss Hayward described as manoeuvring and manipulation.

The three-storey house loomed up before him as he travelled up the driveway. The magnificent ochre stone building dominated the landscape and rivalled the best in England. Mr Hayward might have lied about his daughter, but he had not been deceptive about the extent of his wealth.

The carriage pulled up in front of the house and Mr and Mrs Hayward and a young man in his mid-twenties emerged from the grand entrance and waited under the portico. The parents presented the picture of contented wealth. Mr Hayward's rotund shape and florid complexion suggested a man who liked to indulge, or overindulge, in the finer things in life. His wife's ornate gown and the jewels bedecking her neck, ears and wrists further emphasised this impression.

Unlike most wealthy families, who had accumulated the family jewels over many generations, Mrs Hayward's would have been purchased from the considerable profits of her husband's businesses, which were believed to include shipping lines, railways, mines and manufacturing concerns throughout the land.

Adam drew in a deep, resigned breath and descended from his carriage, determined to get this charade over and done with as quickly as possible.

'Welcome to our humble home, Your Grace,' Mr Hayward said, giving Adam's hand a hearty shake. 'May I present my wife and my son, Thomas?'

Mrs Hayward gave a low curtsey, while Thomas smirked as if enjoying an amusing private joke, before shaking his hand.

'I'm so sorry Georgina is not here to greet you,' Mrs Hayward said as she took his arm and led him into the house. 'She's a bit shy and she really did want to make an extra effort with her appearance. You know what young ladies are like when they are courting.'

Adam merely nodded in response to these outrageous lies.

'Not that she really needs to,' Mrs Hayward said with a small, false laugh. 'My daughter is such a pretty young thing, even if I do say so myself.'

That was something Adam could not dispute. She was indeed pretty.

'And she's so excited to meet you,' she added. 'She had to try on every dress in her wardrobe in an attempt to find the perfect gown.'

Including a maid's uniform, Adam could have added.

'She is so nervous about making a good first impression,' Mrs Hayward continued as they strolled down the entranceway, lined with marble statues the previous owner must have purchased during his grand tour of Europe.

'I don't know what she has to be nervous about,' Thomas said, still smirking. 'Georgina never fails to make a memorable first impression.'

Mrs Hayward frowned briefly at her son, then smiled at Adam as she led him through to the drawing room overlooking the gardens.

'Dorset is lovely at this time of year,' Mrs Hayward said, abruptly changing the subject as she seated herself on the divan with much rustling of skirts.

Adam stifled a sigh. He had forgotten that such social visits required small talk. It was an artform he had never perfected. Rosalie and he had been content to remain in the countryside and take no part in the social whirl the aristocracy enjoyed so much. Now he was going to have to endure an entire Season of commentaries on the weather and endless, mindless gossip.

'Indeed it is,' he responded. Mrs Hayward smiled with delight as if he had just made a witty riposte.

'We visited the Brookshires in Dorset last year,' she said, reminding Adam that name-dropping was another essential aspect of social chit-chat. 'Lord and Lady

Brookshire are such good friends of ours, aren't they, dear?' she added, turning to her husband.

'What? Oh, yes, the Brookshires. They've got some very productive land I was interested in acquiring.'

Mrs Hayward frowned at her husband, then smiled at Adam. 'Oh, let's not talk about business. That's not what this weekend is about.'

Adam could have informed her that business was exactly what this weekend was about. The Haywards were using their daughter to advance their position in Society, and he was in the market for an heiress. It was the depressing truth, but one none of them were going to openly admit to.

The door opened and Miss Hayward entered.

He stood up, surprised by the transformation—and by his reaction. She'd made a pretty maid, but now she was dressed as an elegant, sophisticated young woman, wearing a flowing pale blue lacy dress, with a dark blue sash showing off her slim waist. Her full breasts and rounded hips had been disguised in her shapeless maid's uniform, but they were on display now, as if for his admiration. He knew he shouldn't, but he couldn't help his eyes from sweeping up and down her curvaceous body.

'May I present my daughter, Miss Georgina Hayward?' Mr Hayward said.

She lowered her eyes and performed a low curtsey. 'Your Grace,' she said in a quiet manner.

He wasn't sure why she was indulging in this charade, but if it was to prove her point as to how easily he could be deceived, she was achieving her goal. If he had not already met her, he would have thought her perfect and exactly as her father described—gentle, amiable and content with the idea of such a marriage.

'Now, don't be shy,' Mrs Hayward said to the young woman who Adam suspected had never been shy in her life. 'Come over here and sit beside His Grace.'

Her eyes still lowered, she rose from her curtsey, crossed the room and sat down on the divan. He looked at the Haywards. Both parents were smiling with delight at this performance while Thomas's smile was that of someone watching an amusing play.

'We were just discussing Dorset,' Mrs Hayward said as the men took their seats. 'I believe your family has resided there for many generations.'

'Yes,' Adam responded, somewhat distracted as he watched Georgina's demure performance. 'The Knightly family has lived there since Tudor times, but the sixth Duke of Ravenswood extended the house considerably in the early Georgian period.'

'Did you hear that, Georgina?' Mrs Hayward said. 'A family that can trace its history back to the Tudor period.'

Miss Hayward's eyes remained lowered. 'Yes, Mama,' she said in a barely audible voice.

'Georgian period?' Mr Hayward added. 'I imagine a house built back then would need a lot of upkeep. This house is also Georgian, and when I think about the amount I've spent on it to make it liveable, it would probably have been cheaper to tear it down and build the thing from the ground up.'

Adam merely nodded his assent as Mr Hayward reminded him of yet another reason why he needed to marry an heiress.

'Mama, perhaps I could show His Grace around the estate,' Miss Hayward said, and Adam had to lean forward to hear her quiet words.

'Excellent idea,' Mrs Hayward responded enthusiastically. 'It will give you two a chance to get to know each other better, and His Grace can tell you all about his estate in Dorset.'

Miss Hayward stood up, her eyes still lowered, and glided across the room and out of the door, leaving Adam with no choice but to follow on behind. The moment the door closed behind them, she raced down the hallway and out into the gardens, as if fleeing from armed guards, leaving him following in her wake.

'I believe you can drop this act now,' Adam said when he caught up to her on the gravel pathway.

'Not yet,' she whispered. 'They'll be watching out of the drawing room window. We need to look as if we are complete strangers.'

Adam turned to look over his shoulder to see that all three Haywards were indeed watching them.

'Don't turn around,' she said in a low voice. 'We don't want them to think we're talking about them.'

Adam released an exasperated sigh, but did as she commanded, and followed her down the path and into the formal garden, his irritation at this game-playing continuing to grow.

'There, we're out of sight now,' she said and gave a little laugh. 'These topiaries will hide us from their prying eyes.'

'You don't think you're overdoing the meek and mild act somewhat?' he said as he indicated a stone bench overlooking the garden.

'Nonsense,' she stated in a manner that was neither meek nor mild. 'I was merely following all the instructions I was given at Miss Halliwell's Finishing School for Refined Young Ladies. Miss Halliwell was of the opinion that a young lady could never, ever be too meek or too mild.'

'Miss Halliwell, whoever she might be, never saw *that* performance.'

She laughed as if he had made a joke, rather than stating a fact.

'Surely your parents will know it was all pretence,' he said as he sat down beside her.

'Of course they will. But what do they care, as long as I catch a duke? They'll just be grateful to see that the expense of sending me to Halliwell's to turn me into a proper, refined young lady was money well spent.'

'I'd hate to think what you were like before you were sent off to finishing school and became proper and refined.'

She laughed again as if he had made another joke, which he hadn't.

'You can rest assured that Halliwell's had no effect on me whatsoever, except for teaching me how to *pretend* to be a proper young lady when it suits. But it was worth every penny my father spent as I met my closest friends there, Amelia, Irene and Emily. It was thanks to them that I survived the ordeal.' She looked over at him. 'Irene is the Duchess of Redcliff. That's who I was planning on fleeing to in order to escape…' She shrugged her shoulders and smiled. 'Well, to escape you.'

'I take it the Duchess of Redcliff also failed to become a proper, refined young lady.'

'Yes, she was as hopeless as I was.' She laughed as if this was a great achievement. 'But oh, the four of us had such fun. You can't imagine the things we got up to.'

Adam would rather not.

'We called it Hell's Final Sentence for Rebellious Young Ladies and made a pact that we would continue to rebel, no matter what.'

'A pact that you have obviously managed to adhere to.'

'I have,' she said, not registering Adam's sarcasm.

'So how long do you think we have to remain out here, before we can agree that we are completely mismatched and I can return home?'

'A few minutes more should do it. So, what are you going to tell my father?'

'That we have no wish to marry.'

She turned on the bench and grasped his arm. 'No, don't say that. Then I'll be subjected to a boring lecture about not making enough of an effort, and about how I'm getting old and time is running out, and on and on and on. It's been five Seasons. Five.' The grip on his arm tightened. 'I'm about to start my sixth, and still no marriage prospects. Father will be unbearable if he thinks I let a duke slip through my fingers, and as for Mother, well…' She threw her hands up in the air. 'Please don't get me into any more trouble than I already am.'

'What do you expect me to say?'

She thought for a moment, then gave him a wicked smile. 'Tell him I'm far too passive for your taste. That you want a wife with a bit of pluck. That will teach them.'

'You want me to lie to them?'

She raised her eyebrows and smiled as if she had caught him out in a deliberate deception. 'Don't try and tell me you're incapable of lying. I know you're not because you lied to me!'

'When?'

'When you tricked me into getting back in your carriage. You said you were taking me to the next village, but you were really delivering me back into my parents' clutches and forcing me to endure all this.'

'I was doing it for your own protection. Anything could happen to a young lady alone without a chaperon.'

'Yes, she could get abducted by a duke and held captive in his carriage.'

'I was not… I did not—'

She patted his arm. 'I'm just joking. But just as you meant no harm in lying to me, there will be no harm in lying to my parents. After all, they've been lying to you.'

He nodded slowly. He didn't like it, but she did make a good point. It was not in his nature to tell lies but, given the absurdity of this entire encounter, and the way Mr and Mrs Hayward had contrived to pull the wool over his eyes, there would be a certain satisfaction in letting them think their deception had the opposite to the intended effect.

'So, have you thought about my offer to help you navigate the Season?' she said, obviously assuming the question of what he would say to her father was now settled and he would do exactly as she wanted.

'Yes, and I can see there is some merit in your suggestion.'

'Oh, goodie.' She clapped her hands. 'Let's start

straight away by listing some of the qualities you *do* want in a bride.'

Let's not, Adam wanted to say, but knew that such objections would fall on deaf ears.

'As I said, I need a wife who is happy with the arrangement, and one who will make a kind and loving mother to my children.'

'Right. Kind, loving, happy.' She ticked them off on her fingers. 'What about intelligent?'

'Well, yes, I suppose so.'

She gave him an assessing look. 'Although most men prefer a young lady who agrees with them rather than one who has a mind of her own. When they say a woman is intelligent, that is usually what they mean.'

She gave him a pointed look, and before he could contradict her claim she continued. 'Charming?'

'I don't know what that means.'

'Well, you know, flirtatious, someone who laughs at your jokes, who flatters you, that sort of thing.'

'I do not make jokes.'

'No, you don't, do you?' She laughed as if that in itself was a joke.

'And I have no interest in being flattered or flirted with.'

Her eyebrows drew together and she gave him a shrewd look. 'I suspect you are now the one being deceptive. All men like to be flirted with and flattered.'

'Not this man.'

'Hmm, we'll see. So, a good conversationalist?'

'Again, I don't know what that means.'

'Someone you can talk to.'

'We're talking now. Does that make you a good conversationalist?'

'No. I failed conversation skills when I was at Halliwell's.'

'How could you possibly fail that? You hardly stop talking long enough to catch your breath.'

She smiled at him as if mistakenly believing he had given her another compliment. 'I failed because I'm hopeless at talking to shrubs.'

'Shrubs?'

'Yes, at Halliwell's Hell our lessons in good conversation skills involved walking around the garden, stopping at each shrub and making polite conversation. We had to come up with a different topic with each shrub. That would prove we could circulate at a social occasion and engage every man in interesting conversation.'

He stared at her in disbelief. 'So if a young lady asks me if I get watered frequently enough or enquires as to how much fertiliser the gardener spreads around my roots I'll know she's a graduate of Halliwell's.'

She laughed and leant in towards him. 'I thought you said you didn't make jokes.'

He hadn't lied. He didn't make jokes, but he had to admit it was rather nice to make her laugh. And it *was* a rather pleasant sound. Rosalie was the last woman he had made laugh, and there hadn't been anything worth laughing about since her death.

'I have no idea what sort of woman would make the ideal wife,' he said, bringing all joking to an end. 'As I said, I need an heiress. All that matters is she has no qualms about such a marriage, that she will be kind to my children, and she will be someone with whom I have a sufficient degree of compatibility.'

'Hmm, when it comes to qualities, that is rather vague. Perhaps we should discuss what flaws you want to avoid. We already know you don't want impetuousness or a young woman who takes risks.'

Adam cringed slightly at his bad manners. 'Miss Hayward, I meant no offence in what I said.'

'I know that. You were just being honest and I was just teasing.' She gave another carefree laugh. 'Maybe that's something we should add to the list. You don't want a young lady who teases you.'

Adam had no answer to that claim.

'Although you might have to get used to a bit of teasing during the Season. But don't worry, most young ladies know how to do so in a manner that flatters you, or flatters them, or ideally both of you.'

He huffed out another sigh. 'Once again, I have no idea what you are talking about.'

She gave him an appraising look. 'Perhaps you need a lesson or two. If a young lady ever criticises herself, you have to immediately tell her how wrong she is.'

'So, I should tell you that you're not impetuous, that you don't have a mind of your own and your behaviour is cautious and considered.'

'I can see you need a lot more help than I first thought,' she said, her mock frown showing she was amused rather than disapproving. 'No, if I said, *Oh, the other young ladies at this ball are so much prettier than me*,' she said in a coy voice with much fluttering of eyelashes. 'Then you should say, *No, Miss Hayward, there is none prettier than you,*' she added in a deep, somewhat pompous tone.

'No, Miss Hayward, there is none prettier than you.'

She placed her hand on his arm and laughed. 'It might be better if you said it as if you meant it.'

Adam thought he *had* said it as if he meant it. She was indeed a pretty woman and seemed to be getting prettier the more time he spent in her company. She had a delightful, musical laugh, a vivacious personality, and when she smiled, which was frequently, the dimples that appeared in each cheek were enchanting.

'If that's the best you can do, it might be better to avoid flattery,' she continued. 'And I suspect it won't matter what you say and do. You're an eligible duke. That is all anyone will see.' She gave a small sigh. 'You're a bit like me in that regard. No one ever really sees me, or cares about getting to know me. All they see when they look at me is my marriage settlement.'

'That is surely not true. I'm sure men are attracted to you for many other reasons.'

She gave one of those tinkling laughs. 'That was much better. You are a quick learner. Although perhaps you should have said, *I'm sure men are attracted to you for your beauty and wit,*' she added, once more adopting that rather pompous tone that sounded nothing like him.

'But I mean what I said,' she continued. 'When young ladies talk to you, they'll all be imagining what it will be like to be a duchess. They'll be picturing themselves at the very pinnacle of Society and being able to lord it over their friends and family.'

'That most certainly is not the sort of woman I want.

I do not want a woman with pretensions. I do not want to marry a woman who cares only about becoming a duchess, one who is mercenary.'

Her big blue eyes grew wide. 'If you don't want a woman who is desperate to advance her position in Society then I think you're about to join the wrong game. And as for mercenary…' She tilted her head and raised her eyebrows, as if she needed to say no more on that subject.

Adam huffed out a loud breath. 'Yes, all right. I will no doubt be the most mercenary man present.'

'It's all so wrong, isn't it?' she said with a deep sigh. 'Was your first marriage a love match?'

As if a physical weight had descended on him, Adam's shoulders grew heavy. 'It was,' he said quietly, as if talking to himself. 'I loved her more than life itself, and yet she was taken from me. But before that happened, I vowed to her that I would stay faithful to my love for her till the day I die.'

He closed his eyes, remembering Rosalie's beautiful face, her smile and her laughter.

He felt a hand placed lightly on his arm, reminding him of Georgina's presence. Had he really spoken of Rosalie? He never spoke of the woman he loved to anyone, and yet he had mentioned their love to this flighty young girl who meant nothing to him.

'I'm sorry,' she said quietly.

'I believe we should return to the house now,' he said, standing up and bringing this inappropriate conversation to an abrupt end. 'We have had sufficient time to convince your parents that we have become acquainted.'

'As you wish,' she said, taking his hand and standing up.

They commenced walking arm in arm back to the house in silence. 'So what do you plan to say to my father?' she asked, her voice regaining its usual bubbly sound.

'I will make sure he is left with no illusion that there could ever be a marriage between the two of us, and that it is pointless to try and change my mind. Then I will inform him that I plan to leave immediately.'

'Oh,' she gasped, presumably in response to his stern manner and not his compliance with her plan.

Why was he speaking to her in this manner? It was not this young woman's fault that she was so full of life, joy and vitality. Nor was it her fault that Rosalie's life had been cut short. He had no right to be so terse with her. The fault for Rosalie's death lay with one person and one person only. Him.

'Well, I'd appreciate it if you didn't say anything about the maid's uniform, the drainpipe escape or any of that,' she said.

He nodded. 'I will do everything in my power to convince your father you did your best to capture my heart and you are not to blame.'

'Thank you,' she said, but her gratitude did nothing to assuage his guilt over his terse reaction to the mention of his beloved Rosalie.

They turned the corner, out of the sanctuary of the formal garden and back onto the gravel path.

'Right, no more laughter, no more jokes, no more teasing,' she said. 'We want them to think that we had nothing to talk about and spent the entire time in an uncomfortable silence.'

Adam was indeed feeling uncomfortable, but would have difficulty explaining to Miss Hayward or even to himself, why that should be.

Chapter Four

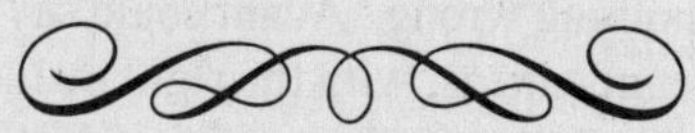

'Did you have a pleasant walk?' Mrs Hayward asked as they entered the drawing room.

Adam merely bowed his assent and remained standing as Miss Hayward took her seat beside her mother, her eyes lowered in that absurd manner. He knew she was playing a game with her parents, just as she seemed to turn everything into a game. But he was not prepared to remain in this house a moment longer to be part of the entertainment.

'Mr Hayward, may I have a word with you?'

The mother's smile grew wider as she took her daughter's hand, while her husband stood, pulled down his jacket, squared his shoulders self-importantly, then ushered Adam out of the room.

'My study would be the best place for this conversation,' Mr Hayward said, escorting Adam down the hallway. 'I've got a rather nice French brandy I've just bought and suspect now will be the perfect occasion to open it.'

Adam said nothing until they were behind the closed

doors of the book-lined study. Mr Hayward sat in a large leather chair and indicated that Adam should take the other one. He declined the offer and remained standing.

'Regretfully, I will not be courting your daughter.'

Mr Hayward sprang to his feet. 'Why not?' Then he sank back into his chair, his face the picture of despair. 'What did she do now? What did she say?'

'She did nothing wrong.' Adam could say that, under the right circumstances, with the right man, Miss Hayward would make a perfect wife, and perhaps they should let her just be herself so she could find a man compatible with an impetuous imp who loved to enjoy life.

'Then why?' Mr Hayward looked up at him, his eyes beseeching.

'I'm afraid she is somewhat too passive and demure,' he said, inwardly cringing at his lie, even if it was a lie that would save Miss Hayward from a reprimand. 'I have a rumbustious five-year-old son who needs a mother, one who is energetic, even feisty, and two daughters who would easily get the better of such a reserved and docile young lady.'

Mr Hayward flinched as if he had been struck. Adam suspected he was desperately wanting to tell him that few young ladies were more energetic or feisty than his daughter, but that would require admitting he had lied in his initial description of his daughter, and her prim and proper behaviour had been designed to deceive him.

'Perhaps over the weekend you will come to see there is more to my daughter than you first thought,' he said. This was becoming embarrassing. The man was actually pleading. 'I'm sure you'll find that Georgina is more than a match for even the most unruly child.'

Adam did not doubt that, but it was hardly the point. He didn't want to marry her. She didn't want to marry him. That was the end of any discussion. He had stayed long enough. To stay any longer would be a trial for all concerned.

'I believe it will be best if you give my apologies to Miss Hayward and your wife.' Adam knew that was somewhat impolite, but for all concerned, including himself, it would be best to leave immediately.

'Are you sure I can't tempt you to stay?' Mr Hayward said with a note of desperation. 'I still have that French brandy.'

'I thank you, but no.'

He bowed to the older man, who had crumpled in on himself in his large leather chair, then headed out of the house and called for his coachman to take him away from this estate as quickly as the horses would allow.

Georgina's father entered the drawing room and slumped into the nearest chair.

'It didn't take you long to see off another one,' Tommy said with a look of unbridled glee. 'You're getting ever more efficient at this, Georgie. So what did you do or say to send this one packing?'

Her father glared at his son. 'This is no laughing matter, Thomas. She's twenty-three, for goodness' sake. She'll be turning twenty-four during the coming Season. I had hoped by marrying her off to the Duke we'd be saved the humiliation of escorting her to yet another

Season. If she doesn't make a suitable match soon…' He sighed and placed his head in his hands.

Georgina almost felt sorry for her father. Almost.

'I believe we have different definitions on what makes a suitable match, Father,' she said, stopping herself from feeling pity for a man who continually thrust her in front of men who anyone with any sense could see would make terrible husbands.

Her father looked over at her through his spread fingers, then dropped his hands and sat up straight. 'We have indulged you far too much, my girl. All we ask in return for all that we have given you is for you to make a suitable marriage to a titled man.'

Georgina matched his glaring look and ramrod posture. 'Why can't Tommy be the sacrificial lamb? Why isn't he being forced to marry a titled lady?'

Her father exhaled loudly and shook his head slowly. 'How many times do I have to tell you? Because if he marries a titled lady, nothing will change. He'll just get a wife and it will make no difference whatsoever to this family. If you married the Duke you would become a duchess and your children would all have titles.'

He scowled in Georgina's direction. 'I would have preferred it if he didn't have a son so my grandson would be a duke one day, but at least we'd have a title in the family.' He shook his head and huffed out a loud sigh through flared nostrils. 'After five Seasons and no takers, we're hardly in a position to be fussy, and at least my grandchildren would have titles.' He lifted his nose into the air. 'That would be part of my legacy.'

Georgina pouted. He was right. Not in his assertion that she should marry a titled man, but that she had heard similar lectures many times before, and frankly it was getting boring. But the other part of his argument was completely ridiculous. Surely his legacy was that he had made bundles and bundles of money. And it wasn't as if Society excluded them. Countless aristocrats attended the Hayward balls. Although she had to admit that was probably because they were the most lavish of the Season. But still, she did not see why she had to be sacrificed for her father's ambitions.

He walked over to the sideboard and poured himself a brandy from the crystal decanter. 'I have been very patient with you, Season after Season, but by the end of this Season you will be married, or else.'

She increased her pouting, while Tommy scoffed at the threat that had been made many times before.

'I mean it, my girl. It's humiliating enough having to drag you to your sixth Season. If you are not married to a titled man by the end of this one, we will be a laughing stock. I have never allowed anyone in Society to laugh at me, and I'm not about to start now. Do you hear me?'

Georgina tried not to laugh as Tommy rolled his eyes.

'Well?'

'Yes, Papa,' she said in her little-girl voice that had won him over so many times before.

'You still haven't told us how she managed to see this one off so quickly,' Tommy said, ignoring his father's wrath and smirking in anticipation of a tale of outlandish misbehaviour. 'Did you do that trick of eating a raw onion?' He looked around the room as if their parents would share his amusement. 'Remember when she did that to Lord Snidley, then breathed onion breath all over him until the poor man was fighting back the tears?'

Her father downed his glass of brandy and poured himself another.

'Or did she try the method she used with the Earl of Granston—?'

'He said she was too passive, too docile, too reserved,' her father interrupted and knocked back another brandy.

Tommy and her mother turned fully in their chairs to look at her with matching expressions of wide-eyed surprise, then Tommy burst out laughing.

'That's a new one, Georgie,' he said, wiping away tears of mirth.

'I behaved in exactly the manner you told me to, Father,' Georgina said, trying to stop herself from smiling and ruining her look of self-righteous indignation. It wasn't entirely a lie. She *had* behaved in that manner in front of her parents.

Her father puffed out his cheeks and released a loud sigh of exasperation. 'Well, it seems this time I was wrong. You should have just been yourself. The Duke doesn't want someone quiet and demure. He wants… well, he wants someone more like the way you usually are.'

Georgina knew that was not the truth either, but if that was what her father thought, who was she to disagree with him?

'You mean he wants someone who is rude and impertinent,' Tommy added.

'Don't be ridiculous,' her father said, glaring at his son. 'He wants a wife who will be a good mother to his young son, and that means someone with a bit of a spark.'

'Georgie has certainly got that,' Tommy said. 'Remember how she continued to box my ears until I got too tall for her to reach. And I've never seen anyone climb a tree the way she can.' He sent her a sly look. 'And I suspect she could still climb down a drainpipe or two if she had to.'

'I doubt if those are the qualities the Duke is looking for in a bride,' her father said, slumping back down in his chair and gripping the crystal glass in his plump hand. 'But it hardly matters what he wants. He's gone and has said she is not the one for him.'

'I wouldn't be so hasty, dear,' Georgina's mother said, smiling and looking strangely like the family's cat, Puffy, after he'd consumed a large bowl of cream. 'I don't believe the Duke is a lost cause.'

'He said he didn't want to marry me,' Georgina stated. 'He left the house. Didn't stay for the weekend. I think that is conclusive evidence that he has no interest in me whatsoever.'

'Nonsense,' her mother said, sweeping her hand in the air as if brushing away all Georgina's statements of fact. 'I saw the way he looked at you when you entered the room. Mothers do not miss such things. Cupid's dart went straight to his heart. The man is smitten.'

Everyone in the room stared at Georgina's mother as if she had lost her senses, while she continued to do her impression of Puffy at his most self-satisfied.

Georgina had not seen the look her mother was alluding to as she had kept her eyes demurely lowered, but nothing about the Duke's behaviour suggested an attraction. Quite the opposite. He had given every impression of being irritated with her, especially when she'd ventured to ask about his wife. He had shuffled her back inside as quickly as he could. Then he was gone.

It was tempting to inform her mother of all this, and that when they'd met in the drawing room they had only been pretending they had never seen each other before. In the unlikely event that her mother was right and he had looked at her as if he found her attractive, that would explain it. He'd been pretending, and obviously doing it rather well. That was something else she needed to thank him for, along with expressing her gratitude for telling her father she was too docile.

No, the Duke was not attracted to her. He most certainly would not have had fantasies of kissing her. Unlike her, he would not have wondered what it was like to be taken in his arms, to taste his sensuous lips. No, he would have had no such thoughts.

'The only thing that put off the Duke was your silly act, Georgina,' her mother continued.

'I behaved exactly as you always said I should,' she said, rekindling her mock outrage while trying to dampen a peculiar, irrational hope that her mother was right. 'I followed all the lessons I learnt at Halliwell's, to the letter.'

'Well, yes, and your father and I appreciate the effort you made, but in this instance I believe it would have been better if you had just been yourself. If you had, I suspect the Duke would have found you irresistible.'

The foolish hope deep within her was further inflamed, before Georgina remembered that she had already been herself in front of the Duke, and that was the person he didn't want to marry, not the meek and mild Georgina.

'When you next meet the Duke just be yourself,' her mother said, while her father and Tommy looked on in disbelief.

'Are you sure that's a good idea, my dear?' her father said quietly, as if being gentle with a person who had lost their reason.

'Well, perhaps don't be completely yourself. Maybe a slightly muted version, but definitely not meek and mild.'

Her mother stood up and began pacing the room, while the three seated Haywards' heads moved as one, following her progress.

'This could all work to our advantage,' she said, pausing and tapping her chin. 'We know he doesn't want meek and mild. If I tell all the other mothers that he rejected Georgina because she's too feisty and he prefers a more docile young woman, then they'll all make their daughters act in an exaggeratedly demure manner. You'll have no competition.'

Georgina decided now was not the time to point out the Duke did not want a feisty young woman. Not when keeping silent meant she would be given permission to act exactly as she wished. Not that she really needed permission. She would do so regardless, but at least if she misbehaved this Season she would not be subjected to endless, boring lectures on how a young lady should behave if she wished to find a husband. This was all working out rather splendidly and boded well for an entertaining Season.

Well done, Your Grace.

'If Georgie suddenly turns from Miss Meekness into Miss Mischievous, don't you think the Duke will notice?' Tommy asked, still smiling as if he found this all to be an entirely amusing diversion.

'Nonsense,' her mother stated. 'Men turn into imbeciles when they're attracted to a young woman. He won't notice a thing.'

It sounded unlikely, but what would Georgina know? No man had ever been attracted to her, including the Duke, although she had had many a man attracted to her dowry, including, unfortunately, the Duke.

'But he has already said he doesn't want to marry her,' Tommy added.

Her mother shook her head, then looked at Georgina, her eyes growing wide, as if to say, *See? Men, they really are imbeciles, including your brother.*

'I saw how he looked at her, even if neither of you men did. He wants Georgina. He just doesn't want a meek and mild Georgina. We just have to show him he wants the real Georgina.'

Except he's already met the real Georgina and he definitely doesn't want her, Georgina could have said. Instead, she sighed.

'Don't sigh like that,' her mother said, frowning. 'And sit up straight.'

'I thought you wanted me to be myself.'

'Yes, but don't be too much like yourself. Just enough to prove that you're perfect for the Duke.'

'What?' Georgina glared at her mother, shocked by her lack of logic.

'And don't let your eyes bulge either. You need to be feisty and strong, but also genteel and agreeable.'

'Isn't that a bit of a contradiction?' Georgina asked rhetorically.

'And don't question everything, in that way that you do. Agree with the Duke, but not so much that he thinks you are overly submissive. And please, keep your more peculiar habits to yourself.'

'You mean like my habit of talking to shrubs?'

All three Haywards looked at her, her parents frowning, Tommy grinning.

'So, let's see if I've got this right,' Georgina said, adopting a mock serious expression. 'You want me to be feisty and strong-minded, but genteel and agreeable. I need to question everything, but not ask too many questions. Be myself, but under no circumstances be peculiar.'

'Exactly,' her mother said. 'And very soon we'll have a duchess in the family.'

Tommy and Georgina both rolled their eyes, while her parents adopted contented grins, as if in competition over who looked more like Puffy the cat at his most self-satisfied.

Chapter Five

Adam missed his children. He missed being in Dorset. And, of course, he missed Rosalie with every fibre of his being. He would give anything for life to return to the time when they were together, deeply in love and believing that they had many happy years ahead of them.

Instead, he was forced to spend the next six months at his London town house, suffering through the social Season, making idle chit-chat with debutantes, one with whom he would hopefully be able to come to a satisfactory arrangement and take home to Dorset as his wife.

He closed his eyes and tried to ready himself for the task ahead. While Rosalie had been alive he had shunned Society, not wanting to subject his lovely, gentle wife to the snobbery and disapproval their marriage had caused.

'*How could you be so stupid as to marry a woman of such low birth?*' his father had said at the time, his face red with anger. '*You're the eldest son of a duke, for God's sake. You were supposed to marry someone with money.*'

On Rosalie's death, instead of offering condolences, he had once again informed Adam of his duty to marry for money.

'*This time, get it right. Lord knows, if your mother would do the decent thing and die instead of gallivanting around the Americas with heaven knows who, then I'd waste no time marrying a sweet young thing with an even sweeter marriage settlement.*'

And now his father's death and the revelation of just how many debts he had accrued had left Adam with no choice but to do exactly what his father had always expected of him.

As his valet brushed down his swallow-tailed evening jacket, Adam stared at the forlorn man reflected back at him in the looking glass. It was not the look of a man in search of a wife. It was more that of a man standing in the dock awaiting sentencing.

'May I offer some advice, Your Grace?' his valet said, standing back and assessing Adam's appearance.

'By all means, Wilson.'

'Perhaps a little colour. It is a ball you are attending. It is supposed to be a joyous occasion. Maybe a more colourful waistcoat.'

They both looked at his black suit and dark grey waistcoat.

'I think not,' Adam responded. There was nothing joyous in what he was about to do. He could only hope that by the end of this first ball an arrangement would be made and this ordeal would have come to a quick and relatively painless end.

He exhaled a loud, despondent breath.

Not for the first time, he wondered if there was another way in which to dig the estate out of the enormous financial hole his father had left. Perhaps he could ask Mr Hayward for a loan. A very large loan. One that would no doubt take many, many years to pay back. He quashed that idea as soon as it surfaced. He knew what that man would expect in return—that Adam marry Miss Hayward. And that was something he would not do.

The memory of Miss Hayward's laughter resurfaced in his mind, and he was reminded of why they were so badly suited. She was so energetic and joyful. She needed to marry a man who could offer her a life full of fun and enjoyment, a man who could love her, and that was not him.

He did not need or want Miss Hayward. The woman he married would be content with a quiet life and would accept being married to a man incapable of loving again. She would not object to having a husband who missed his first wife, his true wife, so much her absence was a constant ache he carried in his heart. She would accept that he was a man who had not wanted to marry again but had no choice.

He drew in another deep breath. He had to stop feeling sorry for himself and dedicate himself to the task ahead.

He thanked his valet, picked up his gloves and hat and headed out of the house towards his waiting carriage. While his children had found it difficult to understand why their father would be spending such a long time away from them in London, Rosalie's mother had understood and made it clear that she did not approve.

But then, Mrs Wainwright had never approved of anything he had done, especially marrying her daughter. It was the one thing she had in common with Adam's father. She too had wanted her daughter to marry a man from the same class and had taken no pride in the thought that her daughter would one day become a duchess.

And she continued to disapprove of Adam. When he'd thanked her for caring for the children while he was in London, she had merely sniffed and said it was never a chore for her to care for her grandchildren. Then she had added a comment that had cut him to the quick.

'I've looked after my daughter's children for the last five years and am happy to continue doing so. You just go off and enjoy yourself with all those other aristocrats and don't give any of us another thought.'

She had then looked at the portrait of her daughter sitting on the sideboard.

He had wanted to tell her that no one would ever replace Rosalie in his affections, that he would never forget her, and he was only going to London and attending the Season because he did care about his children, their future and the future of everyone on the estate. Enjoyment did not factor into it. But he didn't say any of that. Instead, he had kissed the children goodbye and left.

Adam's carriage joined the parade of carriages pulling to a halt in front of the Belgravia house where the ball was being hosted. The other guests were chattering excitedly as they walked up the well-lit steps and gave their cloaks to the servants waiting at the entranceway. The babble of voices assaulted his ears as he passed through the heaving crowd and entered the ballroom.

He looked around the large, brightly lit room, at the debutantes chatting in small groups, all dressed in pretty pastel gowns. They were all so damn young. Far too young to marry, surely. But then, when he had met Rosalie she had been eighteen, he only nineteen. They had not thought themselves too young to fall instantly, hopelessly in love and to run off and marry, despite their parents' objections. But now he was a man of thirty, and was expected to select one of these sweet, innocent young ladies to be his bride. But which one?

Miss Hayward was right. He was hopelessly out of his depth and he needed her guidance. He spotted her standing at the end of the ballroom with her parents and brother, talking animatedly, with much gesturing of her hands. Her parents were looking abashed, but Thomas was amused. The siblings suddenly laughed uproariously, drawing disapproving glances from several nearby matrons.

Still laughing, she looked around the room, caught his eye, excused herself from her now preening parents and crossed the room towards him. The tension he hadn't known he was holding in his shoulders released.

'Miss Hayward, you look lovely tonight,' he said with a small bow when she joined him.

'Well done, Your Grace. Flattery is always a good way to start,' she said with a light laugh.

It was not idle flattery. She did look lovely, as she always did, even when dressed in a sack-like maid's uniform. But tonight she was more appropriately dressed in a pale mauve gown that brought out the myriad shades of blue in her sparkling eyes. A single strand of pearls adorned her neck and matching pearl earrings hung from her pretty ears.

'So, have you had a chance to identify the heiresses

you will be targeting tonight?' she said, looking round the room.

Adam cringed, not just because of her bold statement, but because it was true. He *had* taken the time before he'd arrived to scrutinise the guest list and assess who were the heiresses with the largest marriage settlements, and the ones most likely to being amenable to trading that marriage settlement for the chance of becoming a duchess.

'I believe Miss Arabella Bateman and Lady Cecelia Greville are two of the young ladies deemed to be the most eligible this Season,' he said, reminding himself that he had no need to feel ashamed. He was here to find an heiress and there was no point pretending otherwise.

Miss Hayward snorted and turned back to face him. 'Really? Well, if all you want is an enormous marriage settlement, then yes, they are the most eligible young women on the market this Season.'

'You have objections to the two young ladies in question?'

'No, not at all,' she said with a disapproving sniff.

He waited for further explanation. None came. 'In that case, perhaps you can point them out to me.'

'They're the two staring at you with the most interest. The ones standing beside the mothers who are all but salivating at the thought of marrying their daughter off to a duke.'

His gaze swept the room. Almost every young lady seemed to be staring in their direction, along with their mothers.

'You're going to have to be a bit more precise.'

'Miss Bateman is the one dripping with diamonds,

as if she's carrying an advertising sign that says she is the daughter of one of the richest men in America. Lady Cecelia Greville is the one dressed in an understated beige gown, as if to say, *I have so much money and come from such an impeccable background I do not need to display my wealth in front of all you peasants.*'

A note of pique had entered her voice as if he had caused her great offence. He turned from scrutinising the young women in the ballroom to the one standing beside him. Was she angry with him for some reason?

'I hope your father did not blame you for my decision not to court you.'

'No, not at all.' She smiled up at him and lightly tapped his arm with her fan. 'In fact, I believe I should thank you. Your rejection of me could not have worked out better.'

'How so?'

Her smile grew wider. 'Mother is under the mistaken impression that you are attracted to me. She thinks all I have to do is act more like myself and you'll be mine for the taking.' She clapped her hands together in pleasure before he could respond to this peculiar statement. 'That means I can do whatever I like this Season and they won't be able to object. I can laugh loudly, disagree with whomever I choose. I can be rude to all those horrid fortune-hunters. I can even dance on the tables if I want to.'

The music started for the first dance and she looked towards the tables in the corner, bearing punch bowls and glasses, her expression wickedly joyous.

'Miss Hayward, may I have the pleasure of the first dance?' he said before she made good on her threat.

'Excellent idea,' she said with a wink. 'My parents will think it's working and that you are attracted to the real me.'

He led her into the centre of the dancefloor and placed his hand on her waist. She looked up at him, a cheeky smile curving her lips.

'Oh, and do some more of that,' she said as she placed her hand on his shoulder.

'More of what?'

'More looking at me like that. It's very good. If Mother sees it, she'll think I'm doing something right, maybe being agreeable or witty or flattering you or something.'

Adam was unaware that he had looked at her in any manner worthy of comment. However, he had to admit he *had* registered how slim her waist was when he'd placed his hand on her, and how her rounded hips flared out in a becoming feminine manner, but that was all. And yes, he had noticed the tendrils of hair that had escaped from her ornate hairstyle, and how they drew the eye down her creamy neck to where they curled on her naked shoulders. And yes, perhaps he had noticed the plunging cut of her gown exposed rather a lot of her cleavage to his view. But he was merely making a few observations about her appearance. They meant nothing. And nothing could be read into the manner in which he looked at her.

And even if he *had* been somewhat distracted by Miss Hayward's appearance, that was not why he was here. He was here to find a wife. That was what he needed to focus on, and not on Miss Hayward's hairstyle, her silky skin, nor her shapely figure.

* * *

This was perfect. Georgina could imagine her parents smiling benignly at her from the edge of the dancefloor, delighted to see their daughter in the arms of the Duke.

That was why she was so happy, because she was fooling her parents. It had nothing to do with actually being in the arms of the Duke. It was not because the touch of his hand was like a warm caress on her skin. Nor was it because she was so close to him she could feel the heat of his body and smell his cologne of bergamot, sage and something else. She sniffed as discreetly as she could. It was something rich and musky, something that filled her senses and caused a strange tingling sensation to shimmer through her.

She moved closer towards him and briefly closed her eyes, drawing in that masculine scent. Oh, yes, she was very happy. This Season she would be free to do whatever she wanted and it was all unintentionally thanks to him.

For the first time since that first naïve Season when she had actually thought balls were magical, romantic events—and had had her delusions cruelly ended by the Duke of Cromley's honest but hurtful comments—Georgina had actually looked forward to attending this ball.

She glanced around and decided that no ballroom had ever been grander. No crystal chandelier had ever sparkled more brightly. No parquet dancefloor had looked more inviting. And no band had played more divinely. It just made one want to dance the night away.

And what could be better than to have the first dance with the man who had changed everything? The man who had inadvertently given her the freedom to be exactly who she was.

She looked up at him and wondered if placing her head on his shoulder would be pushing her newfound freedom to be herself just a tad too far. She suspected it would be. While her parents might not object to such boldness, the Duke would not welcome it. After all, he was not here to court her, but to find a bride.

The tingling that had possessed her from the moment she had seen him standing at the side of the ballroom, looking so masculine and so…well, aristocratic, disappeared, overwhelmed by a tight gripping in her stomach and a flare of anger that chased away her happiness.

The unwanted feeling suddenly possessing her was something suspiciously like jealousy, but she could not be jealous. That would be ridiculous. He was a man in search of a loveless, mercenary marriage. She was a woman who was doing everything she could to avoid a loveless, mercenary marriage. Two people could not be more wrong for each other.

No, she was definitely not jealous. She pushed those feelings down and forced herself to smile. What she needed to do was just enjoy this moment. And this moment *was* rather pleasant. She moved slightly closer to his warm, hard body.

No doubt other young ladies watching them dance would think that she had a chance with the Duke. None would realise she had already been assessed and dismissed. And none would realise just how happy she was with this arrangement. It suited her perfectly. It did. It really did. And she wished the Duke all the best in his search. Why else would she have offered to assist him? A jealous woman certainly wouldn't do that.

'So, have you taken some time to practise your flirting skills?' she said, annoyed that she sounded peevish when she was merely trying to be helpful.

'I have not,' came his brief reply.

She forced herself to give a little laugh. 'No, I suppose you don't need to. You're a duke. You can be as boorish and boring as you like and no one is going to care.'

He raised both eyebrows.

'Not that you are boorish or boring,' she added, wishing she could stop talking and just enjoy the dance. It was the first time she was in his arms and it quite possibly would be the last. And that was as it should be. Once he met the young lady he wished to marry he would be dedicating all his time to courting her.

'And will the new, liberated Miss Hayward be flirting tonight?' he asked.

She snorted in a manner that no flirtatious young lady ever would. 'I too have no need to resort to such tactics. The men at this ball fall into two distinct categories. The men who are not the slightest bit interested in me because I am not of their class, and the men who overlook my appalling background because they need my father's money. The first group would look down their raised noses at me if I deemed to try and flirt with them. The second group are falling over themselves to impress me, so I too could be the most boring, boorish woman in the room and they'd still tell me I was an absolute delight.'

She could add there was a third category. Men who

needed her father's money but did not want her. That was a category that included only one person. Him.

'I can assure you, Miss Hayward, you are certainly not boring.'

She laughed at the guarded compliment. 'Are you saying I'm boorish?' She waited with some pleasure for him to look embarrassed, and to rush to assure her that this was not what he meant.

'I believe you take pleasure in being bad-mannered. Isn't that what you said to me before we started to dance? That you were looking forward to misbehaving this Season.'

'Oh, yes, I suppose so,' she said, not sure whether to be disappointed or pleased by his assessment of her character.

'I also believe you were doing what you said all young ladies do. Making a critical statement about yourself so the gentleman will rush to assure you that no, you are not boorish but the most refined, sophisticated young lady in the room.'

Georgina snorted again, with embarrassment at being caught out as much as by amusement. 'And you failed the flirtation test by being far too honest.'

'Is that what you are doing with me, flirting?'

Heat rushed to Georgina's cheeks. Was she?

'Well, if I was indulging in a bit of harmless flirting, it was only to help you,' she quickly responded, willing her cheeks to stop burning. It would be too awful if the Duke did think she was flirting, especially when such behaviour would be so unwelcome.

'So, which heiress do you plan to charm tonight?' she

added, determined to move the conversation away from the flirting she most certainly was not doing.

He huffed out a sigh. 'Miss Bateman and Lady Cecelia are the most likely candidates. I believe Miss Bateman's mother has made no secret of the fact that they are in this country to secure a title for their daughter, and there are few families more socially ambitious than the Grevilles.'

That tightening sensation returned to Georgina's stomach, but she forced herself to keep smiling.

'And there is Lady Gwendolyn Smithers,' he continued. 'Although her fortune is not as vast as the other two ladies, it would suffice and she is reputed to be a pleasant young lady.'

Georgina released a puff of disapproval. 'Lady Gwendolyn? Pleasant? I suppose you do know she is a frightful gossip.' Georgina knew she was not being entirely dishonest. Lady Gwendolyn *was* known to gossip, although no more than practically any other young lady present, including Georgina.

'And as for her family, well, the stories I could tell you.'

He looked down at her, his eyebrows raised in question.

'Yes, all right. I suppose that would be gossiping, but I would be doing so simply to prevent you from making a terrible mistake and marrying the wrong woman.'

'So I shouldn't marry Lady Gwendolyn because she gossips and there are rumours about her family?'

'I'm just saying.' Georgina wasn't entirely sure what she *was* saying, especially as Lady Gwendolyn probably would make an ideal wife. She had attended Halliwell's a few years behind Georgina and had never once got caught sneaking out after hours and was reputed to be able to make fascinating conversation with even the dullest of shrubs.

'And what of Miss Bateman? Is she a gossip? Are there rumours about her family?'

Georgina shrugged. 'Well, her father is an absolute fright. They say he's quite the tyrant.'

'I'm not intending to marry the father.'

'No, but still.' Georgina was unsure of her argument, she just knew that Miss Bateman would not be suitable for the Duke, despite her wealth, her beauty and her grace.

'And Lady Cecelia? Is she a gossip? Are there rumours? Is her father a tyrant? Her mother a shrew?'

'No, but…' Georgina knew there had to be a *but*. Unfortunately, when placed on the spot, she couldn't think of one.

Those annoying, judgemental eyebrows rose up his forehead yet again.

'Well, you did agree for me to help you navigate this Season,' she added, painfully aware she was sounding petulant. 'I'm just trying to give you some good advice.'

He nodded slowly. 'You are right. I am sorry,' he said as the music came to an end. 'I value your insightful comments.'

Was he being sarcastic? It was hard to tell.

He took her arm, led her off the dancefloor and bowed. 'Thank you, Miss Hayward. I shall heed your advice and I wish you well in your Season of misbehaving.'

With that, he turned and walked across the room towards Miss Bateman, quite obviously neither heeding nor valuing her good advice one little bit.

Chapter Six

Adam escorted Miss Bateman onto the dancefloor for the quadrille. Allowing Miss Hayward to guide him through the treacherous waters of the Season was obviously not such a good idea after all. Why would she mention that the young lady's father was a tyrant? If anything, that was surely a good reason to marry her, to rescue her from an unpleasant situation. And as for Lady Cecelia, while he did not particularly approve of gossiping, if that was a young lady's only flaw then it was one he could easily overlook.

He should have known that Miss Hayward would be of no help whatsoever in his quest. All he'd had to do was remember how they'd met. No one would expect good counsel from a young woman who'd escaped from her parents' home on a bicycle dressed as a maid.

He looked across the ballroom to the lady in question. She was talking to Lord Fernley. No, revise that. She was talking *at* Lord Fernley, apparently giving him instructions, but he did not appear to mind. The man had an obviously false smile fixed to his face, as if trying to convince Miss Hayward that everything she said and did was fascinating. Fernley apparently fell into the category of men after her money. Men like himself, but unlike himself—men who did not care whether the arrangement suited the young lady or not.

Fernley opened his mouth to talk, but Miss Hayward took his arm, led him across the dancefloor and joined their group, making up the last of the four couples in the quadrille.

He should be annoyed. He was supposed to be focusing all his attention on Miss Bateman, but Miss Hayward's presence was oddly reassuring, like seeing a lifeboat appear in a turbulent sea. But he was more than capable of rescuing himself. He did not need a lifeboat and he must not get distracted again.

He turned from watching Miss Hayward to his partner. 'Are you enjoying your time in England, Miss Bateman?'

She kept her eyes lowered in a demure manner that could challenge Miss Hayward's act of meekness. 'Yes, Your Grace,' she whispered. This was a surprise. He had been told that American women were confident and effusive, not shy and retiring.

He hadn't meant to, but he looked over at Miss Hayward. The smile she sent him could almost be called victorious. That too was most peculiar. He really was out of his depth, and the sooner he found his bride and escaped the horror of the Season the better.

He turned back to Miss Bateman and racked his brain for a suitable topic of conversation. Perhaps he should have practised on the shrubs before he arrived. Once again, he glanced in Miss Hayward's direction.

Being in her company might be somewhat disconcerting but he never felt this awkwardness, nor did he struggle to find anything to talk about.

The music started. At least there would be little time to make uncomfortable conversation while they moved through the formal steps of the dance. And yet, when Miss Bateman and Miss Hayward approached each other in the centre of the group, there was no ignoring the quick exchange that took place between the two young ladies. For one brief moment, Miss Bateman ceased to keep her eyes lowered. She looked straight at Miss Hayward and said something to cause her to gasp and shoot a quick look towards him.

When she took his hand again, Miss Bateman raised her eyes and gave him the sweetest smile imaginable. Something had just happened and it did not take a man well versed in the machinations of the Season to know it involved him. Nor did he need to be a genius to know he was being played by Miss Bateman, but then, wasn't that exactly what Miss Hayward had warned him about?

This duplicity was far too baffling and the sooner he found a wife and escaped this confusing world the better.

Georgina smiled triumphantly to herself. Mother's plan was working. Miss Bateman, who Georgina knew could talk the hind legs off a donkey, was acting like a spineless ninny without a word to say for herself. Not that it really mattered. That was her mother's plan, not Georgina's. And if it hadn't been for that quick exchange in the middle of the quadrille there would be no reason for Georgina to take pleasure in Miss Bateman ruining her chances with the Duke.

But there *had* been that furious, rather harsh exchange. Mr Bateman was reputed to be a tyrannical businessman and it looked as if the daughter was no different.

'*Back off! This one is mine,*' she had hissed at Georgina. '*Try and get in my way and I will crush you like an ant.*'

Georgina could have told Miss Bateman she had nothing to fear, that the Duke was not interested in her, but instead she had been left uncharacteristically speechless.

She continued dancing, her determination to ensure that Miss Bateman did not win the Duke intensifying every time she looked at them. Georgina had not, and would not, reassure Miss Bateman that she had nothing to fear from Georgina. Quite the contrary. Anything she could do to unnerve that frightful young lady she would take enormous pleasure in doing.

Not for her own sake, of course, but for the Duke's.

As Lord Fernley led her around the square of dances, she continued to watch the Duke and Miss Bateman. She still had her eyes lowered, her long dark lashes sweeping her high cheekbones in what she obviously thought was an enchanting manner. She was rather pretty, Georgina had to admit, but she could see the boredom and frustration on the Duke's face, even if Miss Bateman couldn't.

She smiled with satisfaction. The Duke might not be interested in a woman as boisterous as Georgina, but Mother was right. It was now obvious he really did not want meek and mild either.

That horrid Miss Bateman might think she was enchanting the Duke with this submissive act, but she was doing exactly the opposite.

The dance came to an end and, still feeling surprisingly pleased with herself, she allowed Lord Fernley to lead her off the dancefloor. As he chatted on and on, repeatedly telling her what an elegant dancer she was, she watched the Duke escort Miss Bateman back to her mother, bow, exchange a few polite words then depart, without a backward glance.

He looked over at her and she smiled at him in anticipation. He was going to ask her to dance again.

Perhaps this next dance would be another waltz. Her pulse raced. Not because she wanted to be held by the Duke. Not because she wanted to feel his arms around her or his strong, oh, so manly chest close to hers, but because it would give them a chance to talk without anyone overhearing. If he needed further convincing, she would be able to tell him why Miss Bateman was certainly, categorically, not the woman he was looking for.

The Earl of Cranford stood in front of her, blocking her view of the Duke. 'Miss Hayward, would you do me the honour of this dance?' he said with a low bow and a supercilious smile. The Earl had lost his wealth at the gaming tables and could see no better way of recouping his losses than marrying an heiress. Georgina had been fending him off for five Seasons and yet he still persisted, like a gambler unable to leave the gaming table despite being on a losing streak.

'I'm sorry, I...' Georgina said, leaning to the side so she could see around the Earl. The Duke was not heading in her direction, but had crossed the floor towards Lady Cecelia.

Had that been his intention all along? Was he under the impression that he was not in need of her advice after all? Well, he was wrong. He definitely did need her and it would be remiss of Georgina to stand by and watch him make mistake after mistake with the wrong young ladies.

'Oh, yes, all right,' she said, taking the Earl's arm and leading him onto the dancefloor, as close to the Duke and Lady Cecelia as the crowded ballroom floor would allow.

The music began and it was a galop. As the Earl dragged her around the floor, she moved her head, looking over and between the swirling dancers so she could keep an eye on the Duke and his partner. She would have preferred another quadrille—that way, he would not have Lady Cecelia in his arms. Not that it should really matter but, strangely, it did.

The Earl tried to lead her in a different direction to the one she needed to go, but she put a stop to that. While it might be considered ungainly for the lady to lead the man, needs must. With much tangling of legs and treading of toes she steered Cranford closer to the Duke and his partner.

To her horror, she could see Lady Cecelia was making polite conversation with the Duke, and he was listening to her as if he actually found her interesting.

Had she not got the message? Had her mother's word not got through to Lady Cecelia? The Duke liked meek and mild young women, not ones who made conversation, who smiled at him, who held his attention. Well, perhaps he did. She didn't really know what sort of woman attracted him. All she knew was, she wasn't it. And she also knew she had no reason to object if Lady Cecelia was exactly what he was looking for in a bride.

Hadn't she said she would help him? And surely that didn't just mean preventing him from making a mistake but also assisting him to find the right woman.

Georgina didn't know. All she knew was that she was not enjoying herself any more. And the more the Duke and Lady Cecelia conversed, the less pleasure she was taking in this entire enterprise.

The dance over, the Earl led her to the edge of the dancefloor but did not leave. Instead, he continued to attempt to make conversation with her—conversation she did not hear, her entire focus taken by what was happening on the other side of the ballroom.

The Duke bowed to Lady Cecelia and exchanged a few words with her mother, then departed. Georgina's breath caught in her throat. Maybe this time the Duke would ask her to dance. Yes, that would make more sense. Then they could discuss both young ladies.

But no. Instead, he crossed the room and bowed in front of Lady Gwendolyn.

'Excuse me, I'm afraid I need to go to the ladies' retiring room,' she said, interrupting whatever it was the Earl was saying.

The Earl bowed and left, but her exit was halted by the obsequious Viscount Smarley. Another man drawn like a moth to the flame that was her marriage settlement.

'I'm sorry, my lord. I need to sit this dance out. I must retire to the ladies' room to fix my hair.'

'But your hair is magnificent, like sunlight on a wheatfield in the morning, like—'

'Yes, yes,' she said absentmindedly as she walked away. She skirted around the edge of the dancefloor, her gaze firmly fixed on the Duke and Lady Gwendolyn. She was smiling up at him in a decidedly pretty manner and chatting politely. Georgina stifled a curse that would have shocked the nearby matrons. Lady Gwendolyn had won top honours in conversation at Halliwell's and it seemed she was putting those skills to good use with the Duke.

Georgina knew she should not be objecting. There was nothing actually wrong with Lady Gwendolyn. She was sweet, polite, well-versed in all the skills that a young lady was supposed to possess. And she was nothing like Georgina. That probably made her perfect for the Duke.

Smarley once more blocked her way. The man really was insufferable. Even Georgina knew he kept a mistress, one he was in danger of losing if he did not restore his family fortune in the immediate future so he could keep her in the level of comfort she demanded.

'Miss Hayward, I can assure you, no young lady in the room has more beautiful hair. Would you do me the honour—?'

'I'm not dancing. Go away.' She was not usually quite so blunt but he was being even more insufferable than usual.

'Well, really,' he said, that insincere smile disappearing. 'I don't know why you're acting so high and mighty. You're not the only heiress here tonight and you're far from the prettiest,' he added before striding across the room, his long nose high in the air.

Georgina was tempted to call out to him that he wasn't

telling her anything she didn't already know. Instead, she watched Lady Gwendolyn giggle as the Duke spun her round the room in the polka.

This was definitely not the fun Season full of mayhem and mischief she had been looking forward to. It had hardly even begun and it was turning out to be her worst Season ever, and there was a lot of competition for that title.

Chapter Seven

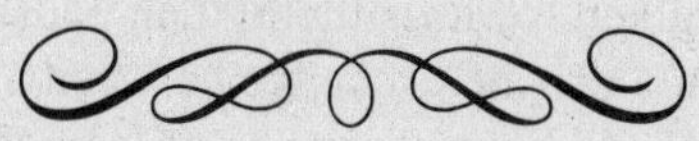

The polka came to an end and Adam led Lady Gwendolyn back to her waiting mother. After the obligatory exchange of pleasantries, he looked around the room to select the next young woman with whom he would dance. He scanned the crowd. He wasn't deliberately looking for Miss Hayward, but he couldn't help but notice that she was nowhere in sight.

During the polka he had seen her have a terse exchange with Viscount Smarley, then he had lost sight of her.

Had something happened to her? Had Smarley upset her? The man was a buffoon, so that would not surprise him. What did surprise him was that Miss Hayward would care about anything that man could say to her. She appeared to be made of much sterner stuff. But then, did he really know her?

Mr Hayward strode across the ballroom towards the exit and he did not look happy. Something *had* happened to Miss Hayward and, whatever it was, he wanted to know. It might not be any of his business but he could not continue to dance if that young lady was in any distress.

At what he hoped was a discreet distance, he followed Mr Hayward towards the exit and into an adjoining drawing room that had been cleared so that supper could later be served. Mr Hayward then disappeared through French windows that led to the terrace.

Adam walked towards them, then paused. Was he intruding on a private exchange between a father and daughter? Would his presence be welcomed or not?

'Your mother said I might find you here,' Mr Hayward said, sounding happy rather than concerned. 'So, my dear, how long will it be before we are posting the banns?'

That drew Adam closer and he leant against a marble pillar, anxious to hear her answer. Was Miss Hayward courting? She gave no impression that was the case. Quite the opposite. If anything, she had asserted she had no interest in marriage, to anyone, including himself.

'I believe you are getting ahead of yourself, Father. The Season has only just begun. You said I had until the end of the Season to find a husband.'

So she *was* in search of a husband, although, again, not him.

'That's as may be,' her father said. 'But your mother has been paying close attention and she is confident that the Duke is on the hook. All you have to do is reel him in. And that's not going to happen if you hide away out here and allow him to dance with other young women.'

Adam closed his mouth, which had inexplicably fallen open. Had he heard correctly? Mr Hayward had said '*the Duke*' and there was only one duke present tonight. Himself.

What was going on? Was Miss Hayward involved in some scheme to marry him herself? If she was, it was an extremely convoluted and confusing scheme. Surely if she was planning on marrying a man she wouldn't run away from him, then inform him that she did not wish to marry him, but would help him find another, more suitable, wife.

And as for being on the hook, well, that was ridiculous. Yes, he had enjoyed his dance with Miss Hayward. Yes, she was a decidedly attractive, shapely young woman who would appeal to any man, and he did enjoy her company, plus she was a delightful conversationalist, despite what those idiots at Halliwell's might think. But she was not for him. Was she? Adam tried to remind himself of what his objections to marrying Miss Hayward actually were. Although he did remember that foremost amongst his reasons was *her* objection to marrying *him*.

'Oh, Papa,' Miss Hayward said with a light laugh. 'You and Mama have got it all wrong. I'm not going to marry the Duke. All I'm doing is helping him find his perfect bride. He's so naïve when it comes to women.'

Naïve? Adam wanted to disagree, but the longer he stayed at this ball, the more he had to admit that women were a complete mystery to him, and this bizarre exchange was not disabusing him of that belief.

'He thinks the way a young lady pretends to be is exactly what they are,' she added.

That was a conclusion he too was starting to arrive at.

'I'm just setting him right, so he doesn't make the wrong choice.'

Adam nodded and ignored the peculiar crushing sensation inside his chest. She had merely repeated what he already knew. She did not wish to marry him. Just as he did not wish to marry her. But he was pleased that Miss Hayward was not, like so many other young women seemingly were, a game player.

None of this would be news to the father either, and Adam waited for his reply. A reply that was taking a long time to come, as the protracted silence stretched on and on.

'You're doing what?' he finally said in a low tone as if he was fighting to control his anger.

Adam braced himself, suddenly on alert. He suspected that Miss Hayward was more than capable of fighting her own battles, and this was not really any of his concern, but he wanted to be on hand in case she needed him. Although what he could do to help her, he had no idea.

'I'm merely assisting him to navigate the Season so he doesn't make a terrible mistake. The marriage mart can be so perilous.'

Adam was relieved that her voice was still light and musical, her father's wrath having no apparent effect on her.

There was another long silence.

'So what about Cranford, Fernley or Smarley?' he said, his voice barely controlled. 'Despite your appalling behaviour towards them, they're still showing their interest.'

Miss Hayward laughed dismissively but made no comment.

There was yet another long silence that appeared to hang in the air.

'I've had it up to my back teeth with you, my girl,' Mr Hayward said, his voice so controlled Adam could tell he was barely holding onto his rage. 'You seem incapable of understanding your situation. You'll soon be twenty-four. You can't possibly attend another Season after this one. You have to marry this Season or it will be a total humiliation for the entire family.'

'Don't be so silly, Papa,' Miss Hayward said dismissively, either oblivious to or unaffected by the controlled rage in her father's tone.

'No, do not act as if this is a joke,' Mr Hayward said, his voice rising. 'This is not a joking matter. And as for helping men find a wife, rather than finding a husband for yourself, well, that is…that is…' He spluttered to a halt.

'I'm not helping *men*. I'm just helping the Duke.'

'My God, girl, are you simple-minded? If you want to help find a wife for the Duke then marry him yourself. And if he still doesn't want you, then marry Lord Fernley, the Earl of Cranford or Viscount Smarley. They're all eminently suitable.'

'You mean they've all got titles,' Miss Hayward mumbled.

'Exactly. So, which is it to be?'

Adam leaned closer and waited for her answer, he suspected with as much anticipation as Mr Hayward.

'I don't know why you're even bothering to ask. I won't be marrying any of them.'

Relief washed through Adam. He could tell himself that it was relief that she still did not wish to marry him but, strangely, it was relief that she was not interested in the other three men either. None of whom seemed at all suitable for a woman with Miss Hayward's spirit.

'You will,' her father said in a low growl. 'You will be married by the end of this Season...or else.'

'Or else what?'

Adam smiled at her defiance. He could imagine how she looked, her eyes blazing, hands on hips, chin raised.

'Or else I will cut you off without a penny.'

Adam's smile died as the implication of Mr Hayward's words hit him. A young woman cut off from her family was placed in a perilous position. With no money of her own, and no means of earning a living, Miss Hayward was completely dependent on her family for support. If that was taken away, she would be set adrift in a world that could be cruel and heartless for a woman.

'You will not,' Miss Hayward said, her voice no longer quite so defiant.

'I will. I've indulged you for far too long, my girl. Your mother has warned me repeatedly that I let you get your own way far too much. Well, that stops right now. You will find a husband with a title this Season or you will no longer be my daughter.'

'Is that all I am to you? Someone who you can use to secure a title for the family?' The strained sound in her words suggested she was holding back tears. Adam felt a strong compulsion to go to her, to comfort her, but what could he say? And he was sure neither father nor daughter would appreciate that he had been eavesdropping.

'Yes, finally, it is getting through that thick skull of

yours. You need to grow up and start doing your duty by the family. You have been given so much, and there is only one thing I expect from you in return and, so far, you haven't even done that. If you don't marry and raise the social standing of the Hayward family, then I can see no point having a daughter.'

'You can't make me marry someone I don't want to.' She still sounded defiant, but the tremulous note in her voice suggested it was pretence.

'No, but I can let you know what the options are. You either marry or you will have to make your own way in the world. Without my support, you would have to find employment and earn your own money. Do you have any skills?'

There was silence.

'No, you don't,' he answered his own question. 'Do you know how to do anything other than cause trouble?'

Again, there was silence.

'No, you don't. The best you can hope for is to become a governess for some family desperate enough to take on a young woman who actually failed at finishing school, something I would not have thought possible. Or you could become a companion to an elderly lady. Although what elderly lady would want the companionship of such a disobedient girl I do not know. And those are by far the best options available to a girl such as yourself. Believe me, there are many more options that are far, far worse than having to marry a titled man and live a comfortable life.'

Miss Hayward still made no reply. All Adam heard was the rustle of silk crumpling as she sat down.

'Do I make myself clear?'

Again, there was no reply.

'Good. Then I'll leave you to contemplate everything I've said, but before the end of this night I expect to see you back on the dancefloor, smiling and flirting with as many titled men as you possibly can.'

Adam moved quickly behind the pillar to avoid being caught in such an inappropriate position, as a red-faced Mr Hayward strode through the terrace doors, across the room and back into the ballroom.

This was not a problem of his creation, and yet it felt like it. He should return to the ballroom and continue his search for his heiress. That was the only reason he was here. But he had to do something. He could not leave Miss Hayward in such a state of distress. Unfortunately, the question was, what on earth *could* he do? And that was a question to which he had no answer.

This was terrible. Georgina rocked slowly to and fro, her head in her hands. She had never felt so miserable. Her father had made threats before, but never any so vile. He'd often alluded to cutting off her dress allowance or confining her to home until she behaved, but she had always managed to get around him and make him see reason.

But tonight he'd looked so fierce, so intractable, as if no argument would move him from his outrageous position of expecting her to marry one of those men. Lord Fernley, Viscount Smarley or the Earl of Cranford. Georgina gripped her head tighter and rocked faster. How could her father possibly condemn her to marriage to one of those men? And as for the Duke—well, despite what her irrational parents thought, that was not an option.

It looked as if she would have to find a way of supporting herself. She looked out at the dark garden through the net of her fingers, the light from the room barely stretching past the dimly lit terrace.

If she did have to support herself, how on earth would she do so? Her father was right. No one in their right mind would hire her as a governess, and she would make a hopeless companion for an elderly lady. If she undertook such work, it would not be long before she was dismissed and tossed out onto the street, and then what would she do?

A shadow passed across her. She released the fingers covering her eyes, looked up and gasped. What was the Duke doing here? She sat up straighter, brushed down her crumpled gown and tried to smile.

'Did you feel the need to take the air as well, Your Grace?' she asked, hoping she sounded lively and did not betray any of her inner anguish. 'It's rather delightful out here, isn't it? Just smell that fresh air.' She sniffed, and unfortunately caught the fragrance of bergamot and sage, sending shivers through her as if the air was not just fresh but decidedly chilly. She did not need the Duke unsettling her and adding to her anguish and yet, at the same time, she did want his company. Wanted it too much.

'Are you tired of dancing?' she burbled on. 'Tired of chasing heiresses?' She gave a little laugh that sounded false to her ears.

'I heard what your father said.'

'Oh,' she said on a gasp. 'All of it?' She hoped he had missed the part when her father had discussed him.

'All of it.'

'I can explain,' she said, turning towards him on the wooden bench. 'I thought it best to let my parents continue thinking that you were interested in me, then they would leave me alone. It was all so silly really. Mother seems to think that you really are interested in marrying me. I suppose she's a bit desperate and sees what she wants to see.' Georgina knew she was gabbling but seemed incapable of stopping. 'I did nothing to encourage her in this misguided idea, but yes, I'm sorry, I also did nothing to discourage my parents from their delusion that you might actually want to court me. It was a bit selfish, but I thought they would stop constantly pestering me about marriage this Season and I could just enjoy myself.'

Her shoulders slumped and she crumpled down on the seat. 'I couldn't have got it more wrong if I tried. Could I?' she added, finally running out of words.

'Is it really such a bad idea?' he said, looking out at the garden.

'What?'

'Marriage. If we did marry, it would solve both our problems.'

'What?'

'It would satisfy your father's need to have a title in the family. It would save you from a terrible fate and, as we both know, I'm in need of an heiress.'

She stared at him, sure that he had gone slightly mad. 'Was that a proposal?'

He shrugged one shoulder. 'Yes, I suppose it was.'

She stared out at the garden, looked at him, then back at the garden, shrouded in darkness. 'It's not a very romantic one.'

'This is not a very romantic situation in which we find ourselves. Neither of us wants to marry, but neither of us has any choice. But, as I said, it would solve both our problems if we did marry.' He turned on the seat to face her. 'You know my situation. You know that I have to marry an heiress. You are an heiress. Your father has given you no real option. You have to marry a titled man. I am a titled man. And, unlike those other men who are trying to court you, I am not lying to you. This will simply be an arrangement that suits both of us.'

'Yes, all right.' The words were out before Georgina could think of the full ramifications of what she was saying.

She looked up at him to gauge his reaction, but could barely see his face in the dim light. Was he looking pleased, surprised, horrified? Had he expected her to say no? Had he hoped she would say no? Was he merely being polite or gallant in making an offer he expected to be rejected?

His silence did not suggest happiness nor any enthusiasm for making her his wife. Should Georgina retract her acceptance?

'Good,' he finally said. 'I am sorry about this, Miss Georgina. It is not an ideal situation for either of us, but I promise I will do everything in my power to make this arrangement agreeable for you.'

Everything except love me, Georgina could say, but

she knew that love had nothing to do with what she had just consented to. As he said, it was merely an arrangement which would save them both from a worse fate.

Chapter Eight

Everything moved so quickly. The day after the ball the Duke visited Georgina's parents and officially asked for her hand in marriage. It came as no surprise to anyone that her father gave his immediate consent. What did surprise Georgina was the way her mother sprang into action. The banns were read, a date was set, invitations were sent out and the wedding gown made all before Georgina had time to fully digest that she was soon to be a bride.

Her parents seemed to care nothing for what rumours such unseemly haste might generate. Obviously, their fear that the Duke might withdraw his offer, or Georgina might try and run off before they got her up the aisle, was greater than their fear of what the twittering gossipmongers might say about such a rushed wedding.

Despite being engaged, Georgina saw little of the Duke leading up to their wedding day, and she was never alone with him. She suspected that too was a deliberate ploy by her mother. She did not want to risk Georgina doing anything to cause the Duke to change his mind, and the best way to achieve that was to ensure they saw as little of each other as humanly possible until they were at the altar. Then there would be no going back.

That meant they had no time to discuss what their marriage would be like. Georgina knew it was an arrangement, but exactly what sort of arrangement she had no idea.

She did, however, have time to discuss the entire disaster with her good friends from her time at Halliwell's. They consoled, they advised, suggested ways in which she could get out of the situation in which she'd found herself, but no one would hazard a guess on what her marriage would be like.

Irene and Amelia also offered her a home, to counter her father's threat to make her homeless, and both said they would be more than happy to support her financially. They had even said they could probably find her employment if she wished, although the tone of their voices when they discussed her prospects suggested that, like her father, they were struggling to think of any job which would use Georgina's skills, or lack thereof.

As she had no desire to take charity, she thanked her friends, and told them she would just have to accept her fate. She was to wed. It would mean doing the one thing she had been determined not to, marrying a man her father had chosen for her. A man who did not love her and was only marrying her for her money. Well, that, and to save her from a life of penury.

If the Duke had not come out to the terrace to take some air. If he had not accidentally overheard her father's threat. If he was not prone to helping damsels in distress, then he would probably have chosen Lady Gwendolyn, Lady Cecelia or Miss Bateman to be his bride.

Instead, their fates were sealed, and within a short month of that hasty, unromantic proposal, Georgina was walking up the aisle of the flower-bedecked local church to the sound of the Wedding March, on her proud father's arm, followed by her closest friends as her bridesmaids, towards her husband-to-be.

Her husband-to-be.

She would soon be his wife. She paused briefly, overawed by that realisation. It would soon be a reality. The handsome, formidable man standing at the altar, dressed in a black morning suit, a red rose in his buttonhole the only splash of colour, would be her husband. Georgina could hardly believe that it was actually happening. And tonight would be their wedding night. She almost stumbled over her feet and came to a halt.

What was their marriage night to entail? They both knew this was an arrangement, not something either was entering into willingly, but what would that mean when they became man and wife? Georgina would discover that tonight, when they were alone in his bedchamber. A tingle of anticipation radiated through her as her eyes quickly scanned the Duke, his broad shoulders, strong arms and those long slim legs.

Alone. In his bedchamber.

'None of your tricks, Georgina,' her father whispered, pulling slightly on her arm to encourage her to continue moving up the aisle. 'You agreed to this, you cannot back out now.'

Her father's words reminded her of what this was.

It was not a love match, but something that suited her father's ambitions. The man standing at the altar was not waiting for the love of his life, he was waiting for his promised dowry.

She commenced her slow walk towards the Duke as the organ music swirled around her. Everyone in the church was smiling as if this was the happiest of days. No one suspected she was a mere pawn in other people's games, or if they did, they did not care. This marriage would mean the Duke would save his estate, her mother could boast connections to the highest echelons of Society and her father would have an aristocrat in the family and grandchildren who went by the titles lord and lady.

She bit her lip. *Children.*

She would be expected to produce children. Another shiver of excitement fluttered through her and her toes curled inside her white satin shoes as an image of being in her future husband's arms crashed into her mind. She looked at the breathtakingly handsome man watching her slow progress. Would he soon be kissing her? Tonight, would he take her by the hand and lead her to his bed? And what would that be like?

As yet, he had not even kissed her. She still did not know what his lips felt like, what they tasted like, what his body felt like pressed up against hers. Warmth enveloped her. Tonight, she would find out.

She reached the altar. Her father handed her over to the Duke and they stood facing the vicar.

Georgina knew she should be paying attention to the service, but her awareness was too focused on the man standing beside her. The man who she would soon be married to, *till death us do part.*

This might not be what she wanted, but it certainly could have been a lot worse. She could have been forced to marry Lord Fernley, the Earl of Cranford or Viscount Smarley.

But she was not marrying any of those appalling men. She was marrying Adam Knightly, the Duke of Ravenswood, a man so handsome that every time she looked at him she had decidedly unacceptable thoughts. Thoughts that would soon be entirely acceptable when she became his wife.

While this marriage had been forced on her, it definitely had some compensations. She smiled up at her husband-to-be and realised the vicar had stopped speaking.

Like the engagement, the wedding service had gone by in a whirl, and she hadn't heard a word spoken. She heard her father cough and she looked at the vicar.

'Wilt thou have this man to thy wedded husband?' he repeated with a note of impatience.

'Oh, yes, I will,' she said.

The vicar prattled on for a bit longer, until finally the church bells rang out joyously as her husband—*her husband*—led her out of the church on his arm, followed by the happy congregation.

On the doorstep, while everyone cheered, he took her in his arms and kissed her lightly on the lips. Like their courtship and their wedding service, it was over before she had barely registered what was happening.

It was their first kiss, and it had been a quick peck in front of her family, friends, relatives, other invited guests and curious locals who had gathered on the lawn outside to watch the bride and groom emerging from the church.

She smiled up at him, willing him to kiss her again, really kiss her, and ignore all who were watching.

But he didn't, nor did he smile at her or say any words of reassurance. Georgina's hopes plummeted. This coldness could not be an omen of what their marriage was to be like, could it? No, it would not be. He just didn't want to kiss her properly in front of the milling crowd. He would save that for when they were alone.

Alone. Alone and married, with no restrictions on what they did and what they shared. Then he would kiss her the way a man kissed a woman, the way a husband kissed his wife.

While the congregation threw rose petals over the heads of the supposedly happy couple, he took her hand and helped her into the open carriage, festooned with white flowers, that would take her back to her family home for the wedding breakfast.

'So, husband,' Georgina said and gave a small giggle as if she had said something rather ridiculous, 'we're now married.'

She looked at him in expectation, waiting for him to laugh, to smile, to say something joyous and encouraging.

'Indeed we are,' he replied in a tone that was neither joyous nor encouraging. 'After the wedding breakfast we shall return to my estate. I believe it would be best if you met the children as soon as possible and I have been away from them for far too long.'

'It's such a shame they couldn't attend the wedding ceremony. The girls could have been bridesmaids, your son a pageboy.'

'I discussed this with the children's grandmother and

she decided that, as it is not long since the children lost their mother, it would be difficult watching their father taking another bride.'

'Would it not have been better for them to have met me before the wedding day? I was surprised you did not insist on that with Father before the engagement was announced.'

'Why?'

'Well, in case they didn't like me. After all, I'm now their stepmother. They might worry that I'm going to be one of those evil stepmothers, like in the fairy tales.' She bared her teeth in her best impression of a witch.

His expression remained impassive, showing he could see no humour in this situation. 'The children are cared for by their grandmother and a nanny. Your duties as my wife will not entail being their mother.'

Her duties as his wife.

She was to have duties and he was to decide what they entailed. Georgina thought not. She might be his wife now, but that did not give him the right to tell her what she could or could not do, what was or was not expected of her.

'Anyway, I am looking forward to meeting them and if I'm not going to be their evil stepmother, I hope we can all become good friends.'

He raised his eyebrows as if he was unsure what to make of the idea of his children becoming friends with Georgina, but made no reply.

The carriage came to a halt in front of the house, and they were soon surrounded by happy guests, so there was no time to further discuss these so-called wifely duties.

Nor did they have time to converse during the wedding breakfast, the whirl of the event making this all but impossible. On the few occasions Georgina did try to converse with her husband, her voice was drowned by the noise of the celebrating guests, the clatter of dishes, the rushing here and there of servants and the toasts and speeches.

When the dancing commenced, the Duke held out his hand and led her onto the dancefloor. She placed her hand on his broad shoulder as he took her other hand, and felt his strong hand move to her waist. She was now in the arms of her husband, a man who was all hers.

Her wifely duties.

Georgina sighed gently. There was one wifely duty she was certainly not going to object to.

Last night, her mother had entered Georgina's bedchamber, her lips pursed tightly, her body held rigidly, and had proceeded to tell Georgina what her wifely duties on her wedding night would entail. Her mother had looked so embarrassed as she'd stumbled over her words, and Georgina had to stop herself from giggling. It was as if her mother was providing her with an instruction manual on what went where, when and why it had to occur.

Her mother's talk would have dismayed Georgina and filled her with qualms if she had not already had a similar conversation with her married friends, Amelia and Irene. Their description of what Georgina was to expect had less to do with what went where, as to what it would feel like, and if it was half as glorious as they described it was going to feel simply wonderful.

She moved closer to her husband and breathed in that

intoxicating scent of bergamot, sage and masculinity. What was expected of her on her wedding night, and throughout her married life, was one wifely duty he would get no dispute over. Whatever he wanted from her, whenever he wanted it and wherever, she would be in full agreement.

Her hand moved slowly along his shoulder, feeling the coiled strength under her fingers, and the fire that had been smouldering deep within her since he'd led her onto the floor ignited further, making her entire body warm and deliciously tingly.

She could stay in his arms, dancing to this music, for the rest of her life and know that she would be content. But the inevitable happened and all too soon the music came to an end. The Duke placed his hand on the small of her back and led her off the dancefloor. They had exchanged hardly a word as he had held her in his arms, and she hoped that it was because he too was contemplating what was to come.

Before they reached the edge of the dancefloor, her brother intervened.

'May I dance with the Duchess?' he said with a wry smile.

Her husband bowed to Tommy, then, surprisingly, gave an equally formal bow to her, before departing.

'Well, you've got what you wanted, haven't you, Duchess?' Tommy said, while Georgina continued to contemplate the Duke's formality towards her.

Surely they should be more relaxed with each other now. And he was yet to ask her to call him by his given name. Did he expect her to keep calling him 'Your Grace'? Well, that wouldn't be happening. From now on he would be Adam, whether he liked it or not. And she would only respond to Georgina, or perhaps Georgie, or maybe even darling or sweetheart. She smiled at the thought.

'I said, you must be pleased to have got what you wanted,' Tommy repeated.

'What?' she said as she looked from the Duke—Adam—and commenced dancing with her brother.

'You got the man you wanted, just as you always get everything you ever want.'

'No, you know that is not the case. Father gave me an ultimatum. Marry a titled man or be thrown out of the house. It was either this—' she lifted her hand off his shoulder to indicate the wedding '—or I would have to become a governess or paid companion, or something equally horrific.'

Tommy gave a small dismissive laugh. 'We both know that isn't true. Father has been threatening you with dire consequences if you don't change your ways since you were a little girl. If you'd wanted to get out of this marriage you would have found a way.'

'Nonsense. I… He… I…' she stumbled, baffled by Tommy's assertion. 'No, you're wrong. Father does make good on his threats. Remember when he threatened to send me to Halliwell's if I didn't change my ways. I didn't change and he did.' She sent her brother a satisfied look to underline the fact that she had proven him wrong.

'You know that if you hadn't actually enjoyed your time at Halliwell's you would have come home, full of tears and tantrums, and Father would have surrendered, as he always did. But you did have fun there, didn't you? You made friends. You enjoyed yourself. So you stayed.'

'Well, yes, I suppose, but it was still a threat Father went through with, so you're wrong.'

'Do you really think Father would have seen his little Georgie thrown out into the street?' Tommy's smile was decidedly smug. 'You've had Father wrapped around your little finger from the first time you smiled up at him from your crib with those little dimples in your cheeks. You're married to the Duke because you want to be married to the Duke.'

'That's not true,' she said, aghast that he should think her capable of doing something so underhand.

Tommy merely raised his eyebrows, that smile becoming even more smug.

She continued to stare at her brother in shock. Was he right? Had she been merely trying to convince herself that this was all against her will? Had she, deep down, intended to marry the Duke from the moment she'd met him?

If that was true, what sort of woman did that make her? One who played games with men in order to get what they wanted? That would make her no better than all those women she had warned the Duke about. Worse, because she had pretended that she was different.

She looked over at the Duke—Adam—her husband, who was talking to her father. Tommy was right. She was attracted to him, and had been from the moment she'd first seen him when he'd stopped to help her at the side of the road. How could she not be attracted to a man with his sublime good looks? But that did not mean she had intended to marry him. And yes, she would admit she had been somewhat jealous when he had shown an interest in Miss Bateman, Lady Cecelia and Lady Gwendolyn, but again, that did not mean she'd intended to marry him herself. And yes, Tommy was perhaps correct in his claim that she had made no effort to change her father's mind and had simply accepted Adam's proposal. But that was because she could think of no alternative, or at least an alternative that wasn't simply horrid.

She shrugged a shoulder dismissively as Tommy led her back to her husband. While her brother was right that she was attracted to the Duke, he was wrong about everything else. Circumstances beyond her control had led to them becoming man and wife. She had no reason to feel the slightest bit of guilt. And, anyway, there was no going back now. All she could do was make the best of the situation in which she now found herself, and that was exactly what she intended to do.

Chapter Nine

It was done. Adam was now married. Again. One moment he was looking at the account books and coming to the daunting conclusion that the only way to save the estate was to marry again, and this time for money, the next moment he was seated beside his new wife and travelling back to his Dorset estate to start their life together.

It was hard to believe it was just over a month ago when he had met Georgina on the side of the road while she was trying to escape from him. Now she was his wife. If this was daunting for him, it must be frightening for her. Although frightened did not describe the chirpy woman sitting beside him in his carriage. Despite her apparent ease, it was still up to him to reassure her she had no need to be anxious concerning their future life together.

'Miss Georgina.' He paused. She was no longer Miss Georgina but the Duchess of Ravenswood.

'Ah-ah-ah,' she said, waggling her finger at him. 'Now that we are married you *must* call me Georgina. And I shall call you Adam.'

'Georgina,' he said, surprised that a softness had crept into his voice. He coughed lightly. 'Georgina,' he repeated. 'Now that we are man and wife, we need to discuss what that will mean.'

'You mean what my wifely duties will be,' she said with a little laugh and a slight colouring to her cheeks.

'Yes, well, no. Your duties, such as they are, will be limited. I have already said I do not expect you to act as mother to my three children. I will expect nothing of you. We both know that this is a marriage of convenience, one that saved both of us from an undesirable future. I believe you should be free to continue to live exactly as you did before you married.'

'Oh, I see.'

He had expected her to smile, to make one of her silly jokes, to do something, anything, to show that she was in agreement with this arrangement. Instead, she looked strangely disappointed.

'Does that not meet with your approval?'

'Yes, I suppose it does.' She looked out at the passing scenery then back at him. 'But I don't really know what that means. Before I married, all I was expected to do was find a husband. Now I have a husband so I'm not sure what will be expected of me.'

Adam too was at a loss. What did young women like her do with their time? Embroider? Paint watercolours? Somehow, he could see neither of those activities occupying a woman such as her.

'You seem to be very good at enjoying yourself. Perhaps you could continue to do that.'

She smiled as if he had given her a compliment, causing Adam to wonder if that was a wise suggestion.

'There's no point climbing down drainpipes now that I'm married, and as for being rude to suitors, well, that's all over and done with now, isn't it?' She shrugged. 'Mother said that once I was married I would have to run the household, but that doesn't sound like much fun for me or anyone else who lives in the house.'

'My former mother-in-law has run the household since my wife's passing. I doubt if she would welcome another woman taking over that task.' Mrs Wainwright had stepped into her daughter's role as soon as Rosalie had become sick and had done so with daunting efficiency. Despite being a somewhat difficult woman, one who never missed an opportunity to let Adam know what she thought of him for marrying outside his class, he owed her an enormous debt of gratitude for managing his household and caring for his children, especially in the early days when he was so stricken with grief he could barely look after himself. He would do nothing to upset her, including challenging her position in the household now that he had a new wife.

'Mrs Wainwright also cares for the children,' he continued. 'I believe that situation should remain, as you have no experience with children.' That had been one of his main objections to marrying Georgina. He could not imagine her caring for children, especially as at times she acted like a child herself.

'Well, she doesn't perform all the wifely duties, surely.' She giggled nervously, then her pink cheeks turned a deep red, making it obvious to what she was referring.

This was the conversation Adam was dreading, but

one he knew he had to have, and the sooner they got it over and done with the better.

'Miss Hay… Georgina, I know this marriage is against your wishes. I am not such a cad that I would expect you to share my bed.'

He turned and looked out of the window, seeing nothing. He might not be such a cad that he would insist that the marriage be consummated, but by God he was enough of a cad that he wanted to.

From the moment he had seen her standing in the doorway of the church on her father's arm he had been powerless to think of anything else, despite spending an inordinate amount of mental energy attempting to ferociously crush it throughout the day.

'I am aware that young ladies are informed by their mothers about what is expected of them in the bedchamber,' he said, still staring out of the window and unable to look at his wife. 'But this marriage is different, and I will not be expecting such duties from you.' He winced at how priggish he sounded. 'And I already have an heir, so…' He came to a halt, uncomfortable that he was suggesting the only reason a man and woman made love was to produce children. But it was essential that Miss Hayward—Georgina—knew she was safe.

'I see,' she said quietly. 'So we are not really going to be man and wife?'

'Yes. Is that not what you wanted?' He turned to face her, and a small flicker of hope sparked within him.

'Oh, yes, yes. I was just making sure.'

The flicker died immediately, as it should. Now that was out of the way he could gratefully move onto other less disconcerting matters.

'I have already discussed your allowance with your father and made provisions with my estate manager. It will be much more generous than the one your father gave you, allowing you complete freedom.'

'That's nice, thank you,' she said, almost dismissively. Was she drawing his attention to the fact that her allowance would come out of her own marriage settlement? If she was, she had every right to do so. It was her money, and his debt to her was enormous.

He turned in the seat to fully face her. 'I am sorry about this, Georgina. I know a marriage such as this is exactly what you were trying to avoid and I understand completely why you would be upset.'

'Do you?'

'Yes, I think so. You have been used by your father and, I'm ashamed to say, used by me. You deserve so much more than this forced marriage. But I promise I will do everything I can to make sure this marriage is tolerable for you. If there is anything you want, please just ask. If there is any way in which you want me to change my behaviour towards you, tell me. Will you promise me that?'

For the first time since they'd started this uncomfortable discussion she smiled. 'Oh, yes, I promise.'

It really was a beautiful smile. But then she *was* beautiful. Radiant, vivacious and so full of life. And he had trapped this spirited young woman in a life she did not want. She should be free to live life to the full, to dance, laugh and fall in love. He had lied to himself and that was unforgivable. He had tried to tell himself he was marrying her to save her from her father's threats, but he knew that was not entirely true. He wanted her.

Even when she'd been dressed as a lowly maid and he knew she was forbidden to him, he had wanted her. When he'd seen her dancing in the arms of other men, he had wanted her. Now he had her, but he had no right to her.

At least now he was being honest with himself. That was something, he supposed. When he'd heard her father threatening her, he had tried to pretend he was acting as her white knight, but his thoughts had been entirely selfish. He had wanted her, in his arms, in his bed. It was almost more shameful than Adam could bear to admit, but it was the truth. And it was wrong, so wrong.

But he would not act on his lustful thoughts. That would be his punishment for his selfishness. That would be his punishment for marrying a spirited young woman for her money. He would have to see this beautiful woman every day, and know that she could never really be his.

'Good,' he responded, to both his thoughts and her agreement. 'I do not want you to feel trapped.'

She shrugged one shoulder. 'I never feel trapped. And if I did, I could always climb out of a window. As you know, I'm very good at shimmying down drainpipes.' She gave a little laugh to show that it was a joke, but that didn't stop Adam from wincing at the memory of how she had tried to escape from him.

'Anyway,' she continued, 'if you knew anything about me, you'd know that I always make the best of any situation and I always get what I want.' The colour that was still tinging her cheeks unaccountably flared again.

'That is good. I too will endeavour to make the best of this unfortunate situation.'

The coach came to a halt in front of her new home, and Adam helped her down from the carriage. It was certainly a house suitable for a duke and rivalled her family home in its grandeur. Three wings surrounded the courtyard, adorned with statuary of what Georgina assumed were Greek or Roman gods, or something like that. While most of the building was in a similar style to her family's home, and built from soft yellow stone, an older section of red Tudor brick could also be seen.

She could imagine her father looking at it with approval, particularly as it had been in the family for countless generations rather than something newly bought.

They entered the house and walked down the long hallway to the drawing room, where they found the revered Mrs Wainwright waiting for them, along with the children.

'I've kept the children up late,' Mrs Wainwright said to Adam, not even looking at Georgina. 'I hope that is all right. They were anxious to meet your new wife.'

Unfortunately, the children did look rather anxious, and not from excitement. Georgina gave her sunniest smile. No one smiled back. Did no one in this household know how to smile, including her new husband?

Well, Adam had given her permission to be herself, to ask for anything she wanted or any changes she wanted made. And the first change she wanted was for these children to smile at her.

'Let me guess,' she said, approaching the children.

'You must be Charlotte. Your father said you were a rare and exquisite beauty. And you must be Dorothea, because you're as pretty as a peach, just as he described you. And you have to be the handsome, indomitable Edwin. Am I right?'

They all turned towards their father with matching looks of trepidation. He had said no such thing, but Georgina was sure that if she had asked that was exactly how he would have described his children.

'Children, greet the Duchess properly,' their grandmother instructed, as if trying to make this occasion as formal and as uncomfortable as possible.

The two girls curtsied while Edwin gave a bow and all three muttered, 'Your Grace...'

'Georgina. That's my name, so please don't call me Your Grace.' She looked to Mrs Wainwright so she would know she was included in that as well. 'And I do hope we can all be the best of friends.'

'May I present Mrs Wainwright?' Adam said, indicating his former mother-in-law.

Mrs Wainwright gave a small curtsey and also muttered, 'Your Grace...' She scowled as if the words were unpleasant in her mouth, but apparently not as unpleasant as calling Georgina by her given name.

'Please, I would really prefer to be called Georgina. Adam says you are simply marvellous with the children and do a splendid job running the household. I do hope you will allow me to assist you in any way I can.'

Mrs Wainwright sent Adam a sideways look, then turned the full force of her glare onto Georgina. 'It's your household now, Your Grace.'

'Nonsense. And please call me Georgina. After all, we're all family now.'

Everyone looked at everyone else, as if needing some clarification of this statement.

'Well, I believe it is past your bedtime,' Mrs Wainwright said to the children. 'I'm sure your father would like to be alone with his new bride.' She glowered at Adam before bustling the children out of the room.

'Well, at least it's not just me she disapproves of,' Georgina said once the door had closed and they were alone. 'Did you see the way she looked at you?'

'Hmm,' was all her husband said.

'And I'm sure the children will warm to me once we've spent a bit of time together. This must be very confusing for them.'

'Hmm,' he repeated. 'It has been a long day. I am sure you would like to retire early.' He crossed the room and pushed the bell to summon a servant. 'I believe your lady's maid arrived earlier today so your bedchamber will be ready and your trunks unpacked.'

Georgina wondered if now would be an appropriate time to mention that he had said if she wanted him to change his behaviour in any way all she had to do was ask. For a start, he could treat her like his wife and not with the polite formality of a guest.

'I have been away from the estate for far too long and there is much that needs to be seen to,' he continued, still standing on the other side of the room. 'Mrs Wainwright will introduce you to the servants tomorrow and show you around the estate.'

No, she was wrong. It seemed she was to be treated like a guest who could be all but ignored. Was this what their married life was to be like? Georgina hoped not. And if it was, that too would be something she would be changing.

A maid entered and gave a quick curtsey, while keeping her eyes lowered.

'Molly, will you show the Duchess to her room, please?'

Georgina turned to face him and waited. Was he going to at least kiss her goodnight? After all, she was his wife.

He bowed. 'Until tomorrow.'

No, there would be no kisses.

'Goodnight then,' she said, and waited for a few more seconds to see if he changed his mind, then departed and stomped down the hallway and up the stairs to her bedchamber.

This was certainly not how she'd imagined spending her wedding night. And certainly not how she wanted her marriage to be. He did not expect her to run the household, thank goodness, as she'd be hopeless at that. He did not expect her to care for his children, which, all things considered, was probably for the best, and now he did not expect her to be a real wife to him either. And that was something she could actually do, was expected to do, indeed, wanted to do.

Her mother had informed her it was the duty of both bride and groom to consummate the marriage as soon as possible, whether they wanted to or not. Until that happened, it was not a real marriage and could be annulled by either party.

She had made consummation sound like an arduous task for the bride, but Amelia and Irene had explained it did not have to be like that and could be glorious. That was what Georgina wanted. Glorious. And she wanted it with Adam, so she could be his real wife.

She came to a halt at the top of the stairs. Somehow, she was going to have to make him realise it was what he wanted as well. If he wasn't going to consummate this marriage out of duty, then she was going to have to convince him he was doing it because it was what he desired.

All she had to do now was work out how one went about making a man desire you so much he just couldn't keep his hands off you. Otherwise, despite being a married woman, she was going to spend the rest of her life living like a lonely spinster, and that simply would not do.

She entered her bedchamber and gave a little giggle over her new plan. When Adam had told her she would be free to do what she pleased, Georgina had been confused, unsure what she actually would do with her time. Now she knew. She would be dedicating her time to making her husband desire her, to convincing him that he simply must make her his real wife.

Smiling to herself, she pulled back the covers and climbed into bed, for the first, and what she intended would be the last, night in which she slept alone.

Chapter Ten

Georgina rose the next morning and dressed with care, in line with her new decision to change her husband's attitude to her, but when she entered the breakfast room he was nowhere in sight. The children and Mrs Wainwright were seated around the table and all stared at her, as if still unsure how to behave in her company.

This uncomfortable situation had to change, and the sooner the better.

'I believe we are all going to have to get to know each other a lot better,' she said, looking from one child to the next. 'After breakfast, shall we go for a nice long walk? You can show me around the estate, tell me all about yourselves, and I can tell you all about me.'

The children all stared at her, then looked to their grandmother as if for approval.

'With your grandmother's permission, of course.'

'It's not my place, I'm sure, to tell you what you can and can't do,' Mrs Wainwright said, her lips pinched.

'Good, that's settled. We'll have a lovely walk and a nice long chat and then we'll all be the best of friends.'

Georgina continued to chatter as they ate their breakfast, with the children giving quiet answers to her questions in as few words as possible, while the formidable Mrs Wainwright barely said a word. It was as if there was a dusty shroud hanging over this house, one that Georgina was determined to whip away and expose everyone to the glorious sunshine. If she was to spend the rest of her life in this house, she wanted there to be fun and laughter. There had to be fun and laughter or she was sure she would be forced to climb out of the window and make her escape to stop herself from going quite insane.

Once they had finished eating, Mrs Wainwright took the children upstairs to dress for their outing. It was a lovely day, and if it had been up to Georgina she would have just taken the children and immediately burst out of the house and freed them from the confines under which they were living. But she was sensible enough to know that it would not be a good idea to antagonise Mrs Wainwright. Not yet.

The children arrived at the entranceway dressed in sensible plain clothing and sturdy boots, a sharp contrast to Georgina, who was still wearing her pretty blue and white striped day dress. One she had chosen because it flattered her figure and colouring and had been intended to tempt her husband. She had to admit it was more suitable for a gentle stroll in Hyde Park than a trek across the countryside. But she had no intention of changing now, and no intention of being sensible.

'Right, let's have some fun,' she said, which elicited no smiles from the children.

'So, I want you to show me everything,' Georgina

went on as they walked down the gravel path. 'I want to know the best trees for climbing, the best lakes for catching frogs, the best places to hide when playing hide and seek or escaping from your grandmother. All the important things.'

The children exchanged curious glances. 'There's a river on the other side of those trees,' Charlotte said, pointing to the woodland. 'And I believe one can find frogs there.'

It was the longest speech she had heard from any of the children.

'Good. Then that will be our first stop. Lead the way, Charlotte.'

While Charlotte walked ahead, Georgina followed with the other two children and was heartened when Edwin put his little hand in hers. She looked down and smiled at him, but he merely gave her a shy look from under his lowered eyelashes.

The estate was magnificent and a perfect place for children. Their stroll took them through extensive areas of grassland, wooded groves, and to a winding river with lovely old arched stone bridges. Georgina could imagine her and Tommy climbing trees, staging mock battles, running around and generally causing mayhem. But these children looked as if they had never run amok or created mayhem in their lives. That would have to change.

'So,' she called out to draw the children's attention. 'What am I supposed to call you?'

Charlotte turned around and all three frowned at her. 'Charlotte, Dorothea and Edwin,' Charlotte said tentatively, as if speaking to an imbecile.

'I know that is what your names are, but what do you call each other? What do your friends call you?'

'Charlotte, Dorothea and Edwin,' Charlotte repeated.

'Hmm, my name is Georgina, but my brother always called me either George or Georgie, never Georgina, and I called him Tommy, and occasionally "you little beast".'

This at least got a small smile from the children.

'I know. I'll call you Lotte,' she said, pointing to Charlotte. 'You can be Dora,' she said to Dorothea. 'And you will be Eddie. I'm surprised no one has called you that before.'

Charlotte looked down at her boots. 'Mother called us by those names. Except Edwin, because they hadn't yet chosen a name for him when…'

The two sisters exchanged pained looks. Georgina knew that Edwin's mother had died only a few days after his birth and regretted having said anything that reminded them of that tragic event.

Charlotte put her arm around her little brother, whose lips had turned down and was blinking rapidly. 'But when she held you in her arms when you were first born she called you her little duke,' Charlotte said, causing her brother to smile.

'Little Duke,' Edwin repeated, looking as pleased as punch.

Georgina's heart clenched for the children. As much as her own mother annoyed her at times, she could not imagine life without her, particularly when she had been young. These children had experienced so much loss, so much unhappiness in their short lives, they deserved, more than anyone, to have some fun, to see that life could be full of wonder and excitement. And she was just the person to provide them with that fun and excitement.

'So, we have Lotte, Dora, Eddie, also known as Little Duke, and Georgie, and we're a band of jolly buccaneers off on an adventure.' Georgina adopted a hearty tone, determined to put an end to this sombre mood.

Eddie's smile grew wider, but the girls did not look quite so convinced and certainly did not look jolly, but they obediently followed Georgina until they reached the edge of the pretty stream, where weeping willows dipped their branches into the gently moving water.

The children came to a halt as if unsure what to do now that they had reached their destination. Georgina picked up a stone and threw it into the water. Eddie followed her example but the two girls stood staring at the water, their arms hanging limply at their sides. Did these children not know how to play?

'Let's see who can throw their stone the furthest.' She picked up a stone and tossed it so it spun across the water and nearly made it to the other bank.

Eddie copied her, his stone plopping a few inches from where he was standing. But this did not deter him and he quickly picked up another and repeated his action. The two girls obediently picked up stones and weighed them in their hands uncertainly, still wearing those confused expressions.

Georgina threw another, which unfortunately did not reach the same impressive distance. Lotte copied her movements and sent her stone skimming across the water almost to the other side. 'Mine went further than yours,' she cried out, picking up another stone to repeat that performance.

Not to be outdone by her sister, Dora picked up a stone, and almost reached the spot her sister's stone had sunk. Soon the girls were competing and arguing good-naturedly, in much the way Georgina and her brother had spent their childhood, while Eddie was content with throwing more and more stones over the edge of the riverbank.

'That almost made it to the bank,' Lotte called out. 'I'm winning.'

'No, it didn't,' Dora said, turning to Georgina. 'She's not winning, is she?'

Georgina stifled a smile at their newfound exuberance and acted as if she was seriously considering the question. 'I believe Lotte's went the longest distance,' she said, causing Lotte to give a look of smug satisfaction. 'But Dora does have an excellent technique so deserves points for style.'

'Exactly,' Dora said.

'So, buccaneers, do you think we should make a raft and sail away on the high seas?' Georgina announced, looking up and down the river as if this was a serious proposition.

'Yes, let's do that,' Dora said, scouring the banks for suitable pieces of wood.

It was something that Georgina and her brother had often attempted when they were children. They'd never actually succeeded in making a raft capable of floating, their enthusiasm being greater than their ship-building skills, but it had provided them with hours of entertainment.

Lotte and Dora began piling up branches, while Edwin added a few twigs.

'Once we've got all the wood we need, we'll have to go back to the house for twine so we can bind it all together,' Lotte announced.

'No, our ribbons will be perfect, and they'll look pretty as well,' Dora said, pulling the carefully tied ribbons out of her plaits.

Georgina was unsure whether Mrs Wainwright would be happy with their silk ribbons being used for such a purpose, but that was a discussion that could be held at a later date. In the meantime, the children were having fun, and that was the one and only point of today.

'We need some bigger pieces,' Dora said, looking at their pile and around the river. 'Some bits like that.' She pointed to a fallen branch that had become wedged in an overhanging tree.

'Perfect,' Lotte agreed as she hitched up her skirts and climbed out on the tree to retrieve the branch. Georgina looked on with proud amazement. Only a short while ago these children were reserved and overly cautious but, thanks to her, they were now having fun and being adventurous. It was the one skill Adam acknowledged that she had and she hoped he would appreciate all her good work.

Her excitement waned as she watched the little girl move out further on the branch. 'Um… Lotte, perhaps you shouldn't go quite so far out—'

Georgina's pride at the girl's adventurous spirit came crashing down, along with Lotte, as she toppled off the branch and, with a large splash, tumbled into the middle of the river. A shriek went up from Dora, who instantly waded into the water, followed by her little brother.

'Eddie, get back here immediately!' Georgina called out, causing the little boy to burst into tears, but at least he returned to the bank. 'Dora, you come back as well. I'll save Lotte. You look after your brother.'

Georgina lifted up her skirts and waded into the brown water, feeling the mud squelch over the top of her shoes. Perhaps sensible walking boots would have been a good idea after all.

Dora fortunately did as she was instructed, returned to the bank and put her arms around the sobbing and hiccupping Eddie.

Before Georgina reached her, Lotte stood up and it became apparent there was no danger. The water was barely at her mid-thigh, and despite the weight of her sodden dress she was able to wade over to Georgina.

'Are you all right, Lotte?' Georgina asked.

Lotte wiped at the mud on her face, but only managed to smear it further. 'Yes, I'm fine. But look, Georgie, your lovely dress is ruined.' She pointed at Georgina's sodden, muddy skirt.

Georgina smiled at the girl. She had called her Georgie. Despite her obvious inability to supervise young children, and despite putting them in apparent danger, the girl had called her Georgie. They were now friends, just as she had hoped.

'I think we'd better return to the house and get you cleaned up,' she said, taking Lotte's hand so they could wade back to the river's edge.

Lotte looked down at her own now filthy dress. 'Buccaneers don't care about such things.'

'No, but grandmothers do, and so do servants,' Georgina said, surprised that for once she was being the sensible one.

They made it back to the shore, where Eddie and Dora were waiting for them, wide-eyed, with an apparent mix of admiration and awe.

'That really was an adventure, wasn't it?' she said, hoping that Eddie would not start crying again. He gave a small hiccup, then smiled.

'But I think that's enough adventuring for today. Let's go home and have some nice hot chocolate.'

This got a cheer of approval from all three, and the dirty buccaneers began their squelching progress back to the house.

As they made their muddy way up the gravel path, Mrs Wainwright and Adam emerged from the house. Georgina was unsure what she was going to say or how she was going to explain the three children returning in this state, not to mention her own filthy appearance.

The closer she got, the easier it was to see the expressions on their faces. The Duke did not look pleased but, to her surprise, Mrs Wainwright was smiling. Could that be right? That dour woman, the one Georgina was sure would tear strips off her, possibly even ban her from having anything more to do with her grandchildren, was actually smiling.

'Well, it looks like you've all had a grand time,' she said. 'But it might be best if you go in through the servants' entrance and not tread mud all over the entranceway.'

'Yes, Grandmother,' the three children said, turning and walking around the edge of the building.

'I can explain,' Georgina said, not entirely sure how she would do that.

'I think it best if you join the children,' Mrs Wainwright said, saving Georgina from doing the impossible. 'I'll ask the maids to prepare a bath for you, but I don't think your lady's maid is going to be too happy about the state of your clothing.'

This was all so unexpected. Mrs Wainwright was not angry with her. If anything, she seemed to approve of Georgina's wayward behaviour. The same could not be said for Adam. He was looking at her as if she was one of his children and he was thoroughly disappointed with her bad behaviour.

'Well, I suppose I'd better get cleaned up,' she said. 'Oh, and I promised the children there would be hot chocolate.'

He made no response, leaving Georgina with no choice but to squelch round the side of the house and join the children, where they were being washed down with buckets of water by one of the stable hands.

Georgina tried to take solace in achieving one aim for today. The children had had fun, albeit dirty and perhaps rather reckless fun, but she was no closer to achieving her second goal. It was now obvious that if one was trying to get one's husband to see you as a desirable woman, appearing in front of him, caked in mud and smelling like a stagnant river was not the way to go about it.

'Well, I'll be...' Mrs Wainwright said after Georgina departed.

'I am so sorry,' Adam said. 'I will have a word with

her and tell her she has to be more careful with the children.'

This was a disaster. He knew Georgina could be impetuous and somewhat childish, but he had not expected that on her first day at the estate she would cause such disruption.

'Nonsense. You'll do no such thing.'

He turned to look at Mrs Wainwright. She was smiling, something he had not seen for a long time.

'Those children need to get out and enjoy themselves. Lord knows I'm too old to play with them, and, well, since Rosalie's passing, I haven't had the energy to do much more than make sure they are cared for.'

'But they were covered in mud,' Adam said, stating what he would have thought was obvious.

'Mud washes off and no harm was done. And the children looked as if they had enjoyed themselves. That matters more than a few muddy clothes ever will.'

He continued to stare at her in disbelief. Mrs Wainwright approved of nothing he did. Was she now approving of his bride's misbehaviour?

'But I can't stand here talking all day. I've got baths and hot chocolates to organise, and clothing to be repaired,' she added in her more familiar brisk tone as if it was Adam who was holding her up from her work.

He watched as she went back into the house. This was not what he had expected when he had looked out of the study window and seen the muddy Georgina and the even muddier children walking up the path. He'd rushed down, certain that he was going to have to mediate a confrontation between Mrs Wainwright and Georgina. Instead, the two women appeared to be on the same side. While he was pleased there had been no disagreement, he was unsure whether having those two women collaborating was going to prove to be a good thing or a bad thing when it came to his own well-being, but that was something only time would tell.

Chapter Eleven

After a warm bath and a change of clothes Georgina was starting to feel like a woman again, and not a mudlark who had spent the day scouring for treasures in the Thames. She had apologised profusely to her lady's maid about the state of her dress, but Betsy was unperturbed, as usual, reminding Georgina that it was not the first time she had had to repair damaged clothing or had to clean mud off her dress and shoes. Although her raised nose did suggest Betsy had not expected to be still doing so now that Georgina was a married woman.

Wearing a clean salmon-pink dress, her hair free of mud, pieces of twig and other flotsam from the river she'd rather not think about, Georgina inspected herself in the full-length looking glass. She wasn't sure if she now looked like a duchess, but her appearance was certainly much more feminine. If she behaved really, really well at luncheon, perhaps she would redeem herself in Adam's eyes for this morning's unfortunate incident and prove to him she was a woman worthy of his attentions.

But all her preparations were for nothing. She joined

the children and Mrs Wainwright in the dining room only to discover that, yet again, Adam was absent. Was she ever going to see him again? Seducing him was going to be difficult enough, but it would be impossible if he never put in an appearance. And even more difficult if the only time he *did* see her was when she was dripping wet and smelling rather unpleasant.

'This morning was such fun,' Dora declared as Georgina took her place at the table. 'When will the buccaneers have their next adventure?'

The other two children looked at her in expectation. It was as if she were in the presence of completely different children than the ones who had looked at her tentatively across the breakfast table just this morning. Even Mrs Wainwright was still unaccountably smiling at her.

'Nothing can stop buccaneers when they are in a mood to rampage across the countryside.' Georgina's comment caused the smiles to grow brighter.

'Will Adam be joining us, Mrs Wainwright?' she asked quietly as the children continued to discuss their future adventures and tried to come up with suitable piratical names for themselves.

The older lady shrugged and frowned disapprovingly. 'No, he has much more important things to do than to spend time with his family.' Her look softened and she smiled at Georgina. 'And if I'm to call you Georgina then I believe it is only proper that you call me Agatha.'

Georgina beamed in delight. She might be failing in seducing Adam, but at least she was winning over the children and Mrs Wainwright.

'Agatha,' Edwin said, looking decidedly pleased with himself, while his sisters giggled.

'You, young man, will continue to call me Grandmother,' Mrs Wainwright said in mock reprimand.

'Yes, Gammie,' he said, then commenced chewing on a piece of bread.

'Thank you, Agatha,' Georgina said, sending a quick wink in Eddie's direction, which caused him to give her a cheeky grin. 'I thought you'd be angry with me after this morning's escapade. I really, really am sorry for letting the children get so dirty.'

Agatha brushed her hand in front of her face as if swatting away Georgina's apology. 'You're a breath of fresh air, my dear, and that is what the children need. I was worried when His Grace said that he planned to marry again. I imagined some snooty young thing coming in here and acting all superior, but that's not you at all, is it?'

'No, you can rest assured I am superior to no one.'

Agatha stared at her for a moment, then gave a small chuckle. 'You are a card, aren't you? My Rosalie would want the children to be cared for by someone who knows how to laugh and play games.'

'Playing games and having fun are my specialities, and I'm afraid I'm not much good at anything else,' Georgina announced proudly, causing Agatha to raise her eyebrows.

'But I have to admit, I am so pleased you are here to help with the running of the house as I'm afraid no one would describe me as a particularly responsible adult.'

'But you will be able to prepare the girls for their entry into Society. That is something I am completely ignorant of,' Agatha said with a sniff, as if her ignorance was something she was rather proud of. 'It is a role a woman from your background should have no problem with.'

Georgina grimaced as the two girls stopped eating and listened with extra concentration. 'If that is something Adam expects of his wife, then I'm not sure if he married the right woman,' she mumbled.

'But you married Father,' Lotte exclaimed. 'You must have been the belle of the ball to capture the heart of a man as handsome as my father.'

'Yes, tell us how you did it,' Dora added, leaning forward in expectation.

Georgina flinched slightly. She did not want to ruin the girls' romantic illusions, and certainly did not want them to know that this marriage was little more than an arrangement for the betterment of both families, as was the case with most Society marriages.

'I don't know what I did,' she said instead. 'I think I was just very lucky.'

'But you will help us be lucky in love as well, won't you,' Lotte said, while Dora nodded.

Georgina forced herself to keep her face straight and not grimace again. 'I promise I will help you negotiate the highs and pitfalls of the Season so you have a thoroughly enjoyable time.'

'And find love, just like you and Father,' Dora added as if this was a statement of fact.

'Hmm,' was the only response Georgina could give. She looked at Agatha, who was eating her meal, seemingly intending to detach herself entirely from this conversation.

'So what shall we do this afternoon?' she said, desperate to change the subject.

'We have lessons,' Lotte said with a sigh.

'Oh.' She looked to Agatha, hoping her horror at this prospect was not written on her face. Georgina had never paid attention to anything her despairing tutors had tried to drum into her and had little interest in anything that could be learnt from books.

'A retired professor who lives in the village visits the house three afternoons a week to give the children instruction,' Agatha said, much to Georgina's relief. 'I help the girls with their needlework, but you might have to instruct them in watercolours as I have never held a paintbrush in my life.'

'Oh,' Georgina repeated. Painting in watercolours was another skill she had never quite mastered. No one could tell what it was she was trying to depict, and the paints tended to run into each other until everything became a strange shade of muddy brown. 'I shall invite my friend Irene Huntington, the Duchess of Redcliff, to visit. She's a renowned artist, you know, which means the girls will be taught by the very best.'

'The Duchess of Redcliff?' Mrs Wainwright said with a frown.

'She's not snooty either. She's really lovely and a famous artist, and I'm sure she would love to give the girls instructions because, believe me, you don't want me anywhere near an open tube of paint.'

Agatha looked unconvinced.

'None of my friends are snooty. Snooty people don't like me because my grandfather started life as a baker and Mother's mother was a seamstress.' She gave a little shudder, remembering all those men who'd shunned her throughout the Season, and all those girls at Halliwell's who'd thought they were oh, so much better than her.

'A baker? A seamstress?' Agatha said as if these were impressive occupations. 'My husband and I were tenant farmers, still are, really.' She looked over at the children, who had gone back to finding more and more outlandish pirate names for themselves and had lost interest in the adults' conversation.

'I still can't forgive the Duke for taking my daughter out of the life she knew and away from the people she loved,' she said quietly. 'But one thing I will say about the Duke, at least he's no snob, although it might be better for everyone if he was.'

Georgina thought it best not to ruin this new cordiality between herself and Agatha by pointing out that Agatha was indulging in a bit of snobbery of her own. It seemed the only reason she was so mean to Adam was because the man had the misfortune of being born a duke and falling in love with a woman outside his class.

'Anyway, that will take care of all the children's lessons, which is good,' she said instead. 'Because, when it comes to children, I have absolutely no experience, apart from having been one myself, and some people, including my father, would say I still am a child.'

'No one has experience with children. I'm afraid it's one of those jobs you learn by doing.'

Despite Agatha's attempt at reassurance, Georgina suspected it was yet another skill she would never acquire. But as long as Agatha was present to do the serious parenting and all that was expected of Georgina was to have fun with the children, then this would all work out rather splendidly.

After lunch, while the children rushed off to prepare for their lessons, Agatha informed Georgina that now would be the perfect time to introduce her to the household staff and discuss what was required in the running of the house.

In Georgina's opinion, it was all rather a waste of time. After all, Adam had told her that managing the household was Agatha's role, one she would be reluctant to surrender to the new Duchess, but she obediently followed Agatha around the house, greeted each servant, listened to all Agatha said, tried to ask questions that weren't too silly, and acted as if she was taking in everything she needed to know.

And so her first day passed, without seeing any more of her husband. When she dressed for dinner, she again took inordinate care in the selection of a lovely pale green satin gown with lace trim, and instructed Betsy to take extra care with her hair.

She entered the drawing room and finally her husband was present, sitting in a wing chair and looking handsome, as always. She paused at the door. He looked up from his newspaper, stood up and bowed.

Was that an assessing look he gave her? Was it one of approval? Had all her efforts been to good effect? She was sure it was. But what did it mean? Was he just pleased that his wife was not dripping mud all over the Oriental carpet? Whatever it was, whatever it meant, as his eyes held hers a tantalising little shiver vibrated within her.

Delightfully aware that his eyes were on her, she

crossed the room with as much feminine grace as she possessed and sat down on the settee. Then she smiled, but before her smile had reached its full beam, he sat down and went back to reading his newspaper.

Oh, well, at least he had looked at her. That was some progress.

Agatha entered with the children and signalled for them to stand in a nice straight line, as if part of some regimental guard, with Agatha standing behind them like their commanding officer.

'Right, children, say goodnight to your father and Georgina.'

'Oh, won't the children be having dinner with us?' Georgina asked.

'No, the children will be taking their dinner in the nursery with their nanny.'

'Oh.' Georgina found that an odd arrangement. She and Tommy had always dined with their parents unless they were entertaining. Even then, they were sometimes included in the dinner party, as long as they promised to be on their best behaviour. Something they did try to do, mostly.

The children performed their well-practised formal curtseys and bow, although, unlike last night, they also gave her small smiles. Georgina stood up and did her own extremely low curtsey with much circling of her hands in response, which caused the children to giggle. Then they turned towards their father and repeated the performance, but he merely wished them goodnight.

Georgina was unfamiliar with a duke's household, but such formality really was a terrible bore, and yet another thing that she intended to change at the earliest opportunity.

'I'll say goodnight then, Georgina,' Agatha said, while Adam looked in their direction and frowned at the informality, causing both women to smile. 'Goodnight, Your Grace,' she added and bobbed a quick curtsey in Adam's direction.

'Aren't you joining us for dinner?' Georgina asked. 'Surely you don't intend to have your dinner in the nursery as well.'

'No, I intend to dine with the servants.' Agatha smiled at Georgina's reaction. 'There's much I wish to discuss with Mrs Browne, the housekeeper.' Then she did something that almost caused Georgina to choke. She winked. Agatha actually winked, before heading out of the door.

Georgina watched the door shut behind her, then closed her mouth, which had unaccountably fallen open, and turned to Adam.

'It looks like it will just be the two of us tonight,' she said in the now quiet room.

'Yes,' he responded, looking up from his paper.

Georgina sent him what she hoped was her most endearing smile. They would be alone. This would be her opportunity to seduce her husband. But there was one rather insurmountable problem. She didn't know how. She had never had to entice a man before, nor had she ever *wanted* to entice a man before and was not sure how to go about it.

Still smiling, she thought back to the lessons she had been taught at Halliwell's. Why hadn't she paid more attention? By the time most of the other girls had left finishing school they knew how to flirt, how to be coquettish, how to converse with a man using one's fan and the fluttering of eyelashes. All Georgina had learnt at Halliwell's was the best way to escape out through the top window, how to sneak back into the dormitory without the staff seeing and how to encourage Cook to give her extra servings of pudding. None of these skills were going to help her now.

One of Miss Halliwell's instructions popped into her head. *Ask them questions about themselves and always look interested in anything they have to say.* That was it. That was one of the lessons she had been particularly dismissive of at the time, but it might just work.

'Did you have a pleasant day, Adam?' she asked and added a small flutter of her eyelashes for effect.

'Yes, thank you,' he responded, his eyebrows drawing together as he looked at her over the top of his newspaper.

'I'd love to hear all about it.'

His frown deepened and she forced herself to maintain her interested smile.

He folded the newspaper and placed it on the arm of the chair. 'I spent the day with the estate manager, going over the books. Do you really want to hear about the expected yield from the farms this season, or the new agricultural machinery we are intending to purchase, or perhaps you want me to discuss the repairs that need to be made to the roof in the west wing?'

Georgina's smile became strained. 'That all sounds fascinating. Yes, I would simply love to hear all about it.'

'Really?'

'Yes, really.' Georgina made herself keep smiling,

despite finding nothing to be amused by. Would another flutter of her eyelashes be a bit too much?

'I doubt that very much,' he said.

He continued to frown at her as Georgina tried desperately to think of something else, anything else, to say.

Nothing came to mind. She needed to try another approach. But what? Flattery. That was another lesson they attempted to drum into her at Halliwell's. *All men respond well to flattery*, according to Miss Halliwell.

'You're right, it will all be far too complex for me to understand, but I'm sure a man as intelligent as you will sort out all those problems and will know exactly what to do.' She gave what she hoped was a coquettish smile.

He did not smile in appreciation as she hoped. Instead, his brows drew even closer together and the creases in his forehead grew deeper. 'Are you quite well, Georgina? Did you bump your head when you fell in the river this morning? Did you catch a chill? Are you perhaps feverish? Should I call for a doctor?'

'What? No, certainly not. I'm perfectly fine.' Then she remembered herself and resumed smiling. Snapping at a man was definitely not something advised by Miss Halliwell. 'I'm just interested in what you did today.'

'Why?'

Because I want you to be attracted to me. I want you to ask me to do my wifely duty. I want you to take me by the hand and lead me up to your bedchamber and do all those wonderful things I've been told that a man does to his wife.

'That is what a wife should do,' she said, in response to her own thoughts, not to his question.

He stared at her, as if she were a curiosity on display

at a fairground sideshow. She suspected this was not how a man looked at his wife prior to expecting her to perform those wifely duties.

'So why are you doing it?'

'Because I'm your wife.'

'I know, but why are *you* doing it?'

'Oh, all right. I don't give a fig about agricultural machinery, the west wing's roof can collapse for all I care, and I have no idea what yields even mean, never mind caring about them.' Georgina knew she sounded like a sullen child, but he really was infuriating.

'That's as I thought.'

'So what are we going to do now? Sit here in silence and glare at each other?'

'You could tell me about *your* day. Falling into the river sounds somewhat more interesting than my discussion with the estate manager.'

'Oh, yes, well, sorry about that. I don't suppose I've made a very good impression, have I?'

'You've made a surprisingly good impression on Mrs Wainwright,' he said, slightly raising one eyebrow. 'And the children do appear to have responded to you warmly.'

'They're delightful, the children, that is,' Georgina said with a genuine smile. 'And Agatha is a surprise. I thought she'd be all gruff and disapproving but she's really rather lovely.'

'Is she? I've known her for more than ten years and have never known her to be anything but gruff and disapproving.'

'Perhaps you need to throw yourself in the river on occasion. That seemed to do the trick.'

He did not smile. Did he ever smile?

'But I am sorry about what happened. Lotte was climbing out onto an overhanging tree to fetch a piece of wood caught in its branches to use for our raft. She lost her grip and slipped. Then, before I had a chance to stop them, Dora and Eddie waded in, thinking they could save her, which was rather sweet of them, even if it was ill-advised. Then I had to rescue the two of them before I could get to Lotte to help her out. It was all really rather silly as the river is little more than knee-deep, but it all happened so fast and I was worried that… Well, that's what happened.'

She shrugged her shoulders, hoping he would see that it was all just bad luck really, and had nothing to do with her lack of skills as a mother.

'It seems no real harm was done,' was all he said but his look was still that of someone trying to hide his disappointment.

My goodness, he could be judgemental.

'No, no harm *was* done. In fact, lots of good was done, as the children enjoyed themselves. Even Agatha could see that.'

He nodded slowly. 'Yes, you are right. I am sorry.'

That almost sounded as if he was pleased with her. His agreement didn't come with a smile, and there was certainly no fluttering of eyelashes, or anything that could be considered flirting, but it was something. And something, as they said, was much better than nothing.

To make up for his lack of smiling, Georgina beamed one back at him, then lowered her eyes. 'Thank you for that,' she said, trying for humility. Humility was another lesson Miss Halliwell tried to teach, and yet another one Georgina had failed to learn.

But her attempt at humility worked as well as her flirting and flattery. She looked up to find those dark eyebrows once again drawn together, a reaction that was, unfortunately, becoming familiar to her.

'Agatha said the strangest thing to me over luncheon,' she continued, determined to ignore his stern expression. 'It seems she's expecting me to help Lotte and Dora prepare for their debut.'

He moved slightly in his chair. It was obviously a sign of discomfort, but it did draw her eyes to his long legs, and those muscles delineated under the fabric of his trousers. Perhaps she should compliment him on them. No, she doubted that would be approved of by Miss Halliwell. In fact, she suspected that noticing a man's body, his muscles, or even thinking about what he looked like under his clothes would have resulted in her having to write pages and pages of lines.

I will not look at a man's legs and will not think about his naked body.

She swallowed and forced her eyes back up to his face.

'I'm afraid, before I left for London, I told the girls that it would be the role of my new wife to help them prepare for the Season.'

'I suppose that was before you and I were engaged.'

'It was.'

'Will that be a role you still expect of me?' She gave a little laugh. 'Do you really want me in charge of turning them into proper young ladies who know how to behave in Society?'

He looked at her under raised eyebrows. 'Perhaps we could send them to Halliwell's.'

She laughed, then stopped. 'That is a joke, isn't it?'

'I'm not in the habit of making jokes, but if you feel incapable of providing them with the guidance they need, then perhaps we should consider a finishing school when the time is right.'

'And have them talk to shrubs like ninnies?'

'It would not have to be Halliwell's.'

'They're all as bad as each other. You do not want to turn your daughters into simpering idiots just so they can get a husband.'

He gave her a long, considered look. 'Then it will be up to you to prepare them for their debuts and what will be expected of their first Season.'

'Yes, right. I will.' She crossed her arms defiantly even though she suspected this was another mothering task that would be beyond her.

'I wish for my daughters to find suitable husbands and to learn how to behave in Society without causing a scene, without upsetting anyone and without embarrassing themselves. Are you capable of that?'

'Agatha can help.'

'Agatha… Mrs Wainwright…is not a member of the aristocracy, as I'm sure she will inform you at every available opportunity. She did not have a coming out and does not know what is expected.' He paused. 'And neither did Rosalie.'

He looked to the sideboard, towards a miniature portrait of a young lady in a silver frame, and his face became wistful. It had to be Rosalie, the woman he had loved, the woman he still loved. A lump formed in Georgina's throat. She was trying to seduce Adam under the gaze of his former wife. No wonder she was failing so dismally.

'I'm sorry,' she said quietly, unsure whether she was apologising to Adam or to the woman staring out at her from the sideboard.

'For what?'

'For everything. For all of this.' She waved her hands around the room to encompass the two of them and the woman on the sideboard as if to say, *For you no longer being married to the woman you love, for your children not having their mother, for Agatha not having her daughter. For you being forced to marry me. For me being me.*

To her surprise, he stood up, crossed the room, joined her on the settee and took her hand. 'You have nothing to be sorry for. None of this is your fault. This was an arrangement forced on you even more than it was forced on me.'

Tommy's words rang in her ear. '*You've got what you wanted.*' She mentally swatted them away. She moved slightly closer to Adam and clasped his hand in return. If he really wanted to reassure her, now would be the perfect time for their first proper kiss.

His gaze *was* on her lips. Yes, he was going to kiss her. Then he would ask her to perform her wifely duties. This was it. Her heart pounding out a frantic beat, her body aching with anticipation, she parted her lips, ever so slightly.

He did not move closer, but he still had her hand in his, his gaze was still fixed on her lips. Would it be too obvious if she ran her tongue along the bottom lip? No, it would be perfectly acceptable. After all, they were rather dry.

A knock on the door and the entry of a servant drew Adam's attention away.

'Dinner is served, Your Grace,' the annoying footman said.

The tip of her tongue retracted as quickly as it had emerged. Damn it all. Did they really need to eat? Georgina certainly wasn't hungry. Well, she was, but not for food.

He stood up and offered her his hand. It seemed, for now, she had no choice but to accompany him into the dining room and eat a meal she did not want.

Chapter Twelve

Adam knew Georgina was an unusual woman, so he should not be surprised by tonight's peculiar behaviour. As they walked the short distance from the drawing room to the dining room, he reminded himself that he hardly knew the young lady who was now his wife. All he really knew about her was that she behaved badly and had not wanted to marry. If he thought she was acting in a surprising manner tonight, all he had to do was remind himself of how they'd met. She had been sitting on the side of a country road dressed as a maid. No behaviour could be more peculiar than that.

But this odd coquettishness was new and difficult to understand. Had she been instructed by her mother that she needed to flirt with her husband? And, if so, why? They were already man and wife. Her mother had done her job and secured a titled husband for her daughter. Any flirting would have been done before the marriage service, and there had been none of that. And if Georgina had been told to flirt with her husband, she was just as likely to do the opposite.

He looked down at her, hoping to glean some understanding. She smiled up at him and did that odd thing with her eyelashes once more. Perhaps she *had* hit her head during this morning's escapade. To be on the safe side, perhaps he should call the doctor in the morning.

They entered the dining room, and he held out her chair. Her smile grew wider, as if a man holding out a chair for a lady was an act of great chivalry, then made a small performance of seating herself, with much rustling of silk and tossing of hair.

'Do the children usually take their evening meal in the nursery?' she asked as he took his seat.

'No, we usually dine together,' he said as he indicated to the footman that he could serve the soup.

'I think Agatha is trying to encourage us.'

He frowned in confusion. 'Encourage us to what?'

'You know. Get to know each other better, become more like man and wife.'

'I find it hard to work out anything that Mrs Wainwright is thinking,' he said. 'But she seems to have accepted you, which is good, and somewhat unexpected.'

'Yes, isn't it?' She smiled and looked decidedly pleased with herself. 'She was so grumpy to me on that first night I thought she was going to try and make my life a misery, but she's not grumpy at all. She's rather lovely.'

Lovely? Mrs Wainwright had never shown a lovely side of her nature in the many years he had known her.

'She is very good with the children, and I don't know what I would have done without her since…' He stopped. He would not mention Rosalie's name so casually in front of his new wife. That would be too much of a betrayal of the woman he loved. 'And the children also seem to have warmed to you.'

'Oh, they're lovely too. Little Eddie is such a treat, and the girls are a delight, I can see we are going to have a lot of fun together.'

He raised his eyebrows. 'There is more to parenting than just having fun.'

She sent him an assessing look. 'It seems to me that it's been a long time since anyone in this family had fun. I might not know much about parenting, but I do know that children need to laugh, to have adventures, to even be naughty occasionally.'

Her words hit him like a blow to the chest. She was right. Before Rosalie's death, Charlotte and Dorothea had been light-hearted and joyful children, and poor Edwin had been born into a house in mourning and knew no other way to live.

'You are right,' he said. 'There has not been enough laughter in this house for some time.' He looked down at the soup in front of him. Had there been any laughter since Rosalie's death? He suspected not.

'And what about you?' she asked quietly.

'I am not a child. I do not need to laugh or have adventures and I certainly do not need to be naughty on occasion.'

To his surprise, she laughed loudly at his response. 'I'm not a child either, but I think it essential to laugh, have adventures, and I hope I continue to be naughty on the odd occasion for a very long time.'

'It seems this is one area in which we differ,' he said, aware that he sounded somewhat priggish and judgemental.

'Oh, come on. Surely you occasionally want to be just a little bit naughty.'

An image of stripping Georgina of her clothing, of his hands and lips exploring her naked beauty, of him burying himself deep within her exploded, uninvited and unwanted, into his mind. He moved uncomfortably in his seat and attempted to rein in his fervid thoughts.

'I can see you are thinking of something naughty you'd like to do right now, aren't you?' she said in a teasing tone.

Guilt ripped through Adam, chasing away that unforgivable image. She was so innocent. If she had known where her talk of being naughty had taken him she would not be smiling at him, or teasing him, she would be outraged.

This marriage was merely an arrangement forced on them, he reminded himself. She deserved to be treated with respect, not to be thought of as an object, the subject of his lustful longings.

And he did not want her or any other woman. He loved Rosalie and would be true to her. He would not lust after another woman, no matter how attractive she was, no matter how beautiful she looked in that green gown. He would not notice how the low cut of the neckline revealed a tempting hint of her cleavage, or how the pearls around her neck drew his eyes to those soft mounds. No, he would not think of such things.

He coughed to clear the restriction in his throat. 'I am not,' he stated, sounding even more priggish.

'Come on,' she said, her tone still teasing. 'Forget about being so sensible and responsible. If you could do one naughty thing, what would it be?'

I would take you right here, on this table. I would wrap your long legs around my waist and enter you hard and deep. I'd make you writhe beneath me until you were begging me for more and crying out my name in ecstasy. I would feel the pleasure of being with a woman...a pleasure that has been denied me for so long.

Adam took a long quaff of his wine. 'I believe this is a pointless conversation and if it is all you wish to discuss, perhaps we should dine in silence.' *And perhaps you could stop torturing me.*

'Come on. Just one little naughty thought,' she said, as if oblivious to the torment to which she was subjecting him.

'I said enough,' he barked, louder than he intended. 'Stop this now.'

Her blue eyes grew enormous, and her hand covered her heart as if he had wounded her.

'I'm sorry, so sorry,' he said, reaching across the table for her hand, then withdrawing it just as quickly. If he wanted to avoid reigniting those inappropriate images, and he most certainly did, then touching her skin was one thing he must not do. 'I'm sorry. I did not mean to be so harsh.'

'And I assume you did not intend to tell me off either,' she said, lowering her hand from her heart and glaring at him. 'I am not one of your children. You will not reprimand me.'

'I said I am sorry.' And he could point out that she was now reprimanding him but, given his own behaviour, he had no right to point that out to her.

'Good,' she said, sending him one more look of reprimand before continuing to eat her soup. 'So, if we can't talk about being naughty, what are we going to talk about? Because I, for one, do not intend to spend every evening sitting in silence.'

He drew in a long breath and exhaled slowly. It seemed once again he had been told off, and by a young lady whose behaviour could never be called exemplary.

'What are your plans, now that you are a married woman?'

'My plans?' she asked, the soup spoon halfway to her mouth.

'As I said yesterday, as this is an arrangement rather than a marriage, you are completely free to do as you please. So, do you have any plans for this freedom?'

She placed the soup spoon back in the bowl and indicated to the footman that she was finished. 'I haven't really thought about it.'

'Do you think you might return to London? I have a townhouse that will be at your disposal.'

'Are you trying to get rid of me already?' She gave a little laugh to indicate this was a joke, but there was no laughter in her eyes.

Yes, he could answer. *I, for one, would be more comfortable if we put some distance between us. If you remain in this house, if I continue having to spend time with you, seeing your womanly body, breathing in your feminine scent, listening to the sound of silk whispering to me every time you move, it is going to be torture.*

'I merely wish for you to feel free to do as you wish. I am aware that this marriage was not what you wanted and I do not want it to be any more of a burden for you than it has to be.'

She shrugged one slim shoulder, drawing his eyes

to her creamy skin. He quickly looked back up at her blue eyes.

'But if I went back to London, I'd miss… I'd miss the children.'

'And I believe they would miss you too.' That he knew to be the truth. After one day she had managed to make the children happy, something neither he nor their grandmother had been capable of doing since their mother's death. It would be cruel of him to encourage her to leave, even though, for the sake of his sanity, he wished she'd go back to London.

'Then it's agreed,' she said. 'I will stay here and we will both make the best of this marriage.' With that, she began eating the dish of salmon the footman had placed in front of her, as if all problems had been solved.

Adam stared down at his plate. It was all so easy for her. She thought they could continue as they were, playing at being a married couple like two innocent children, never knowing the effect her presence was having on him.

Chapter Thirteen

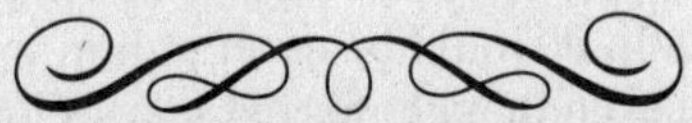

Georgina had tried everything, and failed at everything, and now he wanted her to leave. There was no point trying any of those dimly remembered Halliwell lessons again. They had been a complete waste of time and effort and had resulted in him looking at her as if she had lost her senses.

And now he was trying to drive her away. When it came to seduction, she really was dismal. Perhaps she did deserve all those low grades at Halliwell's. Despite her determination to marry a man who wanted to marry her for herself, she had ended up married to a man who wanted her only for her dowry and, despite her best efforts at seduction, he now would prefer it if she moved out so he could have nothing more to do with her.

And he wanted her to move out before she'd performed her wifely duty even once. She looked at him across the expanse of the dining room table. And, by God, she did want to perform it. Every time she looked at him, her body was aching to do its duty. She only had to look into those brown eyes for heat to engulf her and a persistent pounding to start deep in her body. It seemed no matter what part of him she looked at she reacted in the same way. His hands only made her imagine what it would be like to feel them stroke and caress her, his arms made her remember being in his arms when they'd danced. She could almost feel his strength surrounding her, holding her, leading her where he wanted her to go. And as for his eyes, when she looked into them it was as if she was surrendering herself to those brown depths.

She released a quiet sigh. And then there were his lips. How could she possibly look at his lips without imagining what it would be like to feel them on her own? All she had experienced was that one quick, very public kiss on the steps of the church. But, even then, it had been a glorious hint of what was to come. Except it didn't come, and she'd now been married two whole days.

Perhaps it would have been better if Irene and Amelia had not explained to her what to expect in the bedchamber in such exquisite detail, then she would not be so desperate to experience it.

She sent him a defiant look but he continued eating, oblivious to her torment. If he didn't demand that she perform her wifely duties soon she would do what he wanted. She would move back to London and to teach him a lesson she would take herself a lover.

Her defiant look crumpled. Of course she would not be doing that. All she was doing was trying to fool herself, and it wasn't working. She only wanted one lover. And it was him. A man who had married her for her dowry. A man who hadn't wanted her and still didn't want her.

The meal wore on, course after course, while they made small talk, about what, Georgina hardly knew. Once it was over, he led her back to the drawing room and made a formal bow as she seated herself on the settee.

'I'm afraid I still have much work to do, which I neglected while I was in London. If you will excuse me, I will leave you to…' he looked around the room '…your needlework or something.'

Georgina scoffed. He really didn't know anything about her, did he, if he thought she would want to occupy her time making samplers or putting little flowers on the edges of lace handkerchiefs.

'I don't do needlework.'

'I'm sure you will find something to occupy your time.'

'But—'

'Goodnight,' he rudely interrupted before she could insist that he keep her company, and departed as if he couldn't get away from her fast enough.

Georgina released a deep sigh and looked around the room. It was still so early, and somehow she needed to find a means of occupying herself until it was time to go to bed, alone, yet again.

She walked over to the sideboard and picked up the miniature of Rosalie, his wife. The woman he really did love. The woman he really wanted in his life.

'I'd wager he never suggested you go and live in London,' she said to the pretty young woman staring back up at her.

Georgina had to admit she was extremely attractive, with kind eyes and a gentle smile. If her expression was a true reflection of her nature, she would have made a lovely mother for Lotte, Dora and Eddie. And no doubt the perfect wife for Adam.

They'd all loved her, as, of course, had Agatha, and they had lost her. It was no surprise that there was so much sadness in this house.

'And instead of you, they've now got me,' she told the miniature. 'Someone who has no idea how to be a mother and is proving to be useless as a wife. So useless my husband doesn't even want to stay in the same room as me and is trying to pack me off to London a mere two days after our wedding.'

She sighed loudly into the empty room. 'So do you have any advice for me?'

The pretty woman said nothing, merely smiled her gentle smile.

'Yes, you're probably right. I'm fighting a lost cause.' She placed the miniature back on the sideboard. 'Your husband is still your husband and he's never going to see me as his wife.'

She looked around the room. 'Well, I suppose I'd better try and find a good book to read. It's either that or massacre some innocent handkerchiefs with my embroidery.' She went over to the bookshelf, ran her hand along the boring tomes, then spotted a section full of gothic romances.

'Well, I never.' Georgina looked over at the miniature and smiled. It seemed she and Rosalie did have one thing in common. They both liked tales set in creepy castles where brooding men ravished innocent young damsels. She took the book over to the settee and curled up for a good read. If she couldn't have the real thing, it seemed she would have to settle for the next best thing.

* * *

After a fitful night's sleep, Adam again avoided dining with the family at breakfast time. This would have to stop soon. He could not continue avoiding his wife for the rest of their married life, and he was seeing even less of the children than he had before he'd left for London. That simply would not do.

Despite that command, he retreated to his study, telling himself there was work that simply could not wait. He buried himself in his ledgers, but it wasn't long before a sound he hadn't heard for a long time drew his attention from the account books.

Children's squealing and laughter. He moved to the sash windows and looked out over the estate. On the large lawn at the front of the house, Charlotte, Dorothea, Edwin and Georgina were playing a game. From this distance, it was hard to know what the game entailed. Sword-fighting with imaginary swords seemed to play a major part, but, unlike the controlled, almost balletic movements of a swordfighter, this conflict involved much shrieking and jumping up and down, more akin to the behaviour of screaming banshees. And in the middle of it all was Georgina, making as much noise as the children and flailing her arms with as little coordination as Edwin.

Adam shook his head slowly in amazement. When he'd met Georgina, he had been convinced that she was wholly unsuitable to be his bride. He had wanted someone with the maturity required to take on the care of three young children. And maturity was one quality he could not attribute to Georgina.

But he had to admit the childlike pleasure she took in

everything she did was just what the children needed. Mrs Wainwright was correct. His children had mourned their mother for too long. And Georgina was right. Children needed to play and to laugh, to be naughty on occasion, and that was just what she could offer them.

On the day they had met he had told her father that he could not marry such a passive young woman because he had three young children. He had inadvertently told the truth. His children needed someone with Georgina's spirit, energy and enjoyment of life.

He sighed deeply. That was something he had been unable to offer them since Rosalie's death. He watched as the children continued their progress across the lawn and disappeared into the woodland, then continued standing at the window.

His own enjoyment of life had died the same day as Rosalie. His beautiful, lovely, gentle Rosalie. It should be Rosalie, their mother, who was playing with the children, who was making them laugh. While she hadn't been as rumbustious as Georgina, she'd had a kind, loving manner with the children. He was pleased they were now happy, but he hoped they would never forget their real mother, just as he knew he would never forget his real wife.

But was that entirely true? He clenched his hands tightly behind his back. Only a short while ago, Rosalie had been foremost in his thoughts at all times. But she had not been in his thoughts when he had been lusting after Georgina during dinner last night. She had not been in his thoughts when he'd retired to his bedchamber and spent the night tossing and turning, thinking about Georgina's full lips and that tempting, curvaceous body.

What sort of man was he, who could bring a woman into his life, supposedly to save her from being cast out of her home, and to save his own estate, and then start fantasising about all the different ways he wanted to take her?

He returned to his ledger books, hoping the dull figures would drive out any thoughts of Georgina's hourglass figure, of her parted lips, of her soft skin.

He threw his pen down, sending ink spattering across the page. What on earth was wrong with him? Yes, she was beautiful, but he had never wanted her as his wife. She was simply not the sort of woman he was attracted to. She was silly, impetuous, and thought only of enjoying herself.

He looked back towards the window as he reminded himself of the first time he had met her, dressed in that silly maid's costume. Then of her appearance on her first day in this house, standing at the entranceway covered in mud. How could he possibly be attracted to such an irresponsible, childish, totally unsuitable young woman?

Although at least she was not a vain woman. That was something, he supposed. A vain woman would never have dressed in that sack of a maid's uniform, nor allowed her clothing, face and hair to become soaked in slimy river water. And yet she had every reason to be vain. That thick strawberry blonde hair must be the envy of many a young woman, and those blue eyes that sparkled like cut gems were seemingly created to capture a man's attention. And her lips… Men must have been tempted to write poems about the effect of those full red lips. There was no denying she was a beauty, damn it all. His life would be so much easier if it were not so.

He picked up his blotter and attempted to undo the damage he had done to the columns of figures in the ledger.

The arrival of his estate manager was a welcome reprieve, and he provided Adam with some distraction, saving him from looking out of the window as he heard the boisterous children returning from their morning romp in time for luncheon. It didn't, however, stop him from wondering what state she had got herself into this time.

The estate manager left but Adam still did not feel up to joining his wife. He summoned a servant and informed him he would be taking his meal in his study as he had much work to do. He was unsure why he felt the need to justify his absence from the dining room to his servant but, strangely, he did.

And he remained there for the rest of the day. As the evening approached, he tried to think of further reasons that would keep him away from the dining room. He was unsure whether he could endure another evening in Georgina's company, looking at her and fighting his desire for her. But then, he was the master of the house. He had no need to explain his actions to anyone, including himself. So he summoned a servant who would inform Cook that a small plate of cold meat, cheese and bread was all he required and it could be served in his rooms.

When the knock came on the door he reminded himself he did not need to justify his actions to anyone and he would not repeat that foolish, unnecessary explanation he had given his footman at lunchtime.

The door opened. It was not a servant who entered but Mrs Wainwright.

'I thought this was where I'd find you, hiding yourself away,' she said, getting bluntly to the point as she always did.

'I'm not hiding away. I'm…' He indicated the books opened in front of him on his desk. Hadn't he just told himself he did not need to justify his behaviour to anyone? Although that did not appear to include Mrs Wainwright. In fact, when it came to that woman, he always felt he needed to justify everything, including his very existence.

'I'm sure that can wait. After all, it waited all that time you were up in London, galivanting around in search of a replacement wife.'

Adam winced. He had not been trying to replace Rosalie. That was something he would never do. She would always be in his heart, but that was one thing he did not intend to explain to Mrs Wainwright. And, yes, he had danced at that one ball he'd attended, but he would hardly describe that unwanted ordeal as gallivanting.

'And now that you have brought home a wife, you should at least have the decency to spend some time with her.'

'I dined with her last night,' he said, sounding annoyingly like a child trying to justify his bad behaviour.

'Yes, and ignored her all day today.'

'I had…' Once again, he indicated his books and, once again, he reminded himself that *he* was master of this house, not Mrs Wainwright.

'Well, you can dine with her again tonight. You brought her into this house because you needed her money. The decent thing to do would be to make her feel welcome, not spend all your time working out how best to spend *her* money.' It was Mrs Wainwright's turn to indicate the ledgers spread out in front of him.

He quickly shut the books, shame washing through him. He had indeed taken her money. He was indeed trying to work out the best use that money could be put to, to ensure the estate not only got out of debt but started to turn a profit as soon as possible. But that was not the reason why he was avoiding Georgina, although he could hardly explain the real reason to Mrs Wainwright.

'All right. I shall dine with my wife tonight, but I want you and the children present.'

For protection.

'It would be good if we dine as a family from now onwards.'

You coward. You liar.

As much as he wanted to, and knew he should, spend more time with his children, he also did not trust himself to be alone with his wife.

Chapter Fourteen

Adam knew he was being foolish. Dinner with the family was hardly an event that should disconcert him in any way. After dressing, he entered the drawing room, where the children and Agatha had gathered and were chatting amiably. Perhaps Georgina had decided to take her dinner in her room. He relaxed slightly and sat down in the wing chair.

Charlotte and Dorothea were both talking at once, describing to their grandmother the day's adventures, which included the climbing of trees, the storming of castles and the tracking of wild beasts through the jungle.

'I was the wild beast,' Edwin proudly announced and gave a loud growl. 'And no one caught me.'

'Yes, we did,' Charlotte and Dorothea announced as one.

'Only because I let you!'

This caused the girls' voices to rise louder in dispute.

The door opened and Georgina entered, causing the squabbling to come to a halt as they all looked in her direction, including Adam. The children stood up and rushed towards her, and immediately resumed their chatter. She smiled at them and appeared to listen to their stories with surprising tolerance, given that the volume had risen to an almost unbearable level, and led them over to the settee, where all three children tried to squeeze onto the seat along with her.

Adam realised he was still standing and staring at her, so he took his seat. She looked breathtaking tonight. It must have been the time in the outdoors that had brought such colour to her cheeks and caused her to take on an almost radiant glow. Despite knowing absolutely nothing about female fashions, he had to admit that her pale blue gown suited her admirably, bringing out the various hues of blue in her eyes and seemingly making them sparkle.

The gown was cut low, presenting him with a view of her naked shoulders, tantalisingly covered with sheer lace, and the hint of tempting décolletage. She really was a stunningly attractive woman, and she was his wife.

No, she was not his wife. He looked over at the portrait of Rosalie. Georgina was merely the woman he had married. Composing himself, he turned back to the family. The children were still talking excitedly, discussing what they would do tomorrow, while Mrs Wainwright looked on with pleasure.

His former mother-in-law turned to look at him, still smiling, and there was a wealth of meaning written in that smile. He nodded his agreement. She was right. Georgina had fitted into the household remarkably well, much better than he would ever have imagined possible, and the children were actually happy. You would never suspect that these were children who only a few days ago were still in mourning.

He looked over at Rosalie's portrait, wanting to send her an apology, to let her know that Georgina would never really replace her in the children's hearts, and most certainly would not replace her in his. He coughed and crossed his legs. That was an apology he had no need to make. Of course she would not replace Rosalie in his heart. To even think there might be a possibility was an absurdity.

The footman announced dinner, and the children sprang to their feet and all grabbed at Georgina's hands to pull her up from the settee, causing her to laugh loudly. She looked over at him, still smiling with pure delight, and he smiled back at the happy scene. She raised her eyebrows, her pretty head tilted slightly, and he realised what he had done. He had smiled. It felt like a long time since anything had made him smile. He looked over at Rosalie and sent her another quick apology. It was not Georgina he was smiling at, he informed his wife, it was the joy she was bringing the children—our children. Rosalie smiled back at him, that gentle, loving smile he had once known so well.

When he turned back to the family, the children had already led Georgina out of the door and they were dragging her down the hallway, so he offered his arm to Mrs Wainwright.

'Isn't it lovely to hear the sound of laughter in this house again?' she said.

'Yes, it is.'

'You made a good choice there. Her family is wealthy, and she has friends who are also duchesses, so, unlike your last marriage, this marriage won't result in your wife being alienated from her family, nor will she be forced to move in circles different from the one she grew up in.'

Adam went rigid at the familiar criticism. Mrs Wainwright had never forgiven him for marrying Rosalie and moving her into this house, a place where her parents, siblings and friends had always felt uncomfortable visiting. The wedding had been a trial for all of Rosalie's guests. They had stood in small clusters on the outside of the wedding breakfast, looking uncomfortable and awkward despite Adam and Rosalie's best efforts to include them, and after she'd moved into his house, her friends had turned down every invitation Rosalie had sent for them to visit. And Adam's father had not made things any easier, treating Rosalie and her family as if they were little more than servants. Fortunately, the old Duke had been away in London most of the time, losing the family fortune at the gambling tables, but even his absence had not lured any of Rosalie's friends to what they insisted on calling 'the big house'.

It was not until Rosalie had become pregnant with Charlotte that her mother had started to visit regularly, and even then she had avoided spending time in Adam's company, and never acknowledged the old Duke's presence. A situation that had suited both parents.

And then Rosalie had fallen ill and her mother had moved in to care for her. That had continued with Rosalie's death, when she had taken over care of her grandchildren. There might now be an uncomfortable truce between the two of them, but Adam was still eternally grateful to her for the help she had given him, and that gratitude was something he would never forget. But he did wish she would stop this infernal criticism of him for falling in love with her daughter.

'And you managed to pick another wife who is a born mother,' she added as they headed towards the dining room.

Adam stared at Mrs Wainwright in disbelief. Nothing about Georgina's behaviour would suggest she had the qualities that would make her a born mother. She was impulsive, irresponsible and at times little more than a child herself.

'Don't look at me like that,' Mrs Wainwright said. 'Yes, she's a bit of a flibbertigibbet, but I suspect that's because no one has ever expected her to take responsibility for anything or anyone.' She frowned at him and he knew a reprimand was coming. 'And it wouldn't hurt if you told the poor girl on occasion how much you value the effort she is making, and how good she is with the children.'

Adam hmphed his agreement.

'Now she has the responsibility of three children and has risen to the task admirably. I suspect she would also run this house with equal efficiency.'

Adam stopped walking. 'You're not planning on leaving us, are you?' That would be a disaster, and he wasn't just thinking about the danger of leaving Georgina in sole charge of the house and children. Mrs Wainwright provided a chaperon. While it was ridiculous that a married woman needed a chaperon, it was yet another role played by his former mother-in-law that he deeply appreciated.

'I'm going to have to leave some time. I do have another family as well, you know.' She sent Adam a consoling smile. 'But don't worry. I'll wait until Georgina is completely settled in and has learnt the ropes.'

Adam looked down the hallway, where the children were pulling Georgina into the dining room while she pretended to resist, and hoped it would be a long time before she did indeed settle in.

Georgina looked over her shoulder at Agatha and Adam, who had halted in the hallway, deep in conversation, then gave a whoop of delight as the children pulled her through the door and into the dining room.

It was always fun to play with the children, but she was hoping that some time, later tonight, playtime would be over and she would once more see *that look* in Adam's eyes. The one he had given her when she had entered the drawing room.

That look was just as Amelia and Irene had described it. It was the way a man looked at the woman he wanted with unbridled desire. It was a look that made your body come alive, to cause it to pulsate with longing. It was a look that caused you to forget everything, everyone and made you want him more than anything else in this world.

She had seen that look in his eyes. It might have been fleeting but it had definitely been there. Adam wanted her and tonight he would take her. She could hardly sit still as she took her place at the dining table, and hardly heard a word the children said. Not that it mattered. All they required from her was to smile and nod as they chatted on about what they had done today and what they planned to do tomorrow.

Adam took his seat across from her. She gazed in his direction and saw it again. He was staring at her. His gaze moved slowly over her, from her eyes to her lips, then down lower. She drew in a deeper breath, as if her breasts were arching towards him, wanting him to look, to touch, to caress. His gaze lingered, then slowly moved back to her face, before he flicked open his napkin and signalled to the footman to begin serving the first course.

She smiled, a delighted smile of victory. He wanted her. He might be trying to hide it, but he wanted her as much as she wanted him. And soon he would have her.

Georgina had never possessed a great deal of willpower, and even less patience, and was not in the habit of having to wait for what she wanted, but for now she was going to have to exercise some self-control, act like an adult and wait until she was alone with Adam—alone with her husband. Then she would finally get what she wanted. She bit her top lip to stop herself from smiling brightly like a demented Cheshire cat, and turned her full attention to the children, safe in the knowledge that tonight would be the night. After all, she had seen *that look*.

'After dinner, will you read to us?' Lotte said.

'Oh, yes, I suppose so.' Georgina had never read a story book to a child before, but yes, she could see that would be fun. 'What books are your favourites?'

'*Black Beauty*,' Lotte and Dora said together and gave little shudders of pleasure.

'No, read *Tom Sawyer*,' Eddie called out. 'It's got a really naughty boy on the cover so that's bound to be good.'

'Yes, naughty boys are fun, and horses are lovely, but shall we compromise? Do you have a copy of *Alice's Adventures in Wonderland*?' She looked over at Agatha, who nodded. 'That's got naughtiness, adventures, lots of animals—' she leant down to Eddie '—and a queen who likes to chop off the head of anyone she doesn't like.'

She made a chopping motion to the back of her head, causing Eddie to give a wicked laugh.

The children continued to chatter throughout the meal, with Georgina, Adam and Agatha adding very little to the conversation. Whenever she could, Georgina took a quick glance in Adam's direction to see if he would give her *that look* again. Every time she caught his eye a little shiver of anticipation rippled up and down her spine, and she sent him what she hoped was a knowing smile.

The meal over, they all paraded back to the drawing room and Mrs Wainwright departed briefly to the nursery to find the copy of *Alice's Adventures*. When she returned, she handed it to Georgina and said goodnight.

'I'm sure the children will be ready for bed very soon,' she said. 'Just call for their nanny and she will put them to bed.'

Georgina smiled in gratitude, sure that Agatha was deliberately making it easier for her and Adam to be alone together.

She settled onto the settee with the children and opened the book. Slowly, her awareness of Adam faded as she lost herself in the story of Alice and the White Rabbit. Eddie snuggled up onto her lap, his thumb in his mouth as he looked at the book and gazed in rapture at the drawings of the funny animals. Lotte and Dora leant against her, also enraptured by the story.

This was not what Georgina had expected of married life, but it was decidedly pleasant. These children wanted her, maybe even needed her, and that felt wonderful. She wrapped an arm around Eddie, and gently stroked his hair.

'I think he's starting to fall asleep,' she said quietly to Lotte and Dora.

The two girls nodded, looking rather tired themselves. Adam stood up, quietly moved over towards them and lifted the sleeping boy into his arms.

'I shall put him to bed, while you see to the girls,' he said quietly.

Taking the two girls' hands, they followed their father up the stairs to the nursery. *We're just like a proper family*, Georgina thought as warm contentment washed through her. *And soon I'll be a proper wife.*

The nanny was waiting to help put the children to bed, and once Georgina had kissed them goodnight she joined Adam in the hallway.

This was it. Now he would act on that look.

Georgina paused outside the children's bedrooms. Would he take her hand and lead her to his bedchamber? Yes, that would be lovely. Or would he scoop her up in his arms and carry her to his bed? Even better.

He did neither, merely commenced walking. It was not as romantic as she would have hoped, but she walked beside him, her anticipation mounting with every step that took them closer to his bedchamber.

They reached the door.

He kept walking. Georgina's confidence that tonight

was the night faltered slightly, but then they approached the door of her bedchamber. Yes. That would make more sense. He would want her to be in familiar surroundings for her first time, in a place she felt comfortable.

They passed her bedchamber door. She flicked a look up at him. Could she have been wrong? Had she not actually seen *the look*? No, she most certainly had. So why was he not acting on it? They walked down the stairs and retraced their steps back into the drawing room.

So, this was all going to happen in a formal manner. That was to be expected, she supposed. Adam, unfortunately, was an extremely formal man. And, even more unfortunately, he was not the sort of man who would drag her into his bedchamber and ravish her.

He indicated the wing chair across from the one in which he normally sat. The settee would be preferable for what she had in mind but, wherever it happened, she would be willing and eager. As she sat, she ensured she did so in her most gracious, most feminine manner, while at the same time leaning forward so he could glance down the front of her gown, if he had a mind to do so.

She looked up, and bit her top lip to stop herself from smiling. He most certainly had a mind to. Good, there was no point wearing your gown with the lowest cut top if your husband wasn't going to appreciate your effort.

'Georgina,' he said, coughing lightly as he took his seat.

'Yes,' she said, once again leaning forward as if anxious to hear what he had to say, and once again having the pleasure of his straying eyes.

His eyes flicked up to her face and he coughed again.

'Georgina, I have not yet expressed my gratitude to you, and that has been remiss of me.'

'Gratitude?'

'Yes, I appreciate the effort you have made with the children.'

'Effort? It's no effort. I enjoy spending time with the children.'

'Good. And I can see they have developed an affection for you.'

'And I for them.'

'When we agreed to this arrangement, I have to confess I had some misgivings, but you have fitted into this household admirably.'

'That almost sounds like a compliment. If I didn't know better, I'd think you were flirting with me.' It *was* a compliment, although the matter-of-fact way he said it was far from flirtatious, but what was the harm in pushing him in the direction she knew he wanted to go?

'I am not flirting with you,' he said, as if outraged by such an accusation. 'But yes, I am complimenting you and thanking you.' Georgina was gratified to hear his formality slip, even if just slightly. Now, all she had to do was force it to slip completely, get him to look at her in *that way* again, and she would have him.

She leant forward as far as her corset allowed. 'I am so pleased you appreciate me,' she said, her words dripping with innuendo.

'Yes, indeed,' he said, his eyes straying to where she wanted them to be.

Perhaps you'd like to show your appreciation by taking me in your arms and kissing me senseless.

Georgina always prided herself on being brave, but even she wasn't brave enough to actually say that.

His eyes flicked from her and over to the portrait of Rosalie and he quickly stood up.

'That was all I wish to say to you, so I shall wish you goodnight.'

'Oh, so early.' She looked at the clock ticking on the marble mantelpiece.

'I have much to do tomorrow and wish to rise early.'

'Oh, yes, well, I suppose it is getting late. Perhaps I'll retire now as well.'

He sent her a confused look, seemingly registering her contradictions, then walked to the door and opened it for her. They retraced their steps back up the stairs and along the hallway. When they reached the door of her bedchamber Georgina told herself to be brave, braver than she had ever been before.

She turned to face him, smiling in what she hoped was an enticing manner. 'It's not really that late, and I'm not really tired,' she said, hoping that he would understand the meaning of her words.

He said nothing, but he was looking at her. It wasn't *that look*, but it *was* something. She smiled again, leaned against the door and placed her hand lightly on the door handle. All he had to do was kiss her, she could turn the handle and they would be in her bedchamber.

He picked up her other hand and lightly kissed the back. Georgina swallowed, loving the feel of his lips on her skin.

'Goodnight, Georgina, sleep well,' he said, releasing her hand, giving a formal bow and walking off down the hallway to his own bedchamber.

His door shut, leaving Georgina standing in the empty hallway, unsure whether to feel insulted, outraged or so deflated she could crumple up on the floor.

After several infuriated sighs, she opened her door and, rather than calling for her lady's maid, ripped at her clothing, venting her fury on the hooks and laces.

She climbed into bed and picked up the open book lying on the bedside table. Last night she had left the heroine trembling alone in the medieval castle, fearful that the handsome rake who had taken her captive was going to have his wicked way with her and take her cherished innocence.

She read a few lines then threw the book across the room. That heroine didn't know just how lucky she was.

The book skidded across the wooden floor and landed in front of the door linking her bedchamber with his. Unlike the rake in the book, Adam did not have to scale a castle wall. All he had to do was turn the door handle, enter her room and she would be his. And he couldn't even do that.

Well, she was no trembling maiden. Nor was she going to passively wait for him to do what was expected of him. She would be the one to storm the castle, figuratively speaking, of course. She would be the one to take what she wanted. And she would have her victory.

She slumped back onto the bed. Yes, that was what she would do. But first, she had to somehow find the courage to put those brave words into action.

Chapter Fifteen

Adam didn't go straight to bed after he said goodnight to Georgina. How could he possibly go to bed? How could he even think of sleep when thoughts of her were rampaging through his mind and pulsating through his body?

Instead, he walked out of his bedchamber, strode briskly back down the stairs, out through the entranceway and into the garden, hoping the night air would cool his ardour.

His rapid steps took him down the path, the gravel crunching under his boots. When he reached the country road he stopped. What was he going to do now? Walk all the way to London? He wasn't sure if even that much activity would drive away the circling thoughts of Georgina, of the way she looked, of that tantalising scent of lily of the valley, of the temptation of her soft skin and her full lips.

This was impossible. He had brought Georgina into his house as his wife in name only, and now, every time he looked at her, all he could think of was what she would look like naked, lying on his bed, and what it would feel like to take her, to satisfy a craving for her that was becoming increasingly unbearable.

He was a despicable man. This was an arrangement that suited them both, and that arrangement did not and never had included him satisfying his lustful desires with a woman who had been forced into a marriage she didn't want.

He paced up and down the dark country lane. If only she would go back to London, as he'd suggested. That would give her freedom, but, more than that, it would free him from this torment. But if she did go the children would be devastated. They had already lost their mother, and now that they were getting close to another woman it would break their hearts if she left. It was a level of unconscionable selfishness to even think of separating the children from Georgina. He was just going to have to suffer, and hope that at some time these feelings would pass, or at the very least become more tolerable.

He turned and looked back at the house, which was now almost in darkness. Even the servants had retired for the night. Light shone from only one room, his own. Georgina had presumably gone to sleep.

This was ridiculous. He could not spend the night pacing outside his estate. With a deep, resigned sigh he retraced his path back to the house and fought not to think of what she wore when she slept, or what that long blonde hair looked like when it was released and curling down around her shoulders.

No, he must not think of that. It was hard enough to control himself when he thought of her dressed in the blue gown she'd worn tonight. Throughout dinner it had been impossible to concentrate on anything that was said. All he could think of was pushing down those lacy straps and kissing that creamy white skin. And, to his intense shame, he could not stop his eyes from continually straying where they shouldn't when he was supposed to be doing as Mrs Wainwright commanded and expressing his appreciation. His behaviour was appalling. He was expressing his appreciation for her care of his children, all the while wishing he could fully appreciate those soft, enticing mounds with his hands and his lips.

At a slow pace he walked back up the gravel path, into the house and up the stairs to his bedchamber, trying to drive those torturous images out of his mind.

He passed her door and his pace slowed.

Keep walking. Stop thinking.

He opened the door of his room, knowing that sleep was not going to come easy tonight.

He stopped, his hand still gripping the door handle.

'Georgina?' he said, wondering whether unsatisfied lust could actually drive a man insane and make his fantasies appear to come to life.

'I am here to do my wifely duty,' she said, taking a step towards him.

A low groan escaped his lips as the frantic throbbing of his heart rushed to his groin, making thought all but impossible. She had given him permission to take her, to do what he had been wanting to do from the moment he'd met her. And, by God, he wanted to, with every inch of his pulsating body.

'You don't have to do this,' he said, forcing out the

words he knew he had to say. 'We agreed that I would be content for you to be my wife in name only.'

'No, you don't understand. *I* want to do my wifely duty. *I* want you to show me what happens between a man and wife.'

As if his body had taken over his mind, he was immediately across the room and had her in his arms. He was kissing her like a starving man who had been offered a banquet. Still kissing her, he lifted her into his arms and carried her to the bed, desperate to relieve his hard, pounding need deep within her.

He placed her on the bed and, with frantic fingers, ripped at the buttons of his trousers, all the while staring down at the beautiful woman laid out before him, her long hair curling around her shoulders just as he had fantasised, her white nightdress showing off the curves of her breasts.

She smiled tentatively and lightly bit her bottom lip. His hands dropped to his sides. What was he doing? She was a virgin and he was thinking only of taking her hard and fast, and relieving his own desperate, pulsating need.

'I'm sorry,' he said.

She shook her head and lifted herself up onto her elbows. 'No. What? Why are you sorry? The only thing you should be sorry about is that you've stopped.' She climbed off the bed and reached out her hands towards him. 'Kiss me again, please.'

He released a long, slow breath. It was what he wanted, what he had to have, and she wanted it too, but he had to be gentle.

Taking her chin in his hand, he tilted her head and

lightly kissed her lips, fighting every rampaging impulse raging through his body, an impulse urging him to take what he wanted so desperately. Now, without thought, without control.

Her lips pressed against his more firmly, then her lips parted and her hands wound themselves through his hair.

Go slowly. Be gentle, he reminded himself as his tongue moved along her bottom lip, parting them further and allowing him entry.

Kissing her lush lips was even better than he could possibly have imagined. Her soft, plump lips were designed to be kissed and she tasted wonderful. Honey was never as sweet. He entered her mouth slowly. She gave a small moan of encouragement and moved her body hard up against him, her full breasts pressing into his chest, the nipples hard and tight, making his command to go slowly, to be gentle almost impossible to follow.

She was so beautiful. He had to see her naked. He had to see those breasts, to touch them, to caress them, to kiss them. Reluctantly, he withdrew from her kisses. Her head was tilted back, her lips parted as she waited for more, but instead, he reached down and bundled up the bottom of her nightdress.

'Lift your arms so I can undress you,' he whispered in her ear. 'I want you naked.'

She opened her eyes and looked at him, uncertainty in her gaze. He dropped the nightdress. He was a fool. He had pushed her too far, too fast.

She smiled and lifted up her arms. Before he could question himself again, he grabbed the bottom of her nightdress, pulled it over her head in one quick movement and tossed it to the side of the room.

'You're perfect,' he said on a soft moan as he took in her glorious body—the full breasts, the tight nipples pointing expectantly at him, the curve of her waist, her rounded hips and the dark hair of her mound.

Taking her in his arms again, he kissed her hard, with a desperation that was becoming harder and harder to control, as his hands explored her beauty. Unable to wait another second, he lifted her up in his arms and carried her back to his bed, placing her gently in the middle.

With as much control as he possessed, he undressed, his eyes fixed on the beautiful sight before him, waiting for him. She was breathing quickly, almost panting, those magnificent breasts rising and falling and her legs were parted, as if sending him an invitation—an invitation he was incapable of refusing.

He paused at the foot of the bed, completely naked. Her eyes grew wider as her gaze moved up and down his body, pausing at his groin. 'I will be gentle with you, I promise, Georgina. You have nothing to fear.'

She shook her head. 'I'm not afraid.'

He joined her on the bed, telling himself that it could not be an empty promise. Despite how much he wanted her, he *would* be gentle, he *would* go slowly. He kissed her lips again, and she arched into him. The feel of her silky skin against his naked body was almost more than he could bear. But bear it he must.

Slowly. Gently.

He left her luscious lips and trailed a line of kisses down her neck, savouring the taste and touch of her skin.

Her head tilted, exposing the pale white skin of her neck to his kisses. Cupping her breast, his thumb rubbed over her nipple and she all but purred in response. Slowly, his kisses moved lower, to the soft mounds of her breasts, and he took one hard bud in his mouth, while tormenting the other with his hand.

Her purring grew louder, turning to gasps, matching the rhythm of his caressing tongue. Desperate to explore her body further, his hand moved down to the curve of her waist, over the soft roundness of her stomach and the flare of her hips, to the mound at the cleft of her legs.

A deep moan escaped from him as she parted her legs, knowing instinctively what he wanted. His lips returned to her panting mouth as his hand moved between her legs. His fingers moved along the soft folds, parting them gently, then entered her wet sheath. Hunger for her ripped through him as the soft skin closed around his fingers and he made a deep primal growl of pleasure.

Slowly, gently.

The words emerged through the fog of desire, reminding him that she was a virgin. With a level of control he would not have thought himself capable of, he slowly, gently pushed his fingers deeper inside her, while stroking her engorged nub.

His restraint was rewarded when she gave a loud sigh of pleasure. Lifting himself up onto one elbow, he watched her face as he increased the rhythm of his caresses, his fingers entering her deeper and faster. This was what he had fantasised about. Watching her become more beautiful as her arousal increased. Encouraged by her moans, coming louder and faster as he increased the tempo, he kissed her panting mouth, and she arched up against him, her hard nipples rubbing against his chest.

Her breath caught in her throat. She cried out as the tight walls shuddered against his fingers. She was now ready for him. Kissing her again, he blanketed her body, placing himself between her legs. When her long legs wrapped around his waist he almost forgot himself but, forcing himself to use restraint, he placed himself at the tip of her entrance.

'I don't want to hurt you,' he murmured in her ear.

'You won't,' she whispered back.

'Tell me if it hurts and I'll stop.'

Her hands cupped his buttocks, pulling him towards her.

'Don't you dare stop,' she said, her voice husky.

As slowly as he was capable, he pushed inside her and felt the walls of her sheath clench around him.

'Georgina, my love,' he murmured as ecstasy swamped his mind and senses. 'You are so beautiful.'

Exercising more control than he would have thought possible, he withdrew from her and entered her again, slightly deeper, watching her face, telling himself he would stop if he saw any sign that she was in pain, although not sure if that really was something he was capable of. How could he possibly stop something that felt so right, how could he withdraw from somewhere that was exactly where he had to be?

Her eyes opened and she looked up at him. 'Yes,' she murmured, gripping his buttocks tighter, as if aware that he was holding back.

He pushed into her, harder, deeper, still watching her beautiful face. She closed her eyes and murmured, 'Yes,' once more. With each thrust that word came again, encouraging him to go faster, harder, deeper, until he had forgotten all commands to be gentle.

Gripping her buttocks, he lifted her off the bed and entered her fully, her slick wetness telling him as loudly as her words that this was what she wanted. Her moans matching his rhythm, growing louder and faster, he entered her even deeper, harder. Just when he was sure he could hold back no longer, she released a loud cry, her tight walls convulsing around him, and he released himself deep inside her.

His heart still pounding hard as if trying to escape his chest, he wrapped his arms around her, rolled over on the bed and pulled her on top of him and held her closely.

Her heartbeat thumping against his chest, her breathing as laboured as his own, they lay together. They now really were man and wife. This was not what they had agreed to, but by God it felt good.

Chapter Sixteen

Georgina buried her face against Adam's neck and smiled as total contentment wrapped itself around her as tightly as his arms.

She had done it. She had seduced her husband. She suppressed the little giggle bubbling up inside her. And she had done so without following any of the rules taught to her at Halliwell's. If Miss Halliwell had instructed her to enter a man's bedchamber, dressed only in her nightgown, and ask him to make love to her, Georgina was fairly certain she would have paid attention to that particular lesson.

She stretched luxuriously, rubbing herself against him, loving the touch of his naked skin against every part of her body. When she had been lying in her own bed, facing yet another night alone, the obvious solution to her problem had presented itself. Before she'd had time to think it through completely, to question herself or to find reasons to halt her behaviour, she had grabbed the handle on the door linking their bedchambers, given it a decisive turn and boldly entered his room.

Finding him absent had briefly undermined her confidence, but she had forced herself to not flee back to her room. She *would* be bold. As the minutes had ticked by, her courage had started to fray at the edges. Questions had invaded her mind. How would she cope if he said no? What would she do if he turned her away and sent her back to her room? How would she face him the next day? How would they continue to live together when she had exposed her need for him so blatantly?

But she had pushed those questions to the back of her mind and told herself there would be no turning back. She had seen *that look* numerous times throughout the evening. That look that caused expectation to surge through her. That look that told her he *did* want her. That look she could not and would not ignore.

When he'd finally returned to his room, opened his door and seen her standing beside his bed, his first look had been surprise, then she had seen it again. That look, but this time it was a look that burned through her, sending her temperature soaring. It was the look of a man who liked what he saw, wanted it and had to have it. Immediately. And yet still he had held back, as if he had been told he could look but he could never touch.

So she had taken another risk and told him he could have what she knew he wanted. And now she was exactly where she wanted to be, in his arms, with him still deep inside her, her mind and body still recovering from being taken to the heights of desire and sent crashing over into ecstasy. A sigh of satisfied contentment escaped her lips.

Some wise old sage once said that fortune favoured the bold, and he was right. Fortune had certainly just smiled on her and rewarded her for her boldness in ways more glorious than she could have thought possible.

After her talk with Amelia and Irene she'd had rather high expectations, but what had just occurred was better than they had described. She had not realised making love would be so intense. Nor had she expected to feel so close to him, both physically and emotionally. When he had entered her, it had been as if they were joining as one. She had felt so cherished. So loved.

She stopped smiling. *Loved.* That was exactly what it was like. Now she knew why Irene and Amelia had called it making love. That was the emotion that had taken her over. A deep, abiding, satisfying love.

She nuzzled into him again, kissing his neck, loving the salty, masculine taste of him. She could stay like this for ever, joined to him as man and wife, man and woman.

His heart, which had been pounding against her chest, slowed down to a steady beat. His arms still tightly around her, holding her close, he rolled them over onto their sides and slowly withdrew from her.

They lay together, gazing into each other's eyes.

Love. Was that what she was seeing reflected back at her in those dark eyes? Had he felt it too? She had been confident enough to enter his room, confident enough to seduce him, but she knew she would never be confident enough to ask him that question. Was it because she feared what the answer might be?

She brushed away that question and smiled at him.

'Well, I must say doing one's wifely duty is rather pleasant,' she said with a light laugh. Joking always came so easy to her, and right now it was much better to make light of what had just happened between them than to focus on the powerful emotions still burning within her. 'I have to say I will be happy to do my wifely duty again at any time you wish,' she added, giving him what she hoped was a saucy smile.

He brushed back a lock of hair from her forehead, his face serious. 'I hope I didn't hurt you. I wanted you so much it was hard to hold back.'

He wanted her.

Did that mean he loved her as well?

'Oh, no, it was all so wonderful. Better than expected. No, don't ever hold back. And as for being hard, well, that rather is the point, isn't it, and I've certainly got no complaints.'

He smiled. He actually smiled. She had made him smile. She smiled back, certain she could not be happier.

'You do know how to flatter a man, don't you? And you said you failed that lesson at finishing school.'

'It's not flattery. It's the truth. It was wonderful.'

'There you go again. Well, flattery will get you everywhere.' He kissed her lightly on the lips and Georgina melted into him as her body once more tingled in response to his touch.

His lips left hers, but Georgina would not be having that. She still wanted more, much more. Now that she knew how he could make her feel, she was sure she would never be able to get enough of him.

Her hands curled around his neck and she pulled him back towards her, kissing him hard, her body stroking against his, letting him know what she needed.

His kisses moved to her neck and she sighed in pleasure as his lips caressed her soft, sensitive skin.

'I take it you would like to perform your wifely duty again?' he murmured in her ear.

'Mm, yes, please,' she said, running her inner thigh against the hard muscles of his leg.

His arms surrounded her and in one quick move she was on her back and his caresses and kisses were seemingly everywhere at once, causing her to writhe with almost unbearable pleasure.

'I'm going to need a bit of time to recover,' he said, between kisses. 'In the meantime, I think you're going to enjoy this.' His kisses moved lower. Wherever those wonderful lips went, Georgina knew she would enjoy it. His kisses stopped at her breasts, kissing each hard nub.

'I think you might be right,' she gasped out as he took each bud and suckled, sending powerful waves of pleasure shooting through her. She suppressed a moue of regret as his lips left her breasts. But no, she would regret nothing. She trusted him. He knew what he was doing and, whatever it was, she knew she would love it. His lips moved over her stomach, kissing and caressing. When he took hold of her legs and parted them, Georgina gave a little gasp of surprise and excitement. Was he really going to kiss her there?

He looked up at her, his expression questioning.

'Yes,' she murmured through her daze of desire. She was unsure what she was consenting to, but knew, whatever he did, it would be exactly what she wanted.

He parted her legs wider and looked down at her. A delicious sense of wantonness washed through her. He was looking at her most intimate part with such lust and it felt so wonderfully shameless.

He placed a leg over each shoulder and his head moved

between her legs, licking and nuzzling until Georgina could do nothing other than cry out in pleasure as rapturous waves surged up within her, rising higher and higher until they crashed over her, sending intense pleasure vibrating through her body, starting at the site of his tormenting tongue and consuming her entirely.

His arms wrapped around her, his strong body covering her, and he kissed her gasping mouth.

'Oh, yes, you were right. I did enjoy that.'

He smiled, and lightly kissed her lips again.

'So, if you've recovered, perhaps I can perform my wifely duty again,' she said, wrapping her legs around him. 'Now,' she added with a hint of desperation, arching herself towards him.

'This time I want to watch you,' he said, looking down at her as he pushed himself inside her, filling her up, making her feel whole.

Looking up into his lovely eyes, Georgina wrapped her legs tightly around him, her body immediately burning once more for him. Oh, yes, this was one duty she was never, ever going to tire of performing.

Completely exhausted, Georgina slipped into a blissful sleep. When she awoke the next morning she was still smiling. She rolled over to face the man sleeping beside her. Her husband. After last night's exertions he deserved a long, restorative sleep. She gently ran her finger along the muscles of his chest, causing him to moan slightly in his sleep. Was he dreaming of her? She hoped so.

She stretched, luxuriating in the feel of the sheets against her naked body. There was nothing she would rather do than spend the day in bed with Adam, but she had responsibilities. The children were expecting her to spend the morning with them. With one last, lingering look at the sleeping man, she moved gently to the side of the bed so she wouldn't wake him and retrieved her nightdress from the corner of the room where he had tossed it last night.

'Turn around,' came the command from the bed. 'I want to look at you.'

The nightdress draped from her hand, she turned to the man lying in the four-poster bed, staring up at her. She placed her hand on her heart as she looked down at the man staring up at her. Her husband. That magnificent man lying amongst the tousled bedsheets was all hers and they would be spending the rest of their lives together.

His hungry eyes slowly raked down her body and Georgina felt so beautiful. It was apparent in his eyes that he desired her and, oh, it was so glorious to be desired, and by such a man. As his gaze continued to stroke over her, her body reacted with a now familiar deep, throbbing want.

The temptation to give in was almost more than she could bear. Her body ached for him, her skin craved his touch, her lips tingled for his kisses. All she had to do was cross the room and join him in the bed, and he would stoke that flame that constantly smouldered for him.

But she couldn't. She had made a promise to the children.

'Have you had your fill?' she said, giving her nightdress a saucy little twirl.

He smiled up at her, a slow, sensuous smile that made her legs go weak.

'I doubt if I could ever get my fill of looking at you.'

'Well, I'm afraid that's all you're going to get until tonight, because I have other duties to perform now. I promised the children that we would start an inventory of all the trees in the woodland and rank them according to their climb-ability.'

He laughed. 'Climb-ability? Is that a word?'

'I don't know, but it should be.'

'You're perfect,' he said quietly, his eyes still slowly moving over her naked form.

'Stop looking at me like that! I have to go, and if you keep doing that, I'll get stuck in this bedchamber for the rest of my life.'

'How can I not look at you when you're so beautiful?'

The hunger in his eyes intensified and she took a step towards the bed. No, she couldn't. She had promised the children and, while it wasn't like her to be so responsible, especially when it meant forgoing her own pleasure, she would not disappoint them. She might have fallen hopelessly for this enticing man, but she also loved the children, and would not break her promise to them.

She lifted up her arms, pulled the nightdress over her head and wriggled it down her body. 'There, is that better?' she said when her head emerged. She swept her hand over her now covered body. 'Out of sight, out of mind, and all that.'

'Not really. I can still imagine what you look like under your clothes and that's almost as arousing.'

'Well, you're just going to have to keep thinking about that for the rest of the day, because I have things

I have to do.' She was being such a grown up. It was hard to believe those adult-sounding words were coming out of her mouth.

'Believe me, I will be thinking about your gorgeous body every minute of the day.' He pulled back the covers and his own body was revealed to her, in all its naked glory.

She couldn't help herself and did exactly what he had just done to her. Her eyes raked over his body, taking in those superb muscles. Her fingers twitched with the desperate need to run themselves over those hard, sculptured shoulders, down that firm, moulded chest, over his flat stomach and around the tight, powerful buttocks and thighs. She released a small groan, which caused his lips to quirk into a knowing smile.

When he crossed the room, took her in his arms and kissed her, she was incapable of doing anything other than sink against him, loving the feeling of his strong arms about her, loving the thought that this powerful, virile man wanted her as much as she wanted him.

And want him she did. Her hand moved to her nightgown, crumpling up the fabric, desperate to be free of the cloth that was separating her body from his.

The children.

The surprisingly responsible part of her mind crashed through the powerful pull of desire, reminding her of her promise.

'I have to go,' she said, dropping the fabric as he nuzzled her neck. 'I really do have to go.'

He released her and she tried not to be disappointed.

'Until tonight, then,' he said, gently stroking her cheek.

She looked up at him, her mind still in a daze. 'Tonight,' she repeated, but remained where she was, as if her legs had forgotten how to move.

'The children,' he said, sending her a wry smile. 'Climb-ability? Remember?'

'Oh, yes, until tonight.'

She rushed towards the door, certain that if she remained in the room one minute longer she would forget her newfound sense of responsibility, would throw off her nightgown and do what her body was crying out for her to do—spend the day in bed, being made love to by a man whose touch was as addictive as the most powerful narcotic.

She entered her bedchamber, shut the door behind her and leant against the wall to compose herself. Tonight, he had said. Tonight, she would be back in his bed.

But for now, she had to prepare herself for the day ahead. She pulled the cord to summon her lady's maid to help her dress, then poured warm water from the blue and white china pitcher the maid had left, into the large wash bowl.

As she washed, she caught sight of her bed in the looking glass. It looked as if she had slept the night, but she hadn't, and would not be doing so again. Instead, she would be spending every night in the bed, and the arms, of her lovely husband.

Chapter Seventeen

Climb-ability? Adam smiled to himself as he rang for his valet. Whoever had heard of the word climb-ability?

He looked towards the door that led to the adjoining room. And who would have thought it would be Georgina who would be the responsible one? If he'd had his way, he would have sent a message to the children to tell them they would have to categorise the trees without Georgina's help.

Although he certainly would not inform them of the reason why.

But she was right, and if Georgina could be responsible then so could he. He would follow her good example and do something he had not done since he had brought Georgina into his household. He would join the family for breakfast. After all, he had no reason to avoid her now. He'd had what his body had craved so desperately. Now that he had satisfied that powerful desire for her, he could stop lusting after her like an out-of-control adolescent who wilted at the sight of a pretty young lady.

A dull pain clenched his heart, taking him by surprise—a pain that felt curiously like guilt.

What on earth was happening to him? He had done nothing wrong. She was his wife. She had come into his room. She had asked him to make love to her. It was what she wanted as much as he did. And he was a man, for God's sake. No man could resist what had been offered to him last night, even one who had vowed to love his first wife until the day he died.

His valet arrived to shave him and dress him for the day, and fortunately distracted him from his inner turmoil. He continued to push down all doubts when he left his bedchamber, strode downstairs and entered the morning room.

The children, Mrs Wainwright and Georgina were all seated around the oval table, and all five looked up at him as he entered. The children's smiling faces gladdened his heart. It was good to see them looking so happy, and it was the beautiful woman sitting in the soft morning light that he had to thank for that.

'You're just the same,' Edwin cried out as Adam moved to the sideboard to serve himself a hearty breakfast.

After last night he was famished, and he had every intention of piling his plate with sausages, scrambled eggs, toast and a generous helping of tomatoes and mushrooms. He couldn't remember the last time he'd had such a hearty appetite in the morning, but after last night's antics it was exactly what he needed, and he knew that his appetite was not caused by the long walk he had taken to get Georgina out of his system. It was the other way in which he'd tried to get her out of his system that had stimulated his appetite.

He looked over his shoulder at her and smiled. And thankfully he hadn't got her out of his system last night, so there was only one thing for it. He would have to try again tonight, and every other night that followed.

'He is, isn't he?' Edwin said to his sisters. 'He's exactly the same.'

'I'm the same as what?' Adam asked.

'Before you came in, we were discussing how different Georgie looks this morning,' Charlotte answered for her brother.

Adam stopped what he was doing, a silver serving spoon suspended in mid-air. He turned to look at his family. Georgina's lips were quivering, and she appeared to be fighting her smile from becoming a laugh.

'I don't know what you mean.' Adam turned back to the sideboard and continued to pile food on his plate so the children would not see his discomfort.

'Well,' Charlotte continued as if it needed to be spelt out, 'Georgie is all…sort of shiny, and she keeps smiling, as if… I don't know…and she's glowing or something. And Eddie's right, you are exactly the same. All shiny.'

Adam placed his plate on the table and exchanged a quick, conspiratorial look with Georgina and made a false grimace to say, *How on earth do we get ourselves out of this?*

'I believe it must be the new soap we've been using,' Georgina said, her eyes laughing.

'I think I need to start using that soap,' Mrs Wainwright said, causing Georgina's hand to shoot to her mouth in a failed attempt to contain her giggle.

Was that an innocent comment or a risqué joke? Mrs Wainwright's expression revealed nothing and she merely resumed eating her breakfast.

'So, I hear you're going to spend the morning rating trees for their climb-ability,' Adam said once he had recovered.

'Yes,' all three called out. Thankfully, the children were happy to move on to this more suitable topic.

'And we're going to do it sysmatically,' Dorothea said. 'That way, it can be part of our science lessons.'

'I think you mean systematically,' Adam said.

'Yes, that's what I said.'

Adam exchanged a look with Georgina, who merely smiled indulgently at Dorothea.

'As it is part of your science lessons, and it's such a serious endeavour, would it be all right if I joined you?' Adam asked, surprising himself.

'Yes,' came three loud responses from the children.

'But are you any good at climbing trees?' Georgina asked, her head tilted on one side as if it were a genuine question.

'Yes. It's *one* of the things I pride myself in excelling at.'

'And what would those other things be?' she said, her eyes large in mock innocence. 'Let me see, what else are you good at?' She tapped her finger on her chin and looked up at the ceiling as if in contemplation.

'I'm surprised you have to ask.'

'If there are other things you're good at, I believe you might have to show me before I'm completely convinced.'

She looked back at him and gave him a cheeky little smile that made him long for this day to pass so he could show her, again and again.

'I'm more than happy to show you any time, any place you want, if that is your wish.'

'Oh, yes, it is my wish. It most certainly is my wish.'

As they spoke, the children's heads moved from one to the other, as if following a tennis match, and Adam felt it wisest to change the subject.

'So, tell me about this science lesson of yours,' he said, turning to the children, which resulted in them all trying to talk at once, about how to rate a tree, about branch height and trunk width.

'That does sound very scientific. I can't wait to help you rate every tree in the woodland,' he said, when the children's chatter finally came to an end.

'I take it you no longer have important business that requires you to hide away in your study,' Mrs Wainwright said.

Adam merely nodded, not wishing to explain to Mrs Wainwright the reason for his sudden change in behaviour. Instead, he merely nodded and went back to discussing the day's adventure with the children.

Georgina watched Adam chatting happily with the children. He was a different man, and she took enormous pleasure in knowing she had done that. The power of seduction had unexpected consequences, and they were all good.

Breakfast over, the children excused themselves from the table and rushed off, desperate to be outside. Mrs Wainwright made her excuses and bustled off to do heaven knew what with the servants, while Adam took her arm and led her out into the garden.

This was all so glorious, better than she could possibly have imagined. She had been forced into this marriage against her will, but was now married to the most wonderful man, a man who had made her body sing repeatedly throughout the night and had promised to continue to do so, whenever and wherever she wished.

She moved closer to him and halted his progress. 'Quickly, kiss me while the children are distracted.'

She had expected an objection, perhaps a hesitation, but there was none. She was immediately in his arms, his body hard against hers, his demanding lips on hers. This was no quick peck, but the kiss of a man who wanted her desperately. A moan of pleasure bubbled up inside her. This magnificent, handsome man wanted her—wanted her with passion, with desperation. She kissed him back with equal ferocity, wishing the day could pass so she could be back in his bed.

They broke from the kiss. She looked up at him and saw the fire burning in his eyes—fire for her. A fire that sent the heat of her body to fever-pitch.

'Perhaps we should tell the children to assess the trees for themselves and we could return to bed,' she whispered.

Still encased in each other's arms, they looked towards the children, who had stopped walking and had turned to watch them. Georgina took in the three wide-eyed stares and three open mouths. She dropped her arms to her sides as if caught doing something wrong, and Adam did the same. But she was doing nothing wrong. She had merely been kissing her husband.

'Trees!' Eddie called out. 'You promised we'd climb trees.'

'It looks like we *are* going to have to wait until tonight,' Adam whispered, and lightly ran his hand across her buttocks, causing her body to thrum with delicious anticipation.

'Then I hope you make the wait worth my while.'

'On that, madam, you have my promise.' He sent her a devilish smile, took her arm in his and, leaning in close to each other, they walked over to the children.

They entered the woodland and each child ran to a tree and commenced climbing.

'Remind me again, what is scientific about this?' Adam said with a laugh. 'To me, it just looks like children climbing trees and having a good time.'

'Well, perhaps the experiment proves once and for all that girls can climb trees.'

They both looked at Lotte and Dora, who, despite the encumbrance of their dresses, had already scaled up the trunks of their respective trees, were balanced on branches and were looking up to see how they could climb to greater heights.

'If I had any doubts about that it would have been stripped away when my bride-to-be climbed down a drainpipe to avoid meeting me.'

Georgina laughed. 'Well, if I'd known at the time what would be in store I would have stayed in my room, like a maiden in a tower, and waited for you to whisk me away to your castle and have your wicked way with me.'

'So that's your fantasy, is it? Well, I've no problem with having my wicked way with you, but scaling up drainpipes?' He shrugged.

'What?' She laughed. 'You'd be no use in a gothic novel. Capturing innocent damsels is de rigueur in such novels. Until last night, that's how I've had to entertain myself, reading the gothic novels I found in the drawing room.'

His body went rigid beside her and she cursed herself. They were Rosalie's books, and the last thing she needed to do was remind him of his first wife.

'I need some help,' a small voice called out, breaking the uncomfortable silence that had descended on them.

They turned towards Eddie, who was jumping up and down and trying to reach the first limb of a tree.

'I'm coming,' Adam called out. He raced over to his son and lifted him up onto the first branch, then held his hand as he walked out along the branch.

Georgina joined them, watching the touching scene.

'We men have to stick together, don't we, son?'

Eddie paused, and nodded, his eyes fixed firmly on his feet.

'Good boy. We can't let these women think that they're the only ones who can climb trees.'

Georgina smiled as she watched him with his son. How could she not be in love with such a man?

Eddie reached the end of the branch and looked out at the surrounding woodland. 'I'm the king of the castle!' the little boy shouted out.

Adam smiled at Georgina, his hand still clasping his son's. 'I know exactly how he feels.'

Any discomfort she might have felt through inadvertently mentioning his wife's name floated away. He was once again looking at her in *that way*.

She did not need to worry. He wanted her. That look

proved it. And that shiver that his look always invoked once again cascaded through her body. This was what complete happiness felt like. And oh, it was wonderful, and she intended to do anything and everything in her power to make sure she continued to feel like this.

Chapter Eighteen

As much as she enjoyed spending time with the family—*her* family—Georgina was still pleased when it was time to go inside for luncheon. The children's tutor would soon arrive, and she and Adam would have a free afternoon, and she knew exactly where she wanted to spend that free time.

The suggestive smile Adam gave her across the table when no one else was looking made it clear that he was thinking exactly the same thing.

But it was not to be.

'This afternoon is always the time I discuss the week's menus with Cook and make time for the housekeeper and butler to raise any concerns regarding problems with the servants,' Agatha informed them as the footmen served the meal.

Georgina smiled at her. That was all very nice for her, but she had much better ways of whiling away the afternoon.

'I want you to also be present for those meetings from now onwards,' Agatha commanded. 'As you are now mistress of this house, it is essential you start to take responsibility for those tasks.'

Damn. Wasn't she being responsible enough? It would seem not, and the look on Agatha's face made it clear this was not up for debate. The delights she'd been looking forward to this afternoon would have to wait.

She sent Adam an apologetic smile.

'And I suppose I should occupy myself inspecting the roof in the west wing,' he said, and she could hear his disappointment. That was some consolation, she supposed.

'Good,' Agatha said. 'We will all be occupied gainfully this afternoon.'

Throughout the luncheon the children continued to discuss their tree-climbing prowess until the meal was over and the family dispersed to their respective tasks.

Georgina followed Agatha into the butler's pantry, where Cook, the housekeeper and butler were standing, waiting for the ladies of the house. Agatha indicated for them to sit, and Georgina sat beside her, wondering why on earth she had been dragged down into the lower part of the house.

Cook went through her suggestions for the menus, and Agatha insisted on asking Georgina's opinion on every dish, all of which seemed perfectly acceptable to her. Then they discussed the servants, and Georgina's only contribution was to suggest that if the scullery maid was unhappy, perhaps she should be allowed to work shorter hours and have more days off. Something which resulted in frowns from the butler and housekeeper, but a small smile from Agatha.

'Well, I think that went rather well,' Agatha said,

when the meeting was finally over and they were heading back up the stairs. 'I believe it won't be long before you are more than capable of running a household.'

Georgina frowned, in much the same way as the butler and housekeeper had when she'd made her helpful suggestion regarding the scullery maid. 'Oh, but I'll never be as good as you are at running a house. I think it's all a bit much for someone such as myself,' she said, using the helpless little girl voice that had always resulted in her getting her own way with her parents.

'I suspect there is nothing you are not capable of when you put your mind to it, provided it's something you want badly enough.'

Georgina looked at Agatha's face to see if there was a hidden criticism in her emphatic statement. Did she know that last night she had got what she wanted by seducing her daughter's husband? And if she did know, was she offended?

I'm his wife now, she wanted to cry out. *I have done nothing wrong.*

Still muttering to herself, she returned to her bedchamber to dress for the evening. Instead of selecting an ornate gown to impress her husband, this evening she decided to wear the gown with the fewest buttons and laces. That way, it would be easiest for Adam to remove. As she rolled on her silk stockings and tied on the ribbons of her garters, it was impossible not to imagine him rolling them off her later tonight. But she knew she had to keep such thoughts firmly in place until the time with the family was over.

She joined everyone in the drawing room, where they were already discussing the day's events.

'How was your meeting with the servants?' Adam asked as she took her seat.

'Very satisfactory, thank you,' Agatha responded for her.

'It was,' Georgina added. 'But I think the housekeeper and butler are being a bit hard on the scullery maid. Personally, I suspect that she has a beau and that's why she's so distracted from her work.'

'She has,' Lotte announced, leaning forward in her seat with a gleeful expression. 'He's the blacksmith's son, and she hopes that he'll propose soon.'

'Is that right?' Georgina said, turning to face the girl. She could see that Lotte shared her love of gossiping and the two of them were going to have to spend some constructive time together discussing the goings-on in the house.

'Yes, she goes all funny every time she mentions his name,' Dora added. 'A bit like the way you go every time you look at Father.'

'That's enough, children,' Agatha said. While Georgina did not like to see the children rebuked for gossiping, not when it was one of life's little pleasures, she was grateful that it had distracted everyone's attention from her suddenly burning cheeks.

'So, what did you learn in your lessons today?' Adam said, obviously just as keen to change the subject and save Georgina's blushes.

Dora groaned. 'It was science and it wasn't nearly as much fun as climbing trees.'

'But possibly more systematic and scientific,' Adam said with a laugh as he walked over to the sideboard to pour himself a glass of brandy.

Georgina tensed as he passed Rosalie's portrait.

'And I'm sure it was no worse than spending the day inspecting holes in the roof,' he said, lifting up the brandy decanter. 'After my afternoon, I believe I deserve this small reward.'

'Yes, do tell us all about the roof. I believe we'd all be fascinated to hear,' Georgina said in a rush, determined to hold his attention so he did not look down at the smiling woman in the silver frame.

He gave a small laugh. 'You're still fascinated by that roof, are you? Why, I will never know.'

Georgina tilted her head and forced herself to smile, as if indeed it was a fascinating subject. 'Well, it is the roof over all our heads so it's rather important.'

'I believe we can all avoid the west wing until it is fixed. The rooms have been cleared and the temporary repairs are being undertaken so there will be no further damage until the tilers are able to finish the job.'

'Well, that's good, isn't it, children?' she said, trying to involve them in her attempt to distract their father's attention from their mother's portrait.

He walked back to his seat and sat down, without once looking in the direction of his first wife, and she breathed a sigh of relief, then sent a silent apology to the portrait.

I know he loved you, but I'm his wife now, she secretly told the pretty woman on the sideboard.

Then she turned her genuine smile back to Adam, grateful that she had captured his full attention, and surely it would not be long before she had captured his heart as firmly as he had captured hers.

'You look pleased with yourself,' Adam said, crossing those long legs.

'Yes, well, I had a good day. You know, running the household and all that.' She waved her hand in a circle to indicate the household she now supposedly ran.

'I was occupied with the roof, the children with their lessons, and you and Mrs Wainwright with the household. We were all busy, but no one was doing what they really wanted to.' He sent a quick smile in Georgina's direction which caused her body to do that lovely tingling thing. 'But we can all be proud that we spent the day in a productive manner.'

'Pructive is still not as good as climbing trees,' Eddie added, causing everyone to laugh, and Adam to ruffle his son's hair.

'Perhaps we can climb trees again tomorrow,' Adam said.

'Maybe Father can become a buccaneer,' Dora said, which caused the other two children to cry out their agreement.

'Oh, and you too, Grandmother,' Lotte added politely.

'I believe my buccaneering days are well and truly over.'

'That settles it,' Georgina said. 'We'll induct your father into our gang tomorrow.'

That caused another cheer to ring out from the children, and their discussion on what sort of induction ceremony they should have was only interrupted when the footman announced that dinner was served.

Their loud chatter continued throughout the dinner and didn't stop until they returned to the drawing room.

'I'm rather fatigued,' Agatha announced as the others took their seats. 'I believe I shall retire early and I'll leave you to put the children to bed, Georgina.' With that, she turned and left the room. She really was passing over the running of the household to Georgina, but putting the children to bed was yet another task that she did not object to.

It was not long before Eddie was starting to nod off, and after their hectic day the girls were also starting to yawn.

'Right, bedtime,' Georgina announced.

Adam stood up and gently lifted his son into his arms, and Georgina took the girls' hands and led them up to their bedrooms. The nanny was waiting, but Georgina informed her that she could retire for the night, as she would undress the children and put them to bed.

The nanny bobbed a curtsey and disappeared into her room adjoining the children's.

While Georgina helped the girls out of their dresses and into their nightgowns, Adam carried the sleeping Eddie through to his room. Once the girls were snuggled down in their beds, she picked up the copy of *Alice's Adventures in Wonderland*, which the children had brought up to their room.

'Would you like me to read a bit more before you go to sleep?'

'Yes, please,' the two sleepy girls responded.

Georgina settled herself into a chair and opened at the page where the girls had left their bookmark, the spot where Alice is confronted with the dilemma of whether to drink the potion marked *Drink Me*.

A few pages in, she looked up and saw Adam standing at the doorway, watching her. She had been so caught up in the book she hadn't noticed him enter, and hoped he wasn't thinking her too much of a nincompoop for doing silly voices for each character.

But his soft expression did not suggest disapproval, quite the opposite. Was that the look of love? And if it was, was it directed at her or his two daughters?

'I think they're asleep now,' he said quietly, indicating the two girls in their beds.

'Oh, yes.' Georgina looked from him to the two girls. She had been so caught up in reading she hadn't noticed that her audience had nodded off. She put the book carefully back on Dora's bedside table and as quietly as possible crept out of the room and closed the door behind her.

'So, are you ready for bed as well?' he asked rhetorically, giving her a delightfully wicked smile.

'Oh, yes, I'm very, very tired and I need my bed, right now,' she said, lifting her arms above her head and stretching sensually. 'Or, more accurately, I think I need your bed. Right now.'

'You poor thing. Are you too tired to even walk all the way to our bed?'

She bit her lower lip and shook her head. 'Yes, I'm afraid I am.'

'In that case.' Just as she'd hoped he would, he lifted her into his arms and carried her down the hallway.

She covered her mouth so her giggles would not wake the children and snuggled into the muscular wall of his chest. The flames that had been smouldering within her all day started to burn, sending her temperature shooting up, and she knew there was only one way to quench that fire.

He raced her down the hallway and, when they arrived at his bedchamber, all but threw her onto the bed before ripping off his clothes and joining her. Then slowly, tantalisingly, he removed her clothing, kissing each area as it became exposed to him.

As they made love, Georgina knew her happiness was almost all-encompassing. The only thing that would make it complete was if he loved her the way she loved him, but, given the intensity of their love-making, she knew, just knew, that soon she would have that as well.

Adam lay back on the bed, holding Georgina in his arms, her long hair strewn across his chest. He was exhausted, although he knew that soon his desire for her would well up inside him again and he would be unable to resist the powerful need to lose himself in her glorious body, to forget everything except holding her, caressing her, making love to her.

He lightly kissed the top of her head and she curled in closer against him. Instead of quenching his appetite, each time they made love he wanted more, as if his appetite was insatiable.

All day he had been thinking about having her in his bed and had found it all but impossible to focus on anything else. He had almost been able to feel her soft skin on his fingers and taste her on his lips. Visions of her beauty had constantly intruded on his thoughts. And the reality had been even better than his imagination. As if she had bewitched him, she literally took his breath away every time he looked at her, and she so easily reduced him to an insatiable addict, desperate for more.

He had not expected this when he had taken her as his wife and saved them both from a worse future. He had been grateful at the time that she had agreed to their mutually beneficial arrangement. And by God he was still grateful. Grateful that she wanted to do her wifely duty, as she so amusingly put it.

He had not known what had driven him to ask her to marry him, apart from a desire to save her from being cast out by her father. There were plenty of other heiresses available who he suspected would have been even more accepting of being his wife in name only if it meant becoming a duchess.

But he had not made a mistake. He gently stroked her hair and lightly kissed her shoulder, causing her to wriggle against him in that sensuous manner he loved so much.

Georgina was turning into the perfect duchess, and she was more than happy to warm his bed at night, without expecting any more from him than physical love.

And physical love was all that he would ever be capable of giving her, so thank God she was under no illusions that he would be able to give more. If she had not wanted to consummate their marriage he would have accepted her decision, but he was a man, so he thanked the stars above that she wanted physical love as much and as often as he did. And he thanked the stars yet again that she was content with this new arrangement, aware that he would never truly be hers, as he was still in love with his wife—his *real* wife.

That stab of guilt that he'd fought so hard not to

feel all day pierced deep into his heart. He breathed in deeply to ease the pain, then gently ran his hand over her naked shoulder, down the curve of her back to her beautiful round buttocks.

'Well, that appears to have cured my terrible tiredness,' she said, her buttocks moving sensually in his hands. 'I suspect I could stay up all night now.'

He looked down at the woman in his arms, at her beautiful face, at those full breasts that were lightly caressing his arm, the nipples already tight, pointing up at him in invitation. By God, she was desirable and like an addict enslaved by a powerful drug he was incapable of resistance. And he didn't want to resist. He wanted her. She wanted him. Surely, that was all that mattered.

'So, now that I've been struck by this terrible insomnia, can you think of a way for me to occupy my time?' she said with a cheeky teasing smile as her fingers trailed a slow, tantalising line down his body.

'We could try this,' he said, wrapping his arm underneath her body and pulling her on top of him.

'Yes, this might work,' she replied, laughing, before kissing his lips and nuzzling his neck. Adam released a deep growl as her legs straddled him, her feminine folds rubbing against him, driving him wild with desire.

He looked up at her and saw the triumph in her eyes as she took him deep inside her. She knew she had him hopelessly under her spell, and she would get no argument from him. He *was* spellbound by her, completely and hopelessly.

He held her gaze as her hips began moving slowly, sensuously, then to an increasingly rapid rhythm, taking him higher and higher on an exhilarating, primal ride.

His hands cupped her beautiful breasts, tormenting the tight buds just as she was tormenting him. Through his own delirious passion, he watched her face. Her head was tilted back, her lips parted, panting. She was so beautiful when she was aroused, and that was something else he could never get enough of.

Just as he reached a pinnacle and was sure he could hold back no longer, she gasped loudly, her inner folds tightened around his shaft and his own ecstasy released inside her. She collapsed onto him, her heart pounding as rapidly as his own, her silky body damp with perspiration.

He wrapped his arms tightly around her, turned her over onto her back and kissed her hard and deeply. He knew he had lost himself to her, but also knew that lost was exactly where he wanted to be.

Chapter Nineteen

Despite getting virtually no sleep for the second night in a row, Georgina woke the next day full of energy. She resisted the temptation to stay in bed, knowing the children would be expecting her and Adam to join them at the breakfast table.

The children had no lessons that day and Georgina was sure they would be disappointed if they did not make good on their promise for the buccaneers to go off on one of their adventures.

They entered the morning room together, which seemed to surprise no one.

'We've got all sorts of good ideas for Father's initiation into our gang,' Eddie announced as they served themselves breakfast.

'And some of them are truly ghastly,' Lotte added with delight.

Georgina mouthed 'sorry' to him as they both heaped their plates high with food.

'You know what buccaneers really like to do on a day like this?' she said as she took her seat at the table.

The children looked at her with expectation, and she

pointed to the lovely sunny day through the large French windows. 'They enjoy going on picnics.'

The looks of expectation became quizzical.

'Is that something the servants could arrange at such short notice?' she asked Agatha.

'You're the mistress of the house now,' Agatha replied. 'You make the decisions.'

'Oh, but…um…' was all Georgina could say to that, suspecting this would involve more than just making the decision.

'You will need to go and inform Cook of what you require,' Agatha said, taking pity on her. 'It is usually preferable to arrange these things in advance, but Cook will hopefully be able to use whatever she is preparing for luncheon and pack it in picnic baskets.'

'Good.'

'I've never heard of buccaneers going on picnics,' Eddie said, looking dubious.

'Oh, yes, they always like to have a nice picnic on some deserted island before they bury their treasure. It's a well-known fact.'

Everyone except Eddie raised their eyebrows in question about this little known, and wholly made-up, fact, but Eddie went back to eating his breakfast, seeing her explanation as completely acceptable.

After breakfast, while the others prepared themselves for the day's adventure, Agatha pointed Georgina in the direction of the kitchen, leaving her with no option than to confront the formidable Cook.

You're the lady of the house, remember, she said to herself as she walked down the back stairs. *You're a duchess, a woman of substance, someone more than capable of organising a picnic.*

Cook turned out to be not quite as intimidating as she had expected and also helpfully suggested that Georgina have a word with the butler and housekeeper so footmen, carriages and maids could be arranged to ensure the food was transferred to a suitable site.

Having done that, Georgina returned to the family, feeling rather pleased with herself. 'It's all organised. We're going on a picnic,' she said to the children's cheers and a slight frown from Agatha.

'What?' she asked.

'You might wish to inform the children's nanny so she can dress them in appropriate clothing.'

Georgina looked at what the children were wearing—dresses on the girls, short trousers and a jacket on Eddie. It all looked perfectly appropriate to her.

'Their footwear,' Agatha said, pointing at Lotte and Dora's pretty embroidered shoes, bearing matching blue bows.

'Right. Come along, children.' If informing the nanny about suitable footwear was required, then that was what she would do. So she trudged upstairs, the children following.

Once they were all suitably attired, they finally assembled in the entranceway and waited while the maids helped them on with their coats and the footmen loaded hampers and blankets into the carriage. Agatha did a quick inspection, then finally nodded her approval at Georgina.

'I can see you are well on your way to becoming

the perfect mistress of your own home,' she said. 'Isn't she, Your Grace?'

Georgina didn't hear Adam's response as her attention was taken by the children, who were arguing over who would ride up in front of the carriage with the coachman.

'There's not enough room for all of you, so you're going to have to take turns,' she called out as she rushed down the steps towards them. 'Eddie, you can ride up the front on the way there and Dora and Lotte on the way back.' She turned back to Agatha. 'Eddie will probably be too tired on the way back.'

Agatha joined them and patted Georgina's arm while Adam nodded his agreement. 'Quite right, my dear,' she said. 'A good decision.'

Feeling as if she'd just passed a test with flying colours, Georgina took the footman's hand and entered the carriage, unable to stop from smiling. If Miss Halliwell could see her now, running a household, organising children and married to a wonderful man, and a duke no less, she would never have informed her parents that their daughter was a hopeless failure.

After a delightful trip across the estate, the carriage pulled to a halt close to a particularly pretty part of the river where a grassy area, surrounded by oak trees, swept down to the gently flowing water.

Adam took her hand to help her out of the carriage and gently kissed the back. 'No wading in the river today,' he said with a smile. 'No getting caked in mud.'

'No, today I promise I will act like a lady,' she said, raising her chin high and adopting her most imperious stance.

'Only during the day, I hope,' he whispered as she

alighted. 'I wouldn't want you being too ladylike at night.'

A delicious thrill gripped her. Perhaps she should write to Miss Halliwell and tell her how wrong she had been about Georgina. She wasn't as hopeless as she had said, and one thing she was particularly good at was giving her husband complete satisfaction in bed.

She giggled as she imagined the horror that would have crossed that old biddy's face, especially if she knew of some of the more interesting ways she had learnt to satisfy her husband, and he to satisfy her.

'Believe me, there is no danger of that,' she said, wondering if she could suggest a walk in the woods where she could show him just how unladylike she could be.

He lightly kissed her lips, his hand running down the naked skin of her arm, causing that deep longing for him to erupt again, and making her yearn to drag him off into the woodland right now and have her way with him.

But she would not think of that now. Or, at least, she would try not to think of that now.

While the children ran ahead, they strolled across the soft grass and Adam placed a guiding hand on the small of her back. When it slipped lower and moved across her buttocks, she knew that he too was thinking of the night to come, and she couldn't help but arch her back slightly in anticipation.

They reached the picnic setting and, trying to ignore those inappropriate thoughts, she seated herself on the blankets spread out on the grass. 'You can leave us, thank you,' she said to the head footman. 'I think we can manage by ourselves, can't we, children?'

Without answering, the children instantly started opening hampers to see what treats had been packed.

'You two are all shiny and glowing again,' Eddie said, then commenced gnawing on a particularly large chicken leg.

'They're always like that these days,' Lotte added, holding up a cucumber sandwich which was in danger of losing its contents.

'I know,' Dora said with a giggle. 'And they're always touching each other. Why do you keep doing that?'

'That's what husbands and wives do,' Georgina said, trying not to laugh.

'But I saw Father touching your bottom before. That's rude,' Eddie announced, which caused his two sisters to fall about laughing.

'Bottom, bottom, bottom,' Eddie repeated, obviously enjoying the way that word could make his sisters laugh.

'That will be enough from you, young man,' Agatha said, something Georgina suspected she was supposed to say, but she was laughing too much to do so.

Somewhat chastened, the children resumed eating, but she could see that Eddie was just itching to say his rude word again.

'When we've finished eating, I propose the buccaneers go on another of their rollicking adventures,' Georgina said before they had a chance to return to their favourite topic of discussing her and Adam's supposed shininess.

'But first we have to induct Father into our club and he has to prove he's worthy of becoming a buccaneer,' Dora said, causing raucous cheers to erupt from the other two children.

'We could toss him in the river?' Eddie said. 'Or make him climb up to the highest tree then jump down.'

Adam and Georgina looked at each other with matching looks of mock horror.

'Or perhaps I could give you sword-fighting lessons so you'll be able to defend yourself if another band of pirates attacks you.'

'Yes, sword fight,' Eddie agreed, and Georgina smiled as relief crossed Adam's face.

'Coward,' she mumbled.

'No, clever,' he responded quietly. 'The more we tire them out, the sooner they will go to bed tonight.' He gave her a suggestive smile, and she loved what he was suggesting.

Once the meal was finished, Adam had the children on their feet and marched them off to the nearby field, where he adopted the *en garde* position. The children tried to follow his lead, and a sword fight soon erupted, one that had much more enthusiasm than grace, and seemed to involve a lot more running up and down, whirling in circles and general mayhem than any sword fight Georgina had ever witnessed. While all this took place, Georgina, for once, was happy to sit back, watch and laugh at the antics, taking particular pleasure in Adam's exerted efforts to exhaust the children.

When he picked up a laughing Lotte and Dora under each arm and began running round the field with them, chased by an exuberant Eddie, who was seemingly trying to rescue the captured damsels, she did worry that he might be exhausting himself in the process. That would never do, as she had her own plans on how to try and wear him out, something she had thankfully failed to do so far. But there was no harm in trying yet again tonight.

'He's a changed man,' Agatha said, breaking in on her thoughts. 'And we have you to thank for that.'

She smiled at the older woman, touched by the compliment.

'It's been years since he's played like this with the children. You've really brought him back to life.'

Georgina's smile vanished, and she reached out and touched Agatha's hand, knowing that she must be thinking of her daughter.

'You must miss her terribly,' she said quietly.

'I do.' Agatha pulled her expression into the more familiar stoic one. 'But I'm pleased my grandchildren now have a happy, loving household.'

'I do love them,' Georgina said. 'It wasn't hard to fall in love with them because they're so, well, loveable.'

And it wasn't hard to fall in love with their father either.

She looked over at Adam, who had now collapsed in a heap, his children crawling all over him, the point of the game completely lost on Georgina, but obviously giving the children a great deal of pleasure.

She had fallen in love with him and now had exactly what she had always wanted. From that very first Season she had wanted to fall in love and marry, but had never met a man to whom she was in the slightest bit interested in giving her heart. Not until she had climbed down the drainpipe in a futile attempt to escape her destiny. She might have got the order slightly wrong. One was supposed to fall in love and then marry, but she had married, then fallen hopelessly, completely, passionately in love and now had a man she loved and children she also adored. This was possibly what perfection felt like.

Tommy's words seemed to whisper in her ear.

'*You've got what you wanted...*'

Well, to that she could now reply, *Yes, I have, and what is wrong with that?*

Adam lay on the grass, the children rolling over him, laughing loudly. He could hardly remember the last time he'd played with the children and taken such pleasure in their exuberance. Certainly not since Rosalie's passing.

That familiar tightness gripped his chest as an image of Rosalie making daisy chains with the girls crashed into his mind, before Eddie captured his attention by grabbing onto his shins and attempting to drag him along the ground.

'Aha, me hearties, the blighter is trying to best us,' Adam said, springing to his feet, and doing what he hoped was a passable impression of a pirate.

Eddie slashed at the air, in a chaotic but thankfully harmless manner, with a stick that had been converted to his sword. His sword-fighting was performed with as much vigour as his young arms would allow, while Adam pretended he was hopelessly outmanoeuvred and the girls ran around in circles, squealing as loudly as they possibly could. The reason for that particular behaviour eluded him, but the girls apparently could see some logic in what they were doing, so who was he to question the actions of the bold buccaneers?

Adam felt certain they would never tire of this game, but eventually their energies started to wane and they all headed back to the picnic blankets, where Georgina and Mrs Wainwright were chatting together amiably.

'So, who won?' Georgina asked.

'We did,' all three children answered, while Adam shrugged his shoulders. It was hard to know who'd won when he wasn't actually sure what the game was, and who was on whose side.

Georgina smiled and signalled to the coachman that they were ready to leave. The family packed up the picnic hampers, Georgina having earlier sent the other servants back to the house, and helped load everything into the carriage.

Just as they had expected, the day's activities had exhausted the children. Eddie fell asleep on the carriage drive back to the house, cuddled up against Georgina, and the girls were subdued, which they had rarely been since Georgina's arrival in the house. Even riding on top of the carriage did not result in the expected cries of delight, merely some muted comments of approval.

When they got back to the house, Mrs Wainwright suggested it would be best if the children had their dinner in the nursery as they were far too tired to dine at table, and summoned the nanny to take the sleepy children to their beds.

'I'll come and tuck you in once you're undressed,' Georgina said as the children departed up the stairs, although Adam suspected the moment their heads hit the pillows they would be asleep.

Mrs Wainwright also announced she would not be dining with them this evening and would take a tray in her room, then she disappeared, leaving them alone in the hallway.

'Shall I tell Cook that we are also rather weary and would like to have trays sent up to your bedchamber?' Georgina said, placing the back of her hand on her forehead in a dramatic rendition of weariness and causing Adam to laugh.

'Oh, God, Georgina, you're right. I am hungry—very hungry,' he growled in her ear.

'In that case, you'd better get to bed as well and I'll go and tell Cook to have something sent up to your room.'

It's not food I'm hungry for, he wanted to call out as she hurried off down the hallway towards the kitchen, but a passing footman caused him to hold his tongue.

It was hard to believe that the young woman who was organising him and his family was the same reckless Georgina he had met at the side of the road only a few months ago. She was turning into an efficient manager of his household, not to mention her care for his children. It seemed that wonders would never cease.

While she organised their meal he walked up to his bedchamber, taking the stairs two at a time, anxious to experience more of those wonders that never ceased to amaze him.

Chapter Twenty

The next morning, and every morning that followed, when Georgina woke up, if she wasn't already snuggled up to Adam, that was the first thing she would do. Was there a more perfect way to start the day than in the arms of the man you loved? If there was, Georgina couldn't think what it might be.

And each morning her feelings of love for him increased, along with her certainty that Adam was in love with her. He hadn't said it yet, not in actual words, but every kiss, every act of affection, every time he gave her *that look*, said it louder than words ever could. Although it would be nice to hear those three little words, but Georgina just knew it was only a matter of time. She just had to do what she previously had been incapable of doing, be patient, and she would get what she wanted.

There was always the option of forcing the issue by being the first one to declare her love, just as she had forced the issue by appearing in his room dressed only in her nightgown, but she would not do that. It was going to be so much more special if it came from him first.

And when it did, she just knew her life with him would be even more wonderful than it was now and her happiness would be complete.

He opened his eyes, stretched, smiled at her, and her certainty that he would soon say those three little words surged through her, along with other insistent feelings that only he could satisfy.

His strong arms encased her, and as she melted into his body she realised that her initial thought on waking had been incorrect. There *was* a better way to start the day than being snuggled up to the man you loved. You could start the day by making love to the man you were hopelessly, totally, incurably in love with. And that was exactly what she intended to do.

Her body sated, her mind awash with adoration for the man who made her so happy, she lay in bed and watched Adam as he stood at the washstand and ran water over that magnificent body. It was so tempting to rise from the bed and lick those rivulets of water as they trickled down his superb muscles.

He turned and looked at her, his gaze sweeping over her body. She just loved that hungry look in his eyes and moved sensually in the bed, letting him know the effect he was having on her.

'Don't tempt me,' he said, his gaze still on her. 'Remember you promised Lotte and Dora you would begin their preparation for the Season, and I said I'd help Eddie with his reading lessons.'

'You're right,' she said and climbed out of bed. She had been unable to resist Lotte and Dora's constant pleas, but was unsure what she was actually going to teach them.

'Are you sure you trust me with that task? After all, I hardly had the most successful of Seasons, did I?'

'You managed to catch me,' he said, taking her in his arms and kissing her. Georgina melted into the kiss. It wasn't quite how she remembered their non-courtship. But now was not the time to quibble over little details.

He deepened the kiss, but Georgina reluctantly pulled away.

'Who's trying to tempt whom now?' she said with a little laugh, wondering briefly whether the first lesson could wait a bit longer, before pushing that thought away. 'I need to wash and dress and the children will be wondering what is keeping us. Eddie will probably think you're busy touching my bottom again.'

He laughed, and lightly patted her naked derrière. 'You're right, you need to get dressed, but I'll be wanting you back in my bed and looking just like that again tonight.'

She looked down at her body and smiled. It was amazing how comfortable she had become with being naked in front of him. It felt so natural and was a long way from that first time she had entered his room dressed in her nightgown, feeling nervous and anxious about her own attractiveness. Now, every time he looked at her, she felt more desirable and more powerful, knowing he was incapable of resisting her.

'If you approve of it so much, perhaps I should appear like this in public,' she said, doing a little twirl and looking at him over her shoulder in a coquettish manner. 'I'm sure I would be the belle of every ball I attended.'

He wrapped her gown around her shoulders. 'Don't you dare. That is for my eyes only.'

And your *body is for my eyes only*, she thought, fastening the gown as her eyes raked over his muscular form. You *are for me, and me alone, and that is the way it will always be.*

After breakfast, the family gathered in the drawing room, where Georgina was supposed to give her first lesson on how to conduct oneself during the Season, while Eddie and Adam neglected the book in front of them and watched on in amusement.

'Right,' she said, handing each girl a large book. 'This lesson involves walking around the room with a book on your head.'

'Why?' Lotte asked, looking down at the dictionary in her hand.

'Good question,' Georgina said. 'It's so, should the occasion demand, you can steal books from people's bookshelves without them noticing.'

His daughters stared at her, wide-eyed, and Adam had to suppress a laugh. 'I've never attended finishing school,' he said. 'But I believe that particular exercise has something to do with adopting the correct feminine posture, not theft.'

'Oh, yes, your father's right,' Georgina said. 'Right, here you go.' She placed a heavy tome on each girl's head, which instantly tumbled to the ground.

'It also makes you light on your feet,' she said. 'As you'll get plenty of practice jumping out of the way of falling books. Right, let's try again.'

Adam pulled Eddie onto his lap as they watched the entertainment, the reading book long forgotten. Slowly, the girls got the hang of the exercise and the number of squeals of fright and jumps in the air as the books crashed to the floor diminished. Despite Georgina's joking, he could see his little girls turning into elegant young ladies before his eyes.

Georgina looked in his direction, smiled and raised her eyebrows as the girls performed perfect circuits of the room, their heads held high, their shoulders back and their movements graceful.

He smiled back in approval. It was miraculous. Once again, she was surprising him—as she had done since she'd first arrived at his estate, and continued to do every day, and especially every night.

'Right, you've mastered that,' she said, turning back to the girls. 'I suppose we should discuss the art of conversation next.' She gave a mock scowl.

'You're not going to take Lotte and Dora outside to talk to shrubs, are you?' he said, laughing at the prospect.

The two girls removed the books from their heads and stared at him.

'What?' he asked, looking around the suddenly quiet room. 'That's what Georgina said she had to do at Halliwell's Finishing School—talk to shrubs.'

'You called us Dora and Lotte, not Dorothea and Charlotte,' Dora said, breaking into a smile, a reaction that rippled round the room, until all three females were beaming at him as if he had done something miraculous.

'And I'm Eddie, not Edwin.'

Adam looked down at the young boy smiling up at him from his lap and tousled his son's already messy hair. 'All right, Eddie, Dora and Lotte, let's all concentrate on our lessons, shall we?' Adam said, trying to adopt a stern manner, but the smile quirking his lips made that impossible. 'And Eddie, you haven't even tried to read your book.'

'You've changed,' Dora said, and Lotte and Eddie nodded their agreement.

'Yes, you've become much nicer since Georgie joined our household,' Lotte added.

'Have I? Georgina must be doing something that is good for me.' He sent her a quick wink and was pleased to see a flush of delight on her cheeks. 'So, she's the perfect person to teach you how to be proper young ladies.'

He laughed as Georgina lifted her eyebrows in disbelief.

'Are you sure about that?' she said.

'Well, how to be proper young ladies in the drawing room and how to behave during the Season,' he said, joining in her laughter.

'You didn't used to laugh as much as this before you married Georgie,' Lotte said, looking from him to Georgina and back again.

'No, and you used to spend all your time staring at the little lady in the blue dress and looking sad,' Eddie added, pointing at the miniature of Rosalie on the sideboard.

Adam's smile died instantly as the full impact of Eddie's words hit him hard, like a thump in the chest.

'You mean your mother,' he croaked, his throat suddenly dry and raw.

'No, Georgie is my mother,' Eddie said, still pointing towards the sideboard. 'I mean the little lady in the blue dress who sits over there.'

Eddie slipped down off his lap, crossed the room,

picked up the portrait of his mother and placed it face down. 'That's better. She's not my mother, Georgie is. Now you can always smile at my real mother, and not look sad at the little lady.'

Adam could hardly make sense of what his son was saying. All he knew was that the boy had forgotten about Rosalie, his real mother, just as Adam had forgotten about her, his real wife—the woman he had vowed to love until the day he died. The woman he had hardly thought about since that first night he'd had Georgina in his bed.

Eddie turned and smiled at everyone in the room, then his bottom lip quivered. 'What's wrong? Why is everyone looking at me like I've done something naughty?'

'You haven't been naughty,' Agatha said, crossing the room and taking the young boy's hand. 'Children,' she said, turning to face the girls, 'that's enough lessons today. Let's go outside and play.'

Eddie cheered and raced to the door, pulling his grandmother by the hand, while Dora and Lotte remained standing in the middle of the room, staring at Adam. Georgina wanted to make this right for his children but could think of nothing to say. All she could do was register the weight that had suddenly descended on her body. She gripped the back of the nearest chair, the floor seemingly no longer solid beneath her feet.

'Come on, girls,' Agatha called again. Lotte and Dora followed their grandmother out of the room and the door shut behind them.

'He's just a little boy,' she choked out. 'He doesn't know what he's saying.'

As if she hadn't spoken, as if he was no longer aware of her presence, he crossed the room and picked up the miniature and stroked a finger along the portrait. 'I am so sorry, my darling,' he murmured. 'I will never forget you. I will not stop loving you. My wife, my one true love.'

Georgina's breath caught in her throat, her heart appearing to shatter into tiny pieces. She placed her hand on her chest in a fruitless attempt to ease the pain as she watched the man she loved declaring his eternal love to another.

She was jealous. How could she not be? Those were the words she wanted him to say to her, longed for him to say to her every time he took her in his arms. But it wasn't just jealousy that was consuming her. There was something else. He was in agony, and she hated seeing him that way. It was unbearable to see the man she loved suffer so, even if it was pain caused by another woman. The woman he still thought of as his wife. The woman he still loved.

As quietly as possible, she left the room, closing the door softly, although he was so absorbed in staring at the portrait in his hand she doubted he would have noticed if she had stomped out and slammed the door behind her.

That was what she would once have done when she didn't get her own way, but it was not what she wanted to do now. And, even if she did, what would be the point? No amount of tears and tantrums could make a man love her when he was in love with another.

She stopped outside the drawing room, leant against the wall and fought to slow her gasping breath.

Adam did not love her. That was now clear. She had seduced him into making love to her, but nothing she had done, nothing she could do, would make him love her the way she loved him. As painful as it was, that was something she would have to accept and live with. And her heartache would also have to be her secret. She loved the children too and did not want them to know the extent of her anguish. They'd had too much sorrow in their lives to suffer any further.

She closed her eyes and drew in another series of deep, slow breaths, fighting to ease the painful sorrow in her chest. It didn't work. It seemed this pain was something else she was going to have to learn to live with.

Pulling herself off the wall, she straightened her shoulders in the same manner she had instructed Lotte and Dora and, keeping her head high, strode down the hallway and out through the entranceway.

In the garden she could see Agatha attempting to engage them in a game of tag, with limited success. Eddie was running around like the innocent child he was, while Lotte and Dora made a half-hearted effort to pretend they were enjoying themselves.

The two girls looked at her with concern as she crossed the lawn towards them. Even Eddie looked abashed, knowing something was wrong but unsure what it was. She put on her sunniest smile, placed her arm around Eddie's shoulder and kissed the top of his head.

'So, what game are we playing today?' she asked, hoping she sounded sufficiently chirpy.

'We didn't really feel like playing,' Lotte said.

'What?' Georgina exclaimed. 'How can you not feel like playing? What else is life for, except to play?'

That was exactly how Georgina had felt before she'd met Adam and the children, that life was just one long game that she loved playing. Even when she'd lost, she'd always been able to see it as a win. When men had rejected her during the Season because she did not have the right background, she had laughed off the insult, and seen them as the ones who had lost. When men had courted her for her dowry, she'd seen it as a wonderful excuse to have fun at their expense. But now she had lost the game with the highest stakes of all and knew there was no way in which she could turn this into her own personal victory.

She had married Adam knowing that he did not love her, and that he was still in love with his first wife. The scene in the drawing room had not revealed anything she had not already known. So she would just accept it, get on with life and make certain that her sadness was never, ever passed onto the children.

'It looked to me like you were playing tag,' she said, still smiling as brightly as she possibly could. 'So, let's continue doing that. And you're it,' she said, patting Eddie's arm and running off.

Eddie chased her around the garden, and Georgina squealed each time he nearly caught her, doing her best impression of someone having a jolly good time.

Eventually, the girls joined in, and soon they were all running around in circles, as a happy Eddie chased them on his little legs.

Agatha sent her a grateful smile and soon retreated

back to the house, just as Eddie caught Georgina and triumphantly tagged her leg.

'You're it,' he proudly announced.

'Not for long,' she declared, 'and when I catch you, I'm going to gobble you all up. So, who's going to be my first victim?'

Roaring like a lion and waving her 'paws' in the air, she chased the children, pleased when the girls started to laugh loudly as they dodged around hedges and shrubs.

While she pretended that nothing had changed for the sake of the children, Georgina knew that everything had changed. The man she loved did not love her—would never love her. The man she had married would never see her as his true wife. She was merely the woman he had been forced to marry because circumstances demanded, the woman he took to his bed, the woman he would make love to but never actually love.

With a smile on her face and a pain in her heart, she kept playing with the children, wondering what her future would hold, now that she knew her husband would never truly love her the way she loved him.

Chapter Twenty-One

When luncheon was served, Georgina forced herself to maintain her sunny disposition while she braced herself for seeing Adam again. How she was going to react to being in his company she had no idea, but she had no need to wonder. He did not join them for luncheon and he remained absent for the rest of the afternoon.

Despite her own anguish, she couldn't help but worry about what he was going through. She wished she could go to him, to comfort him and soothe away his grief, but knew that such tenderness would not be welcome. Or worse, he might believe that she was merely trying to seduce him again. That she was trying to divert his attention from the woman he really loved as she shamefully knew she had done in the past.

Tommy had been right when he'd said on her wedding day that she'd got what she wanted. If she hadn't wanted to marry Adam, she would have found a way of getting out of it.

She'd denied it at the time, but deep down she knew she had wanted him. She had wanted him to marry her and then she had wanted him to take her to his bed. Her father had inadvertently helped her achieve the first, and when it had looked as if she wasn't going to get the second, she had presented herself to him and made an offer she knew no man was likely to turn down. And, in doing so, she had made him betray his vow to his wife and caused him such heartbreaking agony.

That had never been her intention, but her intention had most certainly been to get exactly what she wanted, and never once had she thought about anyone else but herself. As she always had.

'Are you all right, Georgina?' Agatha asked quietly.

Georgina was snapped out of her reverie and realised she was holding her empty fork in the air and had been staring into space.

'Oh, yes, perfectly all right. I'm just not so fond of…' she looked down at her plate to see what she was eating '…chicken pie.'

'I thought it was one of your favourites,' Eddie said.

'You're right. Silly me. And this pie is particularly delicious,' she said and took a generous mouthful. She smiled as she chewed, wondering why it tasted like sawdust, and why no one else seemed to have noticed.

Forcing it down her throat, she wondered whether Adam had been served a meal. She also wondered what he was thinking. Was he blaming her? Did he now despise her for seducing him away from Rosalie? Did he know she had deliberately distracted him whenever there was a danger of him looking at her portrait? Did he hold her responsible for the children forgetting about their mother? And if he did despise her, was he right to feel that way?

She continued to move the food around on her plate. To her immense shame, she had even once considered hiding Rosalie's portrait so he would not think of his first wife, but think of her, and only her. She hadn't done so, but, even if she had, it would not have stopped him loving Rosalie, or caused him to love her.

Tommy wasn't entirely right. She hadn't got the one thing she *really* wanted, despite trying her damnedest. Adam's love. She had tried everything and had failed. From now onwards she was going to have to accept that fact and their relationship would have to return to the one they'd originally agreed on when they'd first married. One that involved no kissing, no touching, no lovemaking. Her heart sank, but her mind knew this was as it should be.

Luncheon over, the children's tutor arrived and they disappeared into the rooms for lessons. Finally, Georgina could let go of her artificial smile. She retired upstairs to the privacy of her bedchamber, massaging her sore jaw as she went. It was surprising how much strain an unnatural smile could cause if you held it for too long.

Seeing the bed she had not slept in for some time, she felt the tears she had been holding back all morning course down her cheeks, and she threw herself on the bed, pounding the pillows in frustration. This was where she would be sleeping from now onwards. Alone. She would not be going to Adam's bedchamber. As much as she craved his touch, she could not make love to him now. She could not express the depth of her love for him when she knew he was still in love with another woman.

Her crying was interrupted by a gentle tap on the door. She jumped off the bed and ran to the looking glass, wiping away her tears with the back of her hand, quickly blowing her nose on her lace handkerchief and attempting to repair the damage to her hair.

'Who is it?' she asked, annoyed at the choking sound of her voice.

'It's Agatha. Are you sure you are all right?'

Her heart clenched in disappointment. How could she possibly think that Adam might follow her to her room? When she'd left him staring at his wife's portrait, he had neither noticed that she was still in the room nor registered when she had left. He simply no longer saw her.

'Yes, I'm all right, thank you,' she said with forced cheerfulness.

'Are you sure?'

'Yes, I'm perfectly fine, honestly,' she lied, overdoing the cheerfulness just a tad. 'I'm just quite tired so I think I'll rest this afternoon.'

Agatha made no reply and Georgina put her ear to the door, wondering if she was still there.

'I'm so sorry, Georgina,' she said quietly. 'My son-in-law has always been unworthy of a woman's love.'

Georgina's heart clenched more tightly as Agatha's boots clicked off down the hallway. Did Agatha also blame her for trying to make Adam forget his wife, and for causing the children to forget their mother? And was it blame she fully deserved?

Adam spent the afternoon in the drawing room, Rosalie's portrait in his hands. He knew he'd have to leave eventually, but feared that if he was no longer looking at her lovely face, he would yet again forget all about her. That was something he could not bear to do. But he knew he could not stay in the drawing room for ever. His reaction to Edwin's comments had upset his family and he needed to put things right.

He could not blame his son for what he had said. It was not Edwin's fault that he had forgotten all about the woman who was his mother. While it had wounded him deeply, his son's words were understandable.

Edwin had never known his mother. She had merely held him in her arms a few times before the strain of childbirth had claimed her and taken her from her husband and children.

But while his son forgetting was understandable, Adam's behaviour was inexcusable. Since the moment he had found Georgina in his bedchamber he had hardly thought of his first wife, and when he did, he had pushed the memory of her away so he could indulge himself in the sensual pleasure he was experiencing with his new wife.

Edwin's words had unintentionally made the betrayal of Rosalie painfully clear.

When was the last time he had looked at her portrait? That was something he could easily answer. The day before he'd first had Georgina in his bed. Before that night, he had gazed at her portrait several times each day, his grief hitting him anew each time, the memory of what he had lost coming back to torture him.

Not only had he not looked at her portrait, but the memory of her laughter, of her sweet, gentle ways, was no longer constantly on his mind.

How could he have betrayed her memory so quickly

and so totally? But he had not only broken his vow to Rosalie, he had also mistreated Georgina, neither of which had been his intention.

If only he had not been so damn attracted to Georgina. If he had married a woman who he did not want to bed every time he looked at her, who did not make him laugh so easily, whose company he did not take so much delight in, perhaps he would not have cast his first wife away so quickly. But he could hardly blame Georgina for being who she was. It was not her fault she was so beautiful, so desirable. It was his fault for succumbing so easily.

Nor could he blame her for the way he lost himself so completely when he made love to her. It was not her fault that he could no longer think straight each time he surrendered himself to the exquisite pleasure of her touch.

He was a terrible, terrible man. He had let his desire for one woman drive out his love for another—a love which he had sworn would be eternal.

'I do love you, Rosalie,' he said to the portrait clasped against his chest. 'I will always love you.' But even those words sounded false to his ears. How could they be true when he was still thinking about another woman, still imagining her touch, still remembering the taste of her lips, her feminine scent and the silky softness of her skin?

He placed his head in his hands, the portrait sliding to his lap. He had thought himself a good man, but he had behaved appallingly. He had forgotten the woman he loved because he had been losing himself with a woman he had arranged to marry but had never intended to be anything other than his wife in name only. And, damn it all, he still wanted her, wanted to have her in his arms, to feel her touch, her kisses.

Adam doubted he could hate himself any more than he did now if he tried. Neither woman deserved him. They both deserved a man so much better than he could ever be.

Chapter Twenty-Two

That night Georgina had to face Adam over the dinner table. She forced herself to keep smiling, determined that the children would think everything was still the same, even though everything had changed.

'Did you have a pleasant afternoon?' she said to Adam, keeping her voice polite and cheerful and hoping he would play along with this pretence for the children's sake.

'Yes, thank you,' he replied as he shook out his napkin and placed it on his lap. 'And you?'

'Oh, yes,' she replied. 'I retired to my room and used the time while the children were at their studies to catch up on some reading.'

She sounded ridiculously sunny and was fooling no one, least of all the children. Lotte and Dora were staring at her as if fearing she had lost her senses. After the comfortable way they had been with each other, the way they had laughed and even touched each other at every opportunity, no one could fail to notice that they were now being overly polite, like strangers attempting to make a good impression. Even Eddie was looking at them with a curious expression, and Georgina prayed he would not make another inappropriate comment, the way young children were apt to do. If he mentioned the way Adam touched her or made another joke about his father touching Georgina's bottom, she was sure she would not be able to contain the tears that she was holding back.

Adam would not be touching her again, and she would never again feel the casual stroke of his hand that told her that they were a couple, that they were lovers, as comfortable with each other's bodies as they were with their own.

'Perhaps you'd like to tell your father what you learnt in your lessons today,' she said, forcing herself to keep smiling.

All three children frowned at her.

'What's wrong with—' Eddie started to say before he was interrupted by Agatha.

'Do as Georgina said. Tell your father what you learnt today.' The terseness of her voice made it clear that she would tolerate no argument from the children.

While the children discussed how boring they found mathematics, Georgina nodded along, and could see that Adam was equally distracted, but he fortunately made noises in all the right places, and Agatha filled any awkward silences with questions and comments.

The difficult dinner over, they retreated to the drawing room, where Georgina remained on eggshells, worried that someone would mention the portrait on the sideboard. She fought not to look in that direction and could tell that everyone else in the room was doing the same, even Eddie.

The painfully polite conversation continued, and Georgina was grateful when it became time for the children to go to bed. Maintaining a cheerful façade, she settled them into bed and read some more of *Alice's Adventures* until they finally drifted off.

Then she knew what she had to do. This awkwardness could not continue, if for no other reason than it was confusing the children. She had to talk to Adam.

Ignoring the churning in her stomach, she forced her feet to take her back to the drawing room. She entered to find Adam alone, once again gazing at the portrait of his beloved wife. His eyes quickly moved away as she entered and he sent her an awkward smile.

'I believe we need to discuss what happened today,' she said, surprised at how strong she sounded.

He nodded while exhaling a long sigh. 'Yes. I am sorry, Georgina.'

She sat down in the wing chair facing his. 'You have nothing to apologise for. I knew when I married you that this was merely a marriage of convenience and that you were still in love with your wife. It perhaps should be me who is apologising, for forgetting what this marriage is.'

'No. It was I who forgot,' he said, looking in the direction of the miniature haunting the sideboard.

'Be that as it may, we are married and we need to discuss what sort of marriage we are to have.'

'If you choose to leave, I will understand,' he said. 'I have treated you appallingly. You deserve so much more than what I can offer you. If you wish for a divorce, I will declare myself to be the guilty party.'

She stared at him, astounded that he could even suggest such a thing. 'There will be no divorce and I will not be leaving. It would be too hard on the children. Rightly or wrongly, I am becoming an important part of their lives, and yes, Eddie, and possibly Dora and Lotte, are coming to see me as their mother.'

He drew in a deep breath but said nothing.

'They've already lost their real mother. I will not be responsible for them losing another.'

'As you wish,' he said, staring down at his hands, clasped between his knees.

'But that still doesn't settle what sort of marriage we are now to have.'

'I will abide by whatever arrangement you want.'

I want you to love me, she wanted to scream out.

'I believe it would be best if we now sleep in our own bedchambers,' she said, sounding certain, even though the thought of never feeling his touch again was making her heart and body ache.

He nodded and her heart further shattered within her chest.

'I am sorry, Georgina,' he said, finally looking at her. 'I never meant to deceive you, or to deceive myself.'

'I have already told you that you have nothing to apologise for,' she said quietly. 'You did not deceive me.'

I deceived myself. Tommy was right. I have always got everything I wanted. I wanted your love, therefore thought I would get it, even though you told me you could not love again.

Georgina's father had always eventually given in, even if it took some pouting, the slamming of doors and a few temper tantrums for him to concede defeat. Her mother had usually held out longer, but eventually she too had always succumbed to Georgina's demands.

Even at Halliwell's, where they were supposed to train this wilfulness out of her, she'd managed to turn everything to her advantage.

But the one thing she now knew she wanted more than anything in the world, she simply could not have.

And she would be throwing no more temper tantrums. It seemed, finally, she would be doing what Miss Halliwell had tried to get her to do, what her father had tried to insist on—she would act like an adult.

She would accept that her fate was to live in a loveless marriage, something she had been determined to avoid. Well, that was not entirely true. This marriage would perhaps be easier if it *was* loveless. Instead, she was in a marriage where there was plenty of love, but none of it was directed towards her.

'I'll say goodnight then,' she said, standing up. He too stood up and for one desperate moment she thought he might be going to argue with her. That he was going to say that he wanted them to remain lovers, that he craved her touch as much as she craved his.

'Goodnight, Georgina. Sleep well,' he said, destroying all illusions.

As she left the room, Georgina knew her marriage was now what it was always meant to be—an arrangement, nothing more.

Adam slumped down into his chair the moment Georgina left the room. He now had exactly what he'd wanted when he'd first become aware of the necessity of taking another wife.

Didn't he?

He'd needed a wife whose marriage settlement was

sufficiently large to save the estate. Georgina's dowry had not only paid off the excessive mortgages, it had ensured that everyone who lived on the estate had a secure future, that the house could be repaired and he could now provide generous marriage settlements for Charlotte and Dorothea, so they would have their choice of husbands.

He'd wanted a wife who would care for and love his children. Georgina loved his children and they loved her in return, there was no doubt about that. And he'd wanted a wife who would expect nothing from him, who would respect the fact that he loved another woman, would always love that woman and would never betray her. Now he had that as well.

Yes, he had everything he had set out to achieve when he had first headed to London to partake in the Season. And yet he could not have felt more empty inside, as if he had lost everything.

Adam was very familiar with the feeling of guilt. He had felt deep guilt when Rosalie had died. He had blamed himself for her death. As much as they'd both wanted a son, as much as he loved Edwin with all his heart, he should have taken every precaution to ensure that she not get pregnant again. If he had, his lovely Rosalie would be here with him now.

And guilt was what he was feeling now, mingling with intense shame. He had needed a wife but should never have chosen Georgina, for so many reasons. She was a woman who needed to be with a man who could love her and make her happy. That would never be him. By marrying her, he had deprived her of that opportunity, and he had done so for his own selfish reasons.

When he'd become aware that he must marry again, that had been one of the conditions—he would only marry a woman who was content to marry a title, who wanted the honour of being a duchess and cared nothing for being in a loving relationship. He had known that was not Georgina, and yet he'd ignored that knowledge.

But, worse than that, he should never have made love to her. That had never been part of their arrangement. And, damn it all, despite being racked by the agony of guilt and regret, he wanted to go upstairs, throw open the door of her bedchamber and bury himself in her arms.

He really was a man beneath contempt.

He looked over at Rosalie's portrait, his self-disgust intensifying. He had never deserved that lovely young woman, and he did not deserve Georgina. And thank goodness Georgina had the strength and the maturity to put their marriage back on the tracks it should never have wandered off.

From now onwards, they would live together as man and wife in name only, just as they had originally agreed. He would remain faithful to his wife. He looked towards the door through which Georgina had departed.

But was that fair to Georgina? Once again, was he thinking only of himself, of what he needed to do to loosen the knots in his chest, to relieve the agonising pain in his stomach?

He deserved this punishment. Georgina did not.

She was such a sensual woman it would be cruel not to allow her to continue to explore that sensuality. It just couldn't be with him.

Bile burning up his throat, he came to a decision.

He would have to tell her that he had no objection to her taking a lover. It was what so many members of his class did. In arranged marriages, once the woman had produced the necessary heir, they were often given the same freedom as their husband to find love and satisfaction elsewhere.

He groaned and placed his head in his hands. He and Georgina would have to live in the same manner as so many others did. It was the least he owed her. She had saved his estate, was providing motherly love for his children, and she deserved to find her own love and happiness.

The knot in his chest tightened several notches at the idea of Georgina with another man. If the thought of it caused this much pain and made him rage against that imagined man, how would he cope when she did take a lover?

How would he cope, knowing that another man was holding her, caressing her, making love to her? And, worse than that, how would he cope if it became more than just a physical relationship and she actually fell in love with that man and he fell in love with her?

He stood up and paced rapidly around the room, the desire to hit something, anything, especially this imaginary man, welling up inside him and consuming him like a raging fire.

If merely thinking of her with another man could cause his body to burn with anger and resentment, how on earth was he going to cope when she actually did take a lover, when his beautiful, enchanting Georgina was giving her smiles, her laughter, her joy and…his teeth clenched together so tightly, pain shot through his jaw…her body to another man?

He stopped walking, closed his eyes and forced himself to breathe slowly and deeply. Endure it he would. The ongoing agony he would suffer would be no less a punishment than he deserved for all that he had done to Georgina—to both women.

He would focus on what he had, not what he could never have. Georgina had promised she would never leave his children. That was something he believed would not change. She so obviously loved them, and they her. That care and love was something for which he would be eternally grateful. And if he was to prove that he still had some decency left in him, then he would show his gratitude by granting her the freedom to find the love she deserved.

He slumped into the nearest chair. He would be brave and strong, and at the next opportunity he would tell Georgina of his decision, and then he would just have to find a way to live with it.

Chapter Twenty-Three

Week after strained week had passed without Adam informing Georgina that he had no objection to her taking a lover, should she choose. With one very good reason. He *did* have an objection, even if he had no right to it.

When alone, he practised how he would say it. Straight to the point, making it clear that this was a mature, sensible arrangement for both of them.

And yet, every time he found himself alone in her company, the words would not come. His throat would restrict, as if stopping them from emerging, his heart would pound so loudly he could hardly hear his own thoughts. Then the moment would pass, and relief would wash through him, until that sense of relief was once again chased away by guilt and shame.

He had promised her freedom when they married, now he needed to make good on that promise.

He had to forget his own feelings and set her free. She had a right to be happy. He wanted her to be happy. He could not make her happy so she should find happiness elsewhere. That was logical, but nothing about his feelings, nothing about the way his body ached every time he imagined her with another man was logical. And so he continued to say nothing, and every time he tried and failed to inform her of his decision it reinforced just what a selfish man he was and always had been.

He had selfishly not made enough effort to try and talk Rosalie out of her desire to give him a son. At the time he had known it was what she wanted, but he still should have put his foot down, told her that the risk was too great, instead of giving in to her wishes. And now he was selfishly stopping a woman who had given him so much from finding happiness elsewhere.

And it was obvious that she was not happy. She still laughed, joked and played with the children, but she had a careworn look, one that he had caused. With him she was always excruciatingly polite, and that in itself spoke volumes. Georgina was not polite. She was cheeky, irreverent, mischievous. But now it was as if she were in the company of a very important person and had to be on her best behaviour at all times.

He doubted that even as a child, when Georgina had found herself in such circumstances, she would actually have been so deliberately polite. And that made her courteous manner even harder to bear. He had taken a lively young woman, destroyed her spirit and turned her into this paragon of good manners. That was yet another crime against his two wives he could add to the growing list.

Each evening, after Georgina had put the children to bed, she retired to her own bedchamber, alone, and had even ceased to come back downstairs to say goodnight to him. That did not surprise him. Those exchanges had become the most awkward of all their encounters and a reminder of what they had briefly shared but would share no longer.

And that was exactly what had happened this evening. He had been left alone in the drawing room, contemplating how his inexcusable behaviour was destroying that lovely young woman who deserved so much more from life than what he could offer.

This had to stop. He looked towards the door. He would go upstairs and tell her right now that she did not have to continue living like this, that she could be free to live a life separate from him, and if that included finding a man who could make her happy then so be it.

He shook open the newspaper. It was getting late. He would definitely do it tomorrow. First thing in the morning. This had gone on too long. He had to put an end to her unhappiness.

The door opened and he braced himself. It would not be tomorrow after all. He would have to be true to himself and do it right now.

Mrs Wainwright entered the room and he released his held breath. Thank goodness. He had a day's reprieve.

His former mother-in-law stood in the middle of the room, scowling at him in that familiar manner.

'I thought you had gone to bed,' he said.

'Well, you thought wrong. Again.'

Such criticism was nothing new. She had disapproved of him for marrying Rosalie. Her reaction had irritated him, but now he knew her to be right. If Rosalie had married a man of her own class there would have been no pressure to produce an heir. She would have stopped having children once it had become obvious that her body could not cope with another childbirth. She would still be alive and happy with another man.

'It's time we had a talk,' she said, her glower intensifying. 'I've given you plenty of time to sort out this problem and you haven't done a damn thing about it. So it's time for you to listen to a few home truths.'

Adam nodded, knowing that he deserved this lecture. He signalled to the facing wing chair so she would be comfortable while she berated him, but she chose to remain standing, forcing him to do the same, like a naughty boy about to receive a much-deserved reprimand.

'What are you going to do about your wife? You know she's miserable, don't you?'

Adam exhaled loudly. This was none of Mrs Wainwright's business and he certainly was not going to inform her that he had decided it best that Georgina find happiness with another man. That was a private matter between him and Georgina. Or, at least, it would be a private matter when he finally developed the fortitude to discuss it with her.

'I am fully aware of the problems in my marriage,' he said, adopting a suitably stern tone. 'And I believe I am more than capable of solving them myself.'

She huffed out a humourless laugh. 'It doesn't look that way to me. For God's sake, man, just admit that you love your wife.'

He looked over at the miniature on the sideboard. 'I do love her. You know that I do.'

'Not my daughter. Yes, I know you love her. I mean your wife, Georgina.'

Adam stared at her, aghast. 'No. I do not… I will never… I love Rosalie, with all my heart and soul.'

Mrs Wainwright shook her head from side to side, her expression growing ever more disdainful.

'I made a vow,' he said, for some reason desperate for her to understand. 'A deathbed vow that I would love Rosalie until I die.'

'And you're keeping that vow. I know that.'

Adam released his breath, pleased that she understood and this conversation was now over.

'But you also love Georgina,' she added.

His breath again caught in his throat. He looked towards the sideboard. 'I love Rosalie. I will always love Rosalie.'

Mrs Wainwright sank into the chair with a deep sigh. 'You really are a fool, aren't you? How these bright young women ever managed to become enamoured of such a nincompoop I'll never know. Sit down,' she said, indicating the facing chair. 'And I'll explain this in simple words that even you will hopefully understand.'

Adam did as he was commanded, but remained perched on the edge of the chair, as if wanting to flee from this unwanted conversation at the first opportunity.

'You loved my daughter. Yes?'

'Of course,' he said, bracing himself, uncertain of where this conversation was heading.

'And did she love you?'

'Yes, I believe she did.' He smiled, remembering all the times she had said those words to him. 'I know she did.'

'Did she try and make you happy when she was alive?'

'Yes. We were very happy and very much in love.'

Surely even the disapproving Mrs Wainwright would know that.

'Did she take pleasure in seeing you miserable?'

'No, of course not. What a thing to say. That's not what love is. You only wish happiness for the other person.'

'Exactly.' Mrs Wainwright raised her hands, palm upwards, as if that explained everything.

He shook his head. She surely knew that he and Rosalie had been in love and treasured each other's happiness, so why was she looking at him as if he were an imbecile?

She sighed. 'I can see from that blank expression that you still don't understand. My daughter loved you, heaven help her. She wanted your happiness as much as her own, probably more. Since she died you have been miserable. I understand that. You were grieving the loss of the love of your life. Just as I was grieving the loss of my daughter. But since Georgina entered this house you have again laughed and taken pleasure in life.'

Adam swallowed the lump in his throat. Yes, he had taken pleasure, in ways he never should have.

'I know,' he said, looking down at his hands, clasped tightly in his lap.

'That is precisely what my daughter would have wanted for you. And if you don't realise that then I suspect you never really knew her at all.'

His head shot up and he glared at the judgemental woman sitting across from him.

'How…how can you possibly say that?' he stammered, trying to form the words that would express his outrage at such an accusation. 'I knew Rosalie better than I have ever known anyone in my life.'

'So tell me, what sort of woman was she? Was she a woman who wanted you to be happy?'

'Yes, of course she was.'

'Was she a woman who wanted her children to be happy?'

'How can you even ask that? She wanted that more than anything in the world.'

She sent him a self-satisfied look, as if she had won the argument. But she had done no such thing. All she had done was told him something he already knew.

She shook her head slowly. 'My goodness, how these intelligent women could fall in love with a man who is so dim-witted I will never know.'

'Women?'

'Yes, *women.* Both your wives fell in love with you, although why I'll never understand. And it looks like you know this one as well as you knew my daughter.'

'Now, look here,' Adam said, standing up. He'd had enough of her insults and was not going to listen to another word of this lecture.

'Sit back down and stop pouting.'

Adam glared at her. He had never pouted in his life.

'It was obvious to me that Georgina was in love with you from the moment you brought her home as your wife. And it would be obvious to anyone with a ha'penny worth of sense that she has fallen deeper in love with you with every passing day.'

'No, you're wrong. She never wanted to marry me. This was an arrangement forced upon her, just as it was forced upon me by circumstances outside our control. Her father—'

Mrs Wainwright rolled her eyes, bringing his explanation to an end. She was obviously not going to listen.

'Men are such fools, and you more than most,' she said and released an exasperated sigh. 'She's in love with you. I know it's hard to understand, I certainly can't understand it myself, but there it is. And I'm sure my Rosalie would approve of that love wholeheartedly.'

'But—'

'No buts. And it doesn't take a great deal of insight to see how much your love for Georgina has grown since she first arrived in this house as your new wife.'

'But…' He looked from Rosalie's portrait to Mrs Wainwright, no longer sure what he was going to say.

'And that's as it should be. Do you think Rosalie would want you to mourn her for the rest of her life, for you to be miserable, for her children to be miserable, for this house to be one laden with grief? Is that the sort of woman you think my Rosalie was?'

'No,' he murmured, looking back towards the sideboard.

'Rosalie would be filled with joy that Georgina has come into this house and lifted the pall that has hung over it for the last five years. She would love seeing Georgina playing with the children, making them laugh and filling their days with happiness. Don't you agree?'

'Well, yes. It goes without saying she would want to see her children happy.'

'And she would want to see you in the arms of another woman, knowing that you are happy, married again and in love. To think otherwise would be a disservice to my daughter. It would suggest you think of her as a mean-spirited woman who wanted the man she loved to remain unhappy for the rest of his life. Do I need to say it again? If you think that, then you never knew my Rosalie, never really loved her.'

He stared at her, lost for words.

'Am I right?'

'Yes,' he said, slowly nodding. 'Yes,' he repeated, a heavy weight seemingly lifting off his shoulders. 'Yes, you are right.' He looked over at Rosalie's portrait then back at Mrs Wainwright.

'Then go and make things right with your new wife. Go and show her how much you love her, how important she is to you, and how much you have changed since that lovely, high-spirited young lass was foolish enough to agree to marry you.'

Chapter Twenty-Four

Mrs Wainwright left the room, leaving a stunned Adam staring into space.

In love with Georgina?

Was that what he was feeling? Was that why every emotion felt so intense? Was that why the thought of her with another man caused bile to burn up his throat and almost choke him? Could it be true that when he was consumed by an insatiable desire for her, it wasn't just because he wanted to make love to her, it was because he *was* in love with her?

He looked over at the sideboard. With Rosalie, it had been so clear when he had fallen in love with her, but at the time he had been an innocent young man of nineteen meeting a beautiful, enchanting, equally innocent young woman. With Georgina, it was different. He was a man weighed down by grief and responsibility. He had three children to care for and an estate in peril. There had been no joy in his heart when he'd set out to find a wife, no thoughts of courtship or wooing, as there had been when he'd first met Rosalie. Marriage had been a practical matter that they had both undertaken due to necessity.

And yet…

Mrs Wainwright was correct. He *was* a fool. From the moment he'd first met Georgina he had been unable to stop thinking about her. He had convinced himself that it was because she was always present. At that one ball he had attended, every time he'd turned around, there she'd seemed to be. And yet he had given not a passing thought to any of the other women he'd met at that ball, and would struggle to remember their names, never mind what they looked like. But from the moment he had first met Georgina she had been firmly in his thoughts, and there was more than just her appearance he could conjure up. He could remember her laugh, her smile, her scent, those dimples in each cheek that appeared every time she smiled, the different hues of blue in her eyes.

And he had not hesitated when he'd heard her father giving her an ultimatum. He'd told himself at the time it was because their marriage would be mutually beneficial. It was—but it was so much more. It was what he wanted, even if he had refused to admit it at the time.

It was a love that had made him miserable, simply because he'd refused to admit it, had refused to believe that he was entitled to love again, and to be happy again.

He looked back towards the door through which Mrs Wainwright had departed. She was also correct about her daughter. Rosalie would not have wanted him to be unhappy, just as he could not have borne the thought of Rosalie's unhappiness. Nor did he want Georgina to be unhappy, and yet she was, all because of his foolish behaviour.

He could not be certain that Mrs Wainwright was correct when she said that Georgina was in love with him. Although, if she was, he'd have to agree with his former mother-in-law that it would be foolish for such an intelligent young woman to fall for a man such as he.

But *if* she was in love, there was only one way to find out for sure. He would have to ask her. He walked across the room and picked up the portrait of Rosalie.

'I'm sorry, my love,' he said, gently stroking her cheek. 'It *was* an insult to your memory to ever think that you would not want this house to be full of love and laughter. And I know you would approve of Georgina. I should never have doubted that.'

He lightly kissed the portrait, placed it back on the sideboard and left the drawing room. Smiling for the first time in what felt like an age, he took the steps up to the bedchambers two at a time. When he reached the landing, he stopped.

All he had to do was knock on Georgina's bedchamber door and profess his love for her, but Mrs Wainwright was correct about one more thing. He needed to show Georgina that he was a changed man. That she had changed him, for ever and for the better.

He was not the man she had met on the side of the road. He no longer wanted to be that dour man who had judged her so unfairly for being impetuous, a risk-taker and a woman wholly unsuitable to be his wife and a mother to his children.

She needed to see that he was no longer that uptight man who had no appreciation of her sense of fun, the man who did not value the gift of joy and laughter she had brought into this house, or the love she had given his children and the affection she had shown him.

He quickly retraced his steps back down the stairs, out through the entranceway and around the side of the house. He looked up to Georgina's bedchamber. Light from her candles was spilling out into the dark night. Good, she had still not retired. Mrs Wainwright had said he should prove to her that he had changed and that wise, if somewhat cantankerous, woman was right.

He grabbed hold of the drainpipe and gave it a firm tug. It held. He looked up at her window and his firm resolve wavered. It was a long way up. Had he ever done this before? If he had, it was not since he was a young boy and he was definitely out of practice.

He released the drainpipe. Perhaps there was another, less drastic way of showing how much he had changed? One that didn't risk life and limb.

He took a firm hold of the drainpipe. No, as they said, faint heart never won fair lady. He would not think of the danger.

Trying not to grunt at the exertion, he heaved himself up to the first bracket. So far, so good. He looked up. When was the last time the brackets had been maintained? He ran his thumbnail along the nearest brick. Had the mortar holding the bricks together turned to dust through lack of attention? He was about to find out.

He shimmied up to the next bracket, then the next one, the ground moving further and further away. Then discovered a flaw in his plan. The next bracket was missing. He reached out his foot, trying to find a foothold in the bricks. None presented itself. So he scrambled over to the other side of the drainpipe, hoping to have better luck there.

'What on earth are you doing?' Georgina's voice came from high above him. 'You're making enough noise to waken the entire county.'

He looked up. She was leaning out of the sash window, her long hair hanging loose around her face, the candles creating a halo effect on her blonde hair.

He was like a mortal gazing upon an angel. He sighed. Had he ever seen a more heavenly sight?

'Well, what are you doing?' she repeated. His angel did not sound amused.

'Um…is that not obvious? I'm climbing up the drainpipe.'

'Why?'

'To see you.'

She looked over her shoulder. 'There is a door in my bedchamber, you know?'

'I'm making a point…a romantic gesture,' he said, reaching out his foot and waving it in the air as he searched for that elusive foothold.

'A what?'

'A romantic gesture. But I think I might be stuck.'

She stared at him, her brow furrowed, and then she laughed. That sound made his precarious position worthwhile.

'You're hopeless, aren't you?' she said, still laughing at him. 'I could shimmy up this drainpipe with my eyes closed.'

'Perhaps you're going to have to give me some lessons.'

'I think it might be best if you admit defeat and climb back down and use the stairs.'

'Never,' he said, wrapping himself around the drainpipe and doing an impression of the monkey he had seen at the zoological gardens, or was it more like a snake? Whatever it was, he moved in an ungainly manner up to the next fixed bracket and breathed a sigh of relief when he reached that sanctuary. With the remaining brackets thankfully in place, he was able to scale the rest of the drainpipe with relative ease, and he finally reached her window.

'I told you I could do it,' he said, peeping over the windowsill.

'After that performance, I don't think you should be auditioning for a place in the circus any time soon,' she said, a delightful smile on her lips.

He gripped the windowsill to pull himself in and another problem struck him. How did one climb from a drainpipe, over a jutting windowsill and into a bedroom?

'I think you're going to need my help,' she said, leaning out and grabbing hold of the top of his trousers. 'I hope this holds and your tailor didn't skimp on the stitches or this is going to be highly embarrassing for you.'

With that, she gave an almighty tug while he did his best to gain a footing against the wall and a handhold inside the room. She placed her foot on the windowsill and, with much huffing and puffing from both of them, dragged him into the room.

They collapsed in an untidy pile on the bedroom floor.

Entwined in each other's limbs, they remained where they'd fallen, both breathing heavily. Adam wondered if he was the only one to be reminded of other times when they had lain wrapped together in exhaustion.

When his heartbeat resumed something that resembled a normal beat, he stood up, offered her his hand and pulled her to her feet.

'That was meant to be more like the balcony scene from *Romeo and Juliet* and less like something from a French farce,' he said, still holding her hand and trying to regain as much of his dignity as he could.

'Lucky for you, I enjoy French farces.' She looked towards the window. 'And that was more farcical than most.'

She looked back at him in expectation. Adam suddenly realised that he should have given more thought to what he was to say and less thought to his supposedly grand entrance. After all, this was the most important conversation he was going to have in his life.

'Will you marry me?' he said, causing her to stare at him wide-eyed, as if he had lost all sense of reason.

'Um…we are married. Remember? The church? The white dress? Standing at the altar making our vows?'

'No, I want you to marry me. I want us to be man and wife, not just in name only.'

She looked over at the bed. 'I believe we've done that already as well.'

'Oh, Georgina, I'm making a mess of this, aren't I? In the same way I've made a mess of everything since I followed you out onto that terrace and made that first clumsy, insulting proposal.'

'You mean when you stepped out to get some air and *found* me on the terrace,' she said, eyeing him sideways.

'No, I followed you. I saw that you were distressed

and I was concerned for your wellbeing, then I heard your father's threats.'

'You were concerned about me?'

'Yes, and then I made that foolish proposal, so now I want to do it properly.'

He dropped down onto one knee and took her hands before she could distract him with any more questions.

'Georgina, I love you.'

She gave a small gasp, her eyes growing large.

'I love you with all my heart and soul. Since you came into my life I've learnt how to laugh again. You turned my world from one that was dull and grey to one that is vibrant and filled with colour and light. I'm nothing without you and I want you in my life. I need you in my life. I love you. Will you be my wife?'

She nodded, rapidly and repeatedly.

'That is the proposal I should have made to you when I first asked you to marry me, but I was too stupid to realise I had fallen in love. I was too wrapped up in my grief to realise that the most wonderful woman in the world had come into my life.'

'And if you had made a proposal like that, I would have given the same answer as I did the first time. Yes, although this time perhaps I could add, yes, yes, a thousand times yes.'

'So can we start again? Can we have a marriage that is based on love, not on convenience?'

'Yes, yes, yes.' She stopped smiling, her brow furrowed. 'But...'

'What's wrong, my love?' he asked, his heart suddenly lurching in his chest.

'If we are to start again, then there is something you

must know,' she said, biting her lip. 'When I accepted your first proposal, I told myself it was because of Father's threats. But that was wrong. Father would never have really gone through with his threat. He would never have tossed me out on the street. He simply isn't that sort of man. I could have saved you from this marriage, but I didn't because, even though I pretended it wasn't so, I was in love with you and wanted to be your wife.'

He stared up at her from his bent knee position, surprised at this revelation.

'I'm so sorry, Adam,' she said. 'I know this changes everything.'

'It changes nothing. My love for you sparked into life when I first met you, and it seems it was the same for you. It's just that neither of us was able to admit what was really in our heart.'

'So you forgive me for tricking you into marrying me?'

'There was no trickery, and if there was, you would merely have tricked me into doing what my heart wanted, even if my head did not realise it. So there is nothing to forgive.'

'Oh, Adam, I do love you with my heart, head and soul, and yes, I want to be your wife.'

They continued to smile at each other.

'Um… I think you can stand up now,' she said.

He laughed and stood up, still holding her hands, still looking into those beautiful eyes. 'You are so beautiful,' he whispered. 'You have such a beautiful spirit.'

She sent him a cheeky smile. 'And?'

'And a beautiful face.'

'And?'

'And a beautiful body that I just can't get enough of.'

'Well, that's something you can always try to do,' she said, then bit her bottom lip, a pretty blush on her cheeks.

Her jokes made him smile, but he needed to focus. There was so much more he needed to tell her. He could not let himself become distracted by her laughter, nor by what he was desperate to do with that beautiful body.

'Georgina, I'm sorry it took me so long to realise that what I felt for you was love,' he said, imploring her to understand. 'I always knew that you were a beautiful young woman, and I tried to dismiss my feelings as nothing more than physical desire. But when we made love, the emotions that welled up inside me were so intense they frightened me, so I pushed them away. I tried to tell myself it was nothing more than lust that I was feeling, and that was so wrong. Now I know what I was feeling, what I *am* feeling, is a deep, intense, unfathomable love.'

He clasped her hands to his heart. 'I never wanted to fall in love again, and that is why I tried to push those feelings away. I wanted a wife I would not love, out of a misguided loyalty to Rosalie, but you made that impossible.'

She smiled back at him. 'I've always had a contrary nature.'

'I know, and never, ever change that.'

'Oh, as someone who is contrary, I suppose that will have to be the first thing I'll have to change.'

He laughed, wrapped his arms around her waist and kissed her laughing lips.

'Georgina, I do love you so much,' he said when his kisses had finally stopped her laughter.

'So, do you think we can now consummate our new marriage?' she said with that delightful cheeky smile he loved so much. 'Or after your exertions on the drainpipe do you think you've got the energy left for…?' She tilted her head towards her bed.

'Believe me, I will always have enough energy for that.'

With that, he scooped her up in his arms and carried her to the bed, determined to prove to his wife just how energetic he could be.

Epilogue

Just as she did every Sunday, Georgina gathered the children up, ensuring they were dressed in their best clothes, and with Adam on her arm strolled to the local churchyard to lay flowers on Rosalie's grave.

Adam knew that Rosalie would have loved Georgina, just as he did, and just as their children did.

Mrs Wainwright, or Agatha as she now insisted he call her, had returned to her own home not long after Adam and Georgina had conducted a mock marriage in the garden gazebo for the children's entertainment.

Lotte and Dora had made wonderful bridesmaids, and Adam could see that they would soon be turning into delightful young ladies. Georgina had continued their weekly class to prepare them for their debuts, lessons that seemed to involve more laughter and mayhem than actual instruction.

During the service, Eddie had taken his role as best man very seriously. That was until he'd dropped the ring and sent them all scrambling around on the floor for it, with much laughter and butting of heads.

It was possibly the most chaotic and the most enjoyable wedding Adam had ever attended. And that was how their married life continued, with plenty of chaos and plenty of laughter.

Adam had worn a dove-grey suit for the wedding and, as his valet had once advised him, added colour with a gold brocade waistcoat, while Georgina wore a simple white gown, but adorned her hair and the girls' hair with wreaths of flowers, so they'd looked like carefree nymphs from a fairy tale.

At the end of the service, Agatha had told him she was sure that Rosalie was smiling down on them, enjoying the fact that the man she loved was now happy and that her children were cared for and loved. It had touched him more than he would have thought possible.

Agatha had also informed them that Georgina was now more than capable of running her own household, so there was no need for her supervision.

Georgina had been riddled with nerves, certain that such an undertaking was beyond her, but, to everyone's surprise, including Georgina's, Agatha was proven correct yet again. She'd soon proved herself a more than capable mistress of the house. After a few months she'd even decided she was capable of hosting dinner parties, although, to be on the safe side, the first party had been for her friends, Amelia and her husband, Leo Devenish, Irene and her husband, Joshua Huntington, the Duke of Redcliff, and Emily Beaumont, the only unmarried friend from her time at Miss Halliwell's Finishing School.

Georgina had expected there to be hitches that her friends would either politely ignore or turn into part of the fun, but everything had gone smoothly. And that had become the first of many social events she'd hosted, turning a house that had been in mourning for far too long into a house full of people, laughter and pleasure.

Agatha continued to visit regularly to see her grandchildren, but from that day on it was always as a guest, and she left the management of the house and the servants entirely to Georgina. On each visit, she also never failed to remind Adam how good Georgina was for him, and how grateful he should be to Agatha for pointing out to him that he had fallen in love with his wife.

Adam *was* grateful, but he did not need Agatha to remind him of how much he was in love with Georgina or how good she was for him. He was reminded of that fact every time he looked at his beautiful, impetuous, adorable wife.

* * * * *

Wedded To His Enemy Debutante

Samantha Hastings

MILLS & BOON

Samantha Hastings met her husband in a turkey-sandwich line. They live in Salt Lake City, Utah, where she spends most of her time reading, having tea parties and chasing her kids. She has degrees from Brigham Young University, University of North Texas and University of Reading (UK). She's the author of *The Last Word*, *The Invention of Sophie Carter*, *A Royal Christmas Quandary*, *The Girl with the Golden Eyes*, *Jane Austen Trivia*, *The Duchess Contract*, *Secret of the Sonnets* and *A Novel Disguise*. She also writes cozy murder mysteries under Samantha Larsen.

Learn more at her website: SamanthaHastings.com
Connect with Samantha on social media:
Twitter @HastingSamantha
Instagram @SamanthaHastingsAuthor
Facebook.com/SamanthaHastingsAuthor

Visit the Author Profile page
at millsandboon.com.au.

Author Note

I am so delighted to share another Stringham story! Frederica has been one of my favourites from the very beginning. She is headstrong, fiery, intelligent, adventurous and brave. She will require all these qualities to survive the Battle of Waterloo. Her childhood nemesis turned fiancé, Colonel Lord Samuel Pelford, needs her help to spy on the French before their upcoming attack. Will their temporary truce turn into something more, or will the merry war between them continue?

Alas, because Lady Frederica Stringham is a fictional character, she did not discover or invent carbolic soap nor sell it. Chemist Dr. Frederick Crace-Calvert (1819–1873) is credited with inventing and producing the first carbolic soap in 1857.

The Prince of Orange (later King William II), of the Netherlands, went to school at Eton and served with the Duke of Wellington in the Peninsula wars. He was briefly engaged to Princess Charlotte of Wales before she called it off. He was known to his friends as "Slender Billy." Lord Arthur Wellesley, the Duke of Wellington, was an international hero after Waterloo. He later served as prime minister of England, and it was not until then that he was dubbed the "Iron Duke." Lieutenant-Colonel Colquhoun Grant was Wellington's top intelligence officer for the Battle of Waterloo. He always wore his uniform behind enemy lines and did not consider himself a spy. Colonel George Scovell oversaw communications during Waterloo and he did find a wounded officer in a cowhouse.

DEDICATION

To: Susannah Holden

Chapter One

London, March 1815

'The London Season is abominably dull,' Lady Frederica Stringham said, to no one in particular.

Her mother had once again refused to let her go to the factory with her that morning. It was scandalous enough that a duchess owned a perfumery and actually oversaw its day-to-day dealings. But working there or at the fashionable shop on Bond Street was quite out of the question for an unmarried debutante of the *ton*.

Frederica stood next to a window as tall as a person and three times as wide. She stared at the rain pouring on the cobblestone street of the exclusive Berkley Square—brick and stone mansions in the best part of London. Wishing instead that she was in Greece with her sisters and their father. Papa had accompanied them on their journey, but only planned to stay for a month or two to get them established in a good place. Frederica had spent over a year with her married sister Mantheria in Italy, but Mama now insisted that she attend the London Season. She was one and twenty after all and *unmarried.*

Perish the thought.

And whilst flirting with dandies was delightful and playing cards with Corinthians was charming, no suitor had captured her heart. Although, she did enjoy kissing several of them. Another thing debutantes were *not* supposed to do.

Frederica yawned, walked back to the sofa, and slouched down in her seat. Stacked beside her on the side table were all the Maria Edgeworth books from the lending library. Picking them up, she saw the titles *Belinda*, *Castle Rackrent*, and *Tales of Fashionable Life*. She had read them all. If only she could return them and select more without her mother coming with her. Debutantes in London were guarded more closely than treasure. Listening to the raindrops pelt against the window, she let out another sigh.

A footman with a white-powdered wig opened the door for her mother, the Duchess of Hampford. Her mother was an older version of herself, with the same hazel eyes and brown hair, although showing some grey now. She was an inch or so shorter than her daughter, yet her figure was still trim where it ought to be and generous where she would wish it to be. The fragrant smell of lilacs and rock rose clung to her. She gave her favourite daughter a look of reproach.

'Lawson, you may shut the door,' the Duchess said majestically. 'Frederica, sit up at once. I will not have you slouching like a hoyden. You would think you were a chit out of the schoolroom, instead of a young lady in her twenties.'

Frederica sat up stiffly. All right then. This was going to be a business meeting. 'Yes, Mama.'

Her mother sat on a chair beside her and said in a

more coaxing tone, 'My nerves have been in shreds these last few weeks, but at last, all of my worries for you are over.'

Stretching out her arms, she smiled. 'I do not think I am about to die. In fact, I am in perfect health.'

'Stop it, Frederica,' Mama said in a sharp tone. 'This is no time for funning, Samuel is finally coming up to scratch.'

That wiped the smirk off her face and she lightly touched her throat. 'But his father only died less than a month ago.'

Mama brushed a finite piece of lint off her beautiful pink morning dress in what appeared to be silent frustration. 'Lord Pelford will be arriving this afternoon to make you an offer of marriage.'

Frederica's mouth fell open. 'I cannot believe it! He has not seen me in seven years and he did not like me much then. He was always criticising me and prosing on about proper behaviour.'

Her mother sighed and folded her arms. 'You are acting like this is a surprise. You were named after his mother and a union has been planned between our two families for years.'

Squeezing her hands into fists, Frederica stood up and walked to the window. Her heart palpitated and black spots blocked her vision. 'I thought… I thought after Mantheria's disastrous marriage to a duke, that you would have changed your mind. Glastonbury was not faithful to my sister for even six months.'

Dropping her eyes to her folded arms, her mother sniffed. 'Samuel is not like Glastonbury. I have known him his entire life and he is a steady, intelligent young man. He would never be unfaithful to you. Glastonbury was too old for Mantheria and I was too foolish to realise what a mismatch it would be. I admit that I was blinded to his many weaknesses by his wealth and position.'

'Including Lady Dutton?' Frederica asked, knowing full well that her mother knew about Glastonbury's long-time mistress before he married her sister.

Mama closed her eyes and inhaled sharply. 'We assumed wrongly that he would give her up. You have no idea how much both your father and I regret giving our consent to the match. We resolved to not bring out a daughter at seventeen again, deeming it too young to make a good choice for a spouse. You are more mature at one and twenty. You are well-educated and well-travelled. I believe you will make the right choice.'

Her blood boiling, Frederica threw her hands up in the air. 'But you are not giving me a choice! You are marrying me to a man who will disapprove of everything I say and do.'

'If you had found another young man who caught your fancy when you debuted at nineteen, we would have supported you,' she said slowly as if Frederica was still a small child. 'But after two years, you have not. And I will not attempt to deny that I did everything in my power to secure for my daughter a husband of the highest rank.'

Frederica's hands shook and fluttered. 'Have you bought me a husband?'

'I bought you a title—the husband comes with it.'

A giggle escaped Frederica's lips. Drat her mother for making her laugh when she was trying to throw a proper tantrum. 'It is all about town that Samuel inherited very little beside debts and mortgages from his father, besides a younger brother and mother to keep.'

Mama got up and walked to where Frederica stood by the windows. 'A union between our two families was planned almost from the day of your christening. Lady Pelford has been just as determined as myself for this day to come. She has invited us to stay countless times at Farleigh Palace to improve your acquaintance with her son.'

'Little good it has done either,' Frederica said, folding her arms across her chest. 'I was eight years of age and he eleven, when Samuel and I learned that we could not endure each other's company. And since then when forced together, we have done our very best to make each other miserable.'

'Well, I suggest that you stop trying to make him miserable when he is your husband.'

Frederica let out an airy laugh, but quelled it quickly. 'The last time I saw him, I was fourteen years old, when he stayed with us that summer at Hampford Castle. Samuel gave me a box of chocolates and told me I was immature and badly behaved.'

Mama put her hands on Frederica's shoulders. 'As I recall that summer, you and your little sisters put your papa's pet bear cub in his room in the middle of the night and scared the poor fellow out of his wits.'

Frederica grinned fondly at this memory. 'He didn't have many wits as I remember.'

'But you have both wits and talent,' her mother said, squeezing her daughter's shoulders lightly before releasing her hold. 'And I can think of no better person to leave my perfume company to.'

Her heartbeat raced in her chest as warmth radiated through her body. She grabbed her mother's arm and tugged it. 'You are leaving Duchess & Co. to me?'

Mama smiled like a lioness after a successful hunt. 'I am leaving Duchess & Co. to another duchess. Mantheria is not interested. Please tell me that you will accept Samuel and become a *duchess*.'

Frederica dropped her mother's arm and turned back to the window. She breathed in slowly and exhaled, but it did not slow down her racing pulse. There was nothing in the world she wanted more than her mother's company. She had always been afraid that Mama would leave it to Matthew, one of her elder brothers, who was a fine businessman. Frederica had little experience with running a company, but she had grown up practising languages and mathematics to prepare herself. She even planned to expand her mother's perfume business into red scented soaps with phenol. Adding phenol to the sodium tallowate, sodium cocoate, and glycerine had helped her scratches heal without infection. Three fragrances went well with it: camphor, rosemary, and eucalyptus. Trying different combinations, she had made at least one hundred cakes of them as she waited for something to happen during the early Season.

Gulping, she turned back to her mother. 'When do I get your company?'

The look on Mama's face was triumphant, she knew that she had won. 'I will deed half of it to you when you marry and the other half when I am dead. It is slightly less profitable currently, for I used a large portion of the savings to pay Lord Pelford's family debts.'

Frederica did not want her mother to die any time soon and she knew that she still had a lot to learn from

Mama about how to run her own business. She held out her hand. 'It's a bargain.'

Her mother shook her hand tightly, not letting go. 'You will dress in your blue sprigged muslin and have Wade thread flowers through your hair. Do not forget to put a dab of perfume on your inner wrist. And perhaps if you still look as pale as a ghost, tell Miss Wade that she has my permission to add some rouge on your cheeks.'

Her mother finally released her hand and Frederica threw her arms around her mother's neck, hugging her tightly. She kissed her cheek. 'I won't disappoint you, Mama.'

'With the business or with Samuel?'

Frederica laughed. 'Either.'

'I only met your father once before I married him,' she said, 'and we were not even alone. But any marriage can work, if both parties are committed to its success.'

She thought of Samuel and sobered. She was willing to commit, but she could not be certain that he would be. When they were younger, the harder she'd tried to get his attention, the more he'd ignored her. It had been infuriating. He'd had the unique ability to get underneath her thick skin. No person had ever aggravated her more.

'Yes, Mama.'

Her mother sighed. 'If you wish to love your husband, choose to, as I did. Love is not a feeling, but a choice.'

Frederica nodded again and left the room. She could try to love Samuel, but she doubted whether he would do the same. Was a perfume company worth a lifetime without love? Slumping, she walked up the grand staircase to the second floor. She opened the dark mahogany door to her room and found Wade waiting for her. The lady's maid had already laid out the sprigged muslin day dress that flattered Frederica's figure and colouring. Miss Wade was not yet thirty, but her thin face seemed older because of her perpetual frown. She wore her vibrant brown hair in a severe bun, and her plain dress emphasised her slender figure. She stood and executed a sharp curtsy to her mistress.

'I suppose Mama has already spoken with you.'

Wade curtsied again. 'Yes, my lady.'

'Well then, do your best to make me presentable,' Frederica said, sitting down heavily on the bed. 'For as you, and undoubtedly every other servant in the house, already knows, I am to be engaged to be married today.'

Wade assisted Frederica out of her morning gown and into her prettiest dress in the palest shade of blue. She added fresh white flowers to Frederica's coiffure and carefully added a bit of powder to her cheeks. Frederica held still as the lady's maid put on her gloves, silk stockings, and slippers that were dyed the same shade of blue.

'Thank you, Wade. That is all. I should like to be by myself for a little while.'

Once Wade closed the door, Frederica opened the top drawer of her dresser and pulled out her pistol and powder. It was time for some target practice in the garden.

Chapter Two

When Colonel Lord Samuel Corbin's father died and he'd succeeded to his dignities, Samuel had every intention of selling his commission in the British Army and returning to civilian life. Unfortunately, Napoleon Bonaparte escaped from the island of Elba on the same day. Samuel could hardly desert his friends and his country on the brink of war, despite his bereft mama's many pleadings in her letters. But he had asked for a short leave of absence to return to England and put his affairs in order.

It was seven years since he had last set foot on English soil. His memories of home and his father were still painful. He'd run away from them as a youth of seventeen, but he must face them now as a man.

Samuel fought fearlessly during the Peninsular Campaign, as only a young, stupid officer could. His foolhardiness had come with several rank risings and eventually the Duke of Wellington made him a member of his staff. After the war, Samuel had not returned to England with his regiment; instead, he'd accompanied Wellington to France and to the Congress of Vienna.

There he'd stayed quite happily until the little emperor decided to rule the world again.

Not that Samuel had been avoiding England.

He loved his home, Farleigh Palace.

No.

He had been avoiding his father and a certain young woman: Lady Frederica Stringham.

Samuel knew that if he returned home, he would be expected to make her an offer of marriage. Wisely, he had stayed on the Continent. But with his father's death, followed by insistent letters from his father's many creditors, he'd returned to his encumbered estates and distraught mother. He was relieved to learn that his father was already buried six feet underneath the ground when he arrived. His corpse couldn't be deep enough for Samuel. His sire had made his mother miserable and destroyed his childhood. Samuel only hoped that he could shield his little brother from the entire truth. It was a burden no schoolboy should have to carry.

Donning black gloves, he strolled into his mother's private sitting room, where she sat with her embroidery work. Mama was bedecked in black from her cap, which covered her thick brown hair, to her leather boots. Her face was round and dimpled. She had large pale blue eyes, a pointy nose, and a generous mouth with thick red lips. Placing the hoop and needle on the table beside her, she patted the seat next to her. Samuel dutifully sat beside her and was overwhelmed by the smell of her lavender perfume.

'You asked to see me, Mama?'

She gave her son a fond smile and smoothed a crease out of his coat with her gloved hand. 'There, you look very handsome.'

He grabbed her hand and pulled off the glove. The pale skin was unmarred. 'You are still well?'

Swallowing, his mother nodded and tugged back on her glove. 'As well as can be expected and much better now that you are home.'

'Thank you, Mama, but I do not have time to chatter. I am riding to London to meet with our solicitor and steward. The three of us are going to sort through the tangle of our finances before I return to Wellington's services.'

'Perhaps a little refreshment,' she said, picking up a bell off the table. But before she could ring for her servants, he took the bell.

'Mama, I have no desire for tea and commonplaces. Tell me why you sent for me.'

His mother gave him a tremulous smile as if she was trying to hold in her tears. In the past, he would have promised her anything when she cried, but his years at war had hardened him.

'Oh, Samuel, I hope that you will not dislike it. Before you see Peterson and Fuller, I must tell you something of great importance.'

'Do,' he invited.

She brought a trembling black gloved hand to her mouth and sniffed. He placed a comforting arm around her round shoulders. His mother might be a duchess, but she had endured a long and unhappy marriage.

'The Duchess of Hampford owns all the mortgages to the estate,' she said at last. 'Actually, it is her company, Duchess & Co., that holds them.'

He dropped his arm from her shoulders. 'What? How could that be? Why in heaven's name is Hampford involved in the business?'

A large tear came out of his mother's left eye and slowly fell down her rounded cheek theatrically.

Mama could always cry upon command, he thought. Then chided himself for his callousness. He was one of the few people in the world who knew how much she had suffered and how much she would continue to suffer for his father's choices.

Chagrined, he put his arm back around her and gave her a gentle squeeze. 'Mama, I have been gone for seven years and when I left, I was but a lad. Please explain why Hampford is involved in the business.'

'The Duke of Hampford is not at all involved,' she said, biting on her lower lip as if to stop it from trembling. 'You know about your father's—illness.'

He gave a curt nod. The less that was said about that the better.

'About a year after you left for the Peninsula, he took out another mortgage on the estate and lost a fortune on cards and low company. Before we were entirely ruined, I was able to have him incarcerated for his own protection and that of others. But our finances were in a very bad way. I was forced to order a new gown to placate my dressmaker and additional supplies that we could ill afford to keep them at bay, causing us to fall even deeper into debt.'

A feeling of guilt tightened his chest and Samuel gave her another side hug. He should have been there for her. 'I do not blame you at all for our financial state, Mama.'

His mother exhaled a wobbly breath. 'Your father could not help me and you were not here.'

Samuel's chest felt tight and sweat was forming on his forehead. Guilt settling over him like a sash across his chest. He should have supported her better. Instead, he'd joined the army to escape his family problems.

Sighing, Mama put a hand on her chest. 'So, I confided in my dear friend Selina, Lady Hampford. She brought her son Matthew, and they called in Peterson and Fuller. They went through all the bills and mortgages and established a plan to get rid of the debt. Selina assured me with a little economy, we could be free of encumbrances in around twenty years.'

His ears were ringing and he was seeing black spots. 'Twenty years!'

'Fourteen now. Indeed, Samuel, I know I ought to have consulted with you then, but I did not wish to burden you further,' she explained, pausing to sniff into her handkerchief. 'Selina redeemed half of the mortgages and, with my permission, instructed Mr Peterson to sell the London house and most of the unentailed property to pay off all the moneylenders, tradesmen, and the remaining mortgages. You cannot know what a relief it was to me not to have the knocker banged at all hours of the day, with tradesmen and bailiffs begging for their bills to be paid.'

'I am sure it was very disagreeable,' Samuel said, his skin tingling with discomfort. 'Do you recall the entire sum?'

His mother took another shaky breath, bringing her handkerchief to her dry eyes. 'Two hundred thousand and three pounds, five shillings, and four pence.'

He swore underneath his breath, clenching his fists but still feeling helpless and vulnerable. Swallowing the lump in his throat, he asked, 'And how much money do I still owe Lady Hampford or her company?'

'I am not entirely sure,' his mother said, not looking

him in the eye. 'I believe the total to be over one hundred thousand pounds.'

Samuel's pulse thundered against his skin. His heartbeat quickened as if he were about to face an enemy army with cannons and guns. 'One hundred thousand pounds! My commission is not worth a tenth of such a sum.'

Mama took his fisted hand and stroked the top of it. 'Lady Hampford, Selina, told me that the estate, even without the unentailed property, was worth around ten thousand pounds a year. And if we did not entertain, reduced the staff, and sold the best horses from the stables, we could contrive to live on less than half of that amount and slowly pay back the remaining mortgages. I have enforced the strictest of economies on the estate these last six years and we are in a much better financial position than we were.'

Samuel released his hold on his mother and stood, walking briskly around the room, holding his elbows tightly to his sides. 'Is there anything else I should know?'

Another tear fell down his mother's cheek. 'I hope you know that everything I did, I did for you.'

'I do not doubt that.'

More tears fell down her cheeks, but his mother made no attempt to wipe them with the handkerchief in her palm. He was supposed to see these tears. 'Selina saved our family from ruin and she suggested that you need not pay back the mortgages held by her company... That they could be a part of your wife's dowry in addition to the money from her father of thirty thousand pounds. You would only need to repay the initial mortgage on the estate.'

An unsettling heaviness overcame his body and he felt cold all over. His mother and Lady Hampford were forcing his hand. He knew that they had planned such a union from the time he was a small child, but these sorts of family arrangements were not legally binding and he had never intended to marry Frederica. He'd wanted to choose his own bride.

His mother tried to touch him, but he recoiled. 'Lady Frederica Stringham is the last woman on earth that I should wish to marry.'

'Now, Samuel, you haven't seen her in seven years, and she has become a prodigiously pretty girl and very accomplished,' his mother protested, no longer feigning tears. 'Even your father was quite set upon the match before he went mad. And you could hardly do better than a duke's daughter… Lady Hampford expects you to call on her this very afternoon to ask for her daughter's hand in marriage.'

He felt a sharp pain as he sucked in his cheeks, biting down on them in anger. 'I will not.'

Mama picked up her fan that was attached to her wrist and gently wafted it as if this were an everyday sort of conversation and not the end of his hopes and plans. 'Is there another lady you prefer?'

Gritting his teeth, Samuel shook his head. 'No.'

His mother got to her feet and placed a hand on his arm. 'Dearest son, people of our rank rarely make love matches. And those few like myself who marry for love, are not always happy. Not that it was strictly a love match, for our parents did bring us together several times. As you know, after we were married, your father did not remain faithful to me for very long. Samuel, I beg you to consider Lady Frederica. The Stringhams can trace their line back to William the Conqueror. And I know that I can trust you to be a good and faithful husband to her.'

His own father had been anything but good and faithful. Whenever Papa had been in London, which was most of the year, there was always a prostitute on his arm, usually two of them. His father had also frequented every whorehouse and bawdy club in the city. He'd even brought them into their family's townhouse. Samuel did not regret that his solicitors had sold it to pay his family's debts. He never wished to step foot in that building again.

Samuel tried to swallow again, but was unable to. His throat felt thick. 'For all that Lady Frederica is the daughter of a duke and a descendant of the Conqueror, everyone knows that her grandfather is a wealthy London merchant who purchased Lady Hampford's way into the peerage.'

'That is all forgot,' his mother assured him with a coaxing smile. 'Selina has been the Duchess of Hampford for over thirty years, and her children have married into all the best families. Think of the connections you would acquire. And you would save your family from further disgrace and penury. For how are you to provide for your brother, Jeremy, if you have not a farthing to spare? And you would have to repay the additional mortgages held by the Duchess's company.'

Clenching his fists, every muscle in Samuel's body quivered with anger, resentment, and frustration. 'I take it that both Peterson and Fuller are aware of my approaching nuptials? And no doubt they have already met with Lord Matthew Stringham to discuss the wedding settlements.'

Mama held up her hand. 'Only a preliminary meeting. And Matthew is the Earl of Trentham now.'

He let out a forceful breath. 'What if I were to be killed fighting Napoleon? What would Lady Hampford do with the mortgages then?'

Clearing her throat, Mama said, 'Selina was wishful that you sell out of the army immediately, and we had not yet heard of Napoleon's escape when we initially discussed your marriage. After we learned of Napoleon's uprising, she did say, *most delicately*, that if you were not to come back from war, that perhaps Jeremy might become fond of her youngest daughter, Rebecca. Such a dear girl. She is quite a favourite with me.'

'By Jove! That beats all,' he said, digging his fingernails into his palms. He would not force his little brother into an unwanted marriage. 'Lady Hampford is a fool if she thinks I will go down without a fight. I'll find a way without her money.'

Samuel left the parlour, slamming the door behind him. Passing several servants, he walked through the long portrait gallery of his ancestors. He resented each and every painting.

'Oi, Samuel,' his younger brother, Jeremy, hailed.

Jeremy had inherited his mother's pale blue eyes and pointy nose. At the age of fifteen, he was an ungainly youth with large hands and feet. A smattering of freckles sprinkled over the top of his nose, and his hair and eyebrows were so blond that they looked white.

He gave Samuel a quizzing smile. 'Is Mama still weeping? By golly, I never knew one woman could retain so much water inside her. I daresay she has been weeping for three weeks together, which is perfectly ridiculous, because she did not even like Papa. No one did.'

Samuel grasped his little brother's shoulders for a moment and then let go. 'Have no fear. Her endless stream of tears has finally ebbed. When are you back to Eton?'

Shrugging, Jeremy raised his pale eyebrows. 'Ought to have gone back a week ago, but I was afraid that I would miss your visit.'

Samuel touched his chest. 'I am flattered.'

His little brother laughed, shoving Samuel's shoulder. 'And the food is ever so much better at home and no one expects me to do anything. I am the spare after all.'

Jeremy was not a spare to him. He was Samuel's only sibling and he would not let anything bad happen to him. He loved his brother, and unlike Papa, Samuel would take care of him. 'Well, pack your trunk, I will have Mr Kent drive you back to school tomorrow with a hamper full of Cook's best pastries.'

Leaning his head to one side, Jeremy frowned at him. 'Is there any money for school? Some of my friends at Eton heard that our family was all but rolled up. I thought I could perhaps join the army or the navy?'

Samuel's insides felt knotted and he couldn't get enough air into his lungs. He'd hoped to spare his younger brother the weight of their family problems. Such worries were crushing to a schoolboy, as Samuel had learned all too well and too young. Yet, how was he to raise enough money to take care of his brother's future and keep the family estate? And would he be able to do so in the brief time of his military leave? He didn't wish for his brother to join the army or navy. He'd lost too many friends on the battlefield and couldn't lose Jeremy.

At least if he married Frederica, his little brother would never want for anything. It stung his masculinity and his pride to allow the Duchess of Hampford to win, but there was nothing he would not do for Jeremy. Even marry a badly behaved termagant to pay his family's debts. Samuel pulled Jeremy into a tight hug before letting go. A rare sign of affection. 'We are not destitute and you will return to school. We were obliged to sell the London house and some land, but we are quite well to pass, and since I have no taste for cards, you have no need to worry for your future.'

His little brother did not appear convinced. 'Are you sure?'

Samuel took out his coin purse from his pocket and tossed it to Jeremy, who deftly caught it. 'Don't spend it all in one place.'

His little brother's worried expression turned into a grin. 'I won't!'

He gave his brother a nod, before heading out a side door. Samuel ordered the head groom to saddle his horse—he was to ride to London today. Turning back, he looked at his home, Farleigh Palace. It was one of the few edifices built in the English Baroque style and was as ostentatious as it was ornate. The grey stone building had countless arched windows and looked like three enormous houses connected by covered halls. The centre building was a storey taller than the others and had a great domed roof. The farthest right building connected to the pleasure gardens through several archways. From the outside, Farleigh Palace was cold and stately, but to Samuel, it was the only place he had ever called home. It would have been a wrench to lose it, but to keep it, he would have to marry Frederica.

Samuel had always tried to behave in the opposite manner that his father would have. Serious. Responsible. Thoughtful. Frederica had once called him 'stuffier than a stuffed animal head nailed to a wall'. Perhaps as a young man he had come off as a bit uptight. But he'd had to grow up at a very early age. His mother and his little brother had depended upon him for their emotional well-being.

Frederica had always been his opposite: light-hearted, mischievous, and fun-loving. He worried that she shared some of the same wild traits as his father. She didn't care for society's opinion or approbation. She would always do what she wanted and hang the consequences. And what was worse was that she made *him* feel unsettled and out of control.

He had never been foolish enough to believe that he would marry for love. Dukes didn't. But he had intended to make his own choice. To select a young woman of good birth and family that he both admired and cared for. One that returned his preference. A woman that he could be faithful to for the rest of his life.

The head groom handed him the reins. 'Here is your horse, Your Grace.'

Samuel blinked, still getting used to his father's title. 'Thank you, Jepson. Please advise my valet that I no longer have a London house, so he had better meet me with my gear at Grillon's Hotel.'

'Very good, Your Grace.'

He mounted his stallion and cantered off at a spanking pace. At last being able to work out some of his frustrations.

Chapter Three

Samuel stopped first at his club, Whites, where he freshened up after his ride and had a couple of glasses of ratafia. He next stopped at Manton's, where he shot clay pigeons for over an hour and left no longer feeling as if he was going to backfire like a cannon. His final stop was in Berkley Square. He rubbed his temples, trying to release some of the tension from his body. It didn't help. The butler, Mr Harper, bowed painstakingly to him and asked him to come in. The smiling butler then requested that His Grace follow him upstairs. He had known this man all his life and Harper was clearly aware of what was supposed to happen on this auspicious day. Samuel couldn't help but wonder how many unions planned from the cradle actually resulted in marriage. He wished the number were one fewer.

The butler opened the door to a well-lit room. It was decorated in shades of yellow and the sounds of Beethoven floated from a grand pianoforte. Samuel's eyes alighted on Lady Hampford, who stood to meet him. He sucked his cheeks in. He'd always liked her. She was everything his mother was not: strong, determined, and independent. He'd wished his own mama had half of her resolve. Except now that selfsame resolve was coming for him and he no longer admired it. He resented it and her, greatly.

Lady Hampford raised a white-gloved finger to her lips and looked meaningfully at her daughter playing the instrument. He followed her gaze and saw Frederica. He would have recognised her face anywhere. That stubborn nose. Determined mouth. Slanted eyebrows with diabolical intent. But there were subtle and beautiful changes about her. Even sitting down, he could tell that her figure was tall. Her hair was a rich brown and her lips generous enough to kiss. The fashion for high-waist dresses emphasised her ample chest and trim waist. It was the figure of a woman. A diamond of the first water. He wished that his palms didn't feel sweaty in his gloves or that his collar wasn't quite so tight around his neck.

Her face was slightly flushed as she finished the crescendo and ended the piece with a laugh of triumph, 'Ha!'

His heart jumped, as did his pulse.

Frederica's hazel eyes met Samuel's blue ones, and she immediately stood up from the piano bench. 'I did not hear the door open. Please forgive me, Lord Pelford, for not rising immediately to meet you.'

Samuel was an honest man—especially with himself. He could not deny that the young woman before him was very attractive. Somehow Frederica had managed to grow into her long limbs, for the last time he had seen her she was all knees and elbows. She walked towards him gracefully, with a light step. She held out her hand, and he bowed briefly over it. He caught a hint of her scent, an attractively earthy combination of linden and conifer.

'Why do not we all sit down?' Lady Hampford suggested, smiling at him. 'Shall I ring for some tea?'

He shook his head, holding up one gloved hand. 'Not on my account, please. And if you will forgive my abruptness, I would prefer to speak alone with Lady Frederica. My time is limited and there is a question of great importance I wish to ask her.'

Lady Hampford gave him a dazzling smile and left the room as if she were leaving a pair of young lovers and not childhood enemies. Samuel sat on a chair across from Frederica, where he could readily observe her features. He smiled slightly when he realised that he was not the only one surprised at what he saw. The colour in her cheeks was high and her lips upturned into the slightest of smiles.

'I suppose I ought to apologise for putting the bear cub in your room when last I saw you,' Frederica said, in a completely unrepentant tone. She may have grown into a beauty, but her personality had not changed one whit. Something about her had always irritated him like a rash on his skin.

'Freddie, do not bother apologising,' Samuel said sardonically. 'I should not wish for our relationship to begin with a lie.'

She let out a crow of laughter and gave him a beguiling grin. 'You are not as stupid as you used to be, and no one calls me Freddie any more.'

'And you are not as skinny as you used to be,' he retorted.

She laughed again and more colour came into her cheeks. She was an attractive woman with curves even courtesans would be jealous of. 'I suppose I am not. But then, neither are you. You seem twice as broad as before.'

'Do you wish to marry me?' he asked bluntly, hoping that by some miracle she would be the one to release him from this unwanted obligation.

'No,' she said honestly, raising her eyebrows. 'Do you wish to marry me?'

No, but I wouldn't mind kissing you.

Where had that thought come from? He pulled at his collar, feeling rather hot and betrayed by his own body.

'Heavens no! I do not even know you.'

And I've never liked you.

Frederica laughed loudly at this and his lips twitched. Earlier in the day, he would have thought that there was nothing humorous in his situation. But he'd forgotten that Frederica could be funny; unfortunately, in the past, he'd been the butt of most of her jokes.

She sobered first, clearing her throat. 'Perhaps we could become better acquainted now that we are no longer children? I long for adventure and purpose. And no doubt you have had many adventures and political intrigues whilst on the Continent.'

Samuel stiffened. He hated how the aristocracy glamourized war with their fancy uniforms and formal parades. There was nothing adventurous or exciting about a battle. It was loud. There was so much blood, the wounded, and the burying of your friends. 'Those stories are not fit for a woman's ears.'

Her lips tightened into a straight line. 'Quite a set-down.'

He could not help but smirk back at her as he watched Frederica struggle within herself to be civil. As a child, she would not have even tried. She would have yelled at him, hurled an object, or got her revenge when he least expected it. Usually with a dead rodent or a live snake whilst he was sleeping. Still, he had loved the summers he'd spent at Hampford Castle with her older brothers, avoiding Frederica whenever possible. Her brother Charles had been his best friend and closest companion. He was also the first person he'd seen buried. After his death, Samuel had resented how Frederica had tried to take her brother's place as his friend. She was a poor substitute for Charles, who had been a good listener, clever, and kind.

Little had Samuel known then how many friends he would lose in the war. How many pieces of himself he would bury with them.

After a few moments she said in a lighter tone, 'Shall I receive many set-downs as your wife?'

'I haven't asked you to be my wife,' he pointed out.

Frederica lifted her eyebrows in an arched look and talked with her hands. 'No, you have not. And I have not said yes, but somehow, I believe we will both find ourselves arrayed in finery and in front of the Archbishop of Canterbury before too long.'

'Dreadful thought.'

'I know. It quite gives me the dismals.'

She was so quick-witted. Samuel was smirking at her, as if they were friends instead of old acquaintances who shared a keen dislike of each other. But there was little choice but to make her his wife, so he'd have to make the best of it.

He got out of his chair and kneeled before her. 'I have found in the army, that if something has to be done, it might as well be done at once: Lady Frederica, will you do me the honour of becoming my wife?'

Frederica covered her mouth with her hands and fell into a fit of chuckles.

He caught his breath in surprise, his heartbeat quickened in annoyance. Shaking his head, Samuel asked, 'Why can you never be serious?'

She laughed harder and tears began to form in her lovely hazel eyes. Unexpectedly, her mirth warmed his heart and Samuel struggled to keep his own mouth from forming a smile. Maybe he needed a little lightness in his life.

It was a ridiculous situation that they had found themselves in. Engineered by their meddlesome mothers and his dead father's extravagance.

He handed her his handkerchief embroidered with his initials and the Pelford crest and said in the same exaggerated formality, 'Dearest Lady Frederica, please accept this small token of my high esteem.'

Frederica snorted and giggled harder. Eventually, she stopped laughing and took the handkerchief and dabbed at her eyes, breathing in and out slowly. Her gaze met his and it felt like she was seeing through his ragged soul. He was not sure that he wanted her to see the darkness that raged inside of him now. The terrible secrets that he held in his heart. The burdens he carried.

Taking her hand in both of his, he said, 'Am I to receive an answer, or shall I spend the afternoon kneeling on the floor?'

'My lord duke,' she said with mock formality. 'I should be most honoured to become your wife.'

He kissed her hand before standing up. 'Well, it is about time, my knees were getting sore.'

Frederica got to her feet, as well. They stood eye to eye inches apart, for she was a very tall young woman. Samuel impulsively leaned towards her, placing a hand on her cheek. Frederica did not startle, nor move away. If anything, she leaned towards him. Considering that enough encouragement, he placed his mouth on hers. Her silken lips were cold at first, but warmed quickly. And to his great surprise, Frederica returned his kiss with ardour. Her arms wrapped around him, pulling him closer. Samuel's heart beat fast as his free hand found the dip of her waist and pressed her against him. She tasted of mint and honey, everything that was fresh and wonderful and bright. He was not sure which one of them deepened the kiss, but neither of them seemed to want the embrace to end. Perhaps they had been using their mouths wrongly with each other all these years.

Lips were not made for fighting, but for kissing.

At last, he lifted his mouth from hers. They looked at each other, both breathing heavily. His mind whirled. Frederica put her delicately gloved hands on the lapels of his green coat and pulled him to her for another open-mouthed kiss. He couldn't believe that *she* was kissing *him*! This time her lips were wet, warm, inviting, and deliciously familiar. Samuel put his hands over hers on his chest. Wanting to keep them there. To hold her close. His tongue slipped into her mouth and her tongue tangled with his. If this was another fight, for once he would let her win.

The footman coughed. Samuel and Frederica dropped their hands and quickly parted. He felt more flustered than a raw recruit on the first day. The footman opened the door for the Duchess of Hampford to walk into the room. He stood up taller and nearly saluted her like a general. Lady Hampford had not seen the embrace, and Samuel hoped that she presumed the heightened colour in both of their cheeks resulted from the embarrassment of the situation.

'Have I returned too soon?'

'No indeed, Duchess,' Samuel said, bowing to her. 'Your daughter has been kind enough to accept my proposal of marriage, and I was just begging her leave to write to her father and send an announcement to the newspapers. I do not have much time. The Duke of Wellington demands I return with all possible speed.'

Lady Hampford bit her lower lip, nodding. 'To Vienna?'

Swallowing heavily, Samuel shook his head. 'No, ma'am. I am to meet General Lord Wellington in Brussels, where he will take command of the coalition army.'

'Ah,' Lady Hampford said, tipping her chin. 'I will not detain you any further, Duke. But if you have time to visit us again before you leave, we would be honoured to receive you at any time.'

The Duchess of Hampford held out her gloved hand, and Samuel bowed briefly over it. He then turned back to Frederica and surprised both ladies, and himself, by kissing her on the cheek. Frederica flushed a deeper shade of red and brought her hand to where his lips had brushed her skin. He left the room, escorted by the footman who had opened it.

Feeling lighter than he had all day, Samuel slipped the man a coin and touched his hat. 'Thank you for the cough.'

Chapter Four

'Samuel has certainly become quite broad-shouldered since he went to war,' Mama said after the Duke of Pelford left. 'I scarcely know if I would have recognised him on the street.'

Frederica walked to the window, watching Samuel below hail a hackney coach and get in. She was relieved to see him go. She'd tried to unsettle him with the kiss and it had backfired most dreadfully. Her pulse beat faster than if she'd run a mile. Samuel had changed. Or she had. Perhaps them both.

He was neither short nor tall, but a stocky fellow with thick dark brown hair that he wore shorter than was fashionable. His eyes were a pale shade of blue and his chin jutted out, giving him a determined look. He had left England a boy and returned a man with a powerful upper body. He was too muscular to be shown to advantage in skintight cream pantaloons, nor in the green coat made for him. She thought he would look best in uniform, where his brawn was intimidating.

She turned back to her mother. 'His appearance has changed, but he is still as stubborn and stupid as ever.

He informed me that his adventures on the Continent were not fit for a woman's ears. As if a woman's ears were any different than a man's! Clearly, he has never dissected a cadaver. I can assure you that they are precisely the same.'

Mama raised one eyebrow. 'You obviously did not mind too much, or you would not have let him kiss you.'

Frederica felt a blush suffuse her cheeks. Her mother was too sharp by half. 'It was only on the cheek, Mama.'

Her mother shook her head, a smile on her lips. 'You are not my eldest child. I know the look of someone who has been thoroughly kissed.'

His kisses had been knee-weakeningly wonderful, Frederica admitted to herself. Not that she would admit as such to her mother. 'Samuel's kisses were not as good as the Italian count's.'

Mama snickered, a funny sound, coming from her. 'It would be unfair of us to compare our Englishmen to their Latin counterparts. They will always be deemed inferior.'

Frederica laughed and took a seat next to her mother on the sofa, trying to calm the wild beating in her heart. She didn't want to admit to liking anything about the match. She would lose negotiating ground. Leaning her head on her mother's shoulder, she said, 'Sacrifices must be made in all battles.'

Her mother put an arm around her and sighed. 'That horrid Napoleon has quite overturned all of my plans with his wars.'

'Perhaps he was not considering your convenience.'

Mama chuckled again. 'He certainly was not, or he would have waited to escape for another month or two. The nuisance! Now we must be serious. I do not think we should purchase your wedding clothes until we are able to set a date, which I suppose again will be at the little emperor's convenience. It is bad enough that he has kept most of Europe in war for twenty years, quite making it impossible to visit all my favourite cities. Or sell them my perfumes.'

Frederica sat forward, struck with an idea. 'Mama, why do we not follow Samuel to Brussels? Lady Jersey was bemoaning the other day how so many of the best families are abroad and my dear friend Georgy Lennox is already there.'

Her mother took a deep breath, clearly thinking about Frederica's suggestion. 'I cannot deny that your idea does find favour with me. Like yourself, I wish we were in sunny Greece with your sisters and father, instead of rainy old England. And I do believe a trip to Brussels would alleviate some of the tedium. However, I must have your word that you will behave with the utmost propriety at all times. And that you will do everything in your power to further your match with Samuel. Nothing is final until the vows have been said and the marriage papers signed, and I do not wish for you to do anything that might jeopardise your future.'

Leaning back against the sofa, Frederica put her hands behind her head. 'Sign over half the company to me first and I will behave with perfect propriety.'

Instead of being affronted, her mother smiled. 'I will have Matthew draw up the contract at once, giving you fifty percent of the stocks in Duchess & Co. And we will bring all the soap cakes that you have already made to Brussels with us. I can think of no better advertising than the soap used to tend our wounded, brave soldiers.'

'Thank you, Mama,' Frederica said, kissing her on the cheek. Then she ran up a flight of stairs to her bedroom. She scrambled onto her enormous four-poster bed and jumped up and down—giggling. She would own half of the company and her mother would produce her red scented soaps. At last, her life would have meaning and purpose.

Chapter Five

Brussels, May 1815

They'd settled into their Brussels lodging just the day before, with barely enough time for her maid to unpack her belongings before preparing for their first invitation. Frederica entered the ballroom in a crimson gown with a high waist and a matching crimson gauze overlay, delighted that she was no longer required to wear white like a young debutante. It was a dull colour. Frederica's brown curls framed her face and Wade had intertwined fresh red roses into the chignon on the back of her head. For jewellery, she wore only a single round ruby surrounded by a cluster of diamonds. It hung on a thin silver chain around her long throat. She was not surprised when several eyes focused on her. Both she and her mother were taller than the average height and some of the highest-ranking guests of the party.

Next to them stood the Duchess of Richmond. Lady Richmond was a short woman with large green expressive eyes that missed very little. 'Lady Frederica, may I introduce my nephew, Captain Mark Wallace, as an amiable dance partner?'

A young man not much older than Frederica walked out from behind the Duchess of Richmond. He was tall and fashionably slender. He had curly black hair, dancing blue eyes, and an engaging smile. He bowed to Frederica, and she curtsied. Her mother nodded, giving her permission, and Frederica held out her hand. Captain Wallace took it and led her back to the dance floor. Frederica had more time to study her partner while they performed a country reel. He really was quite devastatingly handsome.

Quirking up one eyebrow, she asked, 'Are you going to speak to me or just smile at me?'

The young captain threw back his head and laughed. 'I am trying to make a good impression. Cousin Georgy suggested that I not say a word.'

Frederica grinned back at him, wrinkling her nose. 'Would you make a bad impression if you spoke?'

'Indubitably,' he said, with a slight Scottish accent and another grin. Both were very attractive. 'I invariably say the one thing that I ought not.'

She laughed out loud as she took his hands in the circular figure. 'You need not worry about my good opinion.'

'No?' he said with a wink, releasing her hand for the turn and then taking it again. 'Has some malicious person already told you that I am a second son?'

Frederica touched her chest and pretended to be shocked for only a moment, before spinning to the correct place to take his hand again. 'No indeed, if they had I would not have danced with you. For I make it my policy to only dance with older sons, in full possession of their fortunes.'

He pulled her closer, his hand on her waist. 'And

I usually only dance with heiresses. But I thought I would make an exception tonight, and dance with the most beautiful lady in the room.'

Nodding her head, Frederica smiled at his compliment. 'Perhaps I am an heiress. How much money do you require for a young lady to be considered for courtship?'

Captain Wallace twirled Frederica around and around. 'Oh, not much more than one hundred thousand pounds.'

'Just a little pocket money.'

He let out another guffaw of laughter and gave her another devastatingly attractive smile. 'I should like to be kept in the same style I have grown accustomed to, when married.'

Her body shook with silent laughter. Frederica turned and saw two people standing on the side of the dance floor giving her a stern gaze. The first was her mother and the second her betrothed. Heat pumped through her body like blood. She had been right. A uniform suited Samuel's muscular form perfectly. He wore a scarlet coat with a high collar, gold braid on the shoulders, and a navy sash across his broad chest. He looked formidable and a bit frightening. He positively glared at her. She hoped that he felt jealous. Growing up she had chased him, wanting to be included with the older children. He'd left her behind over and over again. This time she wanted *him* to do the chasing and she would decide when and if she allowed him to catch her.

Captain Wallace glanced in the same direction. 'Who is that stocky officer over there on the left side of the room that is scowling at me?'

Turning away, she said, 'Colonel Lord Pelford.'

'I have heard of him. He is an aide-de-camp to the

Duke of Wellington. My cousin Alexander has mentioned him several times. Alexander says that he is a positive demon in action. No better man on the field. Do you know the fellow well?'

'When we were children, we hated each other with a passion,' Frederica said, and added conscientiously, 'but not now we are betrothed to be married.'

The captain clenched his fist and struck his heart, his eyes downcast. 'How is it that every beautiful girl is already taken?'

'I have two younger sisters.'

'A poor consolation,' he said with a mournful sigh.

Frederica gave him another beaming smile. She had not met such an amusing fellow in all her London Seasons. 'And how do you know? They could be much prettier than me. You would get along famously with them if you don't mind snakes or mice.'

He stopped mid dance step. 'What?'

Gurgling with laughter, she tugged him to the right place in the line. 'My sisters are both naturalists and extremely fond of all God's creatures. Particularly the animals that no one else seems to like.'

The music ended and they bowed to each other. The captain still grinned and Frederica thought he was either playing at being a fortune-hunter or that he was the most skilled one that she had ever come across.

Captain Wallace took her hand to escort her to the side of the room, not ten feet from Samuel. The captain did not release her fingers; instead, he bent over her hand and kissed it. Thanking her profusely for being his partner. Frederica glanced to her side, to see Samuel looking like he had swallowed an ostrich egg whole. His cheeks were as red as his scarlet coat. The two gentlemen could not have been more different. Samuel scowled and Captain Wallace smirked.

Her betrothed strode purposefully towards her and slightly bowed. 'Lady Frederica, may I have this waltz?'

'Yes.'

He tightly gripped her right gloved hand in his large left one. He led her back onto the dance floor and then put his right arm around her waist and led her in perfect circles around the room. For all his strength and bulkiness, there was a gracefulness to his dancing. A precision that she would expect from a high-ranking officer in the army. She breathed in his scent of leather, boot-blacking, and musk. He wore no cologne, but that did not surprise her. The clean and natural scent suited him very well.

Frederica leaned in a little closer to sniff again—she was going to be a professional perfumer after all. She breathed in deeply before saying, 'You are an accomplished dancer.'

'Wellington requires all of his staff to be adept at the art.'

The corners of her mouth tilted upward. 'And do you always frown at your partners? Or only the ones you are betrothed to?'

Samuel reluctantly returned her smile and nodded his head in the direction of the captain. 'You seemed to enjoy dancing with young Wallace. A Scot, I believe, and the younger son of the Earl of Inverness.'

'I did,' she said in her sauciest voice. 'He is so handsome and there is something irresistible about an accent. I could listen to him speak for hours.'

He snorted, his lips forming a grim line.

If he were one of her unwanted suitors, she would

have allowed him to remain jealous. But he was not. Like it or not, without love, but with a company and a dukedom, they were getting married.

Leaning closer, her nose brushed his. 'Captain Wallace was describing what he is looking for in a wife—a pair of lovely eyes and pots of money. I, alas, do not qualify. Not being nearly rich enough to meet his basic needs as a second son.'

Samuel's lips twitched as if he were fighting them not to grin; his military training must have won out, for he kept his mouth straight. 'Are you ever serious?'

'Occasionally, when the time requires. And never while dancing. I love to dance.'

'Well, I would seriously like to take you outside.'

Was it a challenge? She could not and would not back down. She was not a green debutante, she knew exactly what her betrothed wanted to do out there. Perhaps if they talked less and kissed more, they would have a rather good relationship on the whole. Not that she was eager for his embraces. Of course not. This was a battle for dominance and she intended to win it. 'What a pleasant thought. I should like that very much.'

He turned her abruptly and led her to the opposite side of the room near the door to an antechamber and into the courtyard. They walked past the gravel walkway to the green grass in the centre to a secluded nook behind a statue and shadowed by a large circular bush. Samuel stopped, still holding her hand.

Ignoring the fluttery feeling in her stomach, she shook her head. 'Surely, a seasoned officer like yourself knows better than to stop at the first bush? It is always wiser to go farther back. You are less likely to find a previous occupant, or to get caught kissing by a chaperone.'

One corner of his lips tilted upward. 'Is that why you think I brought you out here?'

'Of course!'

Frederica pulled his hand, leading him farther into the dark garden. She did not stop until they were in a corner that was blocked on one side by a stone wall and the other by a prickly rose bush. 'Now this spot is quite secluded.'

Samuel's grip on her hand tightened slightly. 'Have you been to many secluded spots?'

Wrapping her arms around Samuel's neck, she pressed her body against his. He was all firmness and tight muscles. His brawn made her feel small, a rare thing for a voluptuous woman. 'A lady never kisses and tells.'

'Neither does a gentleman,' he said, before slanting his mouth to hers.

She could feel him everywhere, for he was about her same height. His muscular thighs pressed against hers. It was wickedly exciting. His lips moved over and over hers in a beautiful rhythm, almost like music. Frederica ran her fingers through his short, thick hair, eliciting a soft moan from Samuel. She pulled his hair slightly, before opening her mouth and deepening the kiss. He responded by tightening his hold on her. The pressure of his lips matching the pressure of his arms. It was heaven. Even better than kissing Conte de Ferrari, the fiery Italian she had met whilst her family were staying in Rome.

When he nibbled on her lower lip, it was more exciting than reading the most sensational Gothic novel. Her imagination was nothing on the reality of his embraces. Samuel moved his mouth from hers and made a trail of kisses to her throat, still holding her tightly in his arms. She could hear his heart thundering in his chest. Her own heart was just as loud and wild.

Frederica placed her two hands on his chest and pushed him away slightly, but stayed encircled in his strong arms. 'Why did you bring me here?'

'A singularly stupid question,' Samuel answered, pulling her back to him and kissing her neck in a sensitive spot below her ear.

She could not help herself, she purred like a kitten. She'd always enjoyed kissing and Samuel was rather good at it. She allowed him several more kisses before she gently pushed him farther away from her. 'One more singularly stupid question—have you ever been in love?'

'I think every man of four and twenty has at least imagined himself to be in love once or twice,' he replied lightly. 'And you?'

Raising her eyebrows and shrugging her shoulders, Frederica grinned. 'Oh, several times.'

'Really?'

'The first a footman when I was thirteen. Then an under groom. His name was Jacob, he helped me put the bear cub in your room. Helen and Becca helped, as well. Then there were a few lords and an Italian count.'

He creased his forehead. 'So, you haven't been waiting for me all these years.'

Biting her lower lip, she shook her head. 'No. Did you think I was?'

Samuel stiffened. She could feel the tenseness of his leg muscles. The tightness of his entire body. 'No.'

Frederica gave him a playful shove on his shoulder, before kissing his cheek. 'You are jealous. How delicious! But you need not be. Truly. I never fancied myself in love longer than a fortnight. How about you? Was there a dark Spanish beauty? Or a saucy German baroness? No. I know, a young French comtesse with an elderly husband.'

He stepped back from her and she immediately missed the warmth of his body against hers. The contours of his shape and how they fitted so perfectly against her own curves.

Samuel cleared his throat, then swallowed heavily. 'I suppose I should bring you back to the party before your presence is missed by your mother.'

She linked her arm with his and leaned her head against his shoulder. 'Spoil-sport. I merely wish to know you better. Next time, I will make you confess before we kiss.'

He returned them to the ballroom and they were met at the door by her dear friend Lady Georgiana Lennox. She was a short brunette with large brown eyes. Her hair was a darker shade of brown than Frederica's and her skin was a paler cream. Georgy took Frederica's arm from Samuel's and led her to another antechamber that led to a retiring room.

'What are we doing, Georgy?'

'Fixing your hair,' she replied, deftly arranging several curls in Frederica's hair that had fallen into disorder. 'Did you want the whole room to know that you dallied in the garden with your betrothed?'

'I do not know what I would do without you, Georgy,' Frederica said earnestly. She looked around for a mirror, but could not see one. 'Am I presentable now?'

'Yes.' Georgy linked arms with Frederica again and they walked back to the party. 'Your Colonel Lord Pelford certainly looks strong and—do not eat me when I say this—very handsome.'

Frederica's nostrils flared. 'I suppose he is pleasant to look at. Especially from behind.'

Blushing easily, Georgy laughed. 'Am I to understand that you are more reconciled to your engagement?'

She winked at her friend. 'Of course I am. Why else would I be kissing him in the shrubbery?'

'Sport,' Georgy answered and they both laughed as they left the retiring room.

Captain Wallace walked up to the ladies and bowed. If she had not just kissed Samuel, she might have been tempted to see how the Scots compared to Italian counts.

Bowing her head, Georgy curtsied. 'Cousin Mark.'

'Captain Wallace,' Frederica said, giving him a nod of acknowledgement.

The captain smiled at them and somehow placed himself between them with a lady on each arm. He was certainly a smooth manoeuvrer.

'Any luck finding an heiress?' Frederica asked coyly, squeezing his arm.

Georgy giggled and swatted at her cousin's shoulder. 'You didn't tell her, did you?'

'Lady Frederica,' he said in mock surprise. 'I am shocked that you would treat a fellow's delicate confidences thus.'

Grinning, Frederica tapped his arm with her fan. 'Oh, I am sorry. But it is only Georgy after all, and she is your cousin, so I assumed she was already aware of your matrimonial plans. And is possibly a co-conspirator.'

The captain flashed them both a knee-melting smile. 'If she is "only Georgy" can I be "only Mark"?'

Georgy let go of her cousin's arm. 'I can see that I am not needed for this conversation, I shall go beg a partner for the country dance.'

She walked away from them and 'only Mark' asked Frederica for the next dance. She nodded, looking around the room for Samuel. She saw him making one in the circle of men around the infamous Caroline Lamb, who'd had a public affair with Lord Byron. Lady Caro had a small pixie-like face, surrounded with a mass of short dark curls. She had big brown eyes, a little nose, and a petite red mouth, which she often wore in a pout when she was not laughing. Frederica thought that Lady Caro looked practically naked in her thin white gauzy dress. She must have dampened her chemise. The lady's form was willowy, as unlike Frederica's full figure as possible. Samuel's face was animated when he spoke and Frederica heard Lady Caro's unmistakable high shrill giggle ringing across the room. Frederica scowled across from Mark as they lined up for the country dance. Samuel had not looked so happy speaking with her.

'Is something wrong?' he asked, leading her through the next form.

Frederica gave a ready laugh. She was not some love-struck miss. She had known Samuel her entire life and she was not about to beg for his favour now. 'You tread on my foot!'

Twirling her around, he shook his head. 'Nay, that is impossible. All fortune-hunters are great dancers. It is one of the rules.'

She did not have to fake a smile this time. 'And pray, what are the other fortune-hunter rules?'

'The first,' he said, pulling her towards him. 'You

must be handsome. The second, charming. And the third—'

'Insolvent,' she supplied.

Mark stuttered and missed his step for the first time that night. He grinned at her sheepishly and she thought that he was indeed handsome, charming, and a great dancer. She did not stop smiling until she saw Samuel promenade by with Lady Caro on his arm. Frederica had never liked Lord Byron as a person, his poetry was rather good, but she did not blame him for dropping Lady Caro. She could have happily dropped the woman into the English Channel at that very moment.

Jealousy, she discovered, was a most unpleasant perfume. There was nothing for it, but to ignore Samuel for the rest of the night. She flirted in French when she danced with Belgian nobles, and in English with officers from the British Army. She never lacked for a partner. Unfortunately, neither did Samuel.

Not that she was watching him.

She was not.

Because she did not care about him at all.

Chapter Six

There had been balls in the Peninsula. Parties in Madrid, but nothing like the endless string of entertainments in Brussels. Samuel could have happily missed most of them, but the Duke of Wellington insisted that his staff attend in full dress uniform. He had already attended a picnic that afternoon and he would have preferred an early rest to another night dancing. Being an aide-de-camp to the general kept him busy all day.

Taking a deep breath, he walked up the steps to the rented house where Lady Snow was throwing her ball. He was met at the door by none other than the Prince of Orange.

'If you had any more feathers in your cap, I would have shot you for a bird,' the prince said in a slow English drawl, with only the slightest of accents.

Samuel bowed formally before the young prince. 'I doubt you could hit a bird with your aim. Even one of my size, Your Royal Highness.'

His friend barked out a laugh. 'Only the English know how to insult with pomp and circumstance. You can keep your fine bows for the ladies.'

'I should not wish to steal them all from you, Slender Billy.'

The nickname was one only close friends were allowed to call him. Samuel and the prince had attended Eton together as boys and they'd both served in Spain under the Duke of Wellington. Although they were the same age, they were not at all alike. Samuel was broad, while Billy was angular. Samuel had a thick thatch of dark brown hair, and Billy's thin brown curls had already begun to recede. The prince was a heavy drinker and sometimes silly, while Samuel was known for being sombre. Despite their differences, there was a steady friendship between them.

'You must not steal ladies from me, you know. I have already lost one royal bride,' Slender Billy said, with a curl of his upper lip. 'To lose a second would smack of carelessness.'

'At least you will not have the Prince Regent for a father-in-law.'

The prince sneered. 'Nor the mad grandfather. I wonder if insanity runs in families. I quite thought that Princess Charlotte suffered from it.'

Raising an eyebrow, he asked, 'When she ended your engagement?'

Billy shook his head. 'No. When she entered it in the first place. Completely mad.'

Samuel tried to hold in his laugh, but it came out in several snorts. His friend grinned broadly.

Swallowing his mirth, Samuel said, 'She would have been lucky to have you as a husband, my friend. Just think how envious Princess Charlotte will be when you become the hero of the Napoleonic Wars.'

Billy shook his finger before pointing. 'She will lament the loss of me, I am certain. But over there. Isn't that your filly?'

His gaze followed the direction of the prince's finger. Frederica looked nothing like a horse. Her net gown was a celestial blue that clung to her generous curves and dipped rather low in the front. Samuel quite enjoyed the view, but wished that no other men in the room could. Not that her neckline was at all scandalous, there was simply so much beautifully rounded skin on display. And he knew how she felt pressed against his chest. A surge of desire shot through his body to his belly. He wanted to take her to a secluded spot in the garden again. He needed to feel the soft texture of her lips moving over his.

'For a fellow forced into an engagement,' Billy said, 'you do not seem overly upset by it. I nearly drank myself into a stupor when I had to pay my addresses to Charlotte.'

Shaking his head, Samuel retorted, 'Of course, I don't wish to marry her.'

'I do not claim to read minds, but from the expression on your face, I am pretty sure what you were thinking about her would require marriage banns to be read. She is certainly a goddess of a woman, a pocket of Venus. Ah, and you do not like when other men compliment her either. Am I to understand that you do not want her, but you do not want another man to have her?'

Samuel's hands clenched into fists and his school friend laughed merrily at his expense. 'Of course not.'

'A piece of wisdom, Duke,' Billy said, the first time he used Samuel's new title. 'Lie to others, but never to yourself.'

Clapping him on the shoulder, the prince left for the

card room. Billy was overly fond of drinking, gaming, womanising, and, if the rumours were true, male lovers. He did them all with the enthusiasm of a king. Turning back to see Frederica, Samuel noticed that Colonel Scovell was by her side. The colonel was a man of lower birth who had risen in the ranks with his excellent cryptography skills. In the Peninsula, he'd decoded the Great Paris Cipher and employed army guides as intelligence officers.

Samuel sauntered over to them. Scovell was around forty years of age and quite bald on top with thick sideburns running down his cheeks. His small eyes were keen and Samuel doubted that the man missed any detail. He was Wellington's spymaster after all.

The colonel bowed to Samuel. 'Colonel Lord Pelford, I was just becoming acquainted with your betrothed. I would never have guessed that Lady Frederica was English. Her French is flawless.'

His betrothed gave the spymaster a beaming grin and Samuel doubted that the man was thinking about her French conjugations.

'I am a lucky man, Colonel Scovell,' Samuel said slowly. 'Lady Frederica is a very accomplished young lady.'

Frederica's eyes danced with mischief. 'And you have not even seen me with a pistol, sir! Back at Hampford Castle, I could even best the duke in marksmanship.'

He had expected the proper gentleman, with an even primmer wife, to be shocked by Frederica's unfeminine talent, but it was interest and not censure in the man's countenance. He appeared pleased.

Contrarily, Samuel did not want Frederica to please any man but himself. Taking her elbow tightly, he nodded to Scovell and tugged her towards the dance floor. Like most insipid English balls, it started with a quadrille. He did not release his hold on her arm until she was standing in the right formation and he took his place next to her. The musicians began to play and Frederica weaved through the figures with him.

'That was a cavemanlike manoeuvre,' she whispered when their hands met. 'A gentleman, even a duke, is supposed to ask a lady to dance before dragging her onto the floor.'

Clearing his throat, he felt the blood rush to his face. Frederica did bring out the basest parts of his personality. His spite, resentment, jealousy, and uncontrollable desire. He wanted to grab her and tell everyone in the room that she was his.

They were not allowed to look at her.

Or touch her.

Mine.

Samuel had never known himself to lose control of his emotions or his body before. He did not wish to be a wanton like his father, giving in to his primal lusts to the point that he ignored his responsibilities as a duke and his duties to the family. Samuel wanted to be better. He needed to be the sort of duke and father that his brother could look up to.

Like the Duke of Hampford.

While his own father had been whoring in town, Frederica's father had taught him how to ride a horse, fish, shoot, hunt, swim, and race a curricle. He'd loved going to Hampford Castle in the summers and helping care for the menagerie of animals. He had enjoyed every part of it except for a loud, irritating girl that had followed him around like a golden retriever. She'd demanded to do whatever her brothers and Samuel were doing. And no matter how hard he and Charles tried to shake her, Frederica always found them. She even parroted what they said like their annoying yellow macaw with a missing claw, Mademoiselle Jaune. But what was worse, she always beat him at everything. She was a faster swimmer. A lighter rider. A better aim and swifter on her feet, but that was before she had grown in quite the opposite directions.

Frederica's gaze met his.

'Please forgive my rough handling,' Samuel said, holding her hand for an instant longer than he should have. 'I promise that it will not happen again.'

He would not be like his father. He would remain in control of his body. His emotions.

Wrinkling her nose, Frederica grinned at him. 'I was only teasing, Samuel. I rather liked your caveman treatment.'

'Shall I throw you over my shoulder and drag you to a nearby cave?'

She held her breath. A beautiful blush growing up from her neck and into her face. For all her talk of love and kisses, she was still innocent in the ways that mattered. 'I would say yes, but I do not think we would make it past Mama. As you can see, she has placed herself near the door to the gardens. We will not escape so easily this time. It will be difficult for you, I'm afraid, but you'll be forced to speak to me using real words, instead of grunting like a gorilla.'

His entire body bristled at the comparison to a great ape.

'Alas,' Samuel said in a voice barely above a whisper. 'Talking with you is like speaking to a magpie.'

Frederica shook her head. 'Unoriginal. I expected better from you. But since we cannot converse politely, I suppose we will have to dance instead.'

The hair rose on the back of his neck. Waltzing would have to do, but he wanted to be closer to her. To silence her saucy mouth by tasting her sweet flavour on his lips. Making polite conversation with Frederica was nearly as agonising as a battlefield wound and twice as deadly.

Chapter Seven

Rubbing the sleep from his eyes, Samuel yawned again. He had stayed up too late dancing the night before and keeping an eye on his badly behaved betrothed. Frederica had flirted outrageously with every man she met. From fortune-hunters to generals. She even blew Samuel a kiss when she was dancing with the Prince of Orange. He tried not to react to her blatant attempts to infuriate him. Even as a little girl, she had always been able to get underneath his skin and get him into trouble.

He kept thinking of their stolen kisses from the first ball she'd attended in Brussels, wishing to repeat the experience. Dreaming about it. Her lips were more practised than any incognita. Her shapely figure would be the envy of any woman. And Frederica was too clever by half. All the mischief that she could get up to in Brussels kept him tossing and turning all night long with his desire for her. Frederica was strong, independent, and completely beautiful. He would have to keep an eye on her to save her from falling into scrapes. They were not in England any more and she couldn't rely on her family or her name to keep her out of trouble.

'A word, Pelford,' General Lord Wellington said.

Samuel followed him to his office. Wellington was a tall man with brown hair and brown eyes under thick brows. His nose was rather large and had a distinctive bump. His lips were thin and pressed tightly together. Despite his air of authority, he was a warm, kind man who cared deeply about his staff members. He made Samuel feel like family. Like he was wanted. Like the words that he spoke mattered.

'In the situation that we are placed at present,' the general said, 'neither at war nor at peace, we are unable to patrol the enemy and ascertain his position by view, or to act offensively upon any part of the French line. All we can do is put our troops in such a situation as, in case of a sudden attack by the enemy, to render them easy to assemble, and to provide against the chance of any being cut off from the rest.'

Samuel sighed, nodding. Their position felt precarious.

Rubbing his nose, Wellington cleared his throat. 'Colonel Scovell has an idea, and after ruminating on it, I think it is rather a good one. I should like for you to travel farther into Belgium and meet with Lieutenant-Colonel Grant and bring back his findings.'

He forced himself to keep in a groan. Samuel had worked with the surly Scotsman before. He was a fine intelligence officer, but he made no attempt at stealth. Dignity or not, Samuel's life would be in danger if he was seen in that man's company. At seventeen, death did not scare him. At four and twenty, there was so much he still wished to do.

Samuel took a sharp intake of breath. One did not say no to the general. 'Of course, Duke.'

General Lord Wellington pressed his two hands together until his fingertips turned white. 'I have also heard that congratulations are in order. It took a few weeks to arrive, but I saw the notice of your nuptials in *The Times*.'

He could feel his cheeks growing hot and his collar shrinking around his neck like a noose. He pulled at it. 'Thank you, Your Grace.'

'And I believe that your betrothed, Lady Frederica Stringham, is now in Brussels with her mother.'

'Yes.'

An unwanted and unexpected wave of jealously swept through Samuel. The general was known to like beautiful women. More than like them. Despite being married, he collected mistresses wherever he went. And women seemed to be drawn to a man with power.

Wellington's smile did nothing to ease his discomfort. 'I hear she is a spirited young lady and Scovell suggested that you might wish to bring her with you, when you meet with Lieutenant-Colonel Colquhoun Grant to pick up his reports. It should allay suspicion from your intelligence activities. Hopefully, people will assume that you are going on pleasure rides with your betrothed.'

He did not know if spending more time with Frederica would be a good thing or not. When he was with her, Samuel could never decide if he would rather wring her neck or kiss her. Or both at the same moment. She loved to infuriate him, and even after all this time, she knew how to press all his buttons. Even if Frederica drove him to the brink of madness daily, he still did not want anything bad to happen to her. It would be dangerous to travel farther into Belgium and be seen in the company of a British Army officer. And he doubted Frederica understood the meaning of the word *caution*.

Swallowing heavily, Samuel said, 'I think Scovell's idea is a clever one, but I do not wish to put a lady in danger.'

'Scovell remarked that Lady Frederica spoke French flawlessly,' the general pressed. 'I do not think the danger will be too great. He believes, as do I, that you both will be able to blend into your surroundings. And if anyone notices you, they will only see a young couple devoted to each other.'

Desiring each other was more like it, but he would not dream of telling his superior that.

'Yes, sir.'

Wellington cleared his throat. 'I should like for you and Lady Frederica to meet Grant tomorrow at midday in the town of Genappe. At a public house called The King of Spain Inn. There, he will give letters for me and perhaps more instructions for you.'

Samuel tried to swallow again, but could not. It was as if there was a ball in his throat obstructing his breathing. He saluted the general. 'We will be there.'

He left Wellington's office and went to the room that had a map of the Continent. He placed one finger on Brussels and the other on Genappe. It was close to seventeen miles by road—it could hardly be considered an afternoon jaunt. Even cutting through fields the journey there and back would take nearly seven hours. Not that he thought Frederica wouldn't be more than able to do it. The Stringhams were a hardy set that swam in freezing rivers and wrestled with wild animals. A thirty-four-mile ride would be nothing to her.

After fetching his hat and gloves, Samuel called for his horse and rode to the rented house on Rue de Lombard where Lady Hampford and her daughter were staying. It did not surprise him that it was one of the nicest and most opulent townhouses in Brussels. The Stringhams spared no expense when it came to their own comfort, or that of their guests.

Harper, the Stringhams' butler who had once helped him down from a tree after Frederica dared him to climb it, opened the door. When Samuel asked to speak to Lady Frederica privately, the man grinned and acted like he was assisting in a grand love affair. But the butler could not have been more wrong—this meeting was strictly army business. Harper ushered him into a sunny parlour and bid him wait for his betrothed.

Frederica opened the door a few minutes later, wearing a thin wrap over what appeared to be her nightgown. Only his betrothed would meet a visitor thus arrayed. Or rather, disarrayed. The prim garment buttoned up to her neck, but it did not hide her gorgeous figure or the fact that she had recently risen from bed. Her lustrous brown curls were falling in waves over her shoulders and down her back. Her hair was as untamed as she was. And there were no cosmetics on her face, but her countenance appeared fresh and fetching. Samuel's fingers itched to touch her skin.

She yawned widely, stretching her arms out. 'I hope someone has died. Otherwise there is no good reason for you to have got me out of bed before I have even had time to drink my hot chocolate.'

Samuel's lips twitched. 'Alas, no one has cocked up their toes. I am here at the Duke of Wellington's request. He wants you to do something for him.'

Frederica raised both eyebrows and stepped closer to him. Her breath smelled like mint. He wondered if she had just eaten some. Samuel would not have put it past the proper Harper to give her the herb. The butler thought that this was a romantic interlude after all.

She pinched his left arm sharply. 'If you're having me on, I will murder you.'

Raising his eyebrows, he lifted his free right hand. 'I swear that I am not jesting or pranking. General Lord Wellington requested you by name.'

Moving her hands, she grabbed his lapels and pulled him closer to her until her body brushed his chest. She was most certainly not wearing a corset and a wave of longing shot through him. He took a sharp inhale of breath and tried to think of England. It did not work.

'Tell me. Tell me. Tell me,' she repeated, her lips close to his.

For a moment, Samuel could not think of anything except for how much he longed to kiss her lips. Touch them. Suck them. Bite them.

Frederica pressed the full length of her body harder against his and he could have spontaneously combusted right there on the spot. 'Samuel, please tell me!'

Shaking his head, he managed to clear his mind enough to say, 'The general would like for you to accompany me to pick up letters from an intelligence officer in Genappe.'

She blinked her long eyelashes twice before squealing loudly enough to wake the entire house. 'He wants me to be a spy!'

Most people thought spies were dishonourable; trust Frederica to want to be one. She threw her arms around his neck and hugged him roughly. His whole body was on fire for her.

Trying to keep his wits about him, Samuel said, 'You are not a spy. The appropriate term is an intelligence officer and you would not be one. You are simply going to accompany me to get the letters. Your presence is to allay suspicion from locals.'

Frederica laughed and pressed a hot kiss underneath his ear. 'Oh, Samuel, I have always wanted to do something truly important and I would love to be a spy for the army.'

She nuzzled his neck and he found himself placing his hands on her waist, pulling her closer to him. Frederica's lips made a slow burn from his neck to the corner of his mouth, pausing a hair before reaching his desperate lips.

'Say that I am a spy and I will kiss you.'

'Companion.'

Giggling, she kissed the other side of his face, near his mouth. 'Not good enough.'

'Intelligence officer,' he whispered.

Frederica kissed his chin with a giggle. 'Spy or nothing!'

Looking into her hazel eyes, he knew he would tell her anything when she was in his arms. 'Fine. You are a spy.'

Her lips pressed against his open ones and her tongue entered his mouth. Her lips ravaged his as her tongue stroked his, finding the most sensitive spots in his mouth. When she moaned against his lips, Samuel knew that she was going to be the death of him. Her fingers moved from his neck to his hair and roved through it, claiming everywhere she touched. He knew when her silken mouth slanted over his again, that Frederica was not a novice kisser, but an experienced one with great technique. He had never felt such a thrill. Not on his first horse ride or sailing with the wind in his hair. It was like learning how to kiss all over again. Frederica had remade the art into her own.

Unmarried young ladies were not supposed to be experienced, but Samuel did not care. No, he enjoyed the fact that she knew how to set them both ablaze. Nor did he care about any of the men she might have kissed or the women that he had. They were all in the past. And not worth remembering.

Frederica broke the kiss, but stayed encircled in his arms. They were both breathing heavily. Her face was beautifully flushed from the kisses. Samuel felt a surge of possessiveness that he had never experienced before. She was his now.

'When do we start?' she asked breathlessly. Her breath against his lips.

'Tomorrow morning at nine o'clock,' he said, kissing her neck beneath her ear. 'And we probably won't be home until four or five o'clock in the afternoon. Be prepared for a long and hard ride.'

'I look forward to it,' Frederica said with a giggle, and he realised that his words had a double meaning. A proper young lady would never make such a euphemistic jest, but he had always known that his betrothed was anything and everything but proper. Which in this particular moment did not seem like such a bad thing.

He forced himself to step back from her, his control already slipping, and the butler was just behind the door. 'Try to be dressed next time when I come.'

She smiled at him saucily. 'Are you sure that you would prefer that?'

Rendered speechless, he left the room without a word and was escorted to the door by Harper. Touching his swollen lips, Samuel realised that the butler had been right after all: it had been a romantic rendezvous.

Chapter Eight

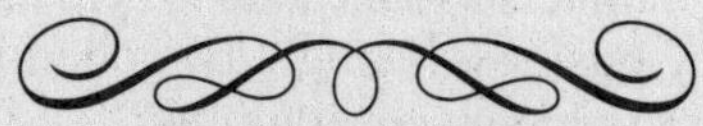

Frederica descended the narrow wooden stairs thirty minutes to nine o'clock the next morning. She wore a lavender riding habit with two rows of brass buttons down the bodice, giving the article of clothing a military look. It was all the rage in London fashion this year. She donned a matching lavender bonnet with feathers that looked more like a sailor's tricorn than a feminine hat. Clutching her reticule, she ensured that her pistol was there and loaded.

Frederica politely asked Harper to call for her horse to be saddled.

The butler bowed to her. 'Shall I have a groom saddle up a horse, as well?'

She shook her head. Spies did not bring along servants. 'No, thank you. Samuel, I mean Lord Pelford, will be my escort.'

The good man raised only one eyebrow. 'Are you sure your mother would approve, my lady?'

Huffing, she hated when Harper caught her behaving badly. Frederica shrugged her shoulders nonchalantly. 'He is my betrothed. It is quite unexceptional for us to go on a ride together.'

'How long will you be gone?'

Holding in her groan, she realised that whilst it might be perfectly acceptable for a suitor or a fiancé to ride with a young lady in the park, it was quite another thing to travel for several miles across country with her. They would not be home until late in the afternoon. And Harper was her friend and not a fool.

'Harper, Samuel has asked me to help him with secret military business. I might be gone for seven or eight hours. Could you cover for me?'

The butler gave her a studied look. Harper had known her since she was a child and could usually tell when Frederica lied. Luckily, this time she was not. 'Very well, Lady Frederica. But be very careful.'

'I am always careful.'

Harper raised one eyebrow again and gave her a dubious look. He knew her too well.

'Fine,' she said with another huff. 'I will be *very* careful. The soul of caution.'

Frederica thought she heard the dear butler mutter that she was *the soul of mischief.* But that did not stop him from calling her a horse and holding the door open for her when it arrived. Jim, her favourite groom, helped her into the side-saddle just as Samuel came down the street. He was not in uniform today, but dressed in a dark riding coat with five shoulder capes. It was severely cut and made him look very handsome. She thanked Jim and gave the butler a wave goodbye, before urging her horse towards her betrothed.

She winked at him saucily. 'I am clothed and ready as requested.'

A little colour stole into Samuel's tanned cheeks. He was obviously attracted to her and Frederica liked having this power over him. When they were younger, he had treated her like an annoying fly that buzzed around him. He either ignored her or tried to swat at her. Now he was practically drooling over her. That Samuel was equally desirable to her, she did not focus on. Or that she had spent the rest of the day after he left thinking about his kisses. He did not need to know that. Being a man and a duke, he already had the upper hand in their arrangement.

'You look—fine,' he said, his eyes avoiding her entire person.

Frederica grinned, directing her horse near his. 'We haven't got all day.'

Samuel nodded, turning his horse around in a circle. Together they weaved through the streets until they had left the city of Brussels. She made to turn onto a small gravel path. Wisely, Frederica had consulted a map for the location of Genappe after he'd left the day before, but Samuel checked her. He told her they would save a mile by cutting through a few fields. She allowed him to lead the way and Frederica revelled in jumping over several fences. They returned to the road and passed the small village of Waterloo. It was not much to look at and nothing worth stopping for.

Over three and a half hours later, Frederica reined in her horse outside of The King of Spain Inn. The building was two stories high and had been painted a crisp white. The only colour was a small black sign, three feet by three feet, that proclaimed the name of the inn. She was relieved to have finally arrived, for her thighs were becoming a bit sore. She was not used to riding this far or hard during a typical London Season. But she would have died rather than admit her weakness to Samuel. He could use it to tease or mock her.

Frederica allowed Samuel to assist her down from her horse and she had to bite her lower lip to keep from groaning. Together, they strode into the taproom of the bar. She tried to walk as normally as possible. A small Belgian man who was several inches shorter than Frederica bowed deeply to her, his long nose almost touching his knees. Samuel requested a private parlour and tea. The owner bowed lowly yet again and directed her to a side chamber with a large window that filled the room with natural light. A round table was placed in the centre of the room and had six chairs around it. The walls were whitewashed and simple, without adornment, but the parlour was clean.

'Monsieur, my betrothed and I are expecting a British gentleman. He is going to help us with our marriage contract. Could you please bring him in here when he arrives?' Samuel asked in French.

The small man nodded vigorously and executed another low bow. Within five minutes, a young waiter with fair hair and innumerable red freckles entered with the tea tray. He set it on the table and asked if the gentleman and lady required anything else. Frederica replied in French before Samuel could that they did not. She wanted to show her fiancé that she spoke French as flawlessly as he did.

Frederica prepared the tea and poured Samuel a cup and then herself. She enjoyed the hot sensation down her throat as she drank it. Somehow, she felt the comfort all the way down to her sore inner thighs. She hoped the British spy would be slow to arrive. She wasn't ready yet for another long and hard ride.

Samuel drained his own cup. 'You're still a bruising rider.'

She could only be glad that she had not mentioned how stiff she was. She realised that it had been seven years since he had seen her ride. 'Did you really join the army to get away from me? My brothers said that you did.'

His cheeks turned as red as a soldier's coat. 'You shouldn't mention that I am a soldier whilst we are here.'

Blushing, Frederica realised that she was not being a very good spy. 'You still have not answered my question.'

Picking up the teapot, he poured himself another glass. The colour in his cheeks fading. 'Believe it or not, Freddie, not all of my life decisions were based upon you.'

She hated that nickname which Matthew sometimes called her and Samuel knew it. She wanted to growl at him like a wolf, but then she would have childishly risen to his bait. She refilled her own teacup. 'Nor have I based my life decisions on you, my sweet baby angel Sammy.'

It was the endearment his mother called him and he hated it more than anything. Hence, Frederica had loved to call him that as children.

Wincing, he took another sip. 'Shall we call a truce on names? I won't call you Freddie and you will refrain from calling me Sammy?'

'Bargain,' Frederica said, holding out her hand. 'Shall we shake on it?'

'I'd rather kiss on it.'

She cursed her fair cheeks, for her body agreed that

was a *much better* way to seal a bargain. But before Samuel could kiss her, there was a knock on the door. They leaned away from each other, both a little breathless.

'Come in,' Samuel said in French.

A gentleman in his mid-thirties entered the small private parlour. He wore a wide-brimmed hat that hid his eyes. His nose was large and straight and his lips a thin straight line. He was neatly dressed in a scarlet uniform with a white cross on the chest.

Samuel and Frederica rose to their feet.

'Lieutenant-Colonel Grant,' Samuel said, bowing. 'Please allow me to present my betrothed, Lady Frederica Stringham.'

She beamed at the man and gestured to the chair. 'Do please sit down. I have never met a real spy before.'

He sat at the table next to Samuel and accepted a cup of tea from her, but his body stiffened at the word *spy*. Oh, dear. She should not have said that word either.

'I am no spy, my lady. I do not believe in subterfuge.'

Disappointed, but undaunted, Frederica asked, 'Do you invariably wear your British uniform while collecting information in France?'

Samuel snorted, but did not say anything.

Grant set his cup down on his saucer with a clatter. Frederica feared he might shatter them both. The china was too dainty for such handling. Her mother would have given the man, spy or no, a sharp reprimand.

'Of course. I am a man of honour.'

He also appeared to be a man who thought quite a lot about himself. This brought a small smile to her lips, but she quelled it. 'But is it not dangerous to proclaim your allegiance by your clothing?'

'This is no place for a lady. But I will have you know that I have never condescended to sneaking about in civilian clothing. And when I was captured during the Peninsular War, my companion who wore plain clothes was shot, whereas I was brought to the general and treated according to my rank.'

Samuel cleared his throat. 'Have a care, Grant, on how you speak to a young woman that also happens to be a lady and the daughter of a duke. Lady Frederica is here at General Lord Wellington's request.'

Frederica handed the intelligence officer a tray of scones. 'I am glad that you were spared, Lieutenant-Colonel.'

Grant grunted at this, but dropped his scone on the table and rifled through his satchel. He handed Samuel a stack of grubby papers. Standing, the spy drained his cup of tea and took his half-eaten scone in his hand. He saluted with it. 'Be here next week. Same time, Colonel Lord Pelford.'

'Very good,' Samuel said, but did not bother to stand as their brusque guest left the small parlour with a slam of the door.

Frederica watched him straighten the papers before placing them in a satchel that he wore around his neck and shoulder. She eyed Samuel closely. His movements were controlled and he did not seem at all alarmed that they were carrying intelligence documents. He had always been terribly brave. It used to annoy her. Samuel never once refused one of her brothers' dares. Even if he did break his foot in that dark cave.

His gaze met hers. 'Sorry about Grant. I have met him a few times before and the fellow is insufferable. He should have treated you with more respect.'

'When you proposed, I asked about your war experiences and you were equally disdainful.'

She watched as he pulled at his cravat.

Samuel's brow furrowed and he shook his head. 'I don't remember.'

'I do,' she said, swallowing and holding up her fingers as she quoted, *'"They are not fit for a woman's ears".'*

Frederica expected him to be embarrassed, not to laugh. But he did and loudly. The sound did something to her inner organs.

He grinned at her. 'I am surprised you didn't box my ears on the spot.'

Her fingers touched her parted lips. 'I wanted to.'

Taking a deep breath, he sobered. 'Forgive me, I was angry and out of sorts that day. I only remember feeling as if I had no choice and resenting it. I know that your ears and the rest of your very beautiful body are more than capable of anything that you set your mind to.'

She could only blink at him. Frederica felt surprised by his apology and his compliment. She had not expected either from him. Moving her hand to her throat, she felt the quick stutter of her pulse and the fluttery feeling in her stomach. 'And do you still resent me?'

He licked his thick lips, making her wish to kiss them. 'I never resented you. I resented that my father's debts did not allow me to make my own choice.'

Sipping her tea, Frederica realised that her cup had gone cold. She set it down on the saucer with a little clatter. She thought of Lady Caro and the other women who had flirted with Samuel at the parties and balls. 'Who would you have chosen?'

As soon as those words left her mouth, she regretted

them. Her heartbeat thundered in her ears. She did not want to hear about a dainty and well-behaved, but less wealthy, young lady that he preferred to her.

'I do not know.'

His answer was better than she could have hoped for, but still disappointing. She knew it was irrational, but she'd wanted him to say her. She wished to be his choice. Frederica got to her feet, her body stiff from her earlier ride, but she could not show Samuel any of her weaknesses. He knew too many of them already.

'Come on, sloth,' she said in a falsely chipper voice. 'We've got a long ride back home and poor Harper can only cover for me for so long.'

They returned to the taproom, where Samuel dropped several coins into the small man's hands. They left the inn, and the innkeeper assured them that he had fed and watered the horses and that they were ready for the trip home. Samuel threw the lad a coin and then assisted her into the side-saddle of her horse. His hands on her waist made her feel strangely breathless. And for once, she actually needed the help. Her leg muscles cramped something awful.

She stroked the neck of her horse and spoke soothingly to it. 'There there, girl. We are almost done.'

If only she could assure her own body of the same thing.

Samuel mounted his mare with ease and they took a more leisurely pace back towards Brussels, only passing a few carriages and wagons. Frederica reined in, placing her right hand over her eyes to get a better view of the area—mostly farms, a few stray trees, and a small blue lake. Her eyes alighted on a black stallion with a slim rider that galloped furiously towards them. Instinctively she gripped the reins of her horse tighter, but then she relaxed them when she saw the face of Captain Mark Wallace.

He rode up beside her and took off his tall hat. 'Good afternoon, Lady Frederica, Colonel Lord Pelford. Off for a bit of exercise?'

She grinned, sighing in relief. 'Yes. And what a superb specimen! Such shoulders and so perfectly black.'

Mark touched his chest. 'Alas, for a moment I was hoping you were talking about my humble self and not my cousin's horse.'

'I hope you haven't stolen it,' Samuel said in a gruff tone.

'No indeed,' he assured them with a confident smile. 'The Duke of Wellington is keeping all of his staff, including my cousin Alexander, so busy training the new recruits that I thought to do him a favour by exercising his horse.'

Frederica raised her eyebrows. 'Is Alexander aware of your kind favour to his beautiful horse?'

Mark winked at her. 'As of yet, no.'

'Perhaps I can ask the general to find something for you to do, Captain,' Samuel said stiffly. 'If you have so much spare time on your hands.'

Frederica's grin widened until it hurt. Despite not choosing her, Samuel seemed quite territorial over his bride-to-be.

'But what of my poor cousin's horse? Someone must take care of him.'

She laughed merrily. 'We are on our way home, Mark. Should you like to accompany us?'

'With pleasure.'

Samuel groaned as Mark brought his horse parallel

to hers and they cantered together to Brussels. He told her blithely about his family's castle in Scotland, his perfect elder brother, James, and cut several jokes at his own expense. He begged to go riding with her again, before bidding her a merry farewell at her door. Samuel was unable to get a word in edgewise. He just scowled at them both. Nor did he bother to tell her goodbye.

Harper opened the front door of the rented house and Frederica saw her mother descending the stairs in a cotton day dress with a little red flower print.

Mama yawned. 'Good heavens! Have you gone riding all afternoon? You should take a short rest before the party tonight. I do not want you looking fagged.'

'Yes, Mama,' Frederica said dutifully and gratefully went upstairs to her room.

Chapter Nine

A few days later, Samuel saw Frederica jumping a high fence on her horse, as if she knew the Belgian countryside as well as her own castle. She was always heedless and fearless like that. Samuel took the same fence on his own horse. Urging his mount to a gallop to catch up with her, he overtook her groom first and then reached her. At least Harper had not let her go out alone. Frederica had a way of twisting people around her little finger.

'What do you think you are doing?' he demanded in a loud voice.

Not at all perturbed, she beamed back at him. 'Oh, hello, Samuel. And I thought it was rather obvious—I am riding.'

Samuel shook his head, a stiffness in his jaw. 'I know that you are riding, but what are you doing jumping unknown fences in a foreign country?'

Frederica slowed her horse down to a trot and glanced over her shoulder at him coquettishly. 'I ride every morning for exercise. I do not know about you, but the ride to Genappe left me quite sore in the most unmentionable places.'

His eyes descended to her curvy body for a moment before he forced them back up to her face. Despite not choosing her for his wife, he wanted Frederica more than was decent. Few women could boast her perfectly balanced and generous curves. And like a courtesan, she seemed to know how to display her figure to the most advantage. In addition, she loved embarrassing him and he too easily fell into her traps. She'd wanted him to stare at her figure and he did.

Pressing his fist to his mouth, he said, 'What if you fell and broke your neck?'

She shrugged her shoulders and raised her eyebrows. 'Then you wouldn't have to marry me after all.'

The thought of not marrying her annoyed him even more for some reason. He clenched the reins tighter. 'You should be more careful. There are all sorts of unsavoury characters about.'

'Like yourself?'

Samuel grimaced. After all these years, Frederica's words still managed to needle him. 'You didn't find me so unsavoury the other day when we kissed.'

She raised one eyebrow. 'Which one were you again?'

He opened his mouth, but then closed it.

Frederica let out a peal of laughter. 'You've always been too easy to tease! Shall we have a race?'

'Very well.'

Glancing back at her groom, she said, 'Jim, you may go home and tell Harper that I am in Lord Pelford's company.'

He doffed his hat to her. 'Very good, my lady.'

Turning back to Samuel, she pointed to a white farmhouse in the distance. 'The first one to jump the fence wins. On your mark, get set, go!'

He watched her spur her horse onward at a spanking pace. Samuel had a little more experience over the terrain and wanted to save his horse's energy for the final gallop. Frederica led the entire race, over the fields, and past a road. Leaning forward, he squeezed his horse's flank with his boots. His mare responded by increasing her speed and flying over the fence, a length ahead of Frederica's grey. Samuel walked his horse a few more yards before turning back to her. The race had brought colour into her cheeks and she looked beautiful.

Frederica grinned at him. She angled her horse next to his and bumped his shoulder with her own.

'Oh, good race, Samuel.'

For all her faults, she was never a sore loser.

'Thank you.'

'I do not know about you, but I am famished! Shall we buy some bread and cheese from the farmer and have a picnic?'

'I need to get back to my duties,' he said gravely.

Frederica laughed in his face. No soldier would have dared to do such a thing. 'I almost believed you for half a moment. You do take yourself rather seriously, don't you? Is that why you do not discuss politics with women?'

Samuel shook his head. 'Must you dredge that up again? I only said that to avoid an argument with you. I am sure if I tell you that I am a Whig, you will proclaim yourself a Tory. Or vice versa.'

'I *am* a Tory and please do *not* try to stop arguing with me. I love quarrelling with you. You have always been such a worthy foe.'

She slid off her horse, tied it to the fence, and walked

off merrily to the barn behind the farmhouse. Huffing, he followed her, half hoping that the owners would rebuff her request. The Belgian farmer was in his late forties, with a scraggly beard that reached his waist, and after a few words exchanged in French, he treated Frederica like his daughter. He ushered them into the house, where a woman wrapped them a loaf of bread, a wedge of cheese, and a carafe of milk. Frederica thanked the woman profusely and paid her with a gold coin. He could not help but be impressed by Frederica's fluency and accent. She sounded like a local and not an aristocratic one.

Frederica held up her newly purchased wares and gave him another smile. The farmer handed him a blanket and told Samuel to be sure to return it.

'I will keep him in line and make sure he does,' she said in French, winking.

Both the farmer and his wife laughed.

Frederica led the way from the farmhouse to a large tree on a slight hill. 'This is the perfect place for a picnic.'

Samuel laid out the blanket, and before he could assist her, Frederica lay down on it and stretched out her arms. 'I am exhausted. I did not see you at the Nottinghams' party last night, but there were plenty of officers there. We frolicked until the early hours of this morning.'

'I am sure you danced with them all.'

She shaded her eyes with one hand. 'Oh, I did!'

Sitting down beside her, he leaned against his elbow. Samuel could not remember the last time they had simply sat together, relaxing. Then he felt her fingers crawl up his side and tickle him just below the arm at his most sensitive spot. He laughed and yelped, trying to grab her hands. But all Stringham girls were experts at torturing boys and she evaded his grasp, causing him to laugh even harder until he could barely breathe. Even then she did not show him mercy, but straddled across his lap and began to tickle his other side.

'You're still ticklish here!'

'Stop! Stop!' he managed between laughs.

Surprisingly, she did. Frederica's eyes widened as she realised that she was all but sitting on his lap. A becoming blush stole into her cheeks, but she did not retreat. He didn't think she knew how to. Instead, she leaned forward and pressed her lips to his. Again, Samuel could not breathe. Her mouth slid over his insistently, until he opened his own and deepened the kiss. Despite already being on the ground, he felt like he was falling. Hard. Fast. And out of control. That was how Frederica always made him feel, but for once he did not fight it. He surrendered. There was no feeling in the world to compare it to. No thrill was equal to this pleasure.

Then just as abruptly as she started it, she ended the kiss. Frederica jumped off him and opened the picnic basket as if she had not been kissing him moments before. She tore off a piece of bread and handed it to him. 'Our second course, Belgian bread.'

He sat back up. 'What was our first?'

She grinned at him, her eyes dancing. 'English lips. Ever so much better than cow tongue.'

He laughed. He loved her wit. Taking a bite, Samuel discovered that the bread was soft and delicious. He tried to concentrate on the flavour and not the fact that Frederica had been on top of him moments before.

She certainly knew how to torment a man, but she always had.

Samuel took a drink of milk from the carafe—there were no glasses. 'Tell me more about yourself. What are your interests? What do you like to do? I feel as if I know everything and nothing.'

Frederica took the jug from his hand and pressed her lips where his had been only moments before. 'What a good line! Have you used it on many ladies?'

Squeezing his eyes shut, Samuel should have known better than to try and converse like an adult with her. 'You are impossible!'

She let out a high trill of laughter. 'Now that is a phrase I do recognise, for you have said it about my poor self at least a hundred times.'

Ripping off a piece of cheese, Samuel ate silently. He was not about to rise to her bait again.

Frederica continued merrily, 'I discovered Mr Foxworth, the latest London poet, going around to different young ladies and comparing them to Miss Elizabeth Bennet from *Pride and Prejudice*. And I can assure you that line worked wonderfully well on myself and many a lady. It was a trifle disappointing to both my heart and my pride that he had not truly meant it.'

The poet's description was not entirely inaccurate, his betrothed was certainly a headstrong girl.

She took a few bites of bread before speaking again. 'Have you read *Pride and Prejudice*?'

As a matter of fact, his mother had sent him a copy in Spain. He had read it out to his fellow officers and they all enjoyed it greatly. 'Yes.'

'I am going to need more than monosyllabic responses if we are going to get to know one another better as adults.'

'Is that what we are doing?'

Frederica waved her chunk of bread at him. 'You asked to know more about me. I love to read. I have just finished reading all the novels by Maria Edgeworth, but Miss Austen's novels are my favourite. *Pride and Prejudice* is a particular treat because there are five sisters in it. And I do think that my sister Mantheria would make a most excellent Jane. And Elizabeth's wit and beautiful singing was just like my late sister, Elizabeth. I miss her every day.'

Her elder sisters were twins, but Elizabeth had died when she was only ten years old. She had been a bright young girl who sang more than she spoke. Samuel had wept when Elizabeth and Charles had died from scarlet fever. Charles had been his dearest friend and so young, only in his first year of school.

'Unfortunately, as the third that would make me Mary,' Frederica continued, counting on her fingers, 'and I cannot help but see some similarities between us.'

'You are anything but plain,' Samuel scoffed.

She smiled at him, but there was a wistfulness in it. 'That is nice of you to say. But Mary plays the pianoforte, like myself, and she tries so hard to be something more, only to be a figure of fun. A caricature of a young woman.'

He had no response. He did not know how a bright and talented young woman could become something more. The most that she could hope for was to be known as a brilliant society hostess and possibly help write her husband's parliamentary speeches. There was no place in politics, business, education, or even the arts for a woman of high birth to succeed. Even though Frederica played the pianoforte with the flare and feeling of a professional, it would never be more than a talent to 'exhibit' at a party.

After a few moments of painful silence, he said, 'Does Becca still draw caricatures? I recall her being very talented at them. Or has she relinquished rodents for suitors and soldiers? Like Kitty and Lydia Bennet?'

Dropping her head, she laughed. 'No. Alas, no. You are right. My two younger sisters are nothing like Kitty and Lydia. Helen and Becca are still more in love with mice and snakes than they are with men. And I do not think Helen could flirt even if her life depended on it.'

He snorted. 'Then it is a good thing that she is always carrying a snake. Perhaps it could save her.'

Frederica wrinkled her nose as she smiled winsomely. 'I am sure she and Becca are finding all sorts of reptiles in Greece. How I wish I was there with them.'

'And not here with me?' The words were out of his mouth before he could stop himself.

Picking up his hand with both of hers, she squeezed it. 'Oh, I am having a lovely time here with you. It is only that sometimes as the middle sister, I feel a little left out. Like poor Mary Bennet. Becca and Helen are closer to each other than they are to me. And Mantheria has always been a bit aloof emotionally since Elizabeth died. She has never tried to make me her confidant. Even when I travelled with them to Italy, she kept everyone at a very polite and correct distance. She is still playing the role of the perfect daughter and duchess. It must be exhausting.'

Samuel understood how she felt. Ever since Charles

died, he had not known where he fit with the Stringham sons. Wick and Matthew were a pair and he trailed behind them. Not that the Stringham brothers had been anything but good to him. He was never bullied at Eton because of Wick, and if he ever needed help with his studies, Matthew had been kind enough to tutor him. But it was not the same being the third person—the one on the outside of the pair.

'They all love you.'

'I know,' she said, bringing his hand to her cheek and rubbing it against her smooth skin.

'I felt the same way when Charles died,' he said in a quiet voice. 'My brother, Jeremy, is so much younger than me, and Charles was like a brother to me. And I resented when you tried to fill his place when we were children.'

A tear slid down her curved cheek as her lips smiled. 'No one could ever fill Charles's place. He was nothing but light.'

Nodding, he swallowed heavily. 'I do not think that I have been very good at letting people close to me since then. I have many friends but, like you, no confidants. And sometimes I think it is easier not to care as much, especially in the army. You bury your friends and must continue on without them.'

'Since you know *everything and nothing* about me,' she whispered, 'could you let me become a close friend? I promise that I will keep your secrets.'

The words had not been a studied line. No other flirtations would ever be like speaking to Frederica. The other women played by the rules and Frederica made her own. They had been childhood enemies, but now could they be friends? Should he trust her with the burdens of his soul? How his mother had leaned on him at such an early age that it was crushing? Could he tell her the truth about his father's life and death? The real reason that he had joined the army. But shame filled his throat and the words would not come.

'When I know more of your nothings, I can tell you my everythings,' he said lightly, steering their conversation away from the deeply personal.

Releasing his hands, her expression became guarded and civil. 'I also devour every Gothic romance I can get my fingers on. I think I have read almost every book in the lending library. Stories help alleviate the boredom of the Season.'

Society and the Season were safe topics. Impersonal ones. He raised one eyebrow. 'You do not enjoy the London Season?'

Frederica took a drink of milk, before shrugging one beautiful shoulder. 'I do not mind it, per se. It is just for once I would like to do something that truly matters. Not simply spend the bulk of my time thinking about my wardrobe and whether or not I will dance every set… Mama used to read out your name in Wellington's dispatches about the important things you were doing. As you know, Papa does not care about politics or wars, but he would always ask her to read it again. He was ever so pleased to hear of your successes. It irritated me to no end.'

A slow smile built upon his lips. She had managed to make the conversation personal again. 'Your father is a good man.'

Leaning forward, she kissed his cheek. 'And he thinks that you will be a great one.'

Touching his face where her lips had briefly resided, Samuel felt himself blushing. Lord Hampford had been his mentor growing up and he could think of no greater compliment. He only wished his own father would have thought of him so highly. That Papa would have been the sort of man that he could look up to and not the cause of his family's shame.

Chapter Ten

Once Frederica's fingers found their places on the keys of the pianoforte, the guests, and the room around her, faded into the background. It was just her and Beethoven having a most marvellous battle for musical predominance. Chopin was too subtle for her taste and Bach too orderly. But Beethoven knew how to wring every bit of feeling out of each note. She loved his minor chords and dissonant cadences. She would never tire of playing his music. Of being transported away to somewhere entirely new.

With one last crescendo, she finished the piece with a flare. Frederica lifted her eyes to glance back at the crowd. It was mostly members of the *ton* with a few foreigners of the highest rank in the mix. Her mother was a notable hostess and even being in a different country did not stop her from being selective in her invitations and expansive in her wine list.

Standing up, Frederica feigned as if she were leaving her place at the pianoforte, knowing full well that she would be asked to play another piece for the company. It was, however, extremely gratifying when none other than General Lord Wellington begged her to favour them with one more. Sitting back down, she pressed the keys loudly to begin Beethoven's 'Piano Sonata 23'. If anyone had fallen asleep, they would be awake now. Her fingers moved quickly on the keys, faster than even her mind could keep up with the notes. Oh, how she loved becoming one with the instrument.

She played the complicated piece until the tips of her fingers were sore. The sound of clapping brought her back to reality with a most unpleasant thud. She slid back on her long dinner gloves, bowing and smiling as she accepted compliments. Georgy took her spot at the pianoforte and began to sing and play a sweet, uncomplicated tune. She had a lovely voice and her fingering was good. Frederica could not help but realise that the audience enjoyed Georgy's simpler performance more than her own. She clapped louder than the rest when her friend finished and was happy that Georgy was asked by Wellington as well to favour them with another piece.

A small, ugly part of herself had to admit that she wished that she was the only person to be asked by the general for a second song. And that the guests would have realised that her performance was equal to a professional male musician. It was not merely a pretty accomplishment to display, Frederica was truly talented and worked extremely hard at practising. Shaking her head, she tried to rid herself of such petty thoughts. They were beneath the person she wanted to be.

'You were extraordinary,' Samuel whispered from behind her. Frederica's knees felt like jelly as he placed a hand on her waist and she could feel his warm breath on her ear. Butterflies danced in her belly. It was terribly annoying that he had this effect on her.

Turning, he kept his hand on her waist. They were standing at the back of the room and everyone else was politely listening to Georgy finish her second song. It was a Scottish air with a playful lilt.

'I didn't notice your arrival.'

It was not the wittiest sentence she had ever uttered, but it filled the silence and the space between them. Their noses were close enough to brush against each other and the bottom of her gown draped over his boots.

'You were well occupied,' he whispered. 'No one could fail to notice you in a room.'

Frederica's eyes lowered to his lips. They were wet, as if he had recently licked them. She would have liked to lick them as well, but she could hardly do that in the middle of her mother's soirée. 'Are you trying to flatter me?'

Samuel brushed his mouth against her cheek in the lightest of touches. 'Possibly. Is it working?'

All too well.

'I missed you today.'

The words were out of her mouth before she could stop them. She could not allow Samuel to know how much she wanted him. She had learned that lesson at the age of eleven: the more she pursued him, the faster Samuel fled. No, she had to make him come to her. Keep him on his toes. 'Fortunately, Mark was around to keep me company. He even let me take a turn riding on Alexander's stallion.'

His hand dropped from her waist and she missed the warmth of his touch and the tender look in his eyes. Lifting her chin, she stood beside him as Georgy finished her song and Lady Anthea took her turn.

Their shoulders occasionally brushed each other,

but the gulf between them felt as large as the English Channel. Perhaps it always would be. Samuel had not chosen her. It was different than when they were children and she'd had to fight for his attention, following him around like a loyal dog. All the terrible tricks and mean words had been her way of getting him to notice her. It was negative attention, but at least he could not pretend as if she didn't exist. Frederica had thought he didn't like her because she was always dirty, bedraggled, and in trouble. At fourteen, she had still been very naughty, but had become more clever about it. Her clothes and hair were tidy, and her womanly shape had already begun to show. Yet, still Samuel had avoided and ignored her more than ever before.

Putting a bear cub in his room had been the final straw, Frederica had made certain that he could not pretend that she was not there any more. Alas, being mauled by claws and requiring stitches did not endear her to him. Samuel hated her more than ever and a few months later he'd joined the army. He did not write to her even once. Or even to her family. She had severed the connection by her unseemly behaviour. Her desperate attempts to get him to see her.

Her arm brushed his, but Frederica was still not certain that Samuel could see her. Or if he wanted to. She knew he noticed her figure, but was he simply making the best of a bad situation? Did he kiss her because she was convenient, or because he felt something for her? And would he ever see her as a friend? A confidant?

It was beyond silly, but after all these years, she wanted him to choose her. Pursue her.

He was so close. But so far from her.

The dichotomy of proximity and distance pinched

at her soul. How could she endure a life of having him near, but not holding his heart? Somehow, she doubted that every bottle of perfume and bar of red scented soap at Duchess & Co. could make up for the lack of love in her personal life. But what could she do, other than what she was doing? Making him work for her kisses and try for her touches. And maybe, just maybe, he might grow to care for her.

Lady Anthea finished her second piece and everyone clapped. The older gentlemen made a swift retreat to the card room with some of the matrons. The chaperones, eligible young ladies, and unattached soldiers stayed in the main room and mingled. Frederica and Samuel stood silently by each other.

'Did your mother send you *Mansfield Park* too?' she asked, desperate to fill the quiet between them.

Nodding, one side of his mouth quirked up into a smile. 'She did.'

'It was my copy, or rather, I sent her both *Pride and Prejudice* and *Mansfield Park*. She must have posted them on to you. Did you read *Mansfield*, as well?'

Samuel swallowed. 'I read it out loud to my soldiers, but we did not enjoy it nearly as much as *Pride and Prejudice*.'

Shifting her weight to one side, she leaned slightly against him. 'I agree. Miss Fanny Price is a very dull character. She is entirely too good. It would have been a much better book if Miss Mary Crawford had been the heroine. She was clever and funny and just the right amount of naughty. Alas, wicked girls are not given happy endings.'

'No indeed. And good girls are given marriages based on their moral behaviour. Miss Elizabeth married Darcy with ten thousand pounds a year and Miss Jane, although good, only got five thousand pounds with Mr Bingley.'

How clever he was!

Frederica grinned, saying, 'And Lydia got Wickham with only his profession to maintain them.'

'And your Miss Mary Crawford received no marriage proposal at all.'

Sighing, Frederica shook her head. 'Precisely. 'Tis most unfair. A man does not have to be virtuous to get a happy ending in a book. Take Tom Jones for example. He was more promiscuous than a tart at Haymarket and he still got Sophie and a fortune in the end.'

Samuel laughed loudly, as if he was genuinely amused by her observations. A few people glanced their way and Frederica felt her colour rising.

'I am surprised, although I know that I should not be, that you have read *Tom Jones*. It is not considered proper for young, unmarried ladies.'

'My parents have never kept any knowledge or books from us,' she said, touching one of her burning cheeks with her gloved hand. 'Good or bad.'

'The problem with most books is that no person is wholly good or bad. We are all a mixture of parts. Take General Lord Wellington for example, he is an excellent military leader, but a terrible husband.'

'The same could be said of the Prince Regent,' Frederica added. She had always felt sorry for his wife, whom he openly despised. His parents should not have forced him to marry his first cousin to pay off his debts. The only good thing to come out of their marriage was their daughter Princess Charlotte, who would one day become queen.

'And I do believe that wicked young ladies deserve happy endings,' Samuel said with a wink. 'But for Miss Mary Crawford, her happy ending would be to elope with the heir, Tom Bertram. Edmund was a dull dog after all. She was much too entertaining to spend her life as a vicar's wife.'

She laughed so hard that she snorted.

Frederica touched his arm. 'You are right! Miss Crawford deserved at least an eldest son.'

Picking up her hand, he tucked it in his arm. 'Shall we go and find the refreshments? I have yet to have my dinner and if we stand here much longer, I might be forced to eat you.'

Frederica could not hold in her giggle. Samuel was hardest not to like when he was witty. 'I suppose so, however, I am not afraid of your bite.'

His eyelids lowered and he whispered, 'I'll remind you of that the next time we are alone.'

'Please do,' she said primly, even though a proper young lady would never say such a thing.

She guided him past the refreshment tables down the stairs and to the kitchens. The light desserts on display would not satisfy a man of his size. In French, she asked the chef to prepare a plate for Samuel. Then they shocked both the English and Belgian servants by sitting at the kitchen table. Samuel ate his chicken like a man who had not tasted food in a week.

'It is a good thing that I didn't know how voracious your appetite is,' Frederica said, raising her eyebrows. 'When I offered to let you bite me, I was thinking of little nibbles.'

A blush stole into his cheeks, but Samuel smiled

at her. 'I have had nothing to eat since this morning. I have been too busy.'

Leaning closer to him, she asked, 'May I ask how?'

She steeled herself for his rebuff as he shook his head slowly.

Samuel cleared his throat, dabbing his mouth with a napkin. 'There is too much to do and not enough soldiers to do it. The dispatches we retrieved from Grant say that Napoleon will go on the offensive to avoid a four-front war. His first target will be us and our allies the Prussians.'

She touched her neck. 'What size is the French army?'

Biting his lower lip, Samuel sighed. 'Currently over two hundred thousand and they are all volunteers—veterans from Napoleon's previous wars.'

'And the British forces?'

'Wellington has called it *"an infamous army, very weak and ill-equipped, and a very inexperienced staff"*.'

Frederica bristled at this, offended on Samuel's behalf. Reaching across the table, she placed her hand on his arm. 'Surely, he does not mean that you are inexperienced. You were also his aide-de-camp in the Peninsular War.'

Covering her hand with his own, Samuel sighed again. 'Thank you, Frederica. When he said it, Wellington did not mean me, Gordon, or Fitzroy, nor his returning staff from the Peninsula, but rather Sir Hudson Lowe. Horse Guards made him chief staff officer without consulting the general. Wellington has written home to complain, but there may not be time before the battle to replace him.'

Frederica did not precisely know how a general's staff worked and it did not help that her mind was equally focused on the pleasant weight and pressure of Samuel's hand upon hers. Even more so now that he was finally confiding in her. She could not let this moment pass. Cudgelling her wits, she managed to ask, 'Is Lowe's incompetence keeping you busy?'

'We are in a very bad way,' he admitted, rubbing his thumb over her fingers. 'We have not one quarter of the ammunition which we ought to have, on account of the deficiency of our drivers and carriages. Our soldiers are inexperienced and ill-equipped. I feel as if I spend from sunup to sundown putting out fires instead of preparing for the upcoming battle.'

Her stomach hardened. Had her presence in Brussels made his life more difficult? She watched him finish off his plate and asked if he would like more.

Samuel gave her a tired smile. 'No, thank you. The general expects us to attend parties and keep up appearances. It was much easier in the Peninsula when we did not have the *ton* watching our progress like a scene in a play.'

'Do you wish I was not here?'

He stood up slowly, like a man twice his age. He must be exhausted. 'I should wish you safely in England, but I am selfishly glad you are here. There is no one else that I'd rather spy with.'

Frederica linked her arm with his. 'You mean intelligence officer with.'

'Call me a spy and I will kiss you,' he said, repeating her words from that fateful morning.

Glancing around the kitchen, there were servants coming in and out. There was no place to be private.

'Scared?' he taunted softly.

Drat, Samuel! He knew that she would never back down from a challenge. Especially not one from him.

Bold as brass, she lifted her chin. 'My Lord Spy.'

With one hand, he cupped her face and angled his mouth towards hers. His kiss was light and sweet, tasting of red wine and decadence. His teeth gently tugged on her lower lip as he broke the kiss. He did bite her after all and she loved it.

'And I do not think that you are a wicked girl,' he said, caressing her cheek. 'I think that you are a different one.'

She gave him a sad smile. 'To the *ton* they are the same thing.'

Samuel twirled one of her curls on his finger. 'You will have such a happy ending that all the books you have read before will pale in comparison.'

Her gaze met his. For once, he had left her speechless. Her heart was pounding like a cannon in her chest and her pulse was racing as if she were going into battle.

'There you are,' Mama said from behind them. 'I have been looking all over for you, Frederica. Your presence has been missed.'

Lady Hampford's expression appeared stern at first, but Frederica knew that she was pleased to see them together. She gave Samuel a knowing smile.

Stepping back from Samuel, Frederica went to her mother. 'Sorry, Mama. Samuel missed dinner and he was positively famished. He nearly ate the curtains.'

'And the chairs,' he added helpfully.

Mama did not appear at all convinced by their flummery. 'I am glad Samuel was not forced to such dire straits. This house has been let after all. The younger members of our party appear a little dull. I thought that you two could begin the dancing.'

Frederica grinned. 'But who will play the pianoforte?'

'You are not the only one who is proficient,' Mama said in her most duchess-like voice. Her mother did not practise often, but she did play well.

Frederica grabbed Samuel's hand and dragged him back up the stairs to dance with her.

Chapter Eleven

Samuel wasn't riding the next afternoon in hopes of running into Frederica.

No.

Of course not.

Why would he want to do that, when he had danced with her three times the night before? The Duchess of Hampford had indeed been a proficient musician and played for nearly two hours while the younger couples danced jigs. Alas, she seemed not to know any waltzes; however, she overlooked Samuel squiring Frederica for a third dance. Only two was considered proper.

He certainly had not woken up early to complete his lists of tasks for the general so that he would be free for most of the afternoon. His horse clearly needed the exercise and Samuel had unaccountably developed an interest in locally made cheeses. He had discovered that no two farms' wares tasted alike. Something he would not have known if Frederica hadn't insisted on visiting a new farm around Brussels each day. With or without him.

And perhaps he had also grown accustomed to a certain young lady's enthusiastic kisses. They no longer felt like falling, but flying. Each kiss sending him closer to the hot sun. Until like Icarus, his wings would melt.

'Yoo-hoo! Samuel!'

He turned to see Frederica and her groom riding towards him at speed. She probably never allowed her poor horse to walk. No. Frederica ran towards life with an exuberance that left uproar in her wake.

'I found us a new farm.'

Samuel reined his horse around to meet hers. 'And cheese?'

She smiled at him and something inside of him broke and was remade. 'The most delicious cheese.'

'Shall we race there?'

Shaking her head, Frederica said, 'No. No. I am tired of losing to your mare. But perhaps we can have a shooting contest when we get there. Jim brought empty bottles for us.'

Sure enough, Frederica's groom had a bag slung around his shoulders and Samuel could hear the clinking of bottles. 'I don't think that shooting in a war zone is wise.'

She leaned over and rubbed his horse's nose. 'What is wise, is rarely fun.'

Samuel half wished that she would rub his nose. What an absurd thought! 'Come, I'll let you lead the way this time.'

Throwing him an arched look over her shoulder, Frederica grinned and cantered towards a large red barn. Instead of stopping, she passed it and rode on until they came to a blanket with a picnic basket underneath a tree, near a wooden fence. She had been waiting for him, and for once, he didn't mind being her prey.

Dismounting, he tied the reins of his horse to the fence. 'What would you have done if you hadn't met me?'

She pushed back her bonnet and let her wild, curly brown hair fall in tresses down her back. 'Found another handsome officer to share my picnic with me.'

He would not rise like a fish to her bait this time. 'You find me handsome.'

Finishing her knot, she grinned at him. 'Very. Which is most fortunate, because we are being forced to marry by our *wicked* mothers.'

His mother's illness was not her fault. 'My mother isn't wicked.'

No. His poor mama carried the burden of her husband's profligacies. And if she had leaned too heavily on him when he was younger, who else did she have? When she first became sick, Jeremy had been toddling about in short coats. Even at a young age, Samuel had wanted to help her. To be someone that she could depend on. And if Mama sometimes cried to get her way, he could not fault her. All the blame rested with his father, who was six feet under.

Frederica giggled, placing her hands on her face. 'My mother is delightfully wicked and I would not want her any other way. She could outbargain the devil himself.'

Lacing her arm with his, she pulled him to the blanket and asked her groom to go to the nearby field to set up the bottles for their shooting match. Alone they ate their picnic and Samuel could not help but yawn several times. In response, Frederica grabbed his head and pulled it down into her lap, stroking his hair. Samuel felt like a contented cat. He had no desire to leave her lap, nor for her to stop touching his curls. She even took off her gloves and he felt her soft skin against his. Closing his eyes, he could have purred.

'Poor Samuel, you look so tired.'

He nodded, unwilling to open his eyes or his mouth.

Frederica continued to stroke his hair. 'I wish that I could help you more.'

Samuel only made a sound in response—a mix between a moan and a sigh. Then he felt her lean down and nip at his ear. His eyes popped open in surprise and he turned his head.

Frederica was above him, her head haloed in light, smiling. 'Do you mind terribly that you have to marry me?'

He blinked. Truthfully, he did not mind at all. In fact, he could barely wait to say his vows and make her his in every possible way. But he was not stupid enough to tell her that. She would only tease him more. 'I can think of worse fates.'

She wrinkled her nose. 'Truly?'

'No.'

Frederica leaned down and pressed her lips lightly against his, tantalisingly brushing them over and over his mouth. He reached his hand up to cup her face and pull her down to him. His tongue slipping between her lips as she gasped. He tasted her moan more than heard it as his tongue stroked hers and teased the sensitive spots in her mouth. Not breaking the kiss, she twisted until her body was lying next to his. Her hands moved to his hair and her fingers raked through his curls. Samuel could not help but deepen the kiss, rolling his chest on top of her soft one. Her curvaceous figure always set him on fire. Pausing for breath, he made a trail of kisses to her neck and then her ear. He licked the lobe and then nipped it, like she had his.

She yelped and wiggled out of his hold. His head hit the ground on the blanket as if waking up from a delightful dream to reality.

Frederica got to her feet, brushing out the wrinkles on her skirt. Her hair mussed and her cheeks flushed. She looked as if she had been properly kissed. 'I only kiss young men who wish to marry me.'

Samuel sat up, running his hands through his own messy hair. Perhaps it was for the best that their embrace ended when it did. Their kisses were growing more frantic and his control was almost gone. He would not be promiscuous like his father, even if Frederica had him hot under the collar all the time. 'And what do you do with young men who don't wish to marry you?'

She pulled a pistol out of her reticule and blew on the barrel. 'Shoot them… Shall we have our match? Jim is waiting discreetly away from us. He's such a dear.'

Frederica offered him her hand and Samuel let her help him to his feet. He went to his mare and took the pistol out of his pack. He would need a weapon he felt familiar with if he wanted to give her a proper match. At Hampford Castle, not even her father or brothers could beat her in a shoot-off.

'If I recall, you're a rather good shot.'

She beamed back at him. 'I am the best.'

'We shall see.'

They walked thirty paces from the fence. Samuel allowed Frederica to shoot first. She barely aimed her weapon before firing it. A green bottle exploded off the fence.

Frederica grinned, pointing her smoking gun at him. 'Your turn.'

Samuel cocked his pistol back and took a few moments to aim, before squeezing the trigger. His shot hit the top of a clear bottle, but it was not central enough to shatter the entire glass. As a boy, he had hated losing to her. But as a man, he could appreciate her rare skill. 'Your point.'

She shot five more times. Each time she hit her mark. Samuel had never seen Frederica's equal with the pistol in any officer in Wellington's army. He was not a bad shot and hit his mark three times, but she never missed a bottle. Each time she aimed, the glass shattered. Frederica beat him handily and her groom, Jim, clapped, hooted, and hollered. The young man was clearly on her side.

'Good match,' Samuel said, giving her mild praise. Nothing annoyed her more. 'You are a fair shot.'

He returned to the picnic blanket and picked up his hat. A bullet whistled past him and he dropped it. Turning, he saw that Frederica had shot his hat out of his hand. He picked up his hat and put his finger through the hole. 'You could have killed me!'

'Don't be a ninny, Samuel,' she said, her hands on her hips. 'I have no intention of murdering you until after I have married you and provided an heir. How else would I be able to keep Farleigh Palace and all your ducal titles?'

Clamping his lips closed, he was determined not to smile at her words or her murderous wit.

Frederica threw back her head, laughing. 'Come on, Samuel, let yourself laugh. That was hilarious.'

His lips twisted up into a small smile. 'Macabre at best.'

She put her pistol back into her reticule. 'Perhaps I am better than *a fair shot*, would you say?'

'Perhaps.'

'Come on then, I have another surprise for you,' she said as her groom helped her mount her horse. 'I have arranged with the servants to give us a formal tour of the gardens and orchard at Château d'Hougoumont. It is quite lovely.'

He mounted his own horse and followed her to a large farmhouse with a garden enclosed behind stone walls and hidden from the road by trees. It looked like a small fortress. Frederica hailed a gardener, who took them through the wooden gate into a new world of flowers and flora. The garden was well-ordered in rows, but had a sense of whimsy. When they reached the orchard, Samuel paid the gardener and groom to go away. He pressed Frederica up against a flowering cherry tree and kissed her until he could no longer think.

Chapter Twelve

The ride to The King of Spain Inn in Genappe did not seem as long the second time. Nor was Frederica so stiff that she could barely walk when she got there. Still, she allowed Samuel to help her down from her horse. And if she pressed her body against his by accident as she slid down, who could blame a poor defenceless young woman getting off a horse? She smirked even if she could not tell if he was groaning in annoyance or moaning in appreciation. The sound he made caused a fluttering in her chest that was almost painful.

The innkeeper recognised them on sight and gave her one of his extremely low bows. He quickly wiped his hands on his apron and led her to the private parlour. 'Tea for two?'

'Trois,' Samuel corrected as the man led them back to the private parlour.

Frederica flashed him a wide smile and winked at him. The innkeeper's red face turned even redder and he nodded vigorously. The next person to open the door was a waiter with a broken nose who introduced himself as Peters. He placed the tea service on the table and asked if they would like anything else.

'No, that is all. Thank you, Peters.'

She and Samuel had drunk two cups of tea before Grant arrived. His wide-brimmed hat shadowed his eyes, but his thick lips were pursed. He still donned his scarlet uniform coat, but it looked a little worse for wear. The cuffs were fraying and the fabric would have been all the better with a thorough washing.

'Ah, Lieutenant-Colonel Grant. We had almost given up on you,' Frederica said, pouring him a cup of tea and placing it on the table near his chair. 'I am afraid the tea may be a little cold.'

''Tis no matter,' Grant said sharply.

'My lady,' Samuel added tersely.

The intelligence officer's cheeks flushed a bright red as he added a reluctant 'My lady'.

The Scot clearly did not like her. Or perhaps, it was just that he did not approve of a woman assisting in intelligence work. If that were the case, then Frederica did not think very highly of *his* intelligence.

Samuel cast her an apologetic look and the fluttering pain in her chest returned. He had never stood up for her before and now he was defending her like a knight in shining armour. Somehow, she seemed to have grown on him. Her lips curved up in a smile as she pictured her little sisters comparing their relationship to a fungus. They would probably compare her to the carnivorous American plant: the Venus flytrap. And like that plant, once she had Samuel in her tendrils, she had no intention of ever letting him go. His assurance, which had once felt insufferable, she now found terribly attractive. She'd never doubted that he was a loyal son and brother, and a noble friend. If he cared for her, there was nothing that he would not sacrifice for her good. She could not think of a worthier man whose heart she'd like to hold. But she couldn't reveal her feelings for him yet. She needed to be sure that he returned her affections first.

'Anything to report, Lieutenant-Colonel?' Samuel asked.

Grant drained the rest of the tea from his cup before pulling out a wrinkled, sealed envelope from his coat. He handed it to Samuel, not sparing Frederica a glance. 'Same time. Same place. Friday.'

Samuel nodded, tucking the dispatch into his plain black coat. 'Very good, Grant. Good day.'

The Scot stood and saluted Samuel before leaving the room in the same abrupt manner that he had entered it.

Frederica delicately sipped her cold tea. 'I am afraid that Grant is not fond of me. I am not saying that it is undeserved, but usually that level of disdain is reserved for people who know me better.'

She watched Samuel rake his fingers through his hair.

He shook his head back and forth slowly. 'I do not think it is personal, Frederica. But rather, he knows how dangerous it is for you and he does not approve of me bringing you here. I do not blame his curtness.'

Lowering her head, she swallowed hard. 'Do you blame yourself?'

Samuel rubbed the back of his neck. 'Yes. No. I do not know. Wellington himself asked me to bring you with me and I could have told him no, but I did not.'

Frederica winced. 'Then you too wish that I was not here?'

His gaze met hers and it pierced into her very soul. 'No, I thought it was a good plan.'

Somehow his words made her feel worse. As if her ribs were growing tighter, making it impossible to breathe. She turned her head, breaking eye contact with him.

'And foolishly,' he continued, 'I wished to spend more time with you and I did not seriously consider the danger I was putting you in.'

Her chin jerked back up.

'You wanted to spend time with me?' She said it slowly, as if each word was a question.

'Well, we are about to be married.'

She hunched her shoulders and said in a small voice, 'A marriage that you do not want.'

Samuel's jaw was set in a tight line. 'Rather, a marriage that I did not choose.'

Frederica did not know what to think or how to feel. She had loved and hated Samuel for as long as she could remember. He infuriated her like no one else could. He also brought out her very worst side. The one that never failed to get her into trouble. But she'd still longed for his attention. His smiles.

'Perhaps you are hoping that I will be killed and then I will never be your wife.' She knew as soon as the words left her lips that they were petty and untrue. But she wanted to hurt him as he had pained her with his indifference. 'Then you can keep my mother's money and live happily ever after.'

With a perfect wife of his own choosing. Who was pretty and not petty or impertinent. Or wicked. Who followed the rules and allowed the man to lead while dancing.

Samuel clenched his fist and brought it to his face. 'It is far more likely that I will die in the following weeks.'

'You survived the Peninsular War,' she said in a small, gruff voice.

He shrugged his broad shoulders. 'It only takes one stray bullet and then *you* will not have to marry me.'

She tried to swallow, but there was a lump in her throat. Standing up, she surprised Samuel by sitting on his lap and putting her arms around his neck. 'Promise me that you will be very careful?'

His arms wrapped around her waist. His face close to hers. 'Are you saying that you wish to marry *me*?'

Leaning forward, Frederica kissed his nose. 'I wish to be a duchess. You happen to be a delightful addition to the title.'

'A side benefit?'

Kissing his cheek and neck, she murmured her agreement. She loved how his skin tasted. The friction of brushing her lips over the stubble of his cheeks. But nothing could compare with his mouth upon hers and his tongue tangling with hers for dominance. Neither of them would concede without a fight in this sensual war. Taking a quick breath before diving back in with another lip-bruising kiss, Frederica thought that perhaps she was winning this battle. Her fingers were in his hair, their bodies close together, and she knew in this moment that she could not bear to lose him. That any hate she felt for him in the past was overwhelmed by love. Samuel was her opposite. Her antagonist. But she would have chosen no other man to stand at her side. He was her equal. Her everything.

Samuel nipped at both her upper and lower lips. The sting of his bites gave both pain and pleasure.

Peters entered the room to take the tea tray and she jumped off Samuel's lap. Turning away from both men, she attempted to straighten her dress and her hair. Her neck and face hotter than the noonday sun.

She heard Samuel thank the waiter and the door close before she spun to face him.

Samuel's lips were red and a little swollen from her kisses. 'Clearly, that servant doesn't know the meaning of a *private* parlour.'

A giggle escaped her lips.

He took a step closer to her. 'And we were so comfortably situated too.'

She held out her hands to him and Samuel's larger ones encompassed hers. 'I still need your promise that you will be careful.'

Samuel brought her right hand to his lips and kissed it, then lifted the other and repeated the action. 'I will be as careful as a cat.'

'My father is a naturalist. I know that cats do not have nine lives,' Frederica protested. 'For once, do be serious. Promise me that you will do everything in your power to come back to me.'

'I promise,' he whispered, and the words felt more solemn and holy than vows spoken in a church.

Frederica felt too overcome to speak, so instead she flung herself into his arms and held him tightly. Wishing that she was brave enough to tell him how she truly felt. Hoping that somehow, he knew.

Chapter Thirteen

Samuel delivered the wrinkled dispatch directly into Wellington's hands. He was slightly curious to know what it contained, but knew better than to ask. The general would tell him what he wished for him to know.

Retrieving the dispatch was becoming more perilous, Samuel thought as he took a drink of water. The waiter, Peters, had entered the private parlour without knocking. Even the greenest of servants knew that they were supposed to wait before coming into a room. The Frenchman had a broken nose and the build of a bruiser. Samuel was pretty sure that the man had once been a soldier and that he was one still, or at least reporting their movements back to the French army. For all he knew, the innkeeper was also an informant.

He should not allow Frederica to continue accompanying him to The King of Spain Inn. Grant was right. It was not safe. But refusing Frederica something only made her want it more. She might even try to go without him. No, the best and only course of action was to go with her and remain alert. And he would need to tell Grant about his suspicions.

Frederica.

Samuel could not recall her becoming maudlin before. Yet, he was certain at the inn that she had been holding back tears and she made him promise to come back to her. From another young woman those words might have been the sentiment of a friend. From Frederica, they were practically a declaration of love. Who would have thought it?

What was even more surprising was that he was eager to marry her and not only to enjoy his husbandly privileges. Although, he would be lying to himself if he did not admit how eager he was to bed her. She had him running hotter than a buck in mating season most of the time. But it was more than desire. He enjoyed her witty tongue and not just for kissing. Her mind was rare and sharp. She would make a wonderful companion and an even better confidant. He could see them building a life together. Theirs would be a marriage of equals. Frederica's gifts and talents would complement his. Their children would grow up in a close and adventurous family, like the Stringhams, whom he had always been so envious of. He could see Frederica slowly transforming Farleigh Palace from a stately building into a warm home. Samuel would become the father that he had always wanted. One like the Duke of Hampford, who taught his children how to ride and swim and shoot. A father who hugged and loved his children. Who made them feel special.

If he survived the war.

Samuel had made her a promise that he could not keep. One that no soldier could. He only prayed that he would be lucky again. His mind whirled with painful memories. Fitzsimmons had not been so fortunate—

a sword through his chest. Neither had McGovern—a bullet to his head. Officers, soldiers, even drummer boys were lost in every battle. He could not depend on his former luck. No. He needed to share his confidences with her now. Before the battle. And he needed to write three letters in case he never returned home. He could not leave these words unshared. The first to his mother. The second to Jeremy. And the last to Frederica.

Taking out a sheet of hot press paper, he dipped the pen in the ink bottle.

Dearest Mama,

If you are receiving this, I am not coming home. Please know how much I love you and please forgive me for not returning sooner and helping you with the burden that you have had to carry on your own. I am sorry that I ran away, from home, from Father, and from our family.

He lifted the nib of the pen to his lips. Samuel had left home at seventeen, still a youth. But seven years in the army had made him a man. And now his brother was fifteen, nearly the same age. He hoped that he would be there to guide Jeremy. To help him when he overran his allowance or prevent him from being taken advantage of by the gulls and captain-sharps of society. To prepare him for a profession or a life in Parliament. One letter would not be nearly enough to convey all that he had learned to his brother.

'Skimping out on working, I see,' Slender Billy said, leaning on the door-frame.

Samuel set down the pen. 'Writing my goodbyes. I never got around to doing them before.'

The prince slunk into the room with the ease of a royal and sat on the edge of the desk. He lifted his fingers up and spoke in a mock, deep voice. 'I really believe that I have got not only the worst troops, but the worst-equipped army, with the worst staff that was ever brought together.'

Sighing, Samuel said, 'I see that you have been talking to Wellington. He is not pleased with any of the arrangements or appointments from the Horse Guards. Nor the promotions made by the Duke of York.'

Slender Billy folded his arms. 'I told you that you should have joined my staff. I have the best troops, the best equipment, and the best staff that has ever been brought together.'

A smile played on his lips, but Samuel tried to squash it. 'Is it better to be overly positive or pessimistically negative about one's chances?'

'Confidence is worth a cavalry in my opinion.'

'In your case, I should say it is worth three companies of cavalry.'

Billy laughed and gave Samuel a playful push on the arm. 'Shall we go out and dance, drink, and be merry before we die?'

Samuel got to his feet. 'Why not?'

Chapter Fourteen

Thanks to her rides with Samuel, Frederica knew every road that led into the great city of Brussels and all the good nooks and crannies for stolen kisses. This morning she did not see Samuel but Captain Mark Wallace, riding towards her on his cousin's black stallion. She waved to him, smiling.

Mark took off his hat, grinning back at her. 'Might I take the place of your fiancé this morning?'

She touched her hat. 'The position of fiancé is already taken, but you're welcome to be my groom.'

He bowed, still sitting on his horse. 'My dearest wish is to serve you.'

Frederica turned to Jim, thanking him, and sending him home. Then she pulled the reins of her horse to angle her mare next to his stallion. 'Shall we race?'

Mark pointed to a fence a couple of hundred yards away. 'First to the fence?'

'First over the fence,' she said, kicking her heels into the horse's flank and yelling, 'Giddyap.'

Frederica did not turn her head to see if he was following. She knew he was. Her grey was a beautiful animal, but it was not in the same class as Sir Alexander's stallion. If she had any hope of winning, she could not lose focus for a moment. She heard the other horse's footfalls behind her. Spurring on her own mount, she let her head fall back and wind rush over her face. It was moments like this where she felt truly free.

Weightless.

'Come on,' she urged her grey as they approached the fence.

Mark soared past her and over the fence, as if it were no more than a small stone in the road.

Her winded grey took the fence, but it was not a victory. 'I suppose you won.'

He grinned at her again. Mark was truly handsome, but he was not Samuel. 'Even after you cheated.'

'If you're not cheating, you're not trying.'

Mark laughed, a merry sound. 'Shall we return to the city?'

She nodded and they cantered together across a green field. Frederica pulled up on her reins when she saw Samuel. Her body was all shivers and tingles at the sight of him.

Mark checked the stallion as well and touched his hand with his chest. 'He's come to steal you away.'

'If you knew me better, you would want me to be stolen,' Frederica told him primly.

Laughing, he bowed his head to her and then to Samuel before riding away. Her betrothed looked furious. His full lips in a tight line. His broad shoulders back and tensed as if he was preparing for a fight. He was a stocky young man and Frederica was certain that Samuel could brawl with the best of them. Her brother Wick had taught him how to throw a nasty left hook.

'What were you doing with Wallace?'

She gave him an arched look. 'What do you think we were doing?'

He grimaced. 'Riding.'

'Nothing that naughty,' she said, shaking her head. 'We were racing.'

Samuel nodded, his expression still murderous. He did not seem to appreciate her euphemistic jest. 'And did you already find bread and cheese for your mid-day meal?'

'Not yet,' she said, pointing to a farmhouse near the road to Genappe. 'And we have yet to try the fare of La Haye Sainte.'

'Far be it from me, to keep you from your cheese.'

She clicked her tongue and urged her mare to a walk on the road. 'This farmhouse is not nearly as large, nor as grand, as Hougoumont.'

'I daresay the gardens aren't as secluded either,' he said dryly.

It was her turn to blush. Unwittingly, her fingers stole to her lips. Samuel had kissed her so thoroughly that day that she had forgotten where she was. He had pressed his hard body against hers and she had melted into his arms. And for the first time in any kiss or embrace, she had lost all control of herself. Of her feelings. Her heart.

When they reached the white farmhouse, Samuel assisted her off her horse and tied their animals to a fence. They walked around the picturesque farm and Frederica wondered if it would be the same after the battle. There was a sort of frantic energy in the air. Like the breath of wind before a mighty gale. Would it ravage this peaceful little farm and all those around it?

After the tour, she purchased some bread and cheese

from a farm worker. Samuel offered to pay, but she liked handling the money herself.

She broke off a chunk of bread and handed it to him. 'Shall we eat like heathens?'

Samuel had already taken a large bite and he said with a full mouth, 'Yeth.'

Frederica let out a trill of laughter and broke off a piece for herself. She liked that he had a large appetite like her. The bread was warm and flavourful and she chewed it slowly. She saw that Samuel had already swallowed his entire piece, so she tore off a large chunk of cheese and gave it to him. Tasting the delicious cheese slowly, she looked about her. She memorised the number of buildings inside the farmhouse enclosure, the doors to the courtyard, and the height of the walls.

Samuel looked at her quizzingly. 'I should dearly love to know what you are thinking.'

Turning back to him, she asked, 'Do you think the fighting will reach here? I was pondering if the walls and courtyard would give enough protection or if they would be a trap to be stuck in.'

He did not answer her immediately, but she didn't mind. He appeared to be considering her opinion and his answer like he had that night in the kitchen.

At last, he said, 'There is a high probability that there will be fighting at this farm and all the others round about it. In the coming days, there will be four armies and hundreds of thousands of men.'

She held up four fingers. 'The English, the French, the Dutch, and the—'

'Prussians,' Samuel said, taking her hand, 'who are our allies, but it is difficult for armies from different countries to fight together. It would not surprise me if lives were lost between ourselves. Lines get blurred. Guns and cannons fill the air with smoke. Officers get shot. Screams make orders hard to be heard and difficult to follow. It is impossible to keep track of every soldier during a battle.'

He caressed the top of her hand with his thumb, holding it in his lap.

'Are battles terrible?'

Samuel was silent and Frederica feared that he would snub her again, or shut her out of his deepest thoughts. He brought his free hand and set it on top of their joined ones.

'When I first enlisted,' he said slowly, 'I was too young and foolish to realise how awful they were. All the sounds and bullets were thrilling for a young man. I thought I was invincible and I fought like it. I even rose quickly in the ranks because I was foolhardy and fearless. But it does not take long for even the most daring of young soldiers to realise that many of his friends are dead. And that his bullets and his sword have dealt death to his enemies' family and friends. In those moments, precious and terrible, you realise the value of life, but you are forced to take it. Killing another person changes you. Murdering many people even more so. And it must, for we are breaking nature's laws.'

She had never thought about it that way. Like so many others, she had been blinded by the spectacle of fancy uniforms and the army parades.

Frederica squeezed his hand. 'You are not a murderer. You are a soldier, defending your country and other countries from cruel tyrants like the Emperor Napoleon. Any creature alive would defend its own. That is the true way of nature.'

He shook his head, regret lining his eyes and mouth. 'That is what the newspapers print and I hope that it is true, but that does not change the fact that I have taken countless lives. And I do not know their names or their situations, the most I can remember is their faces when they haunt my dreams. I wonder who they have left behind and if their sacrifice has any meaning at all. But mostly, if my life and sacrifice would have a purpose.'

Frederica moved her hands to cup his face, his square jaw a little scratchy on her palms. She loved the friction between them. Her eyes met his. 'Your sacrifice has meaning, Samuel. And your actions have made a positive difference in the world. You are a good person and a good soldier.'

Samuel closed his eyes and rubbed his cheeks against her hands. 'I did not join the army to get away from an unwanted marriage, Frederica. I joined it to get away from my father.'

Gasping, she dropped her hands, but he caught them in his larger, warm ones. He was not retreating behind his wall. He was opening himself to her for the first time. Showing his vulnerabilities and scars. If only she could be as brave.

He kissed the back of her hands. 'I should have told you that when you asked me before.'

Her mouth fell open and one word came out: 'Why?'

Dropping his gaze, he no longer met her eyes. 'I had not finished at Eton, when I stopped at my parents' home in London and found my father with a duo of Cyprians there. He offered to share one with me. I was shocked and ashamed. And then I saw the telltale sores on my father's hands. He contracted the French pox soon after Jeremy was born… How much do you know of the disease?'

Frederica could only shake her head.

'When one is first infected, sores form around their mouth and personal areas. They only last a few weeks and heal on their own, but it is just the beginning. Rashes, sores, and fever come next. Then it all goes away. Our family physician called this the latent stage. The illness has no symptoms for ten to thirty years, and then it returns for the tertiary stage, which affects your heart, blood, nerves, and brain.

'That night I entered our London home, I saw that the sores had returned to my father's mouth and hands. Yet he was still whoring around town, no doubt carelessly infecting others. I now understood why my mother kept rooms on the other side of the palace from my father. I left the house immediately and went straight to enlist as a common soldier. And I would have, if I had not run into Sir Alexander Gordon. He convinced me to purchase a proper commission and not a fortnight later, I was off on a boat to fight in the Peninsular War. I never completed my studies. Neither did I say goodbye to my mother or Jeremy. I just wrote a brief letter telling Mama that Father's pox had returned.'

'I knew about your father's illness,' she admitted in a low voice. 'It was my mother's idea that your mother tell people that the duke had had a stroke. His decline was slow and painful.'

He lowered his eyes, shaking his head. 'Not painful enough for what he did. I should have known your mother would have told you. I suppose you deserved to know what sort of family you were marrying into.'

Frederica rolled onto her knees and threw her arms

around her childhood nemesis's neck. Leaning her cheek against his, she shook her head. 'Neither of our mothers told me. I have always been a champion eavesdropper and I taught my little sisters all my tricks. But do not worry, I have never spoken of it to another soul. Nor will I ever betray your confidence.'

'Does it change how you think about me?'

She blinked. 'Your father's choices?'

He nodded his scratchy cheek against her smooth one.

'Of course not, silly,' she said, pressing a kiss against his cheekbone. 'You have always been a very different sort of man. There is no comparison between you, even if you have your father's build and colour of hair. Besides, if you were unfaithful to me, I would not live on the other side of the house or hide in the country, I would simply shoot you.'

Samuel let out a watery chuckle. 'I do not doubt it.' She felt his arms move around her waist and he gripped her tightly. 'Even now, I could not bear to tell my little brother the truth. I did not want him to have to carry the family shame.'

She squeezed him tighter. 'It is not your shame, nor Jeremy's, and you do not have to carry it.'

He buried his head into her neck, moving his head back and forth. 'I should have been there for my mother. I should have helped her. Instead, I ran away.'

She caressed his soft curls with her fingers. He seemed so vulnerable and she wanted to comfort him. 'You were little more than a child and your mother is a very capable woman. She managed to keep your father's condition and confinement a secret from all the *ton*. Your father's mistakes are not your responsibility.'

But as she spoke those words, she realised that they

were not true. The only reason that Samuel was marrying her was because of his father's choices. His debts. Samuel had not chosen her, but she had chosen him. Or at least, she had chosen to accept the bargain with her mother to marry him in exchange for the perfume business. Her hands dropped and she slowly backed away from him. She could not release him from his promise to marry her. It would break her heart to do so.

Frederica got to her feet, her knees a little shaky. 'I am feeling a bit thirsty.'

'Shall I ask that fellow for some water?' Samuel asked, standing beside her. His expression blank, retreating behind his wall of implacability.

'Oh, no,' she said with a forced smile, tucking an errant curl behind her ear. 'I am thirsty for something a little stronger. I believe there is an inn, not too far down the road. Shall we mount up and go find it?'

Samuel held out his arm and they walked back to where the horses were tethered. They led their animals to a trough and allowed them to drink their fill, before Samuel assisted her into the side-saddle. He mounted the magnificent horse, and they rode to a small inn called La Belle Alliance. The paint on the exterior of the building was chipping, and there was no private parlour. Frederica waited in the saddle while Samuel went inside and purchased two tankards of ale. He handed one to Frederica, and she sipped it cautiously. It burned down her throat and she coughed as black spots filled her eyes.

He took several large gulps and laughed at her. 'Not had much experience with tap drinks?'

Taking another sip, she made a face. 'I do not think I have missed much.'

Samuel held out his hand to take the tankard and drained it. 'I shall see if the rascally barman has any milk.'

He returned with a glass of milk.

Frederica took a hesitant sip. It was a little tepid, but otherwise tasted familiar. 'This is much more to my liking.'

She finished the glass and he kindly took it back inside the inn. They set off for Brussels in silence. Samuel had shared his most intimate secrets with her. His shame. And she had been unable to comfort or absolve him. She could not even kiss him, even though she'd wanted to. She was just another burden that he did not want. That he did not choose.

When they reached her house, Samuel helped her dismount her horse and handed the reins to Jim, who stood waiting.

'Shall I see you tomorrow night at the King and Queen of the Netherlands's fête?'

She cocked her head to one side. 'To be sure.'

'May I have your first waltz?'

'I am afraid Captain Wallace has already claimed that dance, but you may certainly have the second.'

'Why do you dance with that Scottish fellow so much?'

'We are discussing military secrets, of course,' Frederica said with a laugh and walked into her house on Rue de Lombard.

It was obvious from the expression on Samuel's face that he did not believe her. Jealousy looked rather good on him.

If only honesty became her.

Chapter Fifteen

Frederica had attended many parties with her mother since arriving in Brussels, but none that impressed her as much as the King and Queen of the Netherlands's fête. It was truly a splendid affair. The rooms were filled with men in a colourful array of fancy dress uniforms. Countless chandeliers hung from the ceilings and their candles burned brightly. She was introduced to the King and Queen of the Netherlands and danced the first country dance with the Prince of Orange. A slender but handsome young man with receding chestnut hair and a winning smile. Unlike Samuel in every way.

'It is a great honour to dance with you again, Your Highness,' Frederica said as they made their first turn of the set.

'No, no, Lady Frederica. I have been most eager to get to know Samuel's fiancée better and could not resist the opportunity to spare myself a dance with one of the old high-ranking frights.'

Raising her eyebrows, Frederica giggled. 'A prince's lot is a hard one.'

Prince William smiled broadly at her and agreed

readily, 'One is always forced to dance with and talk with people whom one would least wish to.'

She shook her head. 'That terrible fate is not reserved only for princes.'

They parted in the dance and circled back to each other. The prince was an elegant dancer. He took her hand and led her in a promenade. 'Well, truthfully, I only dance with a few of them, and then escape to my English friends in the card room.'

Frederica opened her mouth in pretend shock, bringing her free gloved hand to her chin. 'For shame! How long have you known Samuel?'

'Since Eton. Smashing good fellow. No better soldier in the entire Allied forces. I only wish he were my ADC instead of Wellington's, but the duke would not dream of parting with him. Ah, there he is.'

Samuel walked into the room and Frederica was not the only one whose eyes were upon the handsome, broad young soldier. Lady Caro broke from her circle of admirers to greet him at the door. She must have chosen him to be her newest victim now that Lord Byron had spurned her. Frederica had disliked the dashing matron before; now she positively hated everything about her. From her painted toenails to her dampened chemise meant to show every line and curve of her figure.

The music ended and Frederica thanked Prince William for their country dance and then he escorted her to the side of the dance floor where her mother was standing. Her hand was immediately claimed by Georgy's brother, Charles Lennox, the Earl of March. He was a tall, agreeable-looking young man with brown curly hair and matching eyes. He was also a superb dancer, something that she would have appreciated at any other ball but this one. She wanted Samuel by *her* side, laughing at *her* wit, and touching *her* arm.

Over his shoulder, she saw Samuel and Caro join the dancers. For half a moment, Frederica contemplated calling Lady Caro out for a duel. Her mother had once told her a story about how Lady Almeria Braddock took offence at a comment Mrs Elphinstone made about her age and they had a duel in Hyde Park. Both ladies missed their marks with pistols, so they moved on to swords. Mrs Elphinstone was wounded in the arm and promised to write an apology. Swords or pistols, Frederica was more than willing to give Lady Caro a flesh wound. Frederica would not miss with her pistol. Nor would she apologise.

'I feel as if I know you already, Lady Frederica,' Lord March said. 'Georgy talks about you so often.'

She gave him a simpering smile. 'All good things, I hope.'

'The very best and I hear that you are to be congratulated on your engagement to Colonel Lord Pelford. Samuel's a splendid fellow. I only wish Georgy could find such another.'

Frederica felt her body temperature rise. 'Perhaps you should be congratulating him on his engagement to *me*.'

Wiggling his eyebrows, Lord March let out a bark of laughter. 'The reports did not do you justice, my lady.'

Unless the rumours were from Georgy, Frederica was certain that they were not favourable to her at all. Spinning, she decided to change the subject. 'Is it true that you have a bullet inside of you?'

Charles pointed to his puffed-out chest. 'Right here.

Shot at the Battle of Orthez in 1814. It was never removed.'

'Does it pain you at all?'

'Not a bit. I do not notice it at all.'

After Charles, she danced with Mark. But not even his wit could make her smile. Frederica tried to stop her eyes from searching the room for Samuel. Unfortunately, she found him with Lady Caro clung to his arm like she was drowning in the sea.

When the dance ended, Mark escorted her to Georgy's side instead of her mother's. Georgy shooed her cousin away and linked arms with Frederica. They walked around the edge of the ballroom together. Frederica resisted the urge to rub her sleepy eyes. All the late nights and early mornings were catching up with her. She could barely keep her eyelids open.

Georgy whispered in her ear, 'Take care how you flirt with Cousin Mark and my brother, or you shall lose your Lord Pelford to Lady Caro.'

'She is already married and a notorious flirt. Besides, he must be several years younger than her,' Frederica countered. Unlike Samuel, jealousy was not a colour that favoured her.

'You're right and I have heard it rumoured that she is still obsessed with that limping poet who was all the rage.'

'Lord Byron. Mama does not approve of him at all,' Frederica said. 'But he might be respectable now that he married Miss Annabella Milbanke, Lady Caro's cousin. Now that is poetic revenge.'

Georgy squeezed her arm. 'I do not care about Lord Byron. I think you are a great fool if you do not stop Lady Caro from adding him to her string of conquests.'

'What do you suggest I do?'

'Smile at him. Talk with him. Flirt with him. He is your fiancé after all,' Georgy said, steering her to Samuel, who was still standing by the infamous Lady Caro.

'I'd much rather kiss him,' Frederica muttered truthfully.

Samuel arrived late to the King and Queen of the Netherlands's fête. He paid his respects to the current monarchs, then entered the ballroom, where he looked for Frederica. He saw her dancing with Billy, the Prince of Orange. Her hazel eyes flashed with mischief and her cheeks were flushed with excitement. He had not seen her since yesterday and he realised how much he had missed her in that short time. He'd started to walk towards her when he felt a slender hand on his arm. Turning, he saw the petite, pretty, and painted face of Lady Caro.

'Oh, hello, Lady Caro. How do you do?'

'Not well at all,' she purred, placing a hand on his arm like a claw. 'For I have yet to dance with you.'

'Shall we?' Samuel said, leading Lady Caro to the dance floor.

They circled around the room together and she told him of the latest gossip. Lady Caro had a gift for mimicry and he laughed merrily as she parodied their various acquaintances. After the dance was over, she insisted on a second with him. Samuel could hardly refuse her without offence. When the second set was over, he led her by the hand to the side where his friend Sir Alexander Gordon and his new wife were standing. Lady Caro squeezed Samuel's hand before releasing it.

She stayed next to his side as if they were tied together by a string, instead of merely acquaintances.

Alexander was a tall man with thick brownish-red hair and a welcoming smile. He was also an ADC to Wellington and a good man, except for the fact that he let his cousin ride his stallion with Frederica.

His friend bowed. 'Pelford, Lady Caro, allow me to introduce my bride, Lady Gordon.'

Samuel bowed to a short young lady with flaxen hair and brilliant blue eyes. She was pretty in the English style and had the glow of a new bride. 'It is an honour.'

'A pleasure,' Lady Caro purred in a bored voice.

The new Lady Gordon ignored the other woman and turned to face Samuel. 'Alexander has told me all about you and your practical jokes, Duke.'

Ones he had learned from the Stringhams.

Lady Caro cackled and hit his arm with her fan flirtatiously. 'You never told me you were a jokesmith. For shame!'

Samuel was about to step away from Caro and her claws, when he felt a tap on his shoulder. He turned to see the beautiful face of Frederica, her countenance a bit pale.

'I am sorry. I did not mean to startle you,' she said, her neck turning a blotchy red and her cheeks pinker than usual as she smiled at him.

'No, no,' Samuel said, taking her hand in his. 'I was hoping to find you. May I escort you to the terrace? I believe there is to be a fireworks show there.'

He ought to have introduced her to Sir Alexander, Lady Louisa, and Lady Caro, but he forgot his surroundings when she smiled at him. Before he knew it, he was leading her to the terrace to watch the fireworks display. He cursed inwardly that it was so crowded, he would dearly have liked to have kissed her again. He led her to the edge of the crowded terrace and they looked at the crescent moon.

But as soon as the fireworks began, she moved closer to him. Pressing her curves against his side. 'I have decided that I do not like sharing.'

'What are you talking about?' His words were muffled as red fireworks exploded above their heads.

She cupped her hands around his ear. 'You. I do not like sharing *you*.'

He opened his mouth and waited to speak, for another barrage of fireworks was going off at the same time. The sky glittered with gold, but nothing shined brighter than Frederica in her finery.

'Am I not allowed to dance with other women?'

Frederica shook her head. Her curls brushed his cheek tantalisingly.

'Or speak to them?'

'If they try to talk to you, simply run in the opposite direction,' she said primly, but her eyes were dancing with mischief.

Samuel had his own bone to pick with her. 'I shall run from all the ladies, if you promise to do the same from all the men. No more rides with Captain Wallace.'

Her mouth opened. 'But he is just a friend.'

'So is Lady Caro,' he countered.

She gritted her teeth and he tried not to smirk. 'Fine. I shall flee whenever I see him.'

Lifting his hand, he brushed a curl back from her face. It was dark, but the light from the fireworks illuminated her beautiful countenance. 'I never thought to see you jealous.'

'Is jealousy a hideous colour on me?'

He pressed a light kiss to her cheek. 'Quite fetching actually. Perhaps we might find a suitable corner and make our own fireworks show?'

Samuel loved the way Frederica's smile began in her eyes and slowly spread to the rest of her face, finally to her mouth and her beautiful sharp white teeth. She had bitten him before and not only while kissing.

'Yes!'

Putting his hand on her waist, he steered her through the crowd and they were about to make their escape into the gardens, when the Duchess of Hampford appeared in front of them.

He dropped his hand and swore underneath his breath.

Frederica startled and he steadied her with both arms. 'Mama, how…how lovely it is to see you.'

Lady Hampford linked arms with her daughter. 'You know how I enjoy fireworks. Let us watch them together.'

Before Samuel could make his escape, the Duchess had taken his arm into her tight grip. She guided them both back to the middle of the crowd like naughty children. He tried to catch Frederica's eye, but her mother stood directly between them and the Duchess was a very tall woman. And a shrewd one. Samuel was certain that she knew exactly what he and Frederica had been planning to do.

After the fireworks, Lady Hampford dragged them both inside to the dance floor and did not release her hold until the musicians began to play a waltz. 'Ah, should you two like to dance?'

Frederica melted into his arms like she belonged

there. Samuel spun them around together slowly; Frederica's head was practically on his shoulder.

She yawned. 'I am sorry. I am still a little tired from this morning. I woke up early and waited for you, but you never came.'

Samuel did not wish to know if his betrothed had found someone else to keep her company. What mattered is that she wanted him. It was long odds, but he would even wager that she loved him.

'Go to bed early tonight,' he whispered in her ear, 'and we will go riding in the morning. I will come to your house and collect you.'

'Like a package?' she asked with another yawn.

He brushed a light kiss against her sleepy forehead. 'Just like a package.'

After the dance, he returned his tired companion to Lady Hampford and suggested mildly that they might wish to retire early.

Lady Hampford agreed readily and Frederica yawned behind her glove. He walked with them to the entry, where they put on their wraps and called for their carriage.

'I trust we shall see you at Wellington's ball?' Lady Hampford asked in the tone of a command.

'Yes, Duchess,' Samuel said with a slight bow of his head. 'I shall hope for the pleasure of dancing with Lady Frederica.'

Frederica yawned again. 'I will try to stay awake next time.'

Lady Hampford offered her hand. 'Until then.'

Samuel bowed over it and then took Frederica's arm. 'Tomorrow morning, we need to visit the King. Nine o'clock, sharp.'

Her eyes widened and she nodded. Frederica had understood his covert message. He handed her up into the carriage. He thought that she would be asleep in minutes.

Returning to the fête, he saw Slender Billy walking crookedly towards him. It would appear that his old friend had already hit the bottle a little too much that evening. 'Was one of your dreary death letters to her?'

'Not now,' Samuel said, holding up his hands. 'I am afraid that I am in no mood for jokes.'

The prince smiled with only one side of his face. 'I shall not joke with you then. I just thought I would give you a friendly word of advice.'

'Yes?' he said impatiently. Advice from a drunk friend was rarely helpful.

'N-not that I am any great hand at women,' Billy said in a slurred voice. 'The whole world knows of my broken engagement with Princess Ch-Charlotte. I just think that if you are going to marry the girl anyway and you happen to be fond of her, you might do worse than to tell her. Don't make her wait until you are dead to read it in a cold letter.'

Samuel bristled. His relationship with Frederica was like handling a hot coal. One had to be careful or they would get burned. He was certain of his feelings and nearly sure of hers. But like any rider, he did not want to rush his fences. He wanted to wait until the perfect time to tell her. Not some rushed-up job that she might attribute to fear of his impending death.

He laughed. 'Come on, Slender Billy. I think we both could use a drink.'

'Several!' His Royal Highness replied cheerfully.

Chapter Sixteen

Frederica slept poorly. Jealousy burned like poison through her veins. She had dreamed about Lady Caro all night long, except the petite lady had shot her instead of the other way around. Dragging herself out of bed at eight o'clock, she rang for her lady's maid to help her into her riding clothes. Last night her wits had been sleepy and it had taken her a few moments to realise the 'King' that Samuel wished to visit was The King of Spain Inn. She certainly would not mind a visit to a certain *private* parlour.

Watching Jim saddle her horse, Frederica blushed at her words the night before. She had demanded that Samuel not even look at or dance with another woman. While she was a much bigger flirt. The irony was not lost on her. Yet he had not refused her request. He had merely asked her to do the same. Could Samuel actually have feelings for her? Beyond the affection of their childhood memories and family connections? He did not choose her, but could he grow to love her as a man loved a woman? That he was attracted to her, she knew. But she wanted a love as enduring and as rare as the one her parents shared. They were like a team of oxen, equally yoked. They always moved forward together. Not that her parents were at all the same. Papa was an absent-minded naturalist and Mama was a sharp-minded businesswoman, yet their different gifts complemented each other. They supported one another.

How could she create a similar relationship with Samuel?

Smiling wryly, Frederica remembered the story of her mother giving Papa a contract of what she wanted and what he needed. They had not followed it precisely in their marriage, timing and children affected it, but eventually both Papa and Mama had fulfilled all their dreams and ambitions.

Together.

She should tell Samuel about her red scented soaps and her half ownership of the company. And she needed to ask him what he wanted from life. Did he intend to sell out of the army? Become a leader in Parliament? Watch over his estates? She was ashamed to admit to herself that she knew nothing of Samuel's dreams.

Cupping her hands, Jim helped Frederica onto her horse. He led the animal out of the stable by the bridle and into the street just as Samuel arrived on his mare.

Jim tipped his hat to Samuel and then patted the saddlebag. 'I packed your loaded pistol and extra shot. Be careful with it and be careful, my lady.'

Frederica smiled. He was a dear friend. 'Thank you, Jim.'

Clicking her tongue, she urged her horse forward and took her place by Samuel's side.

'Perhaps you should stay home today.'

His words surprised her into pulling up on the reins of her horse. 'Whatever for?'

She saw him swallow, not quite meeting her eyes. 'I think the waiter, Peters, is a French informer. Perhaps even a former member of Napoleon's army. He has the look and the build and his behaviour was not normal. It is dangerous for you to return to Genappe.'

'But not for you?'

Samuel shook his head. 'For both of us. But I would never willingly put you into danger.'

Frederica snorted. She was no simpering miss. If Samuel was going then so would she. 'Jim loaded my pistol and I'll keep it at the ready. Besides, two people are safer than one and perhaps the waiter has not guessed our real purpose.'

They rode silently together through town. There were not many fashionable people about at that time in the morning. The streets were filled with sellers and sweepers. Passing through the last street, they cantered across the field.

Frederica felt like a ball of nervous energy and the quicker pace helped calm her nerves. They rode about five miles, before they slowed their speed for the horses.

Patting her horse's mane, she said quickly, 'I make scented soaps.'

Samuel turned his head towards her. 'Excuse me?'

'I create and make scented soaps,' she said slowly. 'They are red and I add phenol to them to help keep cuts and scrapes clean from infection. I intend to sell them at my mother's perfume shop and distribute the cakes throughout Great Britain. I hope to use her established export routes to expand the reach of my red soaps to Europe and then the Americas.'

He nodded his head, but did not speak.

'You don't mind?' Frederica pressed.

Turning his head to look at her, he said, 'Would it matter if I did?'

She shook her head. 'No, but I still want to know what you think about it.'

'Soap seems like a clean enough hobby.'

The hairs on the back of her neck stood up when he said 'hobby' but then she realised he was gently teasing her. 'It is not a hobby. It is a profession. How do you feel about your duchess working?'

'The more money the merrier,' he said, angling his horse so his leg brushed against hers. Her heartbeat quickened. 'In case you were not aware, my dearest fiancée, I am rather short on funds. We will have to live quite economically for the first few years.'

Frederica wished she could tell how much Samuel was jesting and which words were the truth. 'Yes, poor us. Living on the cheap in a palace.'

His lips twitched before splitting into a heart-stopping grin. 'Precisely. Oh, Frederica, I knew exactly what I was getting into when I asked you to marry me. I am sure that you will be a magnificent duchess and businesswoman like your mother. You take after her in more than appearance.'

These words ought to have placated her, instead they made her feel worse. Samuel understood her, but she did not know him as well and it irked her.

'What do you want to do with your future?'

Samuel's eyes darted back and forth. From the road to the wooded area to a stone fence. 'I wish to live another month.'

She swallowed her disappointment. He must not

be in a sharing mood today. He had already told her about his father, perhaps he was not yet ready to talk about himself.

Urging his horse to a gallop, Frederica had to focus on her own mount to keep up with him for the rest of the ride to Genappe. The road into the small town felt strangely quiet, like Brussels had. There were no people about. When they arrived at The King of Spain Inn, Samuel dismounted and then lifted her off her horse without a word. Taking her hand in a painfully tight grip, he pulled her into the inn.

The innkeeper met them with his typical low bows and immediately escorted them into the same private parlour. He promised to bring them tea and closed the door.

Unbuttoning her pelisse, she took it off and hung it on the rack. She untied her bonnet and shook her hair out. Her entire person felt sweaty and in need of her stringent scented soap after the long ride. She placed her bonnet on top of her pelisse and went to open the latch of the window.

'Don't touch it,' Samuel snapped.

Spinning on her heel, she turned to look at him. 'Which George died and made you king?'

He gritted his teeth and clenched his fists. 'It is not safe. Back away from the window and do not give anyone a clear shot of you.'

She remembered his warning about the French informant. Frederica touched her neck and felt the steady pulse of her heartbeat. She wished to live another month too. Her shoulders were tight, yet her lips trembled.

Taking a seat on the far side of the table, she whispered in French, 'What should I do?'

Samuel moved his chair until it was right next to hers. He sat down and entwined their fingers, as if they were besotted lovers. 'Act normally, but we will not linger today. I only pray that Grant is timely.'

Frederica wished she knew when Samuel was spy acting and when he was not. The sweet brush of his lips against her forehead felt tender. How much did he care? It seemed like a silly question when both of their lives were at stake, but she could not help but think it.

The innkeeper knocked before bringing in the tea tray, followed by Lieutenant-Colonel Grant. His scarlet uniform coat looked more ragged than ever. His eyes narrowed when he saw them holding hands on the table. Samuel pulled away first and Frederica busied herself making the tea once the innkeeper set down the tray with a bow. Grant also moved his chair from the window. Samuel's suspicions must be correct.

The Scot reached into his coat and slid the letter across the table. Samuel pocketed it as Frederica poured three cups of tea. The liquid burned her tongue and throat as it went down. She ate a couple of biscuits, before draining the rest of her burning tea from her cup. Once her cup touched the saucer, Samuel stood up.

'Thank you, Grant,' he said with a deferential nod, before putting on his hat.

Frederica sprang to her feet and pulled on her bonnet, tying the ribbons haphazardly and slipping into her pelisse coat. She did up the buttons so quickly that they were not in the right order, but she did not care. The feeling that they were in trouble only heightened with each moment. They needed to go immediately.

For the first time, Grant stayed in the private parlour and she and Samuel left. He tossed a coin to the ostler and their horses were brought around to the front of the building. She could see that the mare and the grey had been fed, watered, and brushed. Frederica wished her dear grey could get a little more rest, but it was not to be. Samuel grasped her by the waist and lifted her into the saddle without a by your leave. She was both annoyed and impressed. Frederica was not a featherweight, but Samuel had lifted her easily. Swinging up into his own saddle, Samuel nodded to the ostler and signalled for Frederica to lead.

She did not have to be told twice. Easing her heels into her horse's flank, she urged her tired mare forward to a gallop. It was bad manners to canter through a town, but she could not shake the feeling that they were in very real danger if they stayed. They had not ridden a mile out of the small town when Frederica heard a shot. She abruptly swerved her horse and fell out of the side-saddle hard into the dirt. She brushed her dress off—at least she had not been hit. She fumbled with the saddlebag for her pistol and pulled it out, cocking it.

After dismounting, Samuel came to her side. 'Are you injured?'

'No, but I thought I heard a shot.'

Frederica looked around at the surrounding fields and a clump of trees thirty feet from the road. She looked back at the trees and caught a glimpse of a man. She pointed her pistol at the spot and shot. The figure ran away. She must have missed. Pulling out her shot bag, she reloaded the pistol as Samuel went for his own gun.

'Do you think you hit him?'

Shaking her head, Frederica said, 'No, he was too far away for my pistol. He must have had a shotgun. Should we go after the man?'

Samuel grunted. 'No. I say we run for it. He might already be reloading the shotgun behind a tree and we will be sitting ducks.'

'Let's ride.'

He practically threw her back onto her horse, her pistol in her hand. Then slapped the rump of her mare to make it run. Glancing over her shoulder, she saw him swing into his own saddle and gallop towards her. Like herself, Samuel had pulled out his gun and was holding the reins with only one hand. His bigger horse quickly caught up with hers.

'Keep your pistol out and your eyes peeled,' he said.

She swallowed as she nodded. Her throat felt tight and drier than the Sahara Desert. For the first time since arriving in Belgium, she longed for the dull, steadiness of the London Season. They ran their horses for over a mile before Samuel deemed it safe for them to walk. She did not think her poor grey could have gone much longer at their previous speed.

Exhaling slowly, Frederica released the hammer of her pistol and placed it back into her saddlebag. She wiggled her clenched fingers before picking up the reins again. Glancing over at Samuel, she saw that he too had stored his weapon.

He smiled as he sighed. 'That was close. Do you still like being a spy?'

Grinning in return, Frederica nodded. 'I like being useful and proving that a lady can be just as helpful as a man.'

'I've never thought about it.'

'Women's rights?'

Samuel cleared his throat. 'Forgive me, I was speaking about myself and not about you. I meant that I had never thought about my future and what I wanted. I suppose that I assumed that it was already mapped out for me. I would take care of my family's estates and preform my duties in Parliament. I have not considered what *I* wanted.'

'You should.'

'I've always wanted to be like your father.'

A laugh broke from her lips. 'But, Samuel, he is terrible at estate management. My mother oversaw our estates before Wick took charge. And I do not think he has attended Parliament more than a handful of times. He only cares about his family and his animals. The rest of the two-legged world is on its own as far as he is concerned.'

He leaned towards her and their legs brushed against each other. It set Frederica's pulse racing again.

'I did not mean that I wish to become a naturalist or a scientist,' Samuel said. 'Rather, I want to be a father like him. He played with his children. Taught them how to do things. And every time that I visited, he always had a line of little ones trailing behind him. Hampford never acted annoyed or impatient. Quite the opposite, he always seemed delighted that his children wished to be with him.'

Frederica laughed with her mouth closed. Her little sisters, Helen and Becca, were Papa's favourites because they loved animals as much as he did. They still followed him around. They were all three probably exploring the local fauna and flora as well as wildlife in Greece. Her chest ached from missing them.

They were quiet on the rest of the ride. Samuel's keen eyes were watching for threats and Frederica's mind spun with thoughts. She sighed with relief when they reached Rue de Lombard just as the sun began to set. Jim moved to help her from her horse, but Samuel was there first. She slid down into his arms and felt safe for the first time that day. Leaning her head against his shoulder, she hugged him tightly.

Samuel rubbed soft circles on her back. 'You're safe now.'

'You are too,' she mumbled into his shoulder. The bullet could have easily hit him, as well. She wanted him to live another month. Hundreds of months.

Stepping back, he released her waist and back, but moved his hand to her chin. 'I want a future with you. I want to live on the cheap in a palace full of our children. I want to teach them how to ride, swim, and hunt with you. And then I want to help you wash them with your scented soaps after they have got all filthy and scratched up from playing together. I would not mind helping you wash either…in exchange for certain liberties.'

Her face felt warm, as did the rest of her body. It was not just his flirtatious words, although she was not a ninny and understood their sexual meaning. It was the pureness of his dreams. Samuel needed to be the father that his own had not been. But most importantly, he said that he wanted those things with her.

'You have beautiful dreams,' she said, grabbing his

wrist and kissing the palm of his hand, before lightly pressing her lips to his mouth. 'Thank you for letting me be a part of them. I shall have Jim bring you over a cake of soap.'

Chapter Seventeen

The next morning, Samuel's nerves were shot and he felt emotionally drained. These were not uncommon consequences of spending time with his betrothed. Although, it would not be fair to blame her for yesterday. He had felt goose bumps on his arm before he even met Frederica that morning. He knew it had been dangerous to make that trip with her. The battle was getting closer. The air felt charged with it.

He was no longer a lad who wished to prove himself to Wellington—another surrogate father figure. Samuel knew that there was no glory and very little dignity in a battlefield death. An officer's body received more deference than a soldier's, but they were still piled together in a barn or a charnel house until friends or family could take the corpse and have it properly buried. The common soldiers' bodies were thrown into mass graves with no names and sometimes without markers.

No mourners.

No funerals.

This would be the end thousands of his men faced after their battle with Napoleon's armies. At seventeen, he had thought that he had nothing to lose. And now he knew that he had everything to lose. Frederica, his family, a future with a palace full of children. Slender Billy was right. He could not wait until after the war to tell Frederica his feelings. She deserved so much more than a death letter.

Exhaling, Samuel sat in the corner of the room, unnoticed. He watched Colonel Scovell bow to the new chief staff officer, Colonel Sir William Howe DeLancey, a man in his thirties with piercing dark eyes and curly hair. The man towered a head over Scovell as he escorted him to Wellington's office. DeLancey stayed at the door and Scovell entered and left the room alone. Samuel would have loved to hear what they were saying. But it was bad form to spy on your own side.

A few minutes later, the Duke of Wellington opened the door and barked an order that all his staff should come immediately for a meeting. Samuel was one of the first of the twenty men to arrive. He sat next to Lord Fitzroy Somerset and Sir Alexander Gordon. Within five minutes all members of the staff were seated around the dining room. In the centre of the mahogany table was a large map of Europe. Strong and powerful like King Arthur of old, Wellington stood at the top of the oval table.

'The intelligence I received last night from Grant suggests that the bulk of the French army is here in Paris protecting it,' Wellington said, pointing to the city on the map. 'He further suggests that over a hundred thousand men have been moved to the north of France and are coming our way with Napoleon to personally command.'

'Then we have the advantage, Duke,' Samuel said.

'We have nearly ninety-two thousand men, and that is not including the Prussians.'

'Napoleon's presence on the field is worth forty thousand men,' the general said gravely. 'And his soldiers are veterans. They have fought before, unlike most of our soldiers, who are green, and the loyalty of the Dutch soldiers is particularly precarious—many are still committed to France.'

Somerset stood up, knocking his chair over. 'The Prince of Orange has suggested that we go on the offensive and surprise Napoleon on his own turf.'

Wellington pressed his long thin fingers together. 'In regard to offensive operations, my opinion is that, however strong we shall be in reference to the enemy, we should not extend ourselves further than is absolutely necessary, in order to facilitate the subsistence of the troops. His Royal Highness, the Prince of Orange, has presented his plan to me, and I do not approve of an extension from the Channel to the Alps, and I am convinced that it will be found not only fatal, but that the troops at such a distance on the left of our line will be entirely out of our position of the operations.'

Picking up his chair, Somerset sat back down. 'What would you have us do, sir?'

Samuel wondered the same thing.

Wellington pulled out several maps of the local area and pointed out the best spots for a defensive action. 'I have sent several spies to watch over Napoleon's army. We must know which road he will take, so that we can choose the best possible ground to meet him. When word arrives, we need to be prepared to immediately spring into action. All men on my staff must be in constant readiness.'

The general then dismissed his staff, but held a hand on Samuel's shoulder to detain him.

'Pelford, I would like you to stay,' Wellington said in his softest, most penetrating tone. 'I wish to have private speech with you.'

Samuel watched Wellington close the door after every other person had left the room and walk around the large oval table.

'You have been a member of my staff since our days in the Peninsula, and you know I consider my staff to be family,' Wellington said and waited for Samuel's nod of affirmation. 'I would not ask this of you if I did not think it was imperative to our success. I would like you and your betrothed to do more than simply courier information for Grant. I want you two to travel deeper into France and learn which generals and what roads Napoleon will be taking. Information that Grant cannot get whilst wearing his army uniform.'

Riding alone with Frederica was pushing the line of propriety. Travelling alone with her would be ruinous to her reputation.

'The Duchess of Hampford would never agree to it.'

Wellington stopped walking around the table and sat next to Samuel. 'Lady Frederica does not need her mother's permission. Only her husband's.'

It took a few moments for his words to sink in. The general meant *him*. Samuel would not have to wait until after his army duties were over to marry Frederica. To bed her. To make her his in every possible way. He wanted nothing more—but then he would be placing her in terrible danger. He was not sure he could endure many more days like yesterday.

'Unfortunately, it will cause a bit of uproar and perhaps some pernicious gossip,' Wellington continued, 'but Scovell thought that if you left with Lady Frederica from my party tonight, leaving a note that you were being married privately, then no one would expect either of you to return for a few days. I, of course, will not court-martial you for desertion either.'

Samuel could not even form a small smile at the poor joke. 'When will we be married?'

The general cleared his throat. 'Tonight. Scovell has arranged for a Belgian minister to meet you at a chapel not far from the fête. That is, if you are willing?'

Samuel's muscles felt tense and his stomach heavy. How could he risk the life of the woman he loved? How could he make such a large decision about her welfare? Blinking rapidly, he realised that he did not need to. The decision was not his in the first place. It was Frederica's. She did not require his or her mother's permission. She was an intelligent and independent woman. Yesterday, she had proved that she was a capable spy.

Taking a deep breath, Samuel sat up in his chair. 'I am willing if she is, Duke. The only permission Lady Frederica requires is her own.'

'Of course. Of course,' Wellington agreed, vigorously nodding. 'But from all accounts she is a formidable young woman.'

That was putting it lightly, Samuel thought.

Chapter Eighteen

Shaking out his clenched fingers, Samuel entered the large ballroom in his dress uniform. The Duke of Wellington's party was stuffed with fashionable people like a London squeeze. Samuel acknowledged several acquaintances with curt nods before walking over to a large circle where the general stood in the middle.

'I say nothing about our defensive operations,' Wellington said loudly, 'because I am inclined to believe that Marshal Blücher of the Prussians and I are so well united, and so strong, that the enemy cannot do us much mischief. I am at the advanced post of the whole, the greatest part of the enemy's force is in my front, and, if I am satisfied, others need be under no apprehension.'

Samuel wondered how much was bravado, for the general complained about everything from his staff, to the equipment, to the soldiers, in private. Leaving the circle, he walked on and spotted his friend the Prince of Orange moving his way. Slender Billy put his arm around Samuel's shoulders and reminisced about the time Samuel had put soap in the officers' wine and when Fitzroy burped out a bubble. It was during this anecdote that Samuel noticed Frederica standing on the side of the dance floor. Captain Wallace was at her elbow, but she was not dancing with him. Even though her left foot was tapping to the beat of the tune. She wore a light green dress that emphasised her lovely, voluptuous figure. He could hardly wait to take it off this night.

'Well, old fellow,' Slender Billy said, giving him a little shove in the middle of his back. 'You'd best go claim the girl if you are going to ignore who you are speaking to and glower.'

Recalled to his senses, Samuel quickly apologised, but the prince would have none of it. Billy shooed him away with one hand. 'Kiss her once for me. Make that twice. She's a looker.'

Trying to suppress a smile, Samuel strode over to Frederica's side. 'Ah, Captain Wallace, I believe the first waltz is mine.'

He abruptly took Frederica into his arms, waltzing her away from him. Frederica's hazel eyes sparkled as she smiled at him. Samuel felt an overwhelming desire to kiss her there and then.

'Poor Mark, I told him that I was not dancing this evening,' she said with a wrinkle of her nose. 'You have made a liar of me.'

Samuel raised his eyebrows. 'Actually, I hope that I am about to make an honest woman of you. Wellington wants us to elope and go farther into France to discover which generals and what roads Napoleon will take. I told him that I was willing, but that you could decide for yourself.'

Her mouth hung open, but she did not speak for several turns. 'It would be very hard for you to take a wedding trip by yourself.'

'And terribly awkward,' he said with a ghost of a smile playing on the edge of his lips. 'Not to mention disappointing.'

Bright red circles formed on her cheeks and Samuel had a pretty good idea what his betrothed was thinking about. It was all that he had been able to focus on all afternoon.

'I shall try not to be a disappointment,' she parried without her usual sharpness. 'Shall I go and tell my mother?'

He scanned the room and easily located the Duchess of Hampford speaking to Lady Richmond. 'There is no need. After we leave, a waiter will give your mother a billet. I have written to inform her of our private marriage and short wedding trip.'

Frederica looked down at the green lace overlay of her dress. 'I do think I might be a tad conspicuous in the countryside in this gown. In your plans, have you provided for proper clothing for me?'

'Colonel Scovell's wife saw to it,' Samuel said, pressing his hand harder against her waist. 'We are to be middle-class French merchants and will be dressed accordingly.'

The musicians struck the final chord. Reluctantly, Samuel dropped his hand from her waist and took her fingers in his other hand. He led her through several couples and an antechamber. Accepting his hat from the servant, he took the wrap and put it around Frederica. Then he escorted her out the door. Frederica lifted her skirt as she walked down the stairs to where a carriage waited for them. Scovell and his wife sat on the opposite seat with their backs to the driver. The couple matched each other in age and reserved countenances.

'Good evening, Lady Stringham, Lord Pelford,' Colonel Scovell said, bowing his head. 'May I introduce my wife, Mrs Scovell?'

Samuel and Frederica greeted the older woman in unison: 'How do you do?'

'Very well, thank you,' she said in a soft voice.

Awkward silence followed and Scovell broke it. 'We do not have a long drive. The chapel is only a couple of streets away.'

Frederica gave a small smile, but Samuel could see that she was nervous. She kept running her right fingers up her left arm, breathing in and out abnormally fast. The coach stopped, and the Scovells exited first. Samuel followed, offering his arm to Frederica, but she leapt out of the carriage and onto the pavement. She then took his hand and they entered the church.

Several candles cast shadows in the large domed room. A man in black robes stood in front of the crucifix and beckoned them forward. Samuel took Frederica's elbow and directed her past the wooden pews to the front of the chapel.

Nodding, Samuel told the minister to proceed.

The minister was a small man with a lined face. He smiled at Frederica and began the wedding ceremony in French. The minister's sermon was succinct, and Samuel almost missed his cue to say 'I will'.

Frederica said, 'I will,' loudly, and her voice echoed in the empty hall.

The minister then declared them man and wife. They both signed the register and then Scovell witnessed the marriage certificate. The spymaster congratulated them and said that his lodgings were only a step away and that he and his wife would walk. He assured Samuel that both of their trunks were in the carriage and explained that they had rooms booked at the Fleur Blanche Hôtel.

The ride to the inn took almost ten minutes—it was on the edge of the city. Neither Samuel nor Frederica attempted to make conversation. His bride appeared just as nervous as he was and not nearly as excited. He swallowed, his mouth dry.

Samuel stepped out of the carriage first. 'I would hate for you to sprain your ankle before your first adventure.'

Clasping his hands around her narrow waist, he helped her down. He could hardly wait to get her into his arms again.

He directed the coachman to bring in the saddlebags and he opened the door into the inn. The Fleur Blanche Hôtel was a modern building of three stories with an elegant exterior of the palest blue. They were ushered in by a landlord impeccably dressed in a simple suit of black. The landlord looked to be at least seventy years old. His hair was white and thin, but worn to his shoulders. His face was wrinkled, but his figure did not slump. He whistled for a servant to carry the luggage, and he begged Samuel and Frederica to follow him.

The proprietor took them to a second-floor room that was richly furnished in shades of gold. A large four-poster bed with gold bed hangings took up most of the room. A bottle of champagne and two goblets were on a small round dining table. The landlord gave them a knowing smile and wished the new couple a happy marriage. The servant placed the saddlebags near the door, before shutting it behind him.

Frederica walked around the room. 'What a charming apartment. I have never stayed in a hotel so fine.'

It was obvious by the way she chattered that she felt ill at ease.

Samuel coloured with embarrassment and disappointment as he sputtered, 'I did not realise that they would only reserve one room. I do not wish for you to be uncomfortable.'

Frederica's neck and face were flushed, but she looked him directly in the eyes. 'We are married after all—to each other. Will you turn around whilst I change my clothes?'

He would have dearly liked to watch, but did as she requested. He had not considered that shyness could be a hidden quality of his bride. She had certainly never been shy before and he found that he did not particularly like it. He wished for his brazen betrothed.

Samuel felt a hand on his shoulder and jumped.

'Would you undo my buttons?' Frederica asked, her neck as red as her cheeks. 'I cannot reach them.'

She turned away from him.

Lifting a curl off her back, he placed it on her shoulder. He breathed heavily as he fiddled with the small ornate buttons. His heart beat furiously in his chest as though he were in a battle for his life. He felt a frantic heat course through his veins. Frederica turned to look at him and took off her dress, leaving only her shift and corset on. She carelessly tossed it to the ground. Like all aristocratic ladies, she was used to being waited on.

'Could you untie my corset, as well?' Frederica asked, and again turned her beautiful back towards him.

Was she trying to seduce him? Or could she truly not untie her own strings?

Samuel gulped and took several tries before untying the knot and slowly unlacing the whaleboned garment. He let it drop to the floor. He placed his hands where the corset had been around her waist and kissed her shoulder. She made a mewling sound that nearly undid him. He nuzzled her neck and let his hands stray upward.

'I—I—I am not ready.'

With what was left of his slipping self-control, Samuel stepped back from her. He had been preparing for this night all day but she'd had less than an hour. From other officers' bawdy talk, he knew that the first time for a lady could be painful and unpleasant. It was not unnatural that she would be scared, and unlike her feminine peers, a Stringham would know exactly how mating was done. She probably knew many ways, but this thought did not cool down his body.

He clenched his hands and exhaled slowly. 'There is no rush. Would you prefer I asked for a separate room?'

'Do you snore?' Frederica asked, blushing fiercely as she stood before him in the thin material of her shift.

'No.'

'Will you steal the sheets?'

'Never.'

She attempted a tight smile. 'Then I suppose there is no reason why we could not sleep in the same bed.'

Samuel agreed with her gravely. Sleeping beside her would be more torture than pleasure. He would have to keep his hands to himself. He had always prided himself on self-control, but that was before a half-naked Frederica would be sleeping beside him.

Wearing only her shift, Frederica slipped into the bed underneath the covers. Her eyes were as wide as guineas as she watched him unbutton his uniform jacket and then his shirt. She did not avert her gaze and he was not going to ask her to. Nor was he going to fully undress before her. He thought it would scare her and remove his tenuous control of his own body. After putting on his nightshirt, he then pulled off his unpleasantly tight breeches. He brought the bottle of champagne and two wine glasses to the bed. He uncorked the bottle and then poured out the bubbly liquid into the glasses.

He handed one to Frederica and then raised his glass. 'To our marriage.'

Frederica raised her cup and echoed his toast.

Chapter Nineteen

Frederica opened her eyes. For a moment, she did not recognise her surroundings. Beside her in bed, softly snoring, lay her husband. The morning sun shone through the curtains and she pulled the sheets up to her neck. She sneaked another peek at Samuel. His chest rose up and down rhythmically. Extending her hand from under the sheet, she brushed his muscled chest with her fingers. How she had longed to touch him the night before. To try out all the delightfully shocking things her mother had told her about. But she had been too afraid. Not of the act. Nor of the pain that might be part of her losing her maidenhood.

She was afraid that she would be a gauche disappointment. Young men were encouraged to 'practise', for want of a better word, before the marriage night. Their indiscretions were socially acceptable as long as they were relatively discreet with a widow, mistress, or at a brothel. Those women knew how to please a man and enhance the sexual experience. Likely some naughty tricks to extend the pleasure. Frederica had no doubt that she would eventually excel at bed games.

She enjoyed kissing very much and she loved kissing Samuel.

Most young ladies did not know how babies were made. The lucky ones like herself were told by their mother before their wedding night. Some brides knew nothing and had to rely on whatever their husband decided to tell them. Or not tell them. Frederica could readily understand how terrifying sexual congress could be for the unprepared.

She was prepared in knowledge. But what if he laughed at her naivety? Her clumsiness? He had laughed at her so many times in the past and each time it had crumbled a part of her soul. Not that she had been innocent. She had wanted his attention too much to be ignored.

Gulping, she could not resist allowing her fingers to run over his smooth, muscled chest again. A large hand caught hers, and Samuel opened his eyes. Frederica felt heat rush to her cheeks.

'You looked just like that the first time I saw you. You were six or seven years old,' Samuel recalled. 'You had on a yellow frock and your hair was in two braids. Your face looked so worried and full of guilt.'

'I was guilty,' Frederica confessed. 'Elizabeth, Mantheria, and Charles said that I was too young to play with you, so I collected spiders and put them in your bed. When you arrived, you gave me a doll with blue ribbons in her hair. I felt terrible, until the next day, when you pushed me into a mud puddle.'

Frederica felt the laugh vibrate in his chest before she heard it.

Samuel smiled at her. 'We were a pair of hoydens. I daresay you remember every awful thing I did.'

She nodded her head into the pillow. 'I do. Every single dead mouse you put in my shoes, every worm you slipped down the back of my dress, and every mud ball you threw at my head. Shall I go on?'

'No, no,' Samuel said, lifting her hand to his mouth and kissing it. 'That list is incriminating enough. I daresay it was a good thing we only visited each other in the summer.'

Squeezing her eyes shut, Frederica said, 'Let us not talk about the past.'

He kissed the tips of her five fingers as he still held her hand. 'You are right. I would much rather talk about the present and you do not need to be sly about your caresses.'

She gulped. 'I do not think that I am ready yet—for, you know.'

Samuel pressed one more kiss into the palm of her hand. 'You might not be, but your hand certainly is. Well, shall we get an early start of it?'

Frederica readily agreed, and with less embarrassment than last night, she managed to give herself a quick sponge bath and put on a fresh shift. She pulled her corset up, but could not manage to tie it from behind. She felt like a cat chasing its tail. Samuel must have seen her struggles and offered his assistance.

Tying the strings, he kissed her bare shoulder. 'Whoever invented corsets should be awarded a knighthood at the very least.'

Frederica laughed silently, for he had squeezed all the air out of her. She walked over to her trunk and took out a plain grey dress made of coarse material. Pulling it over her head, she returned to Samuel to button up the back buttons. Then she moved to the mirror and combed through her long brown hair, while Samuel finished dressing in a simple dark blue suit, suitable for a merchant. Frederica braided her hair and twisted it into a knot at her neck. Wade would be horrified with her hairstyle. She stuck her tongue out at herself in the mirror.

'Another face that I recall you giving me as a child,' he said, peering over her shoulder in the mirror.

She turned to face him and with one gentle finger traced the white scar on his cheek near his jaw. She heard his breath quicken with her touch.

'You did not have this growing up.'

'No, you are not responsible for this scar,' Samuel said with a heart-stopping smile. 'I did not even get it in a battle. Merely a practice skirmish with a friend.'

'How ignoble.'

He laughed and added in a mock-serious tone, 'Please don't give my secret away.'

'Never,' she whispered, realising that they were no longer playing. Samuel's secrets would always remain safe in her keeping.

'Rica, we had better hurry and eat our breakfast. We should have been on the road an hour ago.'

'Yes, of course.'

They breakfasted in a small private parlour and partook heartily of cold ham and pastries.

She picked up a buttery croissant. 'When did I become Rica?'

'You said that you didn't like the nickname Freddie, so I was trying a new one—Rica,' Samuel said, lifting his glass of juice. 'I suppose, if you would prefer it, I could call you Your Grace, Lady Frederica Maria Ada

Isabella Stringham Corbin, Duchess of Pelford, but it is a bit of a mouthful.'

Frederica's eyes wandered to his mouth. 'I do not like either shortened version of my name. They're juvenile… It is as if you still see me as a child.'

'Nothing could be further from my thoughts.'

Frederica felt her neck and cheeks suffuse with colour. Samuel grinned in triumph and took a large bite of an apple Danish. The filling squirted out onto his lapel and Frederica laughed. Samuel wiped it off with his napkin and joined in her mirth.

She could not help but wonder how her mother had felt the morning after she had married a stranger. Frederica had wed her childhood nemesis. Her emotions seemed to roll all over inside of her; she felt—excited—embarrassed—eager—unsure.

Returning to their golden room, Frederica donned a plain black riding habit and dowdy straw bonnet. Samuel settled with the landlord, and a groom attached their saddlebags to two horses. Samuel put his hands on her waist and assisted her into her side-saddle. She felt breathless from the brief contact. He gave her a small smile and started his horse into a trot. Frederica followed behind him, and they left the city of Brussels.

They rode for over ten hours until they passed the border between the Netherlands and France. There were no soldiers who policed the border, and Frederica saw several peasants pulling carts of their belongings towards France.

'Where are they going?' Frederica asked.

'They are French loyalists returning to the safety and protection of their emperor,' Samuel said. 'Our horses are about spent. We will sleep here tonight and allow the ostlers to attend to the horses.'

Frederica nodded and followed him. She had never ridden so many miles in one day in the saddle. She felt sore and exhausted.

It was early afternoon the following day and the sun was directly above them. The French town they passed through was a small one and boasted no more than fifteen buildings in total—two of which were public houses. Samuel pulled his horse to a stop near the first public house and dismounted. Handing the reins to an ostler, he lifted Frederica out of the saddle and led her into the inn.

Only a handful of customers stood near the bar, and the owner, a round-faced man with a leering grin, met them and asked if they would require a room. Samuel answered in French that they were only stopping for luncheon, but would require a private parlour if one were available. The owner ogled Frederica again, then led them to a cramped room. Samuel ordered the meal and shut the door.

'Stuffy, isn't it?' he said in French, opening the small window. Then he added in a soft tone barely above a whisper, 'Remember, we must only speak French while in France.'

Frederica nodded and took off her hat. She shook her head and yawned widely. 'Where are we going?'

'To Paris perhaps,' Samuel said. 'We will ride until we find the army.'

'You were stationed at Paris with Lord Wellington?'

He looked out the window and then walked up behind her and whispered in her ear, 'This is hardly the time or place to discuss my time with the British ambassador to France.'

Frederica bristled, but remained silent. The owner knocked twice and carried in a tray of food and a pint of ale. They ate in silence and when they were finished, Samuel called for the horses and paid their shot. The owner eyed Frederica on their way out and gave her one last leery grin. She shuddered. Glad that she was not alone.

They rode for another three hours before Samuel slowed his horse down to a trot and she followed suit. 'We should give the horses a rest.'

Frederica nodded, but did not speak a word. They rode side by side for a quarter of an hour before Samuel said, 'I am sorry. I did not mean to offend you.'

'Oh,' was all that she could think to say.

Samuel suggested that they dismount and walk for a little while to rest their mounts. Frederica readily agreed.

'I have always wanted to travel,' Frederica said suddenly. 'That is why I persuaded Mama to take me to Brussels. I loved the year that I spent in Italy.'

'After this is over, I will take you anywhere you wish to go,' Samuel said, taking her hand and holding it.

'I should like to see the places you have lived—France, Austria, and Spain. My little sisters are in Greece with Papa and I am terribly jealous. They write of all the little islands that they visit in their boat.'

He squeezed her hand. 'I hope you are not planning on guiding the boat. When we went punting near Farleigh, you hit a tree branch in the water and nearly toppled into the river.'

Frederica laughed at her younger self; she had fallen into the boat and it had left her covered in bruises. 'Well, I think the blame lies squarely with the person who taught me how to punt.'

'Nonsense, I gave very clear instructions.'

'Don't hit the tree,' she mimicked. 'Not one word about how to move the boat in a different direction, going against the current, and after I fell into the boat and quite scraped up my hands and knees, all you said was "I told you not to hit the tree".'

'I was insufferable,' he agreed.

'So was I, but for quite a different reason than you.'

His hold on her hand tightened. 'What do you mean?'

'You were always trying to avoid me or running away from me.'

'Well, I am not running away now,' he said, winking suggestively.

Frederica gulped audibly, and Samuel pulled her into his arms for a brief kiss. He released her, and she felt her heart in her chest beating against her corset.

'I chased you because you ignored me,' she blurted out. Her face and neck growing hot. 'And the more you ignored me, the greater lengths I went to get your attention. Culminating in putting a bear cub in your room and yet you still acted as if I was beneath your notice. I could never decide if I liked or hated you more.'

One side of his mouth quirked up. 'I would ask if you like or hate me more now, but I am too afraid of the answer.'

'And I am still afraid that you will run away from me or laugh at my feelings for you.'

There.

She had said her greatest fear. The true reason why

she kept him an arm's length from her heart. She was so scared of getting hurt again. Of offering her heart on a platter, only to have him refuse it.

'I noticed you that last summer,' he said quietly, his eyes meeting hers. 'How could I not? You had grown breasts. Beautiful large breasts and I could not stop staring at them. I was afraid that you had caught me more than once, so I tried not to look at you at all. I was seventeen and you were only fourteen. You were too young for me then. I was supposed to be the mature one, but the ragamuffin little girl who had chased me and beat me at everything was turning into a lovely young woman. And I did not want to think of you that way. It made me feel dirty like my father. That is why I gave you the chocolates and told you that you were immature. I wanted you to avoid me. To hate me. But in truth, I was the immature one.'

'And now?'

'I still cannot stop myself from staring at your large breasts.'

Frederica giggled and playfully hit his shoulder. 'Do be serious.'

'I am,' he assured her with a saucy grin. 'But the rest of your figure now commands equal attention. I adore the sway of your hips and the roundness of your bottom.'

At least he was attracted to her now and did not try to avoid her. She could hardly expect him to tell a woman he was compelled to marry because of family debts that he loved her. 'So I could be headless and it would not matter to you.'

'Just because your lush lips and sparkling eyes were not in the top three of my favourite body parts does not mean that I do not appreciate them. Only slightly less than other more obvious endowments. I am also enamoured of your wicked roving hands, but again, they are lower down on the list.'

'Your eyes are the top of my list.'

'That is because you have not seen me unclothed yet.'

Frederica gasped in surprise. Choked and then coughed. Samuel's conversation was dripping with innuendo.

'The sun is starting to set,' he said, glancing over his shoulder. 'We have only another hour or two of light, we had best get back on the horses.'

They rode hard until they reached the city of Valenciennes and found a tiny inn. Samuel personally saw that the horses were rubbed down and fed, while Frederica retired to their small chamber. She took off her hat and let down her hair. She combed through it until Samuel arrived with a bottle of Burgundy and two glasses.

'I was hoping you would need some assistance undressing.'

Frederica stiffened and her hazel eyes nearly popped out of her head.

Light-headed, Samuel roared with laughter. 'Just with the buttons you cannot reach. I daresay we are both exhausted after the hard ride.'

For once his mirth did not offend her. Frederica admitted that she was very tired. Samuel expertly unbuttoned her plain dress and untied her corset. He did not kiss her shoulder this time, and Frederica felt keenly disappointed. They ate dinner together in a private parlour before returning to their room and climbing into the narrow bed. Frederica could feel his warm arm against hers. She felt his body twitch as he fell asleep. She lay there for a long time listening to his steady breathing and wondering if Samuel could grow to love her, as deeply as her father had her mother.

Chapter Twenty

They left the inn early the next morning and rode all day until they reached the town of Roye, and the day after that, they travelled until they reached the outskirts of Paris. Frederica felt bone-tired, but her eyes could not stop moving from one building to another. The old city at sunset was an architectural delight. Cut into perfect sections by the rivers. She wished that she could explore it more fully with Samuel. But that was impossible.

Samuel's eyes did not stop moving either. He was looking for potential threats. Soldiers swarmed the streets with ladies on their arms. Every hotel and public house was filled. The French citizens who could afford to had come to the protection of Paris. For Napoleon had highly fortified the city.

They rode past a fashionable section of town with brightly painted buildings and gorgeous architecture. However, Samuel guided them to a quieter inn, far from the centre of town, where they spent the night. Frederica was becoming more accustomed to having another person in her bed. Samuel did not steal the sheets, but despite his denial, he did snore—a low monotonous drone. She tried to fall asleep but could not. She decided to touch him to see if he would stop snoring and placed her hand on his shoulder. He stirred, turned on his side towards her, and slung his left arm over her waist. Frederica held her breath, but he did not wake up. Exhaling, she closed her eyes and fell asleep with a smile on her lips.

Frederica woke up first, even though it was nearly midday, and mulled over a plan. She tapped Samuel on the shoulder and he moaned and turned over. He placed his pillow over his head. She laughed and began to tickle him.

'I surrender,' he said, turning over to look at her. He pulled her against his hard chest and kissed her passionately until they were breathless.

She loved kissing him and snuggling into the crook of his arm. 'I have a plan, but I am sure you will disapprove of it.'

'Well, I have surrendered.'

'I think we should go to a pub tonight with lots of soldiers and partake of nasty tap drinks.'

Samuel sat up abruptly and shook his head. 'I will not allow my wife—'

Frederica placed a finger on his lips. 'You have surrendered, so you must listen to the entire plan. You and I will flirt and mingle and find out what we can. People are much more inclined to speak freely after a pint or two.'

'It is still too dangerous.'

'I will bring my pistol and my husband for protection.'

'My presence might be a deterrent to the French officers,' he said flatly.

'We will never be far from each other.'

Samuel kissed her fingers one by one. 'It is a good plan. If a man were to ask such searching questions, it might be noticed, but to a beautiful woman, no soldier can resist bragging of his consequence.'

'I will need to purchase a suitable dress and make-up for my face.'

They ate a late repast and then explored several shops to find the necessary purchases. Samuel helped Frederica get ready. She only wore one petticoat and dampened her chemise and the gauzy white second-hand dress they purchased so they clung to her. She had never painted her face before and smudged the rouge on her cheeks. Washing it off with a towel, she tried again. She powdered her face white and painted her eyes. Looking in the mirror, she felt her heartbeat quicken at her reflection—her mother would be scandalised.

Samuel did not seem to mind at all.

'Now where to put my pistol,' Frederica said aloud, taking it out of her reticule in a short, jerky movement. She felt a bit jumpy and her nerves were on end.

'You will not be able to hide it on your person. You can see every curve of your body in that dress,' he said. 'I will carry it in my coat.'

Frederica handed Samuel the weapon and they walked out of the rear entrance of the inn. They followed the noise and the lights to a row of busy taverns. Women of ill repute lingered outside in the shadows and beckoned to Samuel. He held her hand tighter. Still her heart palpitated and her hands shook. This was the moment she had been waiting for her entire life. She could do something that truly mattered. She would be a spy that brought back important intelligence that would make a difference in the upcoming battle. Her life would have meaning.

'Blast,' he whispered in her ear. 'I will be the only man without a uniform.'

'Then we must find you one,' Frederica said, in a higher tone than usual. 'Will you hand me my pistol?'

Samuel placed his hand inside his jacket pocket and pulled out her pistol. 'Try not to make too much of a mess. I will have to wear the fellow's jacket after.'

'And you think the French will notice a large bullet hole surrounded by blood?'

His lips twitched. 'Possibly.'

They hid together in the alley and watched several soldiers pass by, but none that were the same body type as Samuel. They were all slim like Captain Wallace. Or short.

'You are too broad-shouldered,' Frederica complained, kissing his ear.

'Look at the fellow who just got out of the coach.' Samuel pointed out. 'I daresay I could fit into his uniform.'

The man descending from the coach was even broader than her husband. 'You and our elephant.'

Frederica did not hesitate. Stepping out of the shadows, she walked stiffly towards the soldier. Her knees kept locking. She pressed her fist against her thigh, trying not to show her fear.

'Pardon me, sir.' She spoke in French, giggling longer than she should. 'My sandal has become untied. Could you tie it for me?'

The beefy French soldier looked her up and down, smiling his rotten teeth at her. *'Oui.'*

Frederica lifted her skirt to reveal her shapely ankle

and put her sandal forward. Her shoulders felt tight and her stomach was rock-hard. A cold sweat covered her skin and she tried not to flinch.

The man got to his knees and took one of his thick fingers and caressed her ankle. The hairs on the back of her neck and arms stood up. Nausea rose in her throat, but she forced herself to swallow it back down. Wellington had trusted her. Samuel needed her. She would not fail either duke.

Frederica brought down the butt of her pistol hard on his head, knocking him out. Taking a deep breath, she took one arm and Samuel the other, and they dragged him into the alley.

'Couldn't we have picked a lighter fellow?' her husband complained.

The Frenchman began to stir and her heart raced. Samuel punched him below the chin and knocked him out cold. Frederica pinched her own skin between the thumb and forefinger. Over and over again. She watched as he took off the man's trousers and uniform jacket. Tugging the trousers up over his own, he tightened the belt to its last rung. He pulled on the jacket and Frederica helped him button the row of gold buttons. Lastly, he put on the man's hat. Samuel looked very handsome in a uniform, even in an ill-fitting one.

'Not perfect,' Frederica said, eyeing the baggy uniform as she rocked back and forth, 'but I think you will pass.'

Samuel offered her his arm and she placed her shaking hand in the crook of it. They walked out of the alley and down the middle of the street. The air was a curious mixture of open sewage and sweet patisserie.

Her stomach roiled and she fought to control her body. They entered the closest tavern.

The taproom was loud and full of people—some drinking, some talking, and some gambling. The roulette table was swamped with people eager to lose their money, or win their fortune. Several tables hosted male card players. The only women in the room appeared to be prostitutes. They were scantily dressed like Frederica and most appeared to have dyed their hair to stick out from the crowd. One woman's locks were a harsh yellow and another's a brashly bright red. Their faces were heavily painted almost like masks and Frederica wished that she had been more generous with her own cosmetics.

She waved Samuel away and she sauntered through the room, circling. The higher the rank of the soldier, the better the information. She felt a hand on her shoulder and resisted the urge to pull away or punch him in the nose. Turning around, she smiled. The man behind her was old enough that he could have been her father—lines mapped his eyes and mouth. His hair and sideburns were tinged with grey. He licked his thin, colourless lips in what might have been attraction. Frederica only felt revulsion, but she forced her mouth to form a smile.

'You appear to be lost, mademoiselle,' he said in an oily voice.

Frederica looked at his uniform and saw his rank—colonel. The same as Samuel. He would know the highest levels of intelligence.

She smiled coyly. 'Only looking for some company, Colonel.'

He offered his arm, and she placed her quivering

hand on it, ignoring the pit in her stomach that was ever growing.

The older man covered her hand with his callused one. 'Shall I get us a room?'

Frederica swallowed down the bile rising in her throat. 'Later perhaps. I should like first to have a drink and perhaps watch you play a little.'

The colonel led her to a table. A waiter immediately came and bowed before them.

The older man touched her knee underneath the table and began to work his hand up. 'My new little friend and I would like a drink.'

Frederica grabbed his hand with hers and pulled it off. She slapped it playfully and whispered in his ear, 'No play until you pay, Colonel. I know how you officers are. Kissing today and leaving tomorrow.'

She saw him stiffen. Instinctively, she kissed his cheek and then nipped at his ear. She hoped it pained him more than pleased. Her own eyes kept darting towards the exit.

He immediately relaxed and guffawed.

The waiter returned with a bottle of red wine and two glasses. The colonel poured and they both picked up their glasses and raised them for a toast.

'Vive l'emperor,' Frederica said.

'Vive l'emperor.'

Frederica sipped her wine slowly and saw Samuel fifteen feet away playing roulette. The colonel downed his wine with a gulp. She poured him some more, this time filling the glass to the top—well past where she should. He gulped it down, as well. Frederica filled his cup again.

'Are you trying to get me drunk, mademoiselle?'

Frederica gave a high false laugh, chewing the inside of her cheek. 'Impossible, Colonel. I am sure you have too hard a head. I am only loosening you up a bit.'

He guffawed again and gulped down another glass of wine. 'I am ready.'

Swallowing down her fear, she forced herself to wink at him. 'But first I should like to discuss my pay.'

'Fair enough,' he said. 'How much do you charge?'

'Are you requesting my company for tonight only or for longer?' she said, giving him a smile and licking her lips suggestively as he had.

'Alas, only tonight, mademoiselle,' he said with a groan. 'We are to march first thing in the morning.'

Frederica leaned closer and placed her hand on his top button and undid it. 'Colonel, who is your commander so that I may ask his permission to steal you away?'

His eyes opened and Frederica pulled his mouth down to hers. She swallowed down the revulsion of his rank breath and pushed him away when she could tolerate no more.

'Marshal Grouchy, mademoiselle. But he will not mind if I am absent from my post for a few hours,' he said, puffing out his chest as if to impress her. 'Napoleon, himself, will lead us to battle.'

Frederica's face lit up. 'Does the colonel know the emperor?'

He shook his head. 'I have yet to have that honour, but I am slightly acquainted with Marshal Ney, who will be going, as well. Now it is time for you to come with me.'

The older man took Frederica by the elbow in a painful hold and guided her towards the stairs. She clutched her glass with the opposite hand. Glancing over her shoulder, she saw Samuel was still playing roulette and he had not noticed her leaving. The colonel led her up the red velvet stairs and stopped in front of a door. He bent down to open the knob and Frederica brought down the glass as hard as she could on his head. The colonel's head was certainly hard, for he shook off the blow and grabbed her by the shoulders and shook her. His fingers dug into her skin. Kicking him in the shins, she tried to bite his left arm. He struck her across the cheek and pushed her to the floor. Her entire body shivered in fear.

'You like to play rough, mademoiselle. Wait until we get inside.'

The colonel lifted his right arm to strike her again, when Samuel ran into him, sending them both sprawling on the floor. Frederica stood up and edged away from them. Samuel hit the colonel with a left hook and then with a right uppercut. The colonel raised his hands to protect his face from the onslaught, but was helpless before the fury of Samuel's fists. Samuel gave a final punch to the colonel's jaw, which knocked him out cold.

He stood up; his knuckles were bleeding. 'We have drawn too much attention. We had better go.'

Frederica nodded and put her trembling arm through his.

They walked down the stairs and through the main room, past the roulette table and out of the door. Frederica's heart beat in her throat and her legs felt so weak that she was glad to lean on her husband for support. She itched all over. Everywhere that awful old man had touched her.

Samuel hailed a cab and gave directions to the driver. The cab dropped them off a street before the inn. Samuel took her hand and led her between the houses. Shrugging off the French officer's uniform, he threw it in a puddle that smelled of sewage. They walked back to the inn without speaking a word. Samuel took a candle from the owner, and they climbed the stairs to their room. He bolted their chamber door and they both let out a sigh of relief.

Pouring water from a pitcher into the washing basin, she washed Samuel's bloody knuckles with the red soap she'd sent to him. It lifted her heart a little that he had brought it with them. When she patted his knuckles dry with a towel, her hands were almost steady. She took the bloody water and dumped it out the window. After closing the single glass pane, she pulled the curtains shut. Frederica placed the basin back on the dresser and looked at her reflection—a large red welt had formed on her right cheek by her eye. She slumped onto the edge of the bed and tears filled her eyes.

Samuel cupped her face in his hands. 'I am so sorry I did not get there sooner… I did not want to arouse attention. I did not think he would harm you.'

'Ney and Grouchy,' Frederica whispered.

'What?'

She cleared her dry and sore throat. 'Those are the names of the marshals who will be in command with Napoleon…and they are leaving tomorrow morning.'

He inhaled sharply. 'Wellington will want to know immediately. I do not think it would be wise to leave tonight—it might cause suspicion, since we have already paid for lodging. We must leave at first light in the morning and get ahead of the army. It will take them much longer on foot and with their equipment. We should be able to beat them by a couple of days.'

Frederica sniffed and twisted her wrists. Her body flushed with an uncontrollable heat as she realised how close her plan had come to disaster.

'Can you hold me?' she asked in a small voice. 'I had no idea it would be quite so awful.'

Samuel took her into his strong arms. She rested her head against his chest, trying to hold in her tears. But still they fell down her cheeks and onto his nightshirt. She shivered and he held her tighter against him.

He patted her hair and whispered, 'No one will ever harm you again.'

Closing her eyes tightly, Frederica wanted desperately to believe him.

Chapter Twenty-One

Samuel woke up with Frederica still encircled in his arms. Her skin felt hot and flushed against his. The angry red welt on her cheek had turned into a purple bruise. He touched it gingerly, and she turned her head away from him and slept on. He watched the lace of her nightgown rise up and down. He could feel his own heart pounding inside his chest. Never before had she needed his help for anything. He was so used to viewing her as a competent minx. Not that she wasn't very capable, but everyone needed help sometimes. And he could not remember ever seeing her scared until last night.

This trip.

Their wedding journey had been eye-opening in so many ways. He had learned so much about Frederica. He had seen her nervous, shy, scared, and vulnerable. All traits he never dreamed his indomitable wife possessed. Samuel now understood why she danced out of his reach in Brussels and made a point to flirt with other soldiers. She'd wanted him to chase her, as she had chased after him. He even supposed that she worried if she let him catch her, that he would lose interest.

There was very little chance of that.

His body was overly warm and stimulated in all sorts of ways that were most uncomfortable with a shy wife. Shaking his head, he could not help but smile. Frederica felt nervous with him. He would not have believed it possible.

Moaning, she stirred in his arms.

Samuel was not yet ready to let go. He had never felt anything like this before. He wanted to hold her for ever. Protect her. Laugh with her. Love her. Slender Billy was right. Frederica deserved to know how he felt and not just through a death letter.

But how to tell her?

She'd lowered her guard with him on the ride to Paris, but it had been firmly back in place since. Sighing, he realised that they were both very careful with their hearts.

Frederica blinked several times and rubbed her bruised face into his chest. 'Is it morning? Should we be on our way?'

'Not quite yet and if we leave before sunrise, it will draw the kind of attention that we don't want. We cannot appear to be in a rush.'

She kissed his neck and then underneath his chin, making a trail of kisses to his lips. He returned her kisses gently, not wishing to scare her with the force of his own feelings. It felt so right to have her encircled in his arms, to touch her satin-like skin with his fingers, and to lose himself in her wicked mouth.

Frederica kissed him once more before nuzzling her head in the crook of his neck. 'I want more than kisses, but I am scared to disappoint you. And I do not want you to laugh at me.'

Smiling tenderly, he caressed her cheek and then her glorious hair. 'Why would I laugh at you?'

She covered her face with her hands, burying her head further against him. 'At my inexperience. What if I am awkward or, even worse, bad at lovemaking?'

His body temperature rising exponentially, he gently pulled her hands away from her face and gazed into her beautiful hazel eyes. 'What if I promise not to laugh?'

'Stop smiling.'

He pressed his lips together in a thin line, but the edges turned upward.

'You are still smiling.'

'We are in bed together, Frederica,' he said with a light laugh. 'And you said that you wanted me to make love to you. It would be a miracle if I was not smiling.'

Shaking her head, she gritted her teeth. 'I do not know what to do—I mean, I do know, but I have never done it before and I could not bear it if you mocked me.'

He brought her hands to his mouth and kissed her wrists, her palms, and then the tip of each little finger. 'I do not want to mock you. I want to worship you. And you need not worry about being compared to previous experiences. I have never done it before either.'

Pulling her hands away from him, she sat up in bed. The covers fell from her chest, revealing her thin chemise. 'Do not lie to me. I know gentlemen are not supposed to be virgins.'

Scraping his hands through his hair, Samuel sat up in the bed. 'I know, but I could not be like other young gentlemen. I did not wish to get the pox or bring some other bawdy house disease home to my wife like my father did. I should have already told you, but my mother has the French pox too and it's in the latent stage where there are no symptoms. Our family doctor says that the longest time he's seen a patient stay in the latent stage is thirty years. It has been fifteen for Mama and every day I fear that the disease will return. At the most, she will have another fifteen years to live before her organs deteriorate and she goes mad. It will probably be sooner and it is all my lecherous father's fault.'

Placing a hand on his shoulder, she swallowed. 'I did not know that about your mother. I am so sorry. How long have you known?'

'Since I was ten years old,' he said, his voice tight. 'Mama used to say that she depended upon me. Then she called me her sweet baby angel Sammy, but her confidences were crushing. I could see the sores on her hands and mouth and I did not know what or how I was supposed to help her. And after she passed the first two stages of the illness, there was always the worry about my father and his many mistresses. I tried to be the best son I could for her. To do well in school and not chase petticoats or give in to my base desires. So that I wouldn't add to her worries.'

She inhaled deeply. 'That is why you hate that nickname. I wish you would have told me sooner. What a terrible burden for a child to bear.'

Samuel could no longer meet her gaze. 'It was. That is the true reason that I joined the army. Yes, my father's pox coming back contributed to it, but mostly I could no longer live with our family's secrets. I abandoned my mother to deal with it alone.'

Placing her hand on his back, she rubbed circles against his nightshirt. 'I love your mother, I truly do. And I have said it before, she is a very capable woman. But she was wrong to put so much pressure on a child. And you need not remonstrate with yourself any longer—she wasn't alone. After you left, she turned to my mother, who was more than capable of helping her take care of your father and the estates. You are not responsible for your father's, nor your mother's, choices.'

Frederica's words and her touch seemed to ease the tenseness of his muscles. She had given him absolution for his greatest regrets and deepest sorrows. The Duchess of Hampford was nearly the same age as his mother and a much better confidant. She was an adult with experience and resources. Samuel did not blame his mother for depending upon him at such an early age; she must have felt as if she had no other choice. She didn't want society to know the truth. But he also knew that he would never put such pressure or expectations on a child of his own. He would never expect a boy to bear the burdens of a man.

Exhaling, he felt the rest of the tension leave his body. 'You're right. You are right. I am only responsible for my own choices.'

'And do not feel guilt for choosing to leave a difficult situation. When someone is drowning, they cannot save another swimmer. Sometimes, you have to keep yourself afloat and there is no shame in survival.'

Her words were like a balm on his wounded soul. He had done his very best for as long as he could, and when it became too much, he had left. And he hadn't completely abandoned his mother. He wrote to her regularly and came home after his father's death. He'd even promised to marry Frederica because of his mother's pressure. Slightly smiling, he did not hold that particular offence against Mama any longer. Frederica was the greatest joy in his life.

'You saved me once when I was drowning.'

She let out a gurgle of laughter. 'After I pushed you into the river.'

'True.'

And they laughed together.

Frederica leaned her head against his shoulder and her hand brushed across his torso. He was no longer thinking about his parents or his past. His mind and body were focused on his beautiful wife in bed next to him.

'Is it terrible for me to say that I am glad that it is your first time too? That I am the only one that you have been with intimately, so you can't compare me to anyone else, and that you are not diseased.'

He encircled his arm around her waist and pulled her tighter against him. 'No. I am glad that I am your only one too.'

'How do we start?'

He stood up, shucking off his nightshirt and tossing it on the floor. 'Although we do not have any practical experience, we are both bright people. I am sure we can figure it out between the pair of us and I am certainly eager to try.'

She clapped her hands over her mouth and he realised that she was covering a giggle. How quickly their conversations went from serious to silliness. Coming back onto the bed, he moved her hands a second time and kissed that wicked, laughing tongue. Their hands gently explored each other, unsure, but each touch burned. And they came together slowly, tenderly, and thoroughly.

After, he held her in his arms, feeling happier than he had ever been in his entire life. His limbs felt weightless, but full. He couldn't help but hum his favourite bar tune about a buxom maid named Nelly. He was sure that the mythical barmaid had nothing on his wife.

Frederica rubbed her face against his chest and laughed.

'How come you can giggle during the entire act, but if I crack so much as a smile, I am in trouble?'

She giggled again.

How he loved that sound!

All the little noises that she made before, during, and after.

Frederica kissed his bare shoulder. 'Because I cannot help myself. I am too joyful to merely smile—I must laugh.'

Leaning towards her, he brushed her satin lips over and over with his own. He wanted nothing more than to stay with her in this bed. In this room. For ever.

But the sun was rising. It was time to leave. His general and his friends were both waiting for the information.

His wife.

Samuel wanted a lifetime with Frederica and a family. But one short wedding trip might be all the time that they had together. He could not wait any longer. He needed to tell her the truth—that he loved her. Loved everything about her. From every stubborn hair on her head to her sharp heels that she had stomped on his feet with. She had well and truly caught him this time and he would never let her go if the choice were merely his.

But it was not.

He heard his wife moan as she pulled the dress

over her head. The coarse material must have brushed against the bruise on her face. She walked towards him with her shiny brown curls tumbling over her rounded shoulders.

'I finally understand why men as a whole rule the world.'

Samuel pulled up his other boot. 'And why is that?'

She turned around and glanced over her shoulder coquettishly. 'They can do up their own buttons. Men's buttons are on the front of their clothes, and a lady's buttons are always on the back, making them eternally dependent on another.'

Moving his hands to her shoulders, he carefully buttoned her dress up. His fingers shaking a little. 'That is why God made man and woman. To button for each other what the other cannot button. I solemnly promise to always unbutton your dress for you.'

Giggling, she spun around in his arms to face him. 'And button it back up?'

He kissed her hard on the mouth. 'Well, eventually.'

She made a trail of kisses from his mouth to his ear. She licked it and then nibbled on the end. 'That's more than fair.'

They dressed in a hurry and ate a small breakfast, before Samuel paid their remaining shot at the inn. The ostler brought their horses and they were fresh. Samuel helped Frederica onto her grey and then mounted his own mare. They trotted down the street slowly, as if they were not in any hurry to beat an entire army to Brussels. Frederica was unusually quiet as they rode and Samuel felt light-headed. The air felt charged with lightning. The hairs on his arms stood to attention like an ensign before a quartermaster.

Samuel leaned over nearer to Frederica. 'I am going to take us another way. If someone should question us, let me do all the talking. And if I say to make a run for it, do so immediately. With or without me.'

'Yes, of course.'

She would never have agreed to such terms in England. Nor would he have asked them of her, if their situation was not fraught with peril.

They passed several soldiers. Samuel lifted his hat to them, and Frederica waved merrily. She even blew a kiss to one of the soldiers with a shaking hand and a tremulous smile. He could tell that she was scared, yet she still put on a brave face. His bride was truly the most remarkable of women.

They rode under the gates of the city and onto the road that led to Brussels. They urged their horses to a canter and eventually a gallop. After two hours of hard riding, Samuel told Frederica to slow her horse down to a walk for a mile or so. She did and directed her grey close to Samuel so that their knees were touching, a small, but helpful, comfort. He was beginning to depend on her presence. He did not wish to live in a world without her. He needed to get her to the safety of Brussels as quickly as possible.

'Where did you learn to fight like that? With the French colonel?' she asked with a small smile. 'I doubt that it was covered at Eton. You could not even beat Matthew in fisticuffs then and he isn't very good.'

He shook his head, his own lips twitching. 'Your brother is several years my senior, but I learned how to improve my fists and my swordsmanship from an army guide in the Peninsula.'

'You would pummel Matthew now.'

Her brother was an amusing fellow whose best weapon had always been words. 'Seven years. I suppose Matthew has changed a great deal.'

'Not a whit,' she assured him with a chuckle. 'He is still quite nutty about steam locomotives and you should never trust him with a pen. He will write the stockings off your toes and charge you double for them.'

His heart lightened. Matthew had always been a clever cove, but a kind one. 'Didn't he get married a few years back?'

Frederica beamed at him. 'Yes. To Nancy. She is one of my dearest friends. She taught me how to wield a dagger and twirl it between my fingers.'

'A paragon,' he quipped, knowing that weaponry was indeed the way to Frederica's heart.

'She used to be a part of a criminal gang.'

'I look forward to improving my acquaintance with her,' Samuel said and he was not lying. He had forgotten how wonderful it was to be a part of a large and loving family. He had missed the Stringhams in all their absurdity, criminality, and animality. Smiling, he looked forward to being among them again. To belonging.

'And Wick's wife, Louisa, is very nice too,' she added conscientiously. 'She doesn't wield a knife, but she is quite wicked with a sewing needle.'

'You said that Wick has taken over the estate management.'

Biting her lower lip, Frederica nodded. 'Yes, Papa still cannot see past the end of our elephant's trunk.

His animals and his studies are all that he cares about. And Matthew has partnered with our grandfather in his business.'

'He's a businessman?' Samuel tried to keep his tone even, but there was a note of surprise in it. Most gentlemen knew only how to spend money, not earn it.

Her eyes narrowed and she gave him a scowl of disapproval that he recognised all too well. 'Yes, and I mean to be a businesswoman.'

Samuel cleared his throat. 'I remember. Your red soap.'

Frederica's face turned redder than any soap. She looked adorably guilty. 'But I did not tell you everything… It is not just our mothers' fault that you had to wed me. I could have refused to accept the arranged marriage, but I did not.'

'I could have refused my hand, as well.'

She lowered her head, shaking it back and forth. 'Not very easily. I knew that you were in a tight pinch and I wanted you to finally choose me. Not to be forced into proposing to an almost stranger. I told my mother no at first to the arrangement, but then she promised to give me half of her company now and the other half—you know, after she dies.'

His throat felt unaccountably dry and it was difficult to swallow. 'You married me for *perfume* bottles?'

'A lot of perfume bottles. And a company that exports its product to most major cities in Europe,' Frederica said and gulped. 'As you know, I mean to expand the business into red scented soaps.'

He did not speak for several minutes. His mind whirling with these new revelations.

Of course the strong-minded and independent Frederica would not have accepted his proposal of marriage simply because her parents wanted her to. Even if she both liked and despised him, in equal measure. She would have been too proud and obstinate. No, he should have realised that Lady Hampford had sweetened the pot. Frederica was no fool or simpering society miss.

Throwing his head back, Samuel laughed out loud. 'At least we will always be clean and smell good.'

Frederica giggled, covering her mouth with one hand. 'I could use some perfume and soap about now myself. I smell strongly of sweat and horse.'

'Me too,' he said, winking at her.

Her colour was still high in her cheeks. She looked flushed and ready to be kissed. 'Do you mind terribly that I married you for a perfume company? I should have told you before we spoke our vows.'

'Not at all,' he said and meant it.

Samuel would have been too stupid to seek out her company again. Before seeing her, his mind had entangled Frederica and the Stringham family with his father's expectations. And he had not wanted to do anything to please the lecherous old man who was his sire in name only. He might have missed the love of a lifetime by holding on to old grudges. Plus, she had not kept her ambitions from him a secret. She'd told him about her scented soaps and even sent him one that his valet had packed for this very journey. It was very red and strong smelling.

Turning his head, he saw that Frederica was still gazing at him intently. 'At least you did not buy me cheaply. I daresay it cost at least a hundred thousand pounds. And any person would be flattered to be purchased at that price.'

She snorted and then laughed. It was inelegant and utterly adorable. And she was his.

His.

He did not care that his parents had planned the union whilst he was in short coats. Or that his father's debts had made the match inescapable. Or that his bride was bribed to marry him.

How they arrived here did not matter.

She laughed again and he smiled at her. 'I see a town not a mile off. Do you mind if we stop for a few minutes? I have need to—well, you know—'

Samuel readily agreed, and they cantered into the hamlet and found a small, dirty public house. He assisted Frederica to dismount and tied both of their horses to the hitching post. Tossing a coin to the ostler, he asked the lad to bring their mounts some water.

A haggard woman with a scowl and greasy black hair was the proprietor of the public house. Frederica followed the woman to the privy. But something felt off—wrong. Samuel ordered some ale and waited for his wife. Frederica joined him in the taproom, where they quickly drank the ale. He placed a few coins on the bar and led her out of the door by her elbow.

He untied the horses with efficiency, and both were mounted and riding in less than two minutes.

'Why the hurry?' she asked.

'That woman suspected us.'

'How do you know?'

'A feeling.'

He led them away from the road through several wheat fields. He changed directions three times and they did not stop when it became dark. After dismounting, they passed by an apple orchard which cast grotesque shadows in the moonlight. Frederica picked a couple of red apples and tossed one to Samuel. They both ate theirs eagerly. Then they crept through the orchard and towards the large shadow of a barn.

Frederica touched his arm. 'I can't hear any animals.'

Samuel handed her the reins to his horse. 'I will go check it out.'

Opening the barn door as quietly as possible, Samuel blinked to accustom his eyes to the darkness. His other senses came awake. He could smell manure that was not more than a day old. His feet stepped on grain, loose on the floor. There were no animals in any of the stalls. Nor chickens wandering around.

He returned to Frederica. 'Someone left in a hurry. All the stalls are empty and there is a sack of grain spilled on the floor. They were probably trying to avoid having their animals stolen by the army.'

Frederica wrinkled her nose. 'I hope that we are not sleeping on the floor.'

'Nonsense! Only the best for my wife.'

He could see her smile at the comment. It felt unaccountably right to call her *his* wife. To be *her* husband.

Samuel found a few bales of hay, and he cut them open with a knife and spread the clean straw on the dirt floor of the barn. Meanwhile, he heard Frederica feeding the horses apples.

He could tell she was smiling at him in the darkness. 'They are as hungry as we are.'

'I'll fetch them some water,' he said.

She nodded. 'I'll put them in the empty stalls and brush them down.'

It did not take long to locate the well, about twenty-five yards from the barn. He heaved out a bucket and brought it back to Frederica. They both drank first and then washed their faces. Then he fetched two more buckets of water for the horses, before collapsing beside Frederica on the hay. They did not undress, but lay together, huddling for what little warmth they could find.

'I always wanted to sleep in the hayloft as a child,' Frederica said, snuggling up to Samuel. 'But perhaps you could warm me up first?'

He enthusiastically accepted this challenge and after only a few minutes, they were both quite hot. He placed his arm underneath her head and kissed her brow. He felt her body twitch a few times, before she settled into a sleep.

Samuel prayed that he could keep her safe.

Chapter Twenty-Two

Samuel woke up before Frederica. He fed and watered the horses and saddled them up. He touched her shoulder to wake her. Opening her eyes, she smiled at him. He could get used to waking up to her smiles.

'We need to leave before sunrise, just in case this farm isn't abandoned like I thought,' he explained.

Frederica stood and brushed the hay off her riding habit. Samuel gently picked several pieces of hay out of her hair.

Her cheek was still puffy and purple as she touched her disordered brown locks. 'I am sure I look a fright.'

'I think you look beautiful.'

And he meant it. Heaven help him, he meant it.

Frederica only laughed and he led the horses out of the barn, latching the door behind them. Samuel led them back to the road and they made good time until late afternoon. He could see the outline of the city of Valenciennes. Glancing over to Frederica, she gave him a wan smile. He heard his stomach rumble. They were dirty, tired, and hungry. His instinct was to circle around the town instead of going through it, but he could see Frederica's shoulders sagging, her face pale. She was exhausted.

He gently pulled on the bridle to slow his horse to a walk. 'Let us dine in Valenciennes and perhaps stay the night. I think we are both done in.'

She did not respond, only nodded. As if too tired to speak.

They rode slowly into town and there were only a few people in the street. There was an unnatural quiet about the town. The silence before a battle. Samuel stopped at the first inn and helped Frederica dismount. He tied the horses to the hitching post and he watched her stiffly walk in. The owner, a rail-thin man with a skull-like head, met them at the entrance. His dark eyes took in the state of their clothing. He gave them a sinister smile and asked how his humble inn could serve them. Samuel ordered a dinner and asked if there was a private parlour.

'This way, monsieur, mademoiselle,' the owner said with sinister courtesy. He led them to an adjacent room with a dirty square table and four shabby chairs. The owner shut the door with a thud.

Samuel shook his head. 'I am sorry, Freddie. I did not think a nicer inn would allow us in.'

She walked around the table several times. 'No indeed. And there was no other inn on the street. If this place were nicer, we would have been refused entry.'

He watched her touch her reticule for her pistol. Instinctively, he checked his coat for his knife and his pistol. They were there and ready.

Frederica circled the table again, but did not sit down on a chair. 'Something doesn't feel right.'

'I agree. Let us leave,' Samuel said, his stomach roiling with a mixture of fear and hunger. 'We are close to the border. Mons is only another twenty miles, and there are British soldiers there. We will be safe.'

Samuel cautiously peeked into the taproom—he counted ten heavily armed Frenchmen. He closed the door softly and told Frederica to take out her pistol. She did so immediately and cocked down the hammer on it. Pulling out his own weapon, he raised his finger to his lips and then threw open the door.

'Come on!'

Frederica followed him out of the small room with the musket poised in her arms ready to shoot. They ran across the taproom without a word and out the exit to their horses, which were whinnying and fretting. The animals must also have sensed the danger. Samuel pocketed his pistol and started to untie the knots. Glancing over his shoulder, he saw that a Frenchman had followed them and was pointing a pistol at him. He heard a shot and braced his body for the bullet, closing his eyes momentarily. But he felt nothing. The air cracked with a second shot. He opened his eyes to see Frederica standing between him and the body of a dead Frenchman. She clutched her side, which he saw was wet with blood seeping through her gloved fingers. His wife must have stepped between him and death.

Behind her, he could see more men coming towards them. He tossed her onto her horse as she gasped with pain. He mounted his own mare and led both animals in a dead run out of the city. They had to get to the border before the soldiers could stop them. Sweat poured off his face and the horses' bodies. Glancing over his shoulder, he kept making sure that Frederica was still on the back of her grey.

Once he was sure that the soldiers were not following them, he veered off the road and into a small forested area. He didn't stop until they were no longer visible from the path.

After slipping off his horse, he lifted Frederica gently to the ground and helped her lie down. Her legs were too weak to hold her upright. 'Let me see the wound.'

She moved her hand from her side and it was wet and red. Her blood had dripped down her clothes all the way to the hem. Unsuccessfully, she tried to unbutton her riding habit. He brushed her hand aside and quickly unbuttoned it and then took off her dress. With only her shift and corset on, he could see that the bullet had gone clean through her side. Her stays had partially protected her skin, but he still thought that she would need stitching. The fact that she had been able to stand after being shot was incredible. Most soldiers would not have been able to. Nor would they have been able to stay atop a mount for a several-mile ride.

'Bandages. I need bandages,' he said in an undertone to himself.

Frederica swallowed, her face pale and strained. Closing her eyes, she said, 'You can use the bottom of my shift.'

He kneeled down beside her. This delightful garment only grazed the top of her knees. Tearing off the bottom four inches of her shift, he ripped the fabric into long bandages and tied them tightly around the wound at her waist. He lifted her back gently with each wrap. He hoped that would stop the wound from bleeding. Leaning back, he got an eyeful of her long, shapely legs and had to remind himself that she had just been shot. This was not the time for longing thoughts.

'Freddie—I…I…uh…do not know what to say,' he whispered, exhaling slowly. 'You took a bullet for me. I do not think anyone else would have done that for me. W-why did you do it?'

Frederica's lips were nearly as white as her face, but they smiled slightly. 'You cannot bring up the bear cub any more.'

He let out a wet chuckle. 'I won't.'

'And I mean to guilt you about it for the rest of our lives. If ever I am losing an argument, I will say, "Remember that one time in France when I took a bullet for you?" And then you'll humbly let me win.'

A tear slid down his cheek, he was so worried for her that he could barely breathe. She had lost a great deal of blood and they were still several miles away from Mons and safety. He brushed her hair away from her face. 'I will always let you win.'

'Liar.'

Bending forward, he pressed a kiss against her brow. It felt strangely cool. She reached for him and he wrapped his arms tightly around her. She felt fragile to him for the first time and he realised that if the bullet had been a few inches closer to her stomach, that he would have lost her for ever. His fiery, fierce, and formidable Frederica.

Rubbing his face into her hair, he spoke into her curls, 'I am not worth it, darling.'

'You are to me.'

Those four little words nearly undid him. Never before had someone loved him so purely. Not his parents. Not his friends. Not his general. None of them would have sacrificed their lives for his.

Tilting his head back, he brushed his lips against hers before saying, 'Promise me that you will never risk your life for mine again?'

'It is just a flesh wound. I could stitch it myself if I could sew a straight line.'

He squeezed his eyes shut trying not to picture her dead and in a coffin, but the image stayed in his mind. 'Promise me, Freddie.'

She pressed a kiss to his ear. 'I cannot. You know that I cannot.'

Another tear slid down his cheek. 'If you love me, you will live.'

Frederica kissed the tear away. 'I love you and I hate you, Samuel Corbin, and I will do whatever I think is best at the time.'

Samuel wanted to argue with her, but innately he could not fight with her when she was injured for him. When her very life was in the balance. All he could do was ensure that his wife received medical treatment and safety. He had to get her back to Brussels. England would have been better.

Gingerly, he helped her put back on her dress and riding habit before lifting her up into the saddle. Her face paled another shade. Samuel could not meet her eyes. His mouth was dry and his heartbeat raced. He felt so inadequate. The woman he loved had taken a bullet for him, and yet he still could not ensure her safety. Mons was still over an hour's ride away. A hard one.

Samuel leaned closer to her. 'Would you rather ride with me?'

She clenched her teeth together, grimacing and shaking her head. 'The horses are already spent. It would be easier for them if we rode separately.'

Swinging up into his own saddle, he said, 'We will take it slowly. If you need to stop or rest at any time, just say the word.'

Urging his horse into a gentle canter, Samuel's muscles were tensed and his teeth clenched. His eyes kept darting all around to ensure that no danger lurked in the shadows of a tree or a rock. They rode that way until he reached the edge of the city of Mons at dusk. Frederica had not asked to halt, nor had she spoken at all. He thought that she must be using all of her considerable willpower to simply stay on top of her grey. Samuel was in pretty bad shape himself and he did not have a bullet wound.

The road into the city was blocked by British officers wearing dusty scarlet uniforms that would have been all the better for a washing. They pointed their bayonets at them and what was left of Samuel's patience evaporated in the hot air. He needed to get his wife help immediately.

'For heaven's sake get out of my way,' Samuel yelled in English. 'Are you blind? My wife has been shot and needs medical attention immediately.'

The six soldiers looked at each other dubiously. They must have all been of the same rank and it was obviously not a high one. Common soldiers, even cavalry, were often brainless sheep to be herded.

'That is an order!' Samuel yelled, urging his horse closer to their line to intimidate them. 'I am Colonel Lord Pelford and I will see each and every one of you court-martialled, if you do not obey me instantly.'

The officers parted, and Samuel rode through them, pulling the reins of Frederica's horse. Glancing back, he saw her swaying in her seat. They could not arrive soon enough at a respectable inn.

He pointed at a spotted young man on his right. 'I want a surgeon at that inn in less than ten minutes. Do you understand me?'

The spotted young man nodded vigorously, and Samuel rode twenty more feet to the hitching post. He slid off his horse and carried Frederica's limp body in. She gave him a feeble protest, but did not fight him. That worried him more than the bullet wound. Holding her close to his chest, he hollered at the innkeeper in French to take him to a room. The stout man immediately led the way up the stairs to a small room that had a narrow bed, a wooden chair, and a table. The furnishings were humble, but clean, which was all that they needed. The innkeeper pulled down the blankets on the bed and Samuel gently laid Frederica on it. She mumbled something, but it was incoherent. He hoped it was an insult. She was strongest when she was fighting him.

The stout innkeeper went to the door and yelled to his wife in French to come quick and then in broken English. Moments later, a sturdy woman with a kind face and an abundance of red hair came through the entrance.

Her large green eyes widened, and she pointed a stubby finger at her husband. 'Put a kettle to boil, Janssens, and I will get some fresh linen. You can speak English to me, milord. I were born in Dover. Now take off her boots and help your wife get comfortable.'

Monsieur Janssens and his wife immediately left the room. Samuel set about the task that he had been assigned. Perhaps he was a mindless sheep of a soldier after all. As gently as he could, he pulled off her boots and stockings. They were covered in dirt and flecks of blood. Slightly smirking, he remembered that it was not an uncommon state for his bride. During their entire childhood, she'd always had a layer of mud on her boots and often on the rest of her person. She had been an indomitable explorer and a fearless friend. He could not imagine a world without her in it. Telling him what to do. Teasing him. Kissing him. The fear that gripped his heart now was tenfold what it had been during their escape. She simply lay there. Not moving. Not speaking.

Sitting on the edge of the bed, Samuel stroked his wife's hair. 'Just hold on, Frederica, and think of the most marvellous scar you will have. It may be even better than the ones I received from the bear cub's claws.'

He thought he saw a ghost of a smile on her lips. Even wounded, Frederica was the most competitive person that he had ever met. He felt empty at the thought of living without her challenging and loving presence.

'Care to see my scars?'

Her eyes were closed, but his wife only nodded her head slightly. Her countenance was even paler than before. Her wicked fingers had skimmed over his scars on their travels to Paris. His body had tingled when she touched him, skin to skin. Then he had made her his wife. It had been the most transcendent experience of his life, well worth waiting four and twenty years for. There could be no other woman for him.

Mrs Janssens returned first with a stack of linens and a nightgown. She placed them on the table by the bed. Then pointed at him like she had at her husband. 'Milord, would you kindly leave the room?'

'I am not leaving my wife,' Samuel said flatly.

Mrs Janssens nodded and her hair flopped back and forth. 'Wash your hands and help me undress her then.'

She shut the chamber door. Samuel assisted Mrs Janssens in gently taking off Frederica's bloodstained riding habit, dress, and shift. He had never seen her completely unclothed before. She'd kept her chemise on during their first lovemaking; he'd quite enjoyed working around it. And their second time had been in a dark barn where they both had been fully clothed except for the essential areas.

He noticed that Frederica's pale, curvaceous body was covered with sticky black and red dried blood. She seemed smaller and more vulnerable without her clothes. Mrs Janssens lightly touched the bullet wound at her waist and Frederica's body twitched as she cried out in pain. His own chest mirrored the ache. If only he had been faster. If only she had not stepped between him and the man with the gun. If only—

There was a knock at the door and Mrs Janssens took the kettle of hot water from her husband.

'Now I need a basin of cold water,' she said, firmly shutting him out. She cast Samuel a look that seemed to say, *Give me any trouble and you will be kicked out, as well.*

As gently as he could, he washed the dried blood off his wife's body, careful to keep clear of the gaping wound. The blood was brighter there, even if it had coagulated. The skin around it was already red and angry. He hoped and prayed that it would not become infected. In his army experience, infections killed more soldiers than bullets.

Then he remembered her red scented soap. Dunford

had packed it in his saddlebag. He excused himself to go and fetch it. He prayed it worked as well as Frederica said that it did.

When he returned, Mrs Janssens set the kettle near the linen and took another towel, dipping it into the scalding water. She held the rag in the air for a few moments to allow it to cool before she expertly wiped away the dried blood from the wound. Frederica's eyes popped open and she said a few choice words that would have shocked most ladies. She had probably learned them from her father or brothers. Samuel put an arm around her shoulders, wishing that he could give her more comfort. Or laudanum for pain relief. When the rag was saturated, Mrs Janssens took a new towel and dipped it again in the hot water. He had been right. The bullet had only nicked her side.

Samuel held out the cake of red soap. 'Please use this to clean the wound, ma'am.'

The older woman brought the bar to her nose and gave it a sniff before dipping it into the water and lathering it over the wound. The soap smelled of rosemary and an astringent odour that he did not recognise. He hoped the little cake could fight any infection that was beginning to set in. His wife was nowhere near out of danger yet.

Once the area was clean, Mrs Janssens asked, 'Shall I sew you up, milady? I reckon I will do a better job of stitches than the doctor.'

'Y-yes,' Frederica said in a pained whisper.

The Englishwoman glanced at Samuel for his approval too.

'Please. I will pay any price.'

Mrs Janssens left the room with the soiled rags and

returned with more hot water to sterilise the needle. He had to turn his head away as the point of the needle entered Frederica's skin. He expected her to scream, but instead she fainted in his arms. Another thing he could add to his list of surprises. Frederica could faint. *Unfathomable.* He did not try to rouse her immediately, assuming that her consciousness needed a respite from the pain.

When Mrs Janssens finished stitching, she bid Samuel lift Frederica, while she wrapped the bandage around her. Once she secured the bandage, Mrs Janssens directed Samuel to cradle Frederica's head so that she could put the nightgown on her. Mrs Janssens gently placed Frederica's feet underneath the sheets and covered her with the blanket.

There was another discreet knock at the door.

Mrs Janssens rushed over and opened it to take the basin of cold water from her husband. She set it on the table next to the bed. 'Now, milord, let her rest and I will make some broth for when she stirs. Take one of those cloths, dip it in the cold water, and dab at her face. We must prevent her body from becoming feverish, if we can.'

'Yes, of course,' Samuel said, swallowing down the sour taste in his mouth. 'Thank you, ma'am. I cannot tell you how much I appreciate all that you have done for my wife. You are most skilled.'

Mrs Janssens gave him a sad smile. 'You cannot have lived in Europe during the last twenty years, without taking care of a fair share of bullet wounds. Mind you, do not let the doctor bleed her again when he comes. Them doctors is as bad as the leeches they use for sucking blood. And your wife looks as if she has already lost too much.'

With that, she left the room.

Samuel pulled the chair next to the bed and sat down. Dipping a fresh cloth into the cool water, he wiped at Frederica's pale face. She lay so still. He placed his hand on her throat and could feel a light pulse. He took her hand, rocking in his seat. Unable to hold still. Fear gripped his heart and his mind. Not even in the midst of battles in Spain, had he ever felt so powerless and scared. His eyes grew wet and his vision blurred.

Squeezing her hand tighter, he said, 'Do not leave me, Frederica. Please do not leave me. You promised me a lifetime of bickering and I really must insist upon it.'

Frederica's eyes did not open, but her lips moved. Samuel moved his ear closer to her face to hear her say one word: 'Bossy.'

A wet chuckle escaped him and he wiped at his watery eyes, the weight in his chest lightening now that she had regained consciousness. It was a small step, but it gave him hope.

'You also promised me a palace full of children,' he reminded her, watching her lips twitch slightly upward. 'Wild, badly behaved little Stringhams that will probably be covered in mud at least half of the time, and the rest, jumping into rivers fully dressed. Or pushing each other in. I hope our children will be just like you. Just as brave, headstrong, argumentative, and imaginative. And I cannot deny that I am particularly looking forward to the creation of the children.'

She gave a soft, breathy laugh and opened her eyes. 'As am I.'

Leaning forward, he brushed a gentle kiss against her brow. Her temperature was closer to normal now. He hoped that was a good sign.

Mrs Janssens gave two knocks before re-entering the room with a harried man with a small black bag who Samuel assumed was the doctor. 'Monsieur Dubois, the surgeon, milord.'

Samuel stood and held out his hand to the doctor, who reluctantly gave a limp one for him to shake.

'My wife was shot by French soldiers,' Samuel explained, trying to keep his voice even. 'The bullet grazed her side and Mrs Janssens cleaned the wound and sewed it.'

Dubois looked over his long, thin nose at Frederica's still form. He opened his black bag and took out a metal horn-shaped instrument and placed the rounded part against her chest and his ear against the top. He listened to her breathe for a few moments. Then he picked up her wrist and held the pulse, timing it with a golden pocket watch. 'Well, monsieur, if the bullet has already been taken out and bandaged, I think it is best to leave it to heal. I will just take a pint of blood and check on my patient tomorrow.'

Frederica's eyes flew open again. 'No.'

Samuel looked from her to Mrs Janssens, who shook her head slightly.

He swallowed heavily. 'No, doctor. My wife has lost enough blood.'

Dubois gave an exasperated sigh and threw his hands up in the air. '*Sacré bleu!* I was dragged by a British cavalry soldier out of my home, and if you refuse to allow me to bleed her, I will no longer attend the young woman.'

'Do you have any laudanum?'

He shook his head. 'No, monsieur. It is hard to come by these days.'

Without medicine, the doctor would not be of much help.

Glancing at Frederica, she nodded her head forward with a grimace. She did not wish to be bled. Samuel turned back to the doctor. 'Go then. You will have plenty of other patients before the week is done.'

Mrs Janssens and Dubois both looked aghast.

The innkeeper's wife grasped her chest, her face paling several shades. 'Then the rumours are true? Napoleon is coming?'

'You have a day. Possibly two.'

Dubois gave a curt nod and left the room, slamming the door behind him. Samuel wondered if the doctor would try to flee or help. After the battle, every church, school, and public building would be full of wounded soldiers in need of medical attention. Death was often a slow and painful process.

'Samuel,' Frederica said in a weak voice.

Moving to her side, he took her hand with one arm and gently caressed her brow with the other. 'What can I do for you?'

She gave him a small smile, but then winced. 'I am so hungry and everything hurts. And you know that I do not like to miss meals.'

Mrs Janssens cleared her throat and curtsied. 'I'll get milady some broth and bread.'

She left the room.

Perching on the edge of the bed, he continued to stroke her hair and cheek. 'I am so very sorry. I feel terrible that you were hurt under my protection.'

Frederica gave him another pained smile. 'No more sorrys. It was brilliant. You were brilliant. *I* was brilliant.'

This drew a reluctant laugh from Samuel.

She closed her eyes and gasped. 'Except next time, I will try my best not to get shot.'

He kissed her forehead and then her cheek. How he loved her. 'I would prefer that.'

Mrs Janssens returned with a candle and a tray. 'Milord, I prepared the room adjacent to this one for you to freshen up, and Mr Janssens has your dinner in hand. I shall look after the madam.'

Samuel glanced at Frederica, who gave him another weak smile. He thanked Mrs Janssens again and left the room. He found the horses in two stalls in a barn behind the inn. They appeared to have been fed, watered, and brushed down. He was grateful that Monsieur Janssens had taken care of them. The poor animals had run their hearts out for them. Patting his horse's head, he took off his saddlebag. Then he did the same for Frederica's grey.

After returning to the inn, he brought their meagre packs upstairs. The room for him was slightly smaller than Frederica's and not as well aired. Pouring water from a pitcher, he washed his arms, hands, and face. He wished he could wash away the image in his mind of Frederica's blood on his hands. He knew that he should leave her and take the information on to Wellington. It was his duty. But Frederica was his heart.

Chapter Twenty-Three

Frederica ached all over. She felt worse than she did last year when she was kicked in the stomach by a zebra. Clutching at her side, she groaned and tried to sit up gingerly. Falling back on her pillow, she decided to stay exactly where she was. She looked around the room and saw Samuel asleep in a chair by her side. How uncomfortable he must have been! Only an exhausted person could sleep on a wooden chair. His head hung to one side; his jaw was shadowed after several days of growth and no valet. It made him look older, rugged, and even more handsome. He was her husband and even if he did not choose her, Samuel wanted a life with her. A family. She warmed at the thought of it.

'Samuel?'

Blinking, his eyes slowly opened. He leaned forward and took her hand, caressing her knuckles with his strong fingers. 'Can I get you anything? Water? Breakfast? A chamber pot?'

'I am fine.'

He snorted, shaking his head. 'You are a terrible liar.'

'I feel awful,' Frederica said with a grimacing smile. 'How are you?'

Yawning, Samuel shrugged his shoulders. 'Stiff.'

She picked up his hand and brought it to her dry lips, brushing a kiss on the back and then in the palm. 'Please tell me you haven't slept in that chair all night? You must be exhausted.'

'No, no. Only half of it. Mrs Janssens, the innkeeper's wife, took the first shift. She is a most redoubtable Englishwoman and I am sure that you will like her.'

Biting her lower lip, Frederica remembered the red-headed woman who had sewed up her side. 'Yes. How lucky we were to have found her. Will you see if she is willing to help me dress? I do not think I could do it on my own this morning. I cannot even sit up by myself.'

He smiled down at her tenderly. 'And where do you think you are going with a bullet wound in your side?'

Frederica's breath hitched and she wished she didn't have to breathe, for every movement hurt her wound. 'We have to get back to Brussels and warn Wellington about the French generals that Napoleon is bringing with him.'

'We can go tomorrow.'

Squeezing her eyes shut, she shook her head against the hard pillow. 'There is no time to delay. Napoleon's forces are already marching towards us. If our mission is to be a successful one, we must get the information to Wellington as soon as possible, so that he can prepare his plan of attack. You need to leave me.'

'I will not,' he said quietly. 'It isn't safe for you.'

Of all the times for Samuel to be stubborn.

'It isn't safe for you to stay. You know that you should go. You are Wellington's ADC. You are on his staff and he trusts you to bring him this information.'

Moving to the bed, Samuel put his arm around Frederica's waist and kissed her cheek. 'Your health and safety are more important to me than a few hours' notice for a general. And whether that makes me a fool or a traitor, so be it.'

She threw her arms around his neck and pulled him down to her on the bed. Even though it hurt like she was being stabbed repeatedly, she hugged him tightly. Frederica felt alarmed at the thought that he belonged there. She had tried not to let her feelings for him deepen. He already had the most frustrating hold over her heart and mind. Yet here he was, choosing her over his general. The man who had become a father figure to him. A man whose respect he had earned. Samuel was putting her needs above that of his soldiers and his country. She never dreamed that he would be that devoted to her. To anyone. It filled her with a wonder that helped dim some of the pain.

Her eyes watered with unwanted tears. 'Why are you so difficult to hate sometimes?'

Frederica felt his laugh rumble in his chest before she heard it. The warm air brushed her ear and she shivered in his arms.

'Then it is settled. I will go and fetch you some breakfast.'

She nodded her face against his scratchy cheek and watched him leave the room. Slipping one foot and then the other onto the wooden floor, she forced her sore body into a sitting position first and then to standing. She couldn't allow Samuel to betray his general. He would be burdened with guilt for the rest of his life and the poor man already had enough memories that brought him pain. She limped to the window and stared out into the bright morning. Her vision must have been affected, for something large and black clouded the corner of her view. Rubbing her eyes, she opened the window and peered out of it. The black swarm was still there and it was moving.

Swallowing, her mouth went dry as she realised that it was the French army. Napoleon and his generals had taken the same road as Samuel and herself. Her husband had been right. It was not safe for her or for him to stay in Mons for another hour. Let alone another day. She would have to find the strength to leave.

It took several halting steps to make it to the narrow wardrobe where her only other plain dress was hanging. Riding her horse today was going to be a misery, but if Samuel was willing to sacrifice his career for her, she could endure some pain. Mrs Janssens must have cleaned and pressed her gown, because it looked as good as new. Pulling it over her head, she could only be grateful that she was already wearing a shift, for to lift her arms twice would have been torture. She sat on the floor and pulled up her stockings and laced up her boots.

Touching her wild curls, Frederica could not help but wish that Miss Wade was there scowling at her. She had such a way with hair. One that Frederica did not. Lifting both arms again, she braided her curls. She had to hold her breath to stop herself from crying or swearing. Probably both. She tied the end and dropped her arms, gasping in pain.

Frederica was still sitting on the floor when Samuel re-entered the room with a breakfast tray.

Gasping in surprise, he set it on the side table before stooping down beside her. 'What are you doing out of bed? Did you fall?'

She exhaled shakily and pointed to the wall. 'We must go this very morning. Napoleon's army is hot on our heels. Look through that window.'

Samuel moved swiftly to the open window and leaned his head out of it, holding on to the casing.

'Do you see the army?'

She watched him shade his eyes with one hand and lean out even farther. 'I do see a glimpse of something dark. But it is a great distance from us.'

Her eyesight must be sharper than his. 'Help me to my feet. I want to get something in my stomach before our long ride. I will need every bit of strength that I possess.'

Samuel put his hands around her arms and lifted her to her feet. Frederica was relieved that he did not touch her waist. It was smarting something dreadful. She hoped her movements hadn't caused the wound to open and bleed again. Samuel helped her across the room and into the chair that he'd spent half the night in.

She picked up a piece of toast. 'Go and have Monsieur Janssens prepare the horses and supplies. We should leave in a quarter of an hour.'

He placed his hand on her shoulder and gave it a light squeeze. 'Very good.'

Frederica forced herself to eat the toast and eggs, as well as the cherry water and lint weed tea. She'd learned from her mother that they had medicinal qualities. Even if she had no appetite now, she would need her strength for their hard ride. Draining the last of the tea, she felt her chest palpitate and her muscles quiver. She touched her chest and let out an airy laugh. After one and twenty years of age, she was finally behaving like a heroine in a novel: scared and silly.

She cleared her throat—she had no time for such theatrics. She was a spy after all. Frederica got to her feet and left the room, taking the stairs one at a time. The main floor of the inn was as clean and as inauspicious as her bedchamber. There were a few wooden tables, chairs, and a tap. Mrs Janssens bustled out of the kitchen door and bowed to her.

'Is there anything else you'll be needing this morning, milady?'

Frederica put a fist by her sore side. 'Might I have a bonnet? I must have lost my hat yesterday in the scuffle. I promise that my husband will pay for it.'

'Now, never you mind that, milady,' she said, waving her hand. 'Milord has been most generous in settling his accounts. The least I could do fer ye, is give you an old straw bonnet to keep the sun off your face.'

The good woman fetched the hat and even tied it around Frederica's chin. Frederica thanked her profusely before walking outside, grateful not to have to lift her arms again. Samuel stood near both horses and was speaking to Monsieur Janssens. She could see that their packs had been tied to their saddles and that their water jugs were refilled. The innkeeper doffed his hat to her and Samuel kneeled, cupping his hands. Taking a deep breath, she put her boot in his hands and allowed him to lift her onto her grey. She felt a jolt of pain when she sat down in the side-saddle, but forced herself to take the reins. Her fingers closed tightly around them.

Samuel mounted his own horse and they rode to the gates of the city, where several cavalry officers stood guard. They halted for a moment and she heard her husband warn them that the French army was coming and to prepare for battle. He saluted the captain in charge and then urged his horse forward. Frederica followed behind him. The up and down movement caused her wound to throb, but they had to continue. A young woman was not safe near an army, even if she had a bullet hole in her side.

After an hour, she sagged in the saddle and Samuel took the reins of her horse and guided both animals. She could no longer control her grey. It took all her stubbornness to stay seated. More than once, she had to catch herself from slipping off. Placing her hand on her wound, she felt a little blood seeping through her wool dress. She prayed that the stitches would hold a little longer.

How she remained on the back of her horse for another four hours, she did not know. All that she did comprehend is that by the time they reached the edge of the city of Brussels, each and every part of her body ached.

Samuel brought their horses to a halt. 'Shall I return you to your mother's house?'

Frederica shook her head roughly. 'I do not think that I am strong enough yet to deal with her wrath.'

Taking off his hat, he raked one hand through his hair. 'I confess I have always been a little afraid of your mother. Would you mind staying in my room at headquarters until you have been rested? I am sure that it is not as large or as fine as yours.'

Bile rose in her throat and her head felt dizzy. 'At this moment, I could happily lie down in the middle of the street.'

He touched her leg and rubbed it gently with his hand, like you would to calm a spooked horse. 'Hold on for just a little longer.'

With a click of his tongue, he guided their tired mounts through the city to the Rue Royale. Several guards were stationed outside of it and then pointed their weapons at the pair.

Samuel took off his hat again. 'I am Colonel Lord Pelford reporting to General Lord Wellington. Go and fetch a surgeon at once.'

The guards lowered their weapons and two men moved forward to take the reins of their horses. Samuel easily slid out of his saddle and moved to help her down. He put his hands on her thighs, rather than her waist, to lift her off her spent mare. His arms moved to encircle her as her knees gave way. She could not stand or walk. Her head felt like a horse had sat on it. There was not a spot on her body that did not throb in pain. Touching her temples, she winced.

Samuel lifted her up into his arms and carried her into the large house that Wellington and his staff occupied. Several soldiers saluted her husband as he weaved through the hall and up the stairs to presumably his room. He kicked open the door and then set her gently on top of the bed.

'Close your eyes. I will be back in a few minutes to take care of you,' he promised. 'I must first tell Wellington that Napoleon has brought with him Marshal Grouchy and Marshal Ney to command. And that the wily little emperor has taken the path through Mons.'

For the first time in her life, she obeyed him. Closing her eyes, Frederica let oblivion take her.

Chapter Twenty-Four

Samuel waited the next afternoon for the doctor to arrive and check on Frederica again. The night before, all the man had done was prescribe laudanum. It had eased the pain a little, but Frederica said that the hot bath and her red soap had helped more. She ate breakfast with him in bed, but was taking a nap now. Her colour was much better and he hoped that she would make a full recovery. All he could say for certain was that her tongue and wit had returned in full force. When Mr Dunford had found her in Samuel's bed, she'd teased his poor valet until the man was as red in the face as a bowl of cherries and he'd fled the room like a delicately nurtured debutante intent on keeping their reputation unsullied.

While looking out the window, a soldier tapped him on the shoulder and told him to report to Wellington's office. Samuel did so at once, along with several other staff members. The general told them to sit down around the table.

'The Prince of Orange writes that his troops have not been engaged, but the town of Binche is now occupied by the French and the Prussians driven out.'

Slender Billy.

He said a silent prayer of gratitude that his friend was not harmed.

DeLancey breathed in deeply. 'It has begun.'

'Ah, this letter from the Prussians explains that their first corps was attacked around Charleroi shortly after dawn, before five o'clock in the morning,' Wellington said, stabbing the paper with his pointer finger. 'Damn me, this dispatch is vague. Not a word about the size of the French force. This strike could be a trick, a feint, to pull us away from his real target. I dare not offer aid to the Prussians until I am sure of Napoleon's position.'

DeLancey stood. 'Lord Wellington, every ranking officer has been invited to the Duchess of Richmond's ball tonight. Shall I instruct them not to go, but to stand to ready for orders?'

'No,' Wellington said authoritatively. 'All members of my staff will attend the Duchess of Richmond's ball. If we were to cancel it, it would only encourage the Belgians who are loyal to France. No, we will go. We will smile and we will hearten our soldiers. DeLancey, have any dispatch brought directly to me at the ball.'

'Yes, Your Grace.'

Samuel did not think he could dance the night before a battle.

Wellington glanced at the other three men. 'The rest of you, go and put on your best dress uniforms, and I will meet with you again at the ball, where I will give you further orders.'

He would have no choice in the matter.

Samuel walked up the two flights of stairs to his bedchamber. He was met at the door by his valet, Dunford, an impeccably dressed and manicured gentleman in his late thirties. He had a high forehead and his ears pointed at the tips.

Dunford swept his employer an exquisite bow. 'Your Grace, I could not lay out your dress uniform for this evening because your bedchamber is occupied. I have been polishing your boots in the kitchens. The *kitchens*.'

Samuel could hear the indignation in his servant's tone and forced himself not to smile. 'Dunford, I apologise. I will be returning Lady Pelford to her mother's house this very afternoon. I will call for you when I am ready to dress for dinner. I shall be attending Lady Richmond's party this evening.'

The valet swept another perfect bow. 'Of course, Your Grace.'

Samuel opened the door to his room to find Frederica yawning. He shut the door and then rushed over to her. She placed her arms around his neck and pulled him down to the bed, covering his neck and face with kisses.

'Frederica, I am to fight tomorrow.'

She wrapped her arms around his back, pressing all ten fingers against him. 'Hold me.'

His heart pounded as he kissed her hair, her ear, and her neck. 'I would hold you for ever if I could.'

Frederica kissed his shoulder that she was leaning her head on. 'You *will* hold me for ever. That is an order. I am a duchess now and you have to do what I say.'

'Yes, Duchess.'

Bending his head, he kissed her with all the passion in his soul. Knowing that he might never see her again. Hoping to have a lifetime with her. Wishing for more hours in this day. Realising there was no greater pleasure than holding her in his arms. Knowing that she was his.

Out of breath, he leaned his forehead against hers. 'I am to attend the Duchess of Richmond's ball tonight. The Duke of Wellington insists that all members of his staff attend. I wish— I would rather spend the evening with you. Please forgive me, but I must take you now to your mother's house. We have run out of time.'

Frederica nodded her head against his. It took all of his willpower to sit up and stop holding her. She meant more to him than anything in the waking world.

Clutching her right side, she tried to sit up but was unable to. Gently, Samuel took her by the shoulders and helped her to a sitting position. He picked up her newly pressed, but still ugly, gown and eased it over her head, not bothering with a corset. He buttoned up the back, before sliding on her stockings and newly polished boots.

She giggled softly. 'You remind me of a prince in a fairy-tale story—*Cinderella*.'

Looping the lace, he smirked. 'My dear wife, your boot looks absolutely nothing like a glass slipper.'

Frederica gave him a playful push on the shoulder. 'In some renditions, her slipper is made of fur.'

Shaking his head, he tied the other lace and held out his hands to her. She allowed him to pull her to her feet and steal another kiss. Each one could be their last.

Frederica picked up her straw bonnet that was smashed beyond recognition. 'Perhaps you ought to take me out the rear entrance. I daresay I look a fright. Poor Miss Wade. She will be mortified on my behalf.'

He took her elbow. 'She can commiserate with Dunford.'

She laughed as he led her out the door and asked for a servant to call him a carriage. Since the back door led to an alley, they were forced to walk out the front entrance in all their rumpled glory. Samuel found that he did not care. What did wrinkles matter when there was a war to be fought? And a brave and beautiful wife at his side?

He directed the driver to number fourteen Rue de Lombard. Frederica snuggled up next to him, her head resting on his shoulder. Their legs touched. Their arms were entangled and yet it still was not enough for him. He needed to be nearer to her. He could never be close enough.

The carriage stopped abruptly and Samuel cursed underneath his breath. The ride had been entirely too short. He stepped out of the carriage and then helped Frederica out. Holding hands, they walked up to the door of her mother's rented house and he knocked on it. She leaned against him as if standing was too great a task. He hoped that her wound had not begun to bleed again. He regretted having to move her again so soon after their long ride. But she would be safest and best cared for at her mother's house.

Frederica stiffened and stepped away from him, dropping his hand. 'Goodbye, Samuel. I would rather you did not come in. I do not think I could bear to say goodbye to you again.'

His own throat seemed to have closed. He could not manage even the smallest syllable of farewell. Samuel nodded and turned to go. But something pricked from behind his eyes and he knew that he could not leave without saying the words that had been on the tip of his tongue for days.

Pivoting on his toes, he glanced back at her. 'I—I love you.'

Her hazel eyes widened and she opened her mouth, but before she could speak, the butler opened the door.

'My lady! Wade, come at once. Lawson, go and fetch Her Grace and tell her that her daughter is home.'

Mr Harper put his arm around Frederica's shoulders and ushered her through the door without another word.

Samuel's heart fell to his feet. He hoped that his wife loved him more than hated him in this moment. For there was no more hate in his heart.

Love had taken its place.

Chapter Twenty-Five

Mama let out a shriek of relief and ran to embrace her daughter. 'I feared the worst, my dearest.'

The tight hug pulled against her stitches, but Frederica sagged in her mother's arms. 'I am so tired, Mama. Spying is not as glamorous as it seems in trashy novels. I was hit in the face by a nasty French colonel and I got shot. It was not pleasant at all.'

Her mother kissed her cheek and held her tighter. 'I should imagine not and I know about your wound. Samuel sent me a note yesterday. Had you not been staying with a general, I would have stormed through the doors and demanded to see my daughter. Now, let us get you up to your room.'

Her mother put Frederica's arm over her shoulder and helped her up the stairs, not saying a word about Frederica's clothing, nor her hasty marriage. She helped her daughter to the bed as Miss Wade arrived. Together they took off the ugly dress and helped Frederica into a nightgown. Mama tucked her under the covers, like she was still a small child.

Frederica blinked, her eyelids heavy. 'All I have done

for the last twenty-four hours is sleep and yet I cannot keep my eyes open.'

'Then close them.'

And she did.

Frederica slept fitfully for several hours and awoke to see her mother reading in a chair by the window. The sun had gone down, but it was not dark yet. It must have been five or six o'clock in the evening. There was still time to see Samuel again. Time to tell him that she loved him completely. The words that she had not been able to say quickly enough before he'd left earlier that day.

Groaning as she sat up, Frederica said, 'Mama, have you been invited to the Duchess of Richmond's ball?'

Mama closed her book and set it down on the table beside her. 'Yes, of course. But I do not plan on attending with you being indisposed.'

Frederica slid her feet out from the coverlet. 'But I wish to go. I must go. It might be the last time I see Samuel alive.'

Her mother looked at her intently for several moments. The concern in her eyes easy to see, but also respect. Frederica was a grown woman and capable of making her own decisions. 'I will tell Wade to dress you in the white satin frock, and I will lend you my diamond tiara and necklace. We will miss the early dinner, but if we are to go, you will look like a duchess.'

Frederica managed to get to her feet and she hugged her mother, gritting her teeth at the ache in her side. 'I love you, Mama.'

She kissed her daughter's forehead. 'I love you too. But you need a bath and perfume, badly.'

Frederica was too exhausted to laugh, but she managed a small smile. Her mother left the room and the two footmen returned with a metal tub of water. Half of the servants in the house carried hot buckets to fill it. Wade assisted Frederica in removing her nightgown and helped her into the bath. Frederica would have loved to soak her sore body for hours, but now was not the time. She washed herself with the red soap. Her lady's maid put a poultice on her wound, before wrapping it tightly. Then she helped Frederica put on fresh undergarments, and Frederica howled in pain as Wade pulled up the corset, even if it was not tight.

'Should I stop, my lady. I mean, Your Grace?'

'No, no. I want to look my best.'

Wade slipped the delicate white satin dress over Frederica's head and buttoned the round pearl buttons. Then placed the diamond necklace around her throat and the matching tiara in her curls. Frederica gazed at her reflection in the mirror. She looked like a princess.

Like a bride.

Her maid held up a jar of powder. 'Your Grace's mother said that I ought to put some powder on your face to cover your bruises and the circles underneath your eyes.'

'Yes, please, and some rouge.'

Wade held Frederica's train as she walked carefully down the stairs. Her mother sat in the sitting room waiting for her. She wore a black gown with a set of rubies. As always, her mother knew how to best show her daughter to advantage. Mama had dressed as her foil. Together they would catch every eye in the room.

'Are you ready, my dear?'

'Yes, Mama.'

Her mother took her arm and helped her out of the

house and to the carriage. When they arrived at the party, they were directed into a large anteroom with a thirteen-foot-high ceiling. The walls of the room were covered in rose trellis pattern wallpaper. It was hard to believe that a few months before, this had been a storage shed for coaches.

The butler announced, 'The Duchess of Hampford and the Duchess of Pelford.'

Several eyes turned towards the entrance, and her mother took her arm and escorted her into the room near a crowd of foreigners watching the Gordon Highlanders dance a Scottish reel in their tartans and kilts. Her eyes fell on Mark Wallace, who waved to her merrily from the floor. He was dancing with a pretty blonde who no doubt had a generous dowry.

Georgy took her other arm, her countenance wan and sorrowful. 'I cannot believe that you did not invite me to your wedding.'

'Nor I,' Mama said, releasing Frederica's arm.

'It was sudden.'

Her friend pouted and her mother sighed. 'I will go and pay my respects to Lady Richmond, do keep an eye on her for me, Georgy?'

'I will. Two of them.'

Frederica patted her friend's hand that was on her arm. 'I am sorry, Georgy. It was very small and private. Nothing at all like tonight. It looks like every officer in the Continent is here, including General Lord Wellington. What a triumph for your mother.'

She saw that her friend's eyes were filled with unshed tears. 'I sat by your duke and the Duke of Wellington at dinner, and the duke gave me an original miniature of himself painted by a Belgian artist.'

'Which duke?'

Her small jest made Georgy release a watery laugh. 'Wellington, of course.'

Frederica nudged her friend with her elbow. 'I am so relieved. I was about to call you out for a duel.'

Her friend rubbed her already red eyes. 'How can you jest at such a time?'

Frederica let out a shuddering breath. 'What else can I do? If I do not smile, I will weep. If I do not dance, I will drop to the floor.'

More tears fell down Georgy's cheeks. 'I do not think I can dance. All the troops, saving my father's regiment, which is to guard Brussels, have orders to be ready to march before first light.'

Frederica gulped. It was exactly what she expected, but the reality overwhelmed her. If she did not find him at the ball tonight, she might never see Samuel again. She checked her own tears, but others could not or would not. All around her fathers, mothers, sons, daughters, wives, and husbands openly wept and embraced their loved ones with a final goodbye. She watched them leave the ball and prayed that Samuel had not already gone.

She pulled Georgy around the room, searching for Samuel. They passed the Duke of Wellington, who lacked his usual composure. A matron asked him about the rumours.

'Yes, they are true, we are off tomorrow.'

The matron began to sob. 'Oh, my sons! God protect them!'

Frederica steered Georgy away from Wellington and to the door, where several officers were already leaving the ball to change out of their dress uniforms. At last, she saw the broad shoulders and strong back of Samuel.

She dropped her friend's hand. 'I am sorry, Georgy. But I have seen my husband, and I dare not waste another moment in conversation.'

Frederica practically ran to Samuel, ignoring the throb of pain in her side. He turned around at her approach and without a thought to their surroundings took her in his arms and soundly kissed her. He held her in his strong arms, so tightly she could barely breathe. She wished that she could stay encircled in them for ever.

His hands moved to cup her face. 'What are you doing here? You ought to be in bed. How is your wound?'

'I had to see you again,' Frederica explained. Her eyes on him, oblivious to everyone around them. 'I began to worry that I'd missed you. So many officers have already left the ball for the front.'

Samuel dropped a kiss on her hair. 'Wellington requested I remain with him. I suppose I shall fight tomorrow in my evening costume. Now turn around and let me look at you.'

He gently released her. Frederica smiled wistfully and slowly circled. Her nerves felt like pistols all firing at the same time.

Samuel whistled. 'Beautiful. You look like a princess. Like a proper Cinderella. You should always wear white, like a bride. *My* bride.'

But she had no time for flattery. Clutching the lapels of his shiny red coat, she stared resolutely at the top brass button. 'I wanted to tell you that I love you and that I do not hate you even a little bit.'

He lifted her chin with his finger so they were eye to eye. 'I could not quite hear that. Could you say it again?'

Frederica grabbed his finger on her chin and kissed it. 'I love you.'

Samuel gave her a roguish grin and her heart hammered in her chest. 'I still couldn't quite hear that over the din of the crowd.'

With a sobbing laugh, she spoke in a voice loud enough that everyone standing within six feet could hear her. 'I said, I love you!'

Samuel gave an exultant laugh and kissed her brow. A feeling of euphoria settled upon her as he gently pressed her head against his chest, calming her tense nerves. 'I heard you all three times, but I couldn't resist the pleasure of having you repeat it.'

'Be careful, won't you?' Frederica begged, pulling herself tighter against him as tears began to spill down her cheeks. 'Do not take any foolish risks.'

'Never.'

Frederica gave a small watery chuckle. 'I want to grow old with you.'

Samuel ran his palms up and down her back, sending shivers over her skin. 'We will travel the world together and you can take over your mother's company.'

'Where will you take me first?'

'Do you fancy a trip to Scotland? I have a little castle up there on a loch, very private, the perfect place for a wedding trip. That is of course if your mother has not already sold that property. Perhaps we'd better check with her before we set off?'

Frederica let out another watery chuckle. 'A prudent idea.'

Samuel looked past her to the Duke of Wellington, who waved one hand at him. 'I must go, my darling.

We will be marching in front of your house. I will look for you at the window.'

'I will be there.'

He took both of her hands in his and kissed one and then the other, squeezing them before he released them. Frederica watched him walk to Wellington's side, and they left the ball together. It took all her strength to stay standing upright on her own two feet, holding on to her painful side. It felt like he was walking away with her heart and leaving her chest with a large gaping hole. The tears that she had not allowed to fall streamed down her cheeks and onto her white bridal gown.

Mama put a gentle arm around her shoulders and held Frederica for several minutes while she sobbed. She accepted a handkerchief from her mother and wiped her eyes and nose with it. Glancing around the large room that had been full when she arrived, she realised that more than half of the guests had already gone.

'The soldiers are going to march past our house,' Frederica said, sniffling. 'I should like to see them.'

'Then we will leave at once.'

Mama shepherded Frederica to the entrance, where they waited only a short time for Jim and the driver to arrive with their carriage. And back at their house on Rue de Lombard, her mother asked Harper to move two chairs to face the front windows.

They sat together, mother and daughter, watching regiment after regiment pass by—the Brunswickers, Scotch, and English. Frederica did not think she could have slept through it even if she had wished to. Noises filled the air: carts and wagons clattering against the stone road, soldiers blowing bugles and beating drums, horses neighing, and people shouting farewells. Frederica recognised the Gordon Highlanders at once by their tartans and kilts. They marched by in perfect formation and fearlessness. Standing before them was a trio of bagpipe players that played a lively Scottish jig. She saw Mark riding a horse. She waved and smiled. He tipped his hat to her.

Shafts of light peeked through the chimneys and over the rooftops—morning had come. Mama retired to bed, but Frederica stood at the window, determined to stay awake until Samuel came by.

At last, she saw the unforgettable face of the Duke of Wellington, and on his right, mounted on his exquisite mare, rode Samuel. He was still dressed in his bright red dress uniform coat. Frederica tapped against the glass and waved furiously. Samuel kissed his hand to her and was gone from her sight within moments.

Slumping down into her chair, she fell fast asleep.

Chapter Twenty-Six

General Wellington led his staff to Quatre Bras. When they rode into the small Belgian town, Samuel felt the hair on his arms rise—it had already begun. He saw the French army charge against the Dutch Belgians. Instead of holding their positions in the abandoned houses and sheds, the soldiers fled for the Bossu wood in a panic. Samuel saw his friend the Prince of Orange raise his sabre high in the air and yell for his troops to turn and fight, but the soldiers did not heed him.

Wellington swore in disgust.

The Prince of Orange turned on his horse and saw Wellington and Samuel. He galloped towards them in a fury, his thin face red from a mix of exertion and embarrassment.

''Pon my soul, my men were holding fine, returning shots, until the French cavalry charged with their shouts of *"Long live the emperor!"*' Billy explained, 'and my force buckled.'

'Obviously,' Wellington said dryly. 'We have no time for excuses. Go back to the woods and rally your troops to fight man to man in the trees. You will hold the French at Bossu woods.'

Billy saluted Wellington and galloped back to the forest with the same fury he had come with.

Wellington waved Samuel forward with a hand. 'Pelford, we must find some way to hold our position. I have no great confidence in the Dutch Belgians. We cannot lose possession of the Nivelles-Namur road, or we will lose contact with the Prussians.'

Samuel pointed. 'Lord Wellington, look. Picton's forces are not a half a mile down the road. All is not lost.'

Wellington took a small spyglass from his pocket and looked through it. Samuel saw his mouth move as Wellington counted the infantry and light cavalry brigade divisions.

He closed his spyglass. 'Pelford, you must tell Picton that he has to hold the French. No matter the cost.'

Samuel saluted the general and urged his tired horse towards Lieutenant-General Picton and his men. He relayed the message and the Welshman let out a string of vile curses.

'Get on with you, Pelford. Tell Wellington that we'll hold the line.'

Nodding, Samuel returned the same way he came. Glancing over his shoulder, he saw Picton leading his cavalry to charge. He'd been that close to the fighting. The sound of a single bullet pierced the air by his ear. He ducked, only to realise that it was his horse and not himself that had been hit. His beautiful mare stumbled to her knees and fell on her side, with Samuel's left leg beneath her.

Samuel tried to pull his leg out, but the weight of the dead horse felt like a boulder. Looking around him, he saw several other bloody bodies on the ground.

Some were as still as death, while others twitched and moaned waiting for help. If he did not move soon, he might be joining the dead. Touching the buttons on his jacket, he thought of Frederica. He did not want anyone else to help her with her buttons. No one but him.

With a surge of adrenaline, he used all his strength to lift the horse's carcass and shimmy his leg out from underneath it. Samuel rolled to his knees, but his left leg would not bear his weight. Placing his hands on his leg, he felt down it. Nothing felt out of place, or broken, but it hurt like the devil. His knee was bruised and his ankle sprained.

He managed to get onto his feet and swayed in a standing position. Turning slowly, he saw that the French soldiers were swarming the Bossu wood like ants over a crumb. They would reach him in minutes. He stumbled forward and joined other Allies running towards the British line. Samuel met a group of Gordon Highlanders.

Samuel held his side with his hand. 'They are coming.'

He felt a hand on his back and looked up into the face of Mark Wallace, who gave him a crooked grin.

Wallace handed Samuel a flask of whisky. 'Looks like you could use a drink.'

The Scottish whisky burned down Samuel's throat, but it revived him. He stood tall and handed the flask back to Wallace. 'Thank you. Tell your men to get into position, the French will be here any minute.'

Wallace turned to the Gordon Highlander Brigade, wearing their clan tartans, and he yelled in a loud voice for them to make ready for battle. The air echoed with 'ayes' and a trio of bagpipe players situated at the back of the brigade began playing a bonnie tune. Samuel watched each man kneel to prepare to shoot their muskets. Wallace walked through his men giving encouragement.

'First line, fire!' Wallace commanded.

Gun smoke filled the air, and the first line of Highlanders ducked and fell back to reload.

'Second line, fire!'

Several French soldiers fell to the ground, but countless others took their place and continued to charge.

'Third line, fire!' Wallace yelled, lifting his sabre. 'The rest of you, get out your sabres and get ready to charge.'

The third line of Highlanders shot their muskets and fell back in their ranks.

'Charge!'

The Highlanders yelled and held their sabres high above their heads, the silver blades reflecting the sunlight. They charged only ten feet before they met the French soldiers. Samuel stumbled to his feet, raising his sabre to block a blow from another French soldier. He continued to fight, but it didn't seem to matter how many French soldiers they killed or wounded, more continued to pour out of the Bossu woods. The Highlanders fought with fury to the music of the bagpipes.

He stabbed a man through the neck and saw Wallace crumble to the ground, his lower leg bleeding freely. Samuel yelled, stumbling towards the French soldier who had stabbed the captain. The enemy soldier parried a few blows, but was no match for Samuel's strength and speed. Samuel ran him through the stomach. Wallace moved his head and moaned. With the last of his strength, Samuel picked Wallace up by the middle and slung him over his shoulder.

'Fall back!' Samuel yelled to the Highlanders, limping his way back to the crossroads.

He set Wallace's unconscious body into a wagon for the wounded and took off his uniform coat to wrap his leg. Samuel had barely tied the arms together when the driver set off for Brussels. Hopefully the young captain would be operated on by a doctor there.

Glancing around the battlefield, he saw that the British Ninth, Forty-Second, and Forty-Fourth Brigades were putting up a good fight, but that they were greatly outnumbered. British soldiers were falling back to the crossroads. If they retreated farther, they would lose communication with their allies the Prussians.

Samuel looked down the road and to his relief, he saw Colonel Alten leading the Third Division. The troops ran to join the battle. But they were falling like flies. In that moment, Samuel realised that life was fleeting and precious. He wondered if the dead soldiers had sweethearts and wives waiting at home in England. Frederica was only in Brussels, but it felt like a world away from him now. How badly he wanted to make it home to her. He'd give everything to see her smile once more.

He found Wellington mounted at La Haye Sainte farm near the centre of the Allies' position. He thought of Frederica's kisses and their picnics together. Those memories were bittersweet. Samuel borrowed the horse of an officer that had already been killed. Smoke from Hougoumont hung over the field between the two armies. Beneath the smoke, Samuel saw the helmets and feathers of the cuirassiers moving quickly towards them. Cannon and artillery fire fell upon them like rain.

'Hard pounding, gentlemen,' Wellington yelled to the British gunners from his own mount. 'Let's see who pounds the longest.'

Samuel saw a long line of wounded soldiers on the road behind La Haye Sainte. He looked in the other direction and saw the French preparing for another attack—Samuel guessed that they had seen the wounded men and assumed the British were retreating. The French cuirassiers and infantry yelled loudly and ran towards La Haye Sainte farm. They swept past the guards and slaughtered all the British inside. The French now held the centre position of Wellington's line.

'The Brunswickers must fill the gap,' Wellington yelled. 'We cannot let the French break the line and get control of the Genappe road.'

Samuel galloped towards a group of reserves dressed in black uniforms with tall collars and black trousers with a blue stripe down the side. He saluted the captain and relayed to him Wellington's orders. The Brunswickers made four columns and marched to fill the gap on the Genappe road.

'They are fleeing,' Wellington yelled. 'Come, Gordon, Pelford. We must rally the Brunswickers.'

The three men galloped towards the retreating men, and Wellington rode in front of the line, cutting off their path.

Wellington held up his sabre. 'My men, follow me!'

The general then led his horse through them and charged the enemy alone. Samuel spurred his horse to follow and held up his sabre and yelled, 'To Wellington!'

He heard the gallop of Gordon's horse beside him and, for a moment, thought that they were going to be a three-man charge against an entire column of French infantry.

Then he heard the Brunswickers echo his call. 'To Wellington! To Wellington! To Wellington!'

Samuel turned to see the black cloud of Brunswickers running towards him, and he continued onward. He rode straight into the enemy's line and began to stab at every man in his reach. He ducked and heard a bullet sail over his head. Turning his horse around, he circled back towards the Brunswickers, who were slaughtering the enemy before them.

He heard Alexander cry out in agony. His friend had been hit by a bullet in the leg, but he could not stop to help him.

'Go on! Go on!' Wellington yelled. 'They won't stand. Don't give them a chance to rally.'

A bullet whizzed by Samuel's ear.

'Sir, you need to retreat back to safety,' Samuel insisted. 'You're within firing range.'

'Never mind, let them fire away. The battle's gained, my life's of no consequence now. We must clear the field and keep the French retreating.'

Samuel raised his sabre above his head and charged one of the few remaining French squares of soldiers. He stabbed two men, and then he felt a bullet hit him high in the chest. His hands slackened on his sabre and on the horse's reins. Sliding off the horse, he fell face down into the mud and blood. He lifted his head up and fought to keep consciousness. He'd promised

Frederica to do everything in his power to get back to her. Memories of her flashed in his mind: summer days swimming at Hampford Castle, bread and cheese picnics, kissing in the orchard, waltzing at balls, and their precious time as man and wife. Then the darkness consumed him.

Chapter Twenty-Seven

A group of Highlanders yelled in broad Scottish accents, 'Boney's beat! Boney's beat! Boney's beat! Huzzah! Huzzah! Boney's beat!'

Frederica turned to look at the window and saw Highlanders throwing their bonnets in the air and yelling again. She looked for Mark, but did not see him.

It was over.

After months of preparation and days of fear, the great battle was finally over. Great Britain and her allies had defeated Napoleon a second time. Clutching her side, she exhaled with relief. They had been victorious and now all she needed was to see Samuel. To make sure that he was okay. She wanted her quarrelling-ever-after ending. He'd promised her that even girls who do not follow the rules of society could still have happy endings.

'I must obtain news of Samuel.'

Mama was already dressed in her pelisse and bonnet. She kissed Frederica's cheek. 'I will send Jim. I wish I could go for you, but there are so many wounded officers that need my help at the hospital. It is a good thing we brought plenty of your soap. I am almost down to my last bar.'

She didn't doubt that Jim would do his best to find out what he could, but a duchess would learn a great deal more than a footman. 'I am well enough to walk, Mama. I promise you.'

Sighing, her mother nodded her head. 'At least bring Jim with you. The streets are still not safe.'

Her chin quivered and she tugged at her collar. Mama and Miss Wade had spent the previous day from dawn to dusk at a makeshift hospital in a church, whilst she had lain in bed to recover. Mama told her last night that there was so much to do. Men to feed. Wash. And write to their loved ones. Some would survive with missing limbs, others would not. Frederica should be helping them this morning, but her mind and heart were focused on Samuel.

When Harper opened the door for her, Jim, the footman, waited outside. She noticed that he carried a pistol. She wished she had thought to bring her own.

'We'll have to walk, Lady Frederica,' he said. 'Her Grace let the men driving the wagons of the wounded borrow our horses.'

She nodded her head to him. 'On foot is fine, Jim.'

The footman took her elbow and they wandered slowly through the crowded streets of Brussels. Many of the wounded soldiers were still able to walk and they filled the roads with their bloodstained clothes and pale, haggard faces. Frederica thought that half of the city seemed to be standing in the streets waiting for news of their loved ones. She saw women of rank beg eager questions to the lowliest of foot soldiers. Strangers conversed together like friends. There was no ceremony, no false dignity, it was humanity at its core caring and sharing with each other.

A beautiful young woman with a halo of gold hair grabbed the reins of a horse that Frederica recognised. It was Mark's cousin's magnificent black stallion, but a different man was astride it. A boy really. He could not have been more than eighteen or nineteen years old. The brown whiskers on his face were sparse.

'My husband, Colonel Sir Alexander Gordon, have you heard anything of him? This is his horse.'

'I am so sorry, Lady Gordon,' the young soldier said, 'but your husband died this morning in Doctor Hume's arms.'

The young woman's lower lip began to quiver. 'Do you know where his body is?'

The soldier saluted her. 'At Wellington's headquarters in Waterloo.'

He tried to urge his horse forward, but Frederica stepped right in front of the horse's snout and it recognised her scent.

'You were at Wellington's headquarters? Do you know aught of my husband? Colonel Lord Pelford. He is an aide-de-camp to the general.'

The young man would not meet her eyes and shifted in the saddle.

'Tell me!' she shouted over the noises in the crowd. 'You must tell me.'

His eyes were wet when they finally met her gaze. 'He was shot and is currently missing, presumed dead. The general does not know where his body is.'

Stumbling away from the soldier and the horse, she would have fallen over if Jim had not caught her. She felt as if she had been shot a second time, through the centre of her chest. The pain was real and excruciating. She kept swallowing, but nothing seemed to open her constricted throat.

She did not cry.

She could not cry.

She would not believe it.

The possibility of life without Samuel seemed inconceivable.

Who else would annoy her to exasperation?

Disagree with almost everything she believed in?

And kiss her until her toes curled?

'Let us get you back home, my lady,' Jim said, steering her back towards their rented home on Rue de Lombard.

Her own mind was so foggy that she could not have found her way to the rented house. Jim did not leave her at the door, but escorted her inside the parlour and to a chair. He told Harper to make her ladyship some tea.

'Master Samuel? Pelford?' Harper asked.

Jim did not say a word. He only shook his head.

Frederica tried to swallow once more. 'No tea. I just want to be left alone.'

The butler gave her a sympathetic look and then both he and Jim exited the room. Once the door closed, the tears that she had held inside of her spilled out in muffled sobs. Never in her life before had she experienced such despair and it consumed her. She felt as if her head was under the water of a cold river and there was no way for her to breathe as the current dragged her away.

The next morning, her mother came into her room to check on her. Frederica lay in bed. She had no energy and her head felt dizzy. She had dreamed of Samuel dying over and over, until she woke up in a cold sweat. How she wished that her sisters were there with her! She could have used a cuddle from Becca or a blunt observation from Helen. Mantheria would have tried to counsel with her about the proper ways to grieve, but she was not ready to be wise. Touching her swollen eyes, she winced. They were dry and achy like the rest of her body.

Mama lifted the lid of her meal tray. 'You have not touched your hot chocolate nor breakfast.'

Squeezing her eyes tightly shut, Frederica shook her head. 'I am not hungry.'

'That is a first.'

A snort escaped her lips, before she could stop herself. How could she find her mother's wit amusing the day after she learned Samuel was dead?

Anger built in her belly. 'How can you make a joke at a time such as this?'

Her mother placed a gentle hand on her shoulder. 'It was more a dry observation. Dearest, Samuel would not mind you laughing. Even when you were little, he liked nothing more than to make you smile. Whenever he told a joke, he always looked at you to see your reaction.'

Shaking her head, Frederica said, 'He preferred to make me shriek with fury.'

One side of her mother's mouth went up into a half smile. 'That too. The both of you could not bear it if the other one ignored you. Oh, the lengths you two went to for the other's attention. Remember the time when you put salt into his tea?'

Another chuckle escaped her lips. 'It was brilliant. Samuel spat the tea out across the table and it hit both Matthew and Wick.'

Glancing up at her mother, Frederica saw that her eyes were filled with tears. Samuel was not merely a suitor. Her mother had seen him grow up. Not that her mother's pain could reach the depths of her own, but Frederica was wrong to assume that she was not grieving deeply.

She placed her hand over her mother's. 'I am sorry to be snappish, Mama. I know that you loved Samuel too.'

Mama nodded and kissed Frederica's curls again. 'I did and I love you, my dear girl. And although I do not know what it is like to lose a husband, I do know what it is to lose a loved one. My own mother and two of my beloved children. That sort of pain does not go away after days or months, even years. But they are not gone entirely. You carry them with you in your heart wherever you go. So please laugh at salt in tea, bear cubs in bedchambers, and every other happy memory you have of Samuel. It is in your memories that you can keep them alive.'

A sob broke from her throat and her mother wrapped her arms around Frederica as she wept. She cried and cried until she could no more. And then she laughed and snorted.

Rubbing her wet nose with the back of her hand, she said, 'Remember when I was eight and he dared me to eat a grasshopper?'

Her mother cringed. 'I can still hear the sound of you crunching on the shell. I nearly lost the contents of my stomach.'

'He paid me a guinea.'

'You could not pay me a hundred guineas to eat a grasshopper,' Mama said with another shiver of disgust. 'And when I complained to your father, he assured me that it was perfectly good for you.'

Frederica sniffed. 'I'd forgotten. Papa ate a grasshopper with me.'

'And I could not kiss him for a week.'

Leaning her head on her mother's shoulder, she let out another watery chuckle. 'I wish I could kiss Samuel again.'

'Did his skills finally surpass the Italian count?'

Another laugh tore through her. 'Yes. Yes, they did.'

Her mother dropped another kiss on the top of her head. 'I would like nothing more than to relive memories of Samuel with you all day, but I must go. There is too much to do at the hospital. So many men have been wounded and need my help. And you will be helping too. I believe we will go through every bar of red soap that you made.'

Pushing away from her mother's arms, Frederica felt herself snapping out of a trance. 'Just give me five minutes to dress, Mama, and I will go with you.'

'You are still recovering from your wound.'

Frederica shook her head, pushing off her coverlet and forcing her sore body to stand. 'I want to be too busy to think.'

'Well, I can certainly promise you that.'

Her mother helped her change her shift and gown. It made Frederica feel like a little girl again. But after Waterloo, she knew that she had left all childhood behind. Even for a wild young woman who grew up in a castle with exotic animals life was not a fairy tale. Terrible things happened to everyone and all she could do now was save another woman's sweetheart.

They walked down the stairs arm in arm to the landing where Miss Wade stood waiting. She took Frederica's other hand, and they walked in a line down the street to the church. A servant opened the door, and Frederica saw an immaculately clean room with rows of camp beds and each held a soldier—officers and privates mingled together. There were nearly one hundred men in the large room. Most of the men were missing an arm or a leg, besides flesh wounds. Mama put on a white apron and handed one to Frederica and Wade.

'The surgeons are gone,' a woman said in a tired voice. 'They have done what they can do for the men. All we can do now is make them as comfortable as we can.'

Her mother touched the other woman's shoulders. 'Yes, of course. Go home and get some rest.'

'I will return this evening to trade places with you.'

Mama bowed to the woman of inferior rank. 'I do not doubt it.'

Her mother then turned and led Frederica and Wade to the cloister, which was being used as a kitchen. Frederica recognised the cook, for he was their own cook. He stood stirring three large pots of soup that looked to be mostly chicken broth with a few herbs. And one pot was full of tea.

'The tea needs a little more time, but there is no reason why the men cannot drink spirits to celebrate their victory,' Mama said. 'Frederica and Wade, set out the wine that is currently being stored in the confessional booth and help Miss Brady and the other volunteers distribute it.'

Wade and Frederica immediately pulled back the curtain of the confessional booth and saw six cases of wine. They each carried one case back to the cloister and then returned for the other four. The dark-haired woman had already opened the four cases and was efficiently doling out the bottles to the volunteers.

'Start down that line there and only fill the glasses halfway,' the woman said in a businesslike tone. 'We need to make sure that there is enough for everyone.'

Frederica continued to pour wine, until she reached the second to last man in her row. He was not wearing a shirt, and his chest was covered in bandages, his left arm a stump from amputation. She gently touched his shoulder but no response. Touching him again, she realised that he felt cold. She would tell her mother that he was dead, as soon as she served the last man—he was missing his right leg just below the knee. A bandage covered half of his face and his middle.

She looked closer and recognised the face. 'Mark, it is me, Frederica.'

There was no response. His wounds had been attended to, but when she put her fingers on his arm, his skin was on fire. She moved her hand to his forehead, which burned to the touch. If she could not relieve his fever, Mark wasn't going to live through the day. She brought a fist to her chest at the pain and anguish. Looking around her at the hundred other wounded soldiers, she realised that she would not be able to help them all.

Yet, she could not bear for another friend to die. She placed the wine and the glass on the floor near his camp bed and ran back to the kitchen. Grabbing a bucket, she went outside to fill it with fresh cold water from the well. She came back inside and found a stack of clean linens. She took the top few and headed back to Mark. She dipped the first linen in the cold water and laid it on his face where there were not bandages, but without covering his mouth or nose. She unbuttoned his shirt and placed another wet cold linen on his chest.

Mama signalled to her to come. Frederica assisted in serving the soup and changing the bed linens.

But every quarter of an hour, Frederica would take the bucket back to the well for fresh water and reapply the compresses to Mark's hot body. She sat hard on the stone floor next to Mark and breathed in and out. She was so physically exhausted that she could not keep her eyes open. She felt a hand on her head, and she looked up—it was Mark's. He was finally awake.

She scrambled to her feet and poured him a glass of wine and held it to his lips.

He sipped it slowly until it was gone. 'Your husband carried me off the field. Pelford saved my life.'

Frederica nodded and felt a tear slide down her cheek—then another.

Numbly, she went to help another wounded soldier. If Samuel had saved lives, so could she.

Chapter Twenty-Eight

The next day, Frederica slept late. She'd overdone it the day before. Mama and Wade had already left the house for the hospital. Along with Mr Harper and all the kitchen staff. The only servants that remained were the grooms. Jim waited patiently to escort Frederica to the church that was a temporary infirmary. She had not got much rest the previous night and her mother had insisted that she sleep in before coming to help. Frederica still had no appetite and very little energy. She rubbed her chest, but nothing alleviated the heavy sensation in her heart.

There was a knock on their front door.

Jim cleared his throat, shuffling his feet at the bottom of the stairs. 'Should you like me to answer that for you, Your Grace?'

Her new honorific.

Samuel's title.

Chills covered her body. 'Yes, please, Jim.'

She slowly walked down the stairs. The footman, with considerable grace, opened the door for a military man and brought him into the parlour. It took her foggy mind a moment or two to recognise the man. It was Colonel Scovell, the spymaster who had attended her wedding and made the arrangements for her and Samuel to go to Paris. His hair and beard were longer and his uniform a bit ragged.

He bowed to her and she curtsied with shaking knees.

'Lady Pelford, I am afraid that you were misinformed. Colonel Lord Pelford is still alive, but I am afraid that he is not long with us.'

Frederica felt numb and she collapsed to the floor. Bile rose in her throat and she was glad that she had not eaten breakfast or she would have lost it. Her voice cracked as she asked, 'Where is he? Is he at a hospital in Brussels?'

Scovell shook his head, his expression grave. 'Lord Pelford was taken to a small farmhouse in Mont-Saint-Jean near Waterloo. I saw him there this morning and rode immediately to inform you of it. And if it is agreeable, I will escort you there this very moment. In such cases as these even the smallest delay…'

The spymaster did not finish his sentence, but Frederica knew what he meant. She was going to lose Samuel all over again. Yet she would do anything for a few moments with him. For more memories of her husband to hold in her heart.

'Jim!' Frederica said.

The footman rushed to her side and carefully helped her to her feet.

Frederica grabbed his hands. 'Did we get our horses back from the wounded wagons?'

'Yes, my lady.'

'Please, harness the carriage at once.'

Scovell cleared his throat, giving Frederica a pitying

glance. 'A carriage will take more time and the roads are not good.'

'I need to be able to convey his body back with me,' she whispered in a weak voice, touching the column of her throat to feel her own steady pulse. She needed to know where Samuel was. Always. She could not allow his body to be sent to a charnel house and be piled in a large unmarked grave.

Jim bowed to her. 'As you wish it, Your Grace. I will bring the carriage around at once.'

Spinning on her foot, Frederica took the stairs two at a time. She grabbed the last bar of red soap from her room and then she opened the linen cupboard and took out three clean white sheets, placing them in her portmanteau. Going to the kitchen, she took a tea kettle and the remainder of the bread and cheese. She wrapped them up and placed them in the small trunk. She looked around wildly. What else would he need?

Scovell entered the kitchen. 'Excuse me, Lady Pelford. All the wells at Waterloo are spoiled, for soldiers have thrown bodies in them. Fresh water and wine would be the most advisable to bring.'

Frederica thanked him, opening the door to the cellar before carrying out four bottles of spirits. She took the kettle out of the portmanteau and filled it with water. She added lint weed leaves to the concoction. They would be bitter without the cherry water, but she did not have time to ask Jim to fetch some from the market. Nor could she be certain that it would be available with so many wounded soldiers. She packed a jug of water.

Scovell picked up the portmanteau, and Frederica carried the full kettle. She led him through the front door where the carriage stood waiting. Her mother's usual coachman was perched in the driver's seat and Jim sat beside him holding a gun. Recognising Frederica, Jim relaxed his hold on the weapon. She recalled her mother saying that the horses had to be guarded from thieves when the battle began. So many people were trying to run away by any means possible.

Holding her neck again, Frederica said, 'I need to get to Mont-Saint-Jean as quickly as possible.'

Scovell loaded the portmanteau and begged to be excused to retrieve his horse from the hitching post. Frederica thanked him and entered the coach carefully, as to not spill the precious water or lint weed in the kettle. She sagged back against her seat. She felt like Pandora trying to hold on to her small box of hope despite all the terrible calamities in the world.

What if Samuel were already dead before she arrived?

Why hadn't she, like Sir Alexander Gordon's widow, begged for information from anyone about her husband and the location of his body?

He might have suffered less and they could have spent a day and a half more together.

It was not the lifetime that she had hoped for, but at least she could have been with him. Eased the pain. Impatiently, she scratched at her face.

If only.

Leaning out the window for some fresh air, Frederica saw a shocking sight. Rows of soldiers' bodies were being drawn along by fishhooks. The Belgian peasants were dragging them to a large hole in a field to be buried. Frederica covered her mouth with her hand as her stomach roiled. She swore to herself that Samuel would not suffer such an ignominious end. She would bring his body home with her and have him buried where she could visit often. They would never be parted again.

The coach came to a stop beside a wooden farmhouse with a garret, a stable, and a row of cow houses. Scovell dismounted and opened the carriage door. Frederica walked down the steps and saw soldiers using French shields as frying pans over small fires to cook their beefsteaks. Not even the smell of smoke could cover the stench of death.

Scovell picked up her portmanteau and begged her to follow him. He did not lead her to the farmhouse, but to the closest cow house. He opened the door with his free hand. Again, Frederica had to fight not to vomit. The cow house floor was covered in straw and blood, and carrion flies swarmed over the line of wounded soldiers. Infection seeped through the dirty rags that bound their wounds. It was a dirty place not even fit for cows. Let alone soldiers. The brave men who had fought for their country.

She did not see Samuel.

Frederica looked eagerly to Scovell. She was having difficulty breathing. It felt as if her throat was completely closed. Had she been too slow in coming to see him? Her chest felt tight and she struggled to find air.

'They might have moved him inside the farmhouse, Your Grace,' Scovell said, glancing at her. 'When I recognised him this morning, I requested that he be made more comfortable.'

Taking her elbow, Scovell led the way back out of the door of the cow house across a short path to the farmhouse. The air was only slightly less pungent outside.

They were met at the door by a wiry woman with a

mop of grey hair and a lined face. Her simple brown dress was covered in dust, and she had a dazed look in her eyes. 'I stayed the whole battle right there, miss, in that there garret.'

Scovell tried to push past her, but she blocked the door-frame resolutely and repeated herself. He set down the portmanteau, and Frederica thought he was going to forcibly remove the poor, deranged woman.

She placed a hand on his shoulder and asked the woman in French, 'Why did you stay here?'

Her eyes lit up with a wild look. 'I have got a great many cows and calves and poultry and pigs. They is all that I have in this here world, and if I did not stay to take care of them, they would be all destroyed or carried off.'

Frederica gave the woman a friendly smile. 'I promise I am not here to steal your cows or your calves or your poultry or your pigs. I am here only to see my husband. Would you be so kind as to move so that we may look for him in your house?'

The woman's eyes darted back from Scovell to Frederica, then from Frederica to Scovell. She stuck her thin gnarled fingers on her chest and repeated the same phrase.

'Of course you did,' Frederica said soothingly, taking the woman's arm and escorting her into the house. 'Now, why don't you step inside your kitchen, and I will make us a pot of tea while you tell me all about it.'

She did not resist her, but allowed Frederica to pull her into the kitchen. There were bodies of wounded men packed closely together. A lone doctor gave them a nod, but continued to help the soldier in front of him. There were three rooms in the lower part of the house, and the woman proudly showed each to Frederica, as if she could not see the wounded bodies in the first two rooms.

Frederica recognised the faces of Major-General Cooke and Major Llewellyn. The woman opened the third room, which was the size of a closet. She saw Samuel's face on the pillow of a narrow cot—it was devoid of colour. Frederica set the kettle on the table near the bed and took his hand in her own. Scovell quietly placed the portmanteau on the floor. He took the overwrought woman by the elbow and escorted her out of the room, shutting the door behind them. Frederica did not have time to help her right now.

Stepping closer, she saw that Samuel still had both his legs and his arms, but across his bare chest were bandages tinged with a yellowish green. Frederica laid her head on his chest next to the bandages and listened to his laboured breathing. He was burning up and she felt cold all over. But he was alive!

She heard his breathing quicken and she raised her head.

Samuel opened his eyes and looked at her. 'Freddie?'

Her heart lifted at the sound of his voice. She touched her cool fingers to his hot lips and kissed his clammy forehead. 'It's *Frederica*, as you well know.'

'You should not argue with a dead man,' he said in a croaky voice.

A sob escaped her lips, but she quelled her tears. 'If you die, I will kill you.'

A crease formed on his forehead as his eyebrows pulled close together. 'That does not make any sense.'

She brushed his fevered mouth with hers. 'Loving

you does not make any sense and I have never let that stop me before.'

Opening the portmanteau, she pulled out a bottle of wine. She uncorked it with shaking hands and held it to Samuel's chapped lips. She cradled the back of his head as he drank greedily from the bottle and then closed his eyes as if the effort took too much out of him. Setting down the bottle of spirits, she got to her feet and picked up the kettle. She opened the door and Scovell stood right outside it, and she asked if he would boil it for her.

'And please request the surgeon to come as soon as he is available.'

He merely nodded in reply.

She walked over to the bed and carefully took off Samuel's soiled bandages—the stench was overwhelming. She gagged. There was a bullet hole on the right side of his chest just below his shoulder. The wound looked an angry red and a yellow pus oozed out of it. Infection was setting in. She remembered hearing Wick say that spirits could ward off infection, so she poured the rest of the bottle of wine over them. Then she pressed out the pus and scrubbed the wound with her red soap and the small jug of water. Taking out a clean sheet from the portmanteau, she ripped it into two-inch scraps. Once she had a pile, she wrapped them tightly around Samuel's chest and over his shoulder.

Samuel's eyelids fluttered and his breath was shallow and gasping. 'I—I did not know if I would see you again. I—I prayed that I would.'

Frederica kissed his bare shoulder and then his cheek and then his brow, before covering him to his chin with the blanket on the bed. It was slightly cleaner than the rest of the farmhouse. She wished that they were back at her mother's rented house on Rue de Lombard.

Caressing his cheek, she said, 'You will see me every day for the rest of your life. We are going to grow old together, remember? And you are going to take me around the world. You promised.'

He shook his head slightly on the feather down pillow. 'I have run out of time, Frederica. It has taken almost all my will to live this long. I was waiting for you.'

Frederica gulped down a sob and laid her head lightly against his good shoulder. She needed to touch him. To feel his feverish warmth. Now that she had seen him, she could not let him go. She would fight with the devil himself to keep her husband.

'Then you must borrow some of my will. I have enough for two people. Possibly three. I am not losing you again. Do you hear me? Never again. You are mine and I don't share.'

She heard a light tap on the door. Frederica sat up, and Scovell entered the room with a kettle in one hand and a small cup in the other. Taking them from the colonel, she thanked him for brewing it.

Frederica set down the cup and poured the hot liquid into it. 'This will help with the pain.'

Holding his head with one hand, she helped Samuel sip it slowly. His skin was still pale, but she fancied he did not look quite as grey.

'I don't think I can sip another bit of that awful stuff.'

'You will. I brewed it myself.'

'Hire a cook.'

Frederica gave a watery chuckle, but forced him to finish the first cup and drink a second one. His body needed to be cleansed both inside and out. If only she could give him a proper bath. She would burn the clothes he was in.

Samuel gave her another weak smile and closed his eyes. His pulse slowed down and he no longer felt as hot.

He was slipping away from her.

She cupped his prickly cheeks with her hands. 'If you think after all these years, I am going to let you have your way and die, you are most certainly mistaken, Samuel Corbin. You are going to live. And I am going to frustrate you for the rest of your life… You—you are going to exasperate me to no end. And we—we are going to be *so blasted* happy, that we only fight part of the time, instead of all it.'

He nodded so slightly that she almost missed it.

Grabbing his wrist, she eagerly felt for his pulse. It was still there. Samuel had only fallen asleep. Relief flooded over her from her head down to her toes. Where there was life, there was hope. She was a Stringham and they were used to getting their own way.

She intertwined her fingers with his and kissed his hand. 'This is one argument that you had better let me win.'

Chapter Twenty-Nine

Samuel's eyes burned as he opened them. He hoped that this was not hell.

He did not recognise the small room he was in, but he did the woman sleeping next to him on top of the coverlet. It was his wife, Frederica. For a moment, he feared it was a dream. Perhaps he had made it to heaven after all. But then his own odour hit him. He smelled of blood, booze and cow. Turning his head to the side of the bed, he saw a bottle of wine. He picked it up, only to find it empty. It was probably on his chest with the rest of the spirits.

'Did you have to dump out the Bordeaux?'

Frederica's eyes popped open and she sat up next to him on the narrow cot. He felt her cold fingers touching his neck for a pulse. 'Would you have preferred I used a less expensive wine?'

He nodded, but his face was on fire. Grabbing her wrist, he pulled her hand to his forehead. Her cool skin felt better than a wet rag there.

'I boiled the surgeon's instruments in what was left of the tea. He was angry with me, but he got most of the bullet out of your chest. The rest of the shrapnel pieces he said could stay there. Then I washed your chest again with spirits and soap and sewed you back together. My sister-in-law Louisa will be so proud of my needlework.'

'Why the Bordeaux?'

She shook her head and kissed his brow. 'You are very obsessed with the Bordeaux, but I suppose that is a good thing. You have decided to live. I will search Mama's cellars for some after I help you with a proper bath. The sponge bath I gave you did not get everything.'

Despite the agony of pain, his body felt strangely light. Frederica's every touch and kiss filled the empty hole in his chest.

'I smell like a cow house.'

She smiled at his words and a shot of pure joy went through him. He watched as she dipped a cloth into a bowl of water and placed it on his brow.

'That's where Scovell found you.'

Samuel smirked, even though he felt like he was lying on a bed of nails. 'It serves me right for taking off my officer's coat. My body was thrown in with the regular foot soldiers. Will not Grant be pleased to hear that not wearing my uniform landed me in a cow house?'

Frederica shook her head, smiling back at him through tears. 'Oh, no, Samuel. Whatever you do, do not start Lieutenant-Colonel Grant on his diatribe about intelligence agents and uniforms.' She paused and sniffed. 'I am so sorry that I did not find you sooner. I was told by one of Wellington's staff that you were dead and I foolishly believed them.'

He blinked rapidly. The general thought he was dead. Samuel felt a pang of guilt. The poor man would be mourning him and all the other lost officers. Perhaps feeling that he had played a part in their deaths. He was their leader. Their general.

'I ought to go see Wellington and tell him that I am alive. He has been like a father to me and a much better one than my own.'

'Excellent idea, my love.'

He tried to sit up and fell back against the pillows, gasping in pain.

Frederica pressed another kiss to his brow. 'Wellington will have to wait. Besides, you would not wish to see him smelling of cow. Let us just try to get you into the carriage. You can have a bath when we arrive at my mother's rented house and then I will send a note with Jim to the general telling him that you are alive.'

He watched her go to the door and call for a servant. A tall muscular man who looked like a groom entered the confined space. Samuel vaguely recognised the fellow. Somehow, Frederica and the male servant got him to his feet and together they helped him from the house and to the carriage.

Glancing around, he saw that the sun was setting. It would be night soon, but not even darkness could cover the smell of death that hung in the air.

Frederica climbed into the carriage first and the male servant lifted Samuel like a sack of wheat up to her. She placed his head in her lap and his body lay on the seat beside her. His wife stroked his hair and whispered sweet nothings. He closed his eyes for several minutes to regain his strength. The carriage jostled back and forth, but he could not complain about his current location.

Fighting to open his eyes, he said, 'Do you know that I nursed you once?'

She caressed his brow and cheek with a cool hand. It felt wonderful. She smiled down at him. 'When?'

'I brought measles home from Eton when I was thirteen and kindly shared them with you.'

He felt her smile as she pressed another kiss to the side of his head. 'Measles were probably the only gift you gave me freely growing up. Besides the chocolates, when you told me that I was immature.'

Samuel felt his lips twitch into a smile, the pain in his chest subsiding a little. 'My mother and your mother didn't want your sisters to catch the illness, so I was tasked to help with the nursing.'

'That sounds about right. Was I a good patient?'

'Of course not. You dumped the chamber pot on my head.'

Frederica broke out into laughter. His chin jiggled in her lap from her mirth. It hurt his aching head a little, but her pleasure was worth any pain he felt.

'And was it full?'

He closed his eyes again, unable to keep them open despite himself. 'Very.'

Chapter Thirty

It was a week later before Samuel could walk down the stairs with assistance and he no longer smelled like a cow. Happily, his wife and Jim had bathed him with generous amounts of red soap before General Lord Wellington had come to visit. He had embraced Samuel like a son. Samuel had never received so much as a handshake from his own father and was deeply moved by this brief sign of affection.

That was why he was insisting on attending the Duke of Wellington's dinner party despite the objections of both his wife and his mother-in-law. Neither thought that he should leave his bed yet. It was a miracle that he was alive. Samuel ascribed his recovery to his wife's love. Whereas Frederica was certain that it was the anti-infection qualities of her red soap. Either way, his wife had saved his life.

Dunford made sure that Samuel's military uniform and appearance were perfection, but his wife eclipsed him. Frederica wore a sombre grey dress with a delicate black lace overlay. Diamonds hung from her ears and wrists and neck. She was more beautiful than a queen and by some stroke of fate, and a contract involving a large amount of shares in a perfume company that was about to expand to red scented soaps, she was his wife.

Freddie insisted on holding his arm as they walked together down the stairs at a very slow pace. Her hold on him tightened with each step and he was relieved to reach the bottom with circulation still in his fingers. Lady Hampford stood in the entry waiting for them to leave. Raising a hand, she wiped a tear from her eye. It was the most emotion that he had ever seen her display. His mother-in-law was usually as cool as a cucumber and as direct as a drill sergeant.

'Frederica, you look stunning,' she said with a sniff. 'And, Samuel, you look very handsome. I always knew that the two of you would make the perfect pair.'

Releasing her death grip on his arm, Frederica grinned and twirled around for her mother. 'Thank you, Mama.'

Pride filling his chest, Samuel pulled out his pocket watch. 'We had best be going. Wellington is a military man and expects people to be on time. He did say nine o'clock and it is a quarter till. Goodnight, Lady Hampford.'

He surprised the duchess by kissing her cheek and then held out his arm for Frederica. He leaned on her for support, even though they both had bullet wounds. Once they were alone in the carriage, he showed her just how beautiful he thought she looked. He kissed her eyes, her cheeks, her nose, and her mouth. His wife must have thought he cleaned up rather well too, for she returned his kisses with the great enthusiasm of hers that he had grown to love. And he no longer minded that she had to have the last word—or kiss, in this particular instance.

When they arrived at Wellington's headquarters,

Samuel fixed a few of Frederica's curls that had come loose. Nothing he did could dim the glow in her cheeks and the light in her eyes, nor the slightly swollen nature of her lips. They did not detract from her beauty, but added to it. She looked like a woman who was well loved. And he meant to love her well for as long as he lived.

Longer even.

Together, they entered the house and were led to a parlour. He walked slowly like an old man, but Frederica stayed near him. Her bright smile infectious to every person that they passed.

They overheard the Duke of Wellington speaking to Colonel Scovell. 'This is too bad, thus to lose our friends.'

Scovell gravely shook his head. This was the man to whom he owed his life.

Wellington sighed, bringing a fist to his chest. 'I trust it will be the last action any of us see.'

'I hope so,' Frederica whispered into Samuel's ear. It tickled and sent a shiver of pleasure down his spine. He felt recovered enough to help his beautiful wife in their heir-begetting efforts this very evening. He had promised her a palace full of children and by golly, he was going to enjoy every minute of it.

Wellington moved to welcome each of his guests. He kissed Frederica's hand and squeezed Samuel's hand tightly. 'I am honoured that you would come, Pelford. You always were such a dependable member of my staff. Like a son to me.'

Samuel felt too pleased to speak, so he smiled. His own father may not have been worthy of the title, but he had been *fathered* by great men. First, the Duke of

Hampford. And second, the Duke of Wellington. Both men had helped him reach his potential as a man and as a soldier. He did not need to worry any more about becoming like his father. He never would. Samuel would be a father like Hampford and Wellington. One who taught, lifted, and praised.

They sat down at the dining table that had been used to plan the battle. Samuel could almost imagine that was their purpose, for Frederica was the only woman among them. He hoped that she did not feel out of place. But she had helped earn the victory just as much as any man in the room. She had spied on the French and taken a bullet to bring back that important information.

Despite the delicious food and victory fanfare, there was a sober feeling in the room. Samuel was certain that he was not the only person who felt it.

Too many seats were empty.

Too many of their friends would never see their families or homes again.

Frowning, the general twirled his wine in his glass. 'Nothing except a battle lost can be half as melancholy as a battle won.'

'What do you reckon our losses were?' Scovell asked.

Wellington shook his head, setting down his wine glass. 'It has been a damned serious business. Blücher and I have lost thirty thousand men. It has been a damned nice thing—the nearest run thing you ever saw in your life… By God! I don't think it would have done if I had not been there… Indeed, the losses I have sustained have quite broken me down, and I have no feeling for the advantages we have acquired.'

Samuel could not have agreed more. The battle had been closer than anyone liked to admit and without the steady guidance of the general, the result might have been quite different.

Placing both of his hands on the table, Samuel pushed his sore body to his feet. He lifted his glass in the air. 'To Lord Wellington, who held his line like iron until the victory. To the Iron Duke.'

Every person at the table, including Frederica, stood and raised their wine glass and repeated, 'The Iron Duke.'

Epilogue

Frederica and her husband stood on the stony shore of a Scottish freshwater loch, surrounded by green mountains. It was a glorious sight and she eagerly turned her head to see every angle. The glen was bathed in sunlight and she was glad to be carrying a white parasol that matched the little flowers on her blue morning gown of figured muslin. Her parasol had a dual purpose: to block the sun and to use as a weapon.

The wife of the Duke of Pelford always needed to be prepared.

Samuel wore a plain brown jacket and buckskin breeches. He had taken off his boots and his feet were bare. From his clothing, no outsider could have guessed that he was a decorated soldier and duke. He was so rugged and handsome that it took her breath away and butterflies danced in her stomach. She watched him untie the rope from a post and step into a small rowboat. Once he found his balance, he held out his hand to her.

Cautiously, she took his hand and put one foot into the boat, then the other. All her senses were on high alert. Neither she, nor her husband, could be trusted near bodies of water. 'I do not want to get wet. You must promise not to push me in.'

He gave her a roguish grin that set her heart thumping. 'You pushed me into a river and I did not even know how to swim.'

She had been ten years of age at the time. Frederica might have felt bad if Samuel's younger self had not got his revenge the next day by flinging a pile of elephant droppings at her. They had been a pair of rapscallions.

Lifting her nose in the air, she sniffed, trying not to remember the pungent smell. 'Promise me.'

He gave her another raffish grin that put her on her guard. 'I promise that I will not push you into the loch. We will have a nice little sail to the castle.'

Frederica had barely sat down when Samuel shifted his weight back and forth, causing her to lose her balance and teeter from side to side. Before she fell into the cold water, Samuel placed his hands around her to steady her. One hand covering the puckered scar at her waist. A small price to pay to have him by her side. Even if he meant to dump her into a cold lake.

She kissed his cheek. 'I hope this is not going to be a repeat of the punting lesson.'

Frederica felt his lips grin against her own as he lightly kissed her. Then he pressed his mouth harder against hers to deepen the kiss and she felt it all the way to her toes.

All too soon he lifted his lips from hers. 'I still maintain that my directions were very clear.'

'And yet, I ended up covered in bruises.'

'You were going to hit the tree in the river and I told you *not* to hit the tree.'

She laughed merrily and he helped her sit down on

the seat in the small boat. She pushed open her parasol in front of her, *accidentally* knocking Samuel's oar out of his hand, and into the freezing water.

Frederica placed a gloved hand over her mouth. 'Oh, dear! How clumsy of me.'

Samuel pulled the oar out of the cold dark blue water, his sleeve wet to the shoulder. 'If that is the worst thing that you do to me on this trip, I shall consider myself lucky.'

Feigning innocence, she twirled her parasol. 'You *are* the luckiest man alive. You married *me*.'

The smoulder he gave her caused her pulse to race and heat to pool in her belly. 'Luckier than I knew.'

Samuel began to row the boat towards a small island with a castle. According to Samuel, it was six hundred years old. She could well believe it. The narrow structure was three stories tall and made from grey weathered stones. Green moss grew up the walls, and a large stone staircase led to the front door. It was truly magnificent, like something out of a fairy tale or a Mrs Radcliffe novel. But *The Romance of the Forest* had nothing on her own love story, and she was living her very own happy ending.

Frederica dipped her free hand in the icy water and let it slide through her fingers. 'I am glad Mama didn't sell your Scottish castle after all.'

'So am I,' Samuel said soulfully. 'I shall finally have you to myself. There will be no carriages. No friends stopping by at all hours to visit. No relatives inviting us to never-ending dinner parties. No mother-in-law in the same house only a door or two away. No father-in-law giving me a herd of pigs as a wedding gift, or plenty of practical advice on the use of their dung.'

She giggled, making her shoulders shake. 'I thought that was a very conservative choice for Papa. I was expecting an alligator.'

'You come from a family of alligators,' he retorted. 'Each and every one of your brothers and sisters threatened me.'

Frederica could not help but beam at him. 'With their teeth?'

Samuel continued to row. 'No, Wick threatened to throttle me with his bare hands if I did not treat you right.'

She spun her parasol, laughing. Her eldest brother was quite handy with his fists. 'Well, your past treatment of me was not the best. He did see you push me out of the hayloft.'

'You were eleven and you had put a snake in my bed. I am sure Helen helped. Besides, you are interrupting. No Matthew trying to get me to invest in steam locomotives and railroads.'

Her second brother was a businessman who never seemed to take a day off. 'It is fine that you did not. I already own five percent of the stock in his company and I will share a portion of the proceeds with you when I make my fortune.'

Samuel huffed, lifting his eyebrows. 'No Mantheria, giving me lessons via correspondence on how to be a duke.'

Frederica continued to twirl her parasol. Her eldest sister was married to the Duke of Glastonbury, who was in poor health. She ran his estates with the exactness and efficiency of a good housekeeper/steward. 'I hope you kept all of her notes and study them regularly.'

'No Helen writing me letter after letter from Greece

trying to convince me to take you on a wedding trip to South America, with herself as your companion.'

Her younger sister and her snakes. She missed them both. Helen was one of a kind. 'I hear that there are lots of very interesting reptiles there. I am sure she would love it. But I do not know if we will be able to get her to leave.'

Samuel gave an exaggerated sigh. 'No Becca, sending caricatures of me caught in a spider's web or with a yoke on my shoulder like a pair of oxen.'

'I thought her drawings of you were terribly clever and rather accurate. You are trapped in my web for life.'

'And you in my yoke,' he said, giving her a warm look. Then he ruined the moment by adding, 'Nor my little brother pestering me for every detail of the battle.'

Jeremy had been more persistent than a dog with a bone wanting to know every detail. He'd even got on Frederica's nerves. 'You cannot blame him for wanting to know all about the most famous battle of our age from the ADC to the Duke of Wellington, himself. And, you have not mentioned your mother at all. I love her dearly, but she cried on my shoulder no less than ten times. Thanking me for saving your life. I wish she would have shown my favourite dresses more consideration and saved *them* from wet spots.'

Samuel waved this aside with his oar. 'Like I said, it will finally be only the two of us.'

She had been looking forward to their wedding trip as much as her husband, but she could never resist teasing him. Frederica held out her lace gloved hands and began to count. 'There will also be your butler, the housekeeper, Mr Dunford, Miss Wade, a couple of footmen, various maids, and the cook.'

He continued rowing as if he had not heard her. 'Only the two of us…on an island, in a lake, surrounded by massive mountains. Alone, in a castle, with nothing to do.'

Tilting her head to one side, Frederica licked her lips suggestively. 'Oh, I am sure we can find something to entertain ourselves with. I brought several good books.'

Samuel laughed and scooted forward on his seat. Frederica leaned forward too and brushed her lips against his. Her limbs tingled with joy and her heart sang. Samuel sat back on his seat and began to row more vigorously towards the castle, causing her to laugh.

Once they reached the island, he placed the oars in the bottom of the boat and jumped out into the shallow water of the shore. Grabbing the rope, he pulled the boat onto the sand and tied it to the post so it would not float away. He held out his hand to Frederica and she stepped out of the boat. He lifted her up by her waist and twirled her around and around. She felt as if she were flying. Like one of Papa's birds.

Samuel set her feet down on the sandy beach and whispered, 'Only the two of us.'

Frederica placed his hands on her still flat stomach. 'Only the three of us…'

His eyes widened and his mouth dropped. She had finally succeeded in surprising him. Her husband let out a loud whoop and he picked her up again, spinning her around once before carefully setting her on the sand.

'Should I not lift you?' he asked, his tone filled with concern.

Throwing her arms around his neck, she shook her head. 'No, you should kiss me instead.'

Slanting his lips towards hers, Frederica knew that she was living her very own happily-ever-after.

* * * * *

Keep reading for an excerpt of a new title
from the Historical series,
SPINSTER WITH A SCANDALOUS PAST
by Sadie King

Chapter One

June 1818

As the carriage rattled along the road towards Lowhaven, Louisa Conrad wondered what on earth she had been thinking. The sound of braying horses rang in her ears, and if she closed her eyes she could still feel herself tumbling down, could still feel her body thud against the coach's solid wood as it landed on its side and took her with it.

In her lap, her hands tremored. She clasped them together and pressed her lips into a tight smile, forcing calm where there was none to be found. Her gaze moved between the two brothers sitting before her, but only one of them returned her smile. The other did not even look at her, apparently preferring the country views offered through the small carriage window.

Briefly she furrowed her brow at him, before giving her full attention to his sibling as he struck up a conversation once again.

'I'm sure that you will find Juniper Street to your liking,' Mr Liddell said.

'I'm sure I shall, sir,' she replied crisply. 'And I believe that after the journey we've had I will appreciate it all the more.'

'Indeed, indeed. A wholesome meal and a good night's repose cures most ills, I find.' His eyes shone, almost teasing. 'You have both had quite an adventure.'

Beside her, Nan shifted, gripping the cushioned seat so hard that her knuckles turned white. Louisa couldn't decide what was distressing her maid more. The terror of the stagecoach accident, or everything that had happened since.

'I'm not sure I would describe it quite like that,' Louisa answered him. 'Those poor horses were dreadfully frightened after the coach turned over. I'm quite sure that the coachman was beside himself with concern for their welfare.'

'Of course—well, until the next time he's whipping them relentlessly so that he might travel at a dangerous speed,' Mr Liddell countered, a smile playing on his lips.

Louisa gave him a small nod, suppressing her own smile but finding that she could not, in earnest, disagree. Nan, meanwhile, chose that moment to clear her throat, no doubt to remind Louisa of the impropriety of their situation. They would have words later, that was for certain. Strong words about getting into the carriage of some unknown gentlemen, about reckless decisions and their consequences, about the manifold horrors which might have occurred.

Louisa had already prepared her defences. What else could they have done when they were stranded in the middle of nowhere, miles from the nearest inn? Were they not fortunate that the gentlemen happened upon them just moments after the coach had overturned?

Her hands trembled again, reminding her that she was not certain of her own argument. After all, Nan's undoubted reservations would be more than justified. Shaken and disorientated, the coach stricken and their luggage scattered on the ground, she could hardly claim to have been thinking clearly. No, instead she had allowed them to be swept along, embracing the notion of rescue without reservation. In those few moments she had been utterly unguarded. And Louisa, more than most, ought to remember the dangers inherent in letting down one's guard.

'Forgive me, Miss Conrad, I am making light of a difficult day, but you might have been seriously injured. I would urge you to consult a doctor once you are settled at your aunt's house. I can ask our physician to pay a visit to you, if you wish?'

'That's very kind of you, sir,' she replied, 'but I'm sure there's no need. We are, as you see, unharmed.'

She forced a smile, ignoring the ache in her ribs which served to remind her that she was not being entirely truthful.

'My brother is right.'

Louisa blinked, startled by the low timbre of the voice which had interjected. The other brother looked at her now, fixing his deep blue eyes upon her so intently that she almost wished he'd return to looking out of the window. Sir Isaac, Mr Liddell had called him during their fraught introductions earlier. Sir Isaac Liddell of Hayton Hall. As she stared back at him now, Louisa realised that this was the first time Sir Isaac had spoken to her in the several hours they'd been travelling together.

'My brother is right,' he repeated. 'We will send our physician.'

Louisa nodded her assent, sensing it was not worth her while to disagree. This appeared to satisfy him, as he said nothing more, but continued to look at her for a little longer than would be deemed polite. Louisa dropped her gaze, and after a moment she sensed him resume his interest in the scenery outside.

'What did you say your aunt's name was, Miss Conrad?' Mr Liddell asked, apparently keen to break the awkward silence which had descended in the carriage.

'I'm not sure that I did, but it is Miss Clarissa Howarth.'

'Miss Clarissa Howarth,' he repeated. 'I know that name. Is your aunt the rector's daughter from Hayton?'

Reluctantly Louisa nodded, feeling immediately guarded at this new line of questioning. 'That's correct, sir.'

Mr Liddell nudged his brother. 'Do you remember Reverend Howarth, Isaac?'

'Of course,' Sir Isaac muttered, not troubling himself to tear his gaze from the window.

From across the carriage Louisa found herself observing him, both offended by and grateful for his apparent lack of interest. With his striking blue gaze safely averted, she felt able to note his other features: near-black hair, a strong, angular jawline, and a sun-kissed complexion which hinted at time spent outdoors. He was dressed from head to toe in black, apart from the white shirt which she glimpsed beneath his coat, and it struck Louisa that he would not look out of place as a character in one of Mrs Radcliffe's gothic romances.

He was handsome, she concluded, but disagreeable. Not that either aspect of Sir Isaac Liddell mattered to her.

'It must be some time now since Reverend Howarth's passing?' Mr Liddell continued.

She nodded, returning her attention once more to the talkative brother. Unlike Sir Isaac, his features were fair, his hair the colour of sand and his eyes a pale blue-grey. In both looks and demeanour, it was hard to believe that they were related.

'Yes,' she replied, 'almost fifteen years.'

'And now your aunt lives on Juniper Street,' he said, in a way which seemed to be neither a statement nor a question.

'She does, yes.'

Now it was Louisa who turned to look out of the window, emulating Sir Isaac's aloof posture in the hope that it would signal an end to the conversation about her family history. Answering questions about Aunt Clarissa was all very well, but she was not keen to see where Mr Liddell's enquiries might lead. He'd already discovered where she'd come from, not long after they'd settled into the carriage.

'Berkshire…?' he'd pondered, before remarking upon how far she'd travelled and recounting a tale of some arduous journey south he'd previously undertaken.

She'd only half listened, and after a while he'd seemed to sense her weariness, smiling an apology and insisting that she needed to rest. Now, so close to her destination, she was determined that they would not revisit the subject. Louisa Conrad was a stranger here, and that was how it was going to remain.

Fortunately, it appeared she wouldn't have to deflect his attempts at conversation for much longer. Outside the carriage window, the wild Cumberland countryside had given way to a gentle townscape of smart grey and white buildings, and the streets were alive with coaches, carts and crowds, as people went about their business.

Her first glimpse of Lowhaven was a reassuring one, and she recalled the excitement she'd first felt when her parents had proposed this sojourn to her. A change of scenery, they'd called it. An opportunity to travel, just as she'd always wished.

She suspected there was more to their desire to send her away than mere broadened horizons, but she didn't care, and had loved the idea from the very first moment. Her eagerness had been dampened somewhat by the travails of the journey, but now, as it reached its welcome conclusion, it returned with renewed vigour. Even Nan looked happier, staring wide-eyed out of the window, her mouth agape at the town as it unravelled in front of her.

'Juniper Street is not far from the port,' Mr Liddell informed them. 'I do hope you won't find the noise and traffic too disturbing.'

Louisa thought about her family's estate, enveloped in rolling green fields and an almost unendurable silence. About the large country house, containing too few people and too many opportunities to ruminate on what might have been. Without doubt, she'd had her fill of living quietly in recent years.

'If it's near to the port then it is near to the sea, which will do very well for me,' she countered cheerfully. 'Besides, lively places can be very diverting.'

Mr Liddell let out a soft laugh. 'If diversion is what you seek, Miss Conrad, then I do believe you will find it in Lowhaven.'

The carriage drew to a halt on a dusty street, lined on either side by rather humble-looking stone townhouses, uniformly built, but with little embellishment. After a moment the coachman opened the door and Mr Liddell exited, offering Louisa his hand as she descended the steps, with Nan following closely behind her.

Louisa smoothed her palms over the crumpled, muddied skirt of her day dress as she took her first breath of Lowhaven's fresh sea air. *Yes,* she thought, *this will do very well indeed.*

'Our driver will fetch your luggage to the door for you, Miss Conrad,' Mr Liddell said.

Louisa turned to face him, realising then that Sir Isaac had not followed them out of the carriage. Instead he remained within, his sombre countenance visible through the little window to which he'd given so much of his attention throughout the journey. Briefly Louisa shook her head at his rudeness, before regarding Mr Liddell once more. There might have been two gentlemen in the carriage today, she thought, but really only one of them could be regarded as their rescuer.

'Mr Liddell, I must thank you most sincerely for coming to our aid today. Truly, you are a good Samaritan. I only hope we have not caused any significant delay to your own journey.'

The gentleman shook his head. 'None whatsoever. Our home is merely a few miles up the road. It was a pleasure to escort you, and to see you safely to your destination, and I will see to it that our physician calls upon you later. I hope that your stay in Lowhaven is agreeable. It is not comparable with the fashionable resorts of the south coast, but nonetheless it has its charms.'

'I'm obliged to you, sir. Will you not stay for some

tea? I'm sure my aunt would be glad to welcome you both,' she added, glancing warily once more towards the carriage.

'You're very kind, Miss Conrad, but I'm afraid we must take our leave,' he replied, tipping his hat briefly. 'Perhaps our paths will cross again, while you are here.'

Before Louisa could respond, Mr Liddell had climbed back into the carriage and closed the door behind him. Through the window he gave her one last broad smile, before his coachman cracked his whip once more and they were off.

For a moment Louisa just stood there, staring after that handsome carriage, surrounded by the luggage which Nan was frantically trying to put into order. After the ordeal of their journey, it seemed miraculous that they had finally arrived. In fact, it almost didn't seem real: the accident, the rescue, the kind gentleman, the rude gentleman—all of it.

Louisa let out a weary sigh. What a long and strange day it had been.

Then, behind her, a door opened and a voice she hadn't heard for years rang out in delight.

'Louisa! Oh, my dear Louisa! Is it really you?'

Louisa turned around and walked straight into the outstretched arms of her Aunt Clarissa, who embraced her quickly before stepping back to regard her niece. The woman looked older than Louisa remembered, her face heavily lined, her once blonde hair now silver and peering wildly from beneath a lace cap. Thinner, too, Louisa thought. She could compete with the minuscule Nan in terms of slenderness.

'You look well, my dear, all things considered,' her aunt said carefully, and Louisa couldn't help but suspect that she was referring to more than just the long journey. 'Your mother was right; you've grown into quite a beautiful young lady.'

Louisa laughed aloud, gesturing at her mud-spattered travelling clothes. 'I look far from beautiful right now, Aunt! And I don't believe I merit being described as "young" any more, either.'

Clarissa raised a curious eyebrow. 'Oh, nonsense—you're barely five-and-twenty; you're not allowed to deny your youth for a few years yet!' She placed a gentle hand on Louisa's arm and steered her towards the door. 'However, you do look as though you've become acquainted with our Cumberland countryside already. Come, let's get your luggage brought in, then we can have some tea and you can tell me all about it.'

'Tell you all about what, Aunt?'

'Your journey, of course—I'd say it's quite a story, judging by the state of your dress.' Clarissa smiled, a look of amusement sparkling in her keen blue eyes. 'But above all you must tell me—how on earth did you come to be accompanied here by Samuel Liddell of Hayton Hall?'